**Angela Huth** has written eleven novels, four collections of short stories as well as plays for radio, TV and the stage. *Land Girls* was made into a 1998 feature film starring Rachel Weisz and Anna Friel. She is also a well-known freelance journalist, critic and broadcaster. Angela is married to an Oxford don, lives in Warwickshire and has two daughters.

Praise for *Land Girls*

'A first-class writer.'                                      *Sunday Telegraph*

'Riveting . . . evocative and entertaining.'                      *Daily Mail*

'Huth's controlled, eloquent style has been compared to Jane Austen's, but her talent is entirely original.'                      *The Times*

'Piquant, witty and entertaining.'                                      *Tatler*

'Huth is a master of this sort of novel, steeped in period atmosphere and gentle irony.'                      *Daily Telegraph*

'A good story, told with wit and a keen observation of detail.'
                                      *Times Literary Supplement*

# ONCE A LAND GIRL

Angela Huth

Constable · London

Constable & Robinson Ltd
55–56 Russell Square
London WC1B 4HP
www.constablerobinson.com

First published in the UK by Constable,
an imprint of Constable & Robinson Ltd, 2010

This edition published by Constable, 2012

A copy of the British Library Cataloguing in
Publication Data is available from the British Library

ISBN: 978-1-84901-275-1

Typeset by TW Typesetting, Plymouth, Devon

Printed and bound in the UK

1 3 5 7 9 10 8 6 4 2

*For Sally and John*

# Chapter 1

'How much longer do you want to be staring at an empty field?' said a voice behind her. 'Nothing to see, is there?'

Prue stood on the third rung of the gate, the gate she remembered for its soggy wood, which was gentle against her knees as it always used to be. She stared at Lower Pasture, empty now of animals. No crops had been sown this year. Its hedges were no longer as trimmed to the neatness Mr Lawrence had always required. The long grass bent carelessly in the wind. In the far corner she could see the haystack in flames, the petrified cows leaping away from its heat, so strong that the air quivered like a mirage. She could hear the cows screaming and the smaller voices of Stella and Ag, sticks in hand, trying to urge them into the clover field across the lane. She could feel again the piercing sweat beneath her arms as she ran on clumsy legs to join them.

'Come along. We'd best be getting back.'

Prue did not move. She needed a moment longer. The hedge that ran along the west side of Lower Pasture was now so overgrown it would have been impossible to see what she had seen that day – Stella in Joe's arms, their two bodies sagging with relief that the fire was finally under control, but tense with the thrill of their first embrace. They had left the scene of devastation a few moments before she and Ag had linked arms, swiped at

1

their tears, and taken a last look at the sickening remains of Nancy, the one cow that had taken a direct hit from a bomb: the one cow Mr Lawrence had agreed not to sell. Once in the clover field, Prue remembered, the rest of the herd still roared their fear – oddly high-pitched squeals from such hefty animals. They still bucked and reared, their black and white jagged skins making a mad pattern that snagged Prue's streaming eyes. The incendiary flames had been colours of terrifying beauty, but the smoke they left behind was a vast black rock in the sky. It showed no sign of evaporating. Its vile smell was in Prue's nostrils – even now, today, four years after some German had dropped the bomb on his way home.

'I said, come on. We've been here long enough. Beats me what you're staring at.'

Prue climbed down from the gate, ignoring her husband's offered hand. Even though he had heard something of her days as a land girl, he did not seem to understand that she was able to get off a gate without help. He knew nothing of the country. Rural life was of no interest to him though he professed he was proud that his wife had served her country as a land girl. On their honeymoon he had made a promise that one day he would drive her back to Hallows Farm, take a look at the place if it would give her pleasure. Four years later, here he was, carrying out his promise, and a god-awful day, in his opinion, it had been too, manoeuvring the Humber along narrow lanes, mud and worse splashing its pristine paint. He hoped this visit would be a once and for all: he didn't fancy any more such journeys down these rotten little memory lanes. The only blessing was that he'd decided to bring the Humber rather than the Daimler: God knew what the country would have done to the Daimler.

The parked Humber blocked the lane.

'Lucky no tractors wanting to come down this way.'

Barry took off an orange pigskin glove, holes punched on its knuckles, and stroked the bonnet of his car. He then gave a more cursory pat to his wife's shoulder. He opened the passenger door for her with the flourish of one who has observed many a hotel doorman. By now Prue had become used to travelling in this huge, comfortable vehicle with its fabric seats and mahogany dashboard. Barry, so proud of his car, urged her to observe its finer details on almost every occasion they travelled together. Prue climbed in, wriggled her back against the seat. She had hoped that Barry would show some interest in the country round Hallows Farm, but the comfort of the car eased her disappointment. She wound down the window to try to reduce the permanent smell of cigar smoke.

'I should close that,' said Barry, pressing the starter button with the kind of reverence that Mr Lawrence, the farmer she had worked for during the war, had never shown to his old Wolseley. 'Don't want to let your country smells into a car like this.'

Prue wound up the window. Whatever Barry asked of her, today, she would do without argument. Nothing mattered to her. She was in another time, another place – startled, shaken once again by the remembrance of it all.

'So, what now? Do you want us to drive up to the farmhouse?' Barry glanced at his watch.

Prue knew they were in no hurry, but she had no desire to go to the house, the yard, the barn, in the company of someone whose impatience was almost tangible. This whole outing, she could see, was not Barry's idea of fun. Besides, unknown to him, this was not the first time she had returned to the farm. Just a few weeks ago, sick of waiting for his invitation, she had come here on another visit which she thought prudent not to mention. 'I don't think we'll bother,' she said. 'It'll be dark soon. We'd better be getting back.'

Such generosity of understanding spurred Barry's particular kind of benignity. 'There's my girl. We'll stop somewhere for a drink. Treat ourselves to something bubbly. How about that?'

'Fine.' Prue didn't care where they stopped or what they drank. She wanted desperately to take a further look at the outside of the farmhouse, the bleak yard, the barn. But she wanted to go on her own, or with Stella and Ag. Not with Barry.

The car moved slowly forward. Barry was unused to the hazards of lanes and he had no intention of further soiling the immaculate Humber. They passed the cottage where Ratty, the single labourer on the farm, used to live with his sometimes mad wife Edith. It had clearly been improved by new owners: window frames painted, front door a garish green that clashed with the garden. No lights in the windows. Prue wondered if the new inhabitants, despite their renovations, could sense a shadow of the misery that had soured the place when Ratty and Edith lived there.

'Must be hard for you,' Barry said, 'coming back. Myself, I wouldn't want to return to a place that had meant . . . whatever all this meant to you.'

Prue shrugged. 'Curiosity,' she said.

They passed the wood where she and Joe had so often made love. After Joe, Prue and Barry One had gone there for the same reason. It was a hidden place, safe. The moss had been beneath them. Birdsong, from birds they were too busy to notice, was the only sound. With Barry One, as Prue recognized at the time, it was real love in the undergrowth. When he was killed and his friend Jamie had come to console her, she had eventually agreed to sessions in the same place – out of habit, she supposed. But it hadn't been the same with Jamie.

Barry tightened his grip on the huge steering-wheel and accelerated gently. Prue was revolted by the pigskin gloves, which meant so much to him. They made her think of Sly, the Lawrences' querulous old sow who had endeared herself to all three land girls. The idea of Sly or any pig turned into gloves was so horrible that—

4

'Tell you what,' Barry was saying, 'I'll run you up one of my special salmon-paste sandwiches when we get home. Lots of paste, a sprinkling of cress. How about that?'

'Lovely.'

It was dark by now so Barry could not see the tears that ran down her cheeks. She wanted to scream at him, 'Stop! It's left here. Mrs Lawrence will be waiting for us with a huge stew and turnips and a suet pudding.' But in the confusion of past and present she dared not speak a word lest she broke down, and Barry's moment of kindness would turn to impatience.

They turned into the wider road that led from the farmhouse to the village. For a moment Prue fancied the shadows from the overhanging trees were the flock of bumbling sheep that she had so often driven down this road, and felt herself smile. Then she saw that her mind was playing tricks. There were no sheep. 'Stupid,' she said to herself.

'I was thinking,' said Barry, 'that what we should go for next is a Sunbeam Talbot. How does that strike you? Lovely red machine, leather seats. Turn heads, a Sunbeam Talbot would.'

'Why not?' said Prue. She was trying to remember how many times she and Joe had shagged in the wood, and if it was more than she and Jamie had, and if they were added together they would come to more than the occasions with Barry One, whom she had loved more than either of them.

At the end of the war, while her fellow land girls Stella and Ag went off to get married, Prue had gone back to live in Manchester with her mother in whose hairdressing shop they both worked. It was not a happy arrangement. Before the war Prue had enjoyed it, and at Hallows Farm she had kept up her skills on Stella and Ag, often surprising them with her experimental cutting and bleaching. But her years as a land girl seemed to have destroyed her enthusiasm for working all day in a small shop that smelt of

5

shampoo and peroxide, and clumps of hair mistakenly burnt by curling tongs. She never managed to accomplish a permanent wave to her mother's satisfaction, and now she didn't care if she never became a skilled hairdresser, let alone under-manager in the business, which once had been her ambition.

She spent the days dreaming of a husband who could take her away from this narrow life and provide her with money, luxury. Even though Stella and Ag had teased her over her desire for gold taps, she still hankered for them. But there were few signs of available young men, let alone those seeking matrimony. Some of the boys she had known as a child had been killed. Others had returned wounded. She would go to the pub by herself most nights, survey the gathering of old men, and return to her mother's claustrophobic little house in a state of acute dejection.

One day after work mother and daughter walked to the bus stop in a downpour. At the best of times buses were infrequent and when it rained they seemed to give up altogether. They stood there for half an hour, drenched. Then a large car pulled up, sloshing water from the gutter onto their feet. Mrs Lumley gave a long and noisy sigh against the rain. 'A Daimler!' she cooed. 'A wedding car. Whatever can it want?'

A man leant across the empty passenger seat and wound down the window. 'You look like drowned rats,' he said. 'Can I give you a lift somewhere?'

'You certainly can. Much more of this and we'll melt.' Mrs Lumley was breathless with the wonder of such a car pulling up beside them, its driver proposing to rescue them from the rain.

'Mum, do you think we should?' Prue, between clients, kept abreast of stories of post-war rape and murder in the *Daily Mirror*.

'Don't be daft, child. Two of us could beat an attacker any day. Get in quick.' Mrs Lumley scrambled into the front seat without giving her daughter a glance.

Prue opened the back door and fell into a seat that seemed to her more like the softest sofa.

The man turned to her. 'You all right?'

'Fine, thanks.' She could just see very wide-apart dark eyes above a certain pudginess of cheek.

'Where to?'

'Twenty-five Wimberly Road, if you don't mind.'

Prue was certain the question had been to her, but her mother's swift reply made her realize that Mrs Lumley's excitement at the possibility of adventure was even greater than her own.

'Delighted. It's on my way.'

The Daimler swooshed forward, parting the deep water on the street.

'I'm afraid we'll be making wet marks on your seats,' said Mrs Lumley.

'That's no matter. Easily taken care of.'

Prue sat back, closed her eyes. Despite the discomfort of her soaking clothes this, she realized, was as near to bliss as a girl could come when she was not lying beneath a wonderful lover.

'I'm Barry Morton,' said the man, suddenly, breaking a fraction of silence.

'Pleased to meet you, Mr Morton. I'm Elsie Lumley. In the back it's my daughter Prudence – Prue, we call her.'

'Very nice.'

'So . . . how come you have such a lovely car?'

'I'm in cars. Buying and selling. Ten years from now there'll be a very big demand for cars, all sorts. The market will explode. Mark my words.'

'I see. Very interesting.'

'And what line of business are you in yourself?'

'I have my own hair salon: Elsie's Bond Street Hair Salon, it's called. Prue helps out.'

'I often pass it. I've noticed it several times.' He knew how to flatter, thought Prue, though it was just possible he spoke the truth.

'Very kind of you to say so.'

Prue wished the journey would never end. This was no ordinary car: this was a moving cloud, a velvet box, a jewel. Its engine made no sound. There was sheepskin carpet at her feet, tickling her wet ankles. And there, bugger it, far too soon, was their road.

Barry Morton drew to a stop very slowly. Neither of his passengers moved. Mrs Lumley pushed back a strand of wet hair that clung to her cheek – Prue knew her mother was wishing she'd put on more lipstick before they left the shop, but she couldn't have known that an ordinary journey home was to be trans-formed by a millionaire rescuer – for presumably he was a millionaire.

Mrs Lumley turned to him, puckering her lips in the way she did when fondling a cat, or catching sight of some man across the street whose looks she fancied. 'Well here we are, Mr Morton. I can only thank you for your true kindness.'

'Do call me Barry.'

Why call him Barry when he was about to drive off and they would never see him again? Prue wondered. She still did not move. She wanted to remember the touch of the seat against her shoulders. She wanted to remember it when she was on the bus, or walking towards another dreary day.

'Ba-rry', said Mrs Lumley, after a pause to contemplate just how she should graft the name of this remarkable stranger on her tongue. She leant very slightly towards him, put a brief finger on his shoulder. 'We mustn't detain you,' she said sadly.

'My pleasure,' said Barry. Prue could not work out the logic of his reply, but sensed he was enjoying her mother's appreciation. 'Let me open the door for you.'

It would have been foolish to get out in such heavy rain when all he had to do was lean across his passenger. Prue could understand that. She watched, fascinated, as Barry leant as discreetly as a bulky man can across a strange woman and opened the door. A shaft of rain flung into the car. Prue managed to open the back door on her own, helped only by an encouraging smile from the millionaire driver. 'You'd better hurry,' he said.

'Can't make much difference, we're so wet already.'

Barry's remark had been addressed to Prue this time, but Mrs Lumley's quick response showed that she was now happily in charge of any remaining fragments of conversation. She gave the sort of laugh that Prue remembered had come so often to her mother before the war.

They hurried up the concrete path, heads bowed against the wind, eyes blurred with rain. In the small kitchen Prue lit the gas fire and Mrs Lumley put on the kettle. The white walls blazed in the light of the forty-watt bulb that hung beneath a raffia shade from the centre of the ceiling. Prue remembered how she used to think this was how the perfect kitchen should be, and at first had been shocked and repelled by the kitchen at Hallows Farm, with its peeling dun walls and a rabbit waiting in the sink to be skinned. Now she thought that the perfect kitchen. Her mother's neatness and brightness, the china plates and Bakelite mugs with matching poppies, jarred her senses in a way she found puzzling.

'Well I never,' Mrs Lumley was saying. 'Talk about the unexpected. But there again, surprises do turn up once in a while. It was nice he – Ba-rry – noticed the shop.' She went to her pile of souvenir biscuit tins and chose the top one which housed a precious store of gingernuts, only brought out on special occasions. There was lightness in her step. Prue recognized a flame of hope. The pathos in her mother's small toss of her head was alarming.

'You never know,' Mrs Lumley went on, dithering among the biscuits. 'He knows the salon. He might drop in one day.'

A week later there was still no sign of Barry Morton. Mrs Lumley never mentioned him after the night they had met, which Prue guessed was an act of considerable self-will. She knew her mother could think of little else. In silence as she stirred tinned soup in a saucepan, her lips would move into the familiar provocative pout and she would run a hand through her thin, decorous hair. She had started to paint her nails scarlet, a new colour by Peggy Sage.

One evening she turned from the saucepan to Prue. 'I shouldn't really be saying this to you, Prue,' she began, 'but sometimes I don't half fancy lying back and thinking of England again under some nice fella.'

'Oh Mum. Something will happen.' Prue had no wish to be party to her mother's private yearnings. She put an arm round her shoulders, felt the bone of the blades through the skin.

'I hope so.'

The next afternoon there was no one booked into the salon. Prue and her mother sat on the two chairs placed in front of mirrors, contemplating their own faces. They waited patiently for a surprise appointment. Occasionally someone one would drop in on a whim, attracted perhaps by the photographs of Margaret Lockwood and her Drene-brilliant hair in the window.

'I wonder, Mum,' said Prue, who was so bored that even the act of wondering tired her, 'if anyone actually thinks Margaret Lockwood gets her hair done here?'

'Must do. Else they wouldn't come in, would they?'

Mrs Lumley, exhausted by hope, moved her eyes from her own reflection to the door of the shop. Thus she was the first to see the delivery man knock, not in reality but in the mirror image. He held a large bunch of flowers. Then Prue saw his reflection in her mirror. As Mrs Lumley leapt up, knocking hairbrushes, combs and tongs to the ground, Prue kept her seat. This was her mother's moment: she had no intention of detracting from it.

At the door Mrs Lumley gave the delivery man the sort of smile she had not exercised for a week. 'Those'll be for me,' she said. 'Thank you, dear.' She signed a receipt with a shaking hand, returned to her seat. Then everything went into slow motion. She pulled at a red bow of pre-war satin ribbon, let the tissue paper fall in a cloud onto the floor. She buried her head in a bunch of pink roses, searching for scent that did not exist, but the surprise caused her to cry out with joy.

'Who can they be from, Mum?' Prue asked, knowing how much her mother would enjoy the answer.

'Who do you think, silly?'

'Where's the card?'

'The card? Oh yes. Silly me, this time.' She bent down, ruffled through the tissue paper, noting in the still practical part of her mind that there was a lot of hair on the floor that Prue should have swept up. She found the small envelope. 'Here, take these while I open it.' She handed the roses to Prue.

Mrs Lumley slit open the envelope with her best cutting scissors. To Prue, impatient to know what Barry Morton had said, her mother's every movement was maddeningly slow.

The card was pulled from its miniature envelope by two scarlet nails – chipped, now, sign of fading hope. Then there was a pause while Mrs Lumley found her glasses in the pocket of her apron. Finally she held up the card so slowly it might have been a great weight, and turned it towards the grey light in the window. Prue watched, horrified, as her mother's slow eyes trudged back and forth over some short message, and the skin round her rouged cheeks turned a deadly white.

'They're for you. They're not for me.' She handed Prue the card.

'Oh, Mum. There must be some mistake.'

11

'No. Read it.'

Prue scanned Barry's politely phrased invitation to a 'proper ride' in the Daimler and a drink on Friday evening. He added that he would be honoured, should she accept. 'It could still be a mistake,' she said. 'He may have meant Mrs.'

'No. The handwriting's quite clear.'

Prue could see her mother was beginning to disintegrate. Her feet were shuffling on the floor among the unswept hair. She kept licking her lips.

'Well I won't go,' said Prue. 'Of course I won't go. Who'd want to go for a drink with a strange man just because he has a bloody great car?'

Mrs Lumley looked her daughter in the eye, suddenly fierce. 'You will, my girl,' she said. 'You certainly will. I want to know what game Mr Barry Morton's playing. You'll go.'

'If you say so,' said Prue. Concerned by her mother's disappointment, she was in no state to anticipate what the date with Barry Morton might bring.

Mrs Lumley watched Barry's arrival from her bedroom window. She had been waiting behind the net curtain for twenty minutes and was surprised when the Daimler drew up at precisely six thirty for she had begun to think he might be a cad rather than a punctual man of honour. After all, he had been so friendly to her that rainy night, scarcely exchanging a word with Prue in the back seat. He couldn't have caught more than a glimpse of her.

As Barry strode down the front path she could see that he was a man of means: camel-hair coat, carnation in his buttonhole, box of Black Magic in hand – well, obviously a man who could pull strings even in these days of sweet rationing. She could also judge better, in daylight, his age: definitely a touch older than she had supposed. If things had turned out for her and Barry she would have been accused of cradle-snatching. If possible romance came to fruition (she had found the phrase in a romantic novel and it had stuck in her mind) for Prue and him, it would be said her daughter was associating with (marrying?) an older man.

She heard voices downstairs but could not make out the words. Prue had begged her to be there to greet Barry, to 'make things easier'. But Mrs Lumley had been insistent. She certainly wasn't up for making conversation with a man who had shown his colours so strongly, then changed his mind. All the same, when Prue and Barry, halfway down the path, stopped, turned and waved up at her window, Mrs Lumley relented. She waved back, knowing the gesture would be unclear behind the net curtain. After that, she observed Barry put a hand under Prue's elbow and guide her to the car.

Several faces peered from neighbouring houses. This Mrs Lumley noted with satisfaction. Her sense of vicarious importance increased when several children ran up for a closer look at the car. One stretched out a hand and touched its bonnet. That, too, was gratifying. Mrs Lumley had always been accused of bringing a touch of class to the neighbourhood – though the accusation was never voiced, she was positive it existed. She had always been able to feel it. And now here was proof. Rich man, swanky car, pretty daughter taken out. Curiously soon, considering her dreadful week, Mrs Lumley found that she was able to transfer her hopes for herself to hopes for Prue. She came downstairs, sat in the kitchen surrounded by her precious souvenir tins, and as she ate several of the best biscuits – surely extravagance was permissible on such an occasion – she imagined the couple fox-trotting in some posh hotel in the city centre.

Barry Morton made no suggestion about fox-trotting, but drove instead to a large pub on the outskirts of the city. There, Prue felt overdressed. She had chosen – encouraged by the mother – the dress she had worn at Buckingham Palace for the tea party the

King and Queen had given for land girls. It had been perfect on that unforgettable day. Several of the other girls, who had had to alter their mothers' pre-war dresses or run something up from lace curtains and parachute silk, had congratulated her. An almost bluebell blue (not quite dark enough to Prue's keen eye for colour, but no one else noticed this imperfection) with a sweetheart neckline and a flirty skirt, the dress had, as she recounted back at the farm, dazzled their Majesties.

In the smoke-filled bar, at the table Barry chose, furnished only with a tin ashtray advertising Colman's mustard, she feared it was too much. On the way to the table she was conscious of many turning heads – mostly of men, some in uniform. When she crossed her legs her knees were more exposed than she would have liked, but the shortage of even artificial silk meant the skirt had to be short. Still, she was wearing her only pair of nylon stockings, which gave her legs a burnished sheen, a sight that Barry Morton was able to admire as he lit his cigar.

'So, Prue,' he said, 'where do we begin?'

Several ideas skittered through Prue's mind, rendering her silent. In truth she was aware of a clutch of disappointment in her stomach. She had imagined that a man with a Daimler would head straight for the poshest hotel in the area, not this dreary pub. Perhaps, she thought, he was putting her through some kind of test.

'Here's to . . .' he said, breaking the silence at last. He held up his glass of champagne, urging Prue to do the same with a nod. Their glasses clicked.

'Here's to what?' asked Prue, with a smile.

'Who knows?' Barry smiled too. Somewhere towards the back of his mouth there was a very large gold tooth. So perhaps he had gold taps as well, thought Prue. He leant back in his chair, allowing a spread of light from a corner lamp to illuminate his heavy but adequately proportioned features. Prue guessed he must be forty, or thereabouts. A touch young for her mum but, she reckoned, if he gave her some sort of opening, she'd try to find out what he had made of her, though she had little hope for this plan. What mattered was that he had a nice face, kindly. The wide-apart, frog-like eyes blinked slowly, taking her in so intensely she felt herself blush. She fixed her eyes on his maroon tie – not, she knew, artificial silk but the real thing. Then they moved over the pin-stripe suit, stripes a little too wide for her taste but a fine bit of cloth. Pre-war, she supposed. Everything about Barry Morton, including a visible paunch, indicated money.

'What a lucky man I was,' he said, 'finding you like that the other night. I was only being a good Samaritan. The bonus was that you and your mum turned out to be a couple of good-lookers. I thought, They've got something, those two. Took me a week to decide whether I should follow up our meeting. Then I decided, what the hell? Go for it, Barry. They can only say no. When I say "they", of course I meant you. Threesome's aren't much fun, and I'm a touch on the young side for your mum, lovely lady though she is.'

'Yes.' The idea of recommending her mother's qualities was quickly blasted.

'But I imagine what you'll be wanting to know about is me.'

Prue nodded, hoping her expression was suitably enthusiastic. She finished her drink quickly. Barry Morton waved at a woman behind the bar, signalled that she should bring two more glasses. It seemed he was the only man in the bar who did not have to get up and fetch his own drink.

'Born and brought up in Manchester. Father a scrap-dealer. Not a bean to begin with. My two brothers and I shared a bed, outdoor toilet, all that. But did that man work! My dad? Ended up with a bit of money, took my mother for a Southend holiday, tried to make up for all the years of hardship, bought a nice bungalow – all that. Left each of us a small lump sum, enough to buy my first car. I'd always been car mad. I resprayed it, sold it for a profit, and I was off. Ended up buying a house, then another for rent, and now I own most of a street. Well, I exaggerate, if the truth be known. I own a couple of other houses in my street. But twenty, thirty years from now they'll be worth a fortune. Prue, I tell you, I'll be a very rich old man. When the country's back on its feet again the housing market will shoot up, mark my words.'

In the next two hours Barry furnished Prue with many details of cars he had bought and sold, the size of the profit he had made on each one. He went on to describe his house: 'Lovely place, wall-to-wall carpets, chandeliers, three-piece suite in the best leather money can buy—'

'Gold taps?' Prue, who had not spoken for so long, put the question with a laugh in her voice so that he should not think she was serious.

Barry paused, fussed at his dying cigar with a new match. 'Ah. There, Prue, you've caught me out.' He laughed. 'No gold taps so far, though there could be one day if ever I find a wife who wants such things. I've got a nice line in brass taps, mind. Take a bit of cleaning, but worth the effort.'

Prue cast him a look of profound understanding – the kind of look that would indicate she would never be that kind of wife. She glanced at the clock above the bar: time for Barry to ask his first question.

'And you, Prue? What's been your life?'

As the question did not reverberate with an aura of deep interest, she decided to mention just one era. 'I was a land girl,' she said.

Three glasses of champagne had made Barry's cheeks a lively red – a cranberry red, Prue thought.

'Very interesting,' Barry said. 'Admirable, admirable. I used to look at photos of land girls in *Picture Post*. Sexy, weren't they?'

The tip of his tongue slithered halfway along his bottom lip, making it glisten.

'I don't know about that. We were just ordinary girls, really.'

'Was it a good life? Better than munitions factories, I dare say.'

Prue sighed. The champagne had made her sleepy. Barry's interest did not seem keen enough to spur the energy for a proper reply. Here, in this doleful pub, the lights an ugly orange, the air thick with smoke, she knew she could not begin to convey to this stranger the highs and lows of the time at Hallows Farm. And she didn't want to. They were private, stored in her mind for revisiting when hours in the salon became almost unbearable. 'It was a good life,' she said at last.

That was enough to satisfy Barry. He suggested it was time to take her home.

They did not speak in the car. Prue found it hard to keep her eyes open. He took her arm as they swayed up the garden path, and when she faced him to thank him for the evening, he put a hand round her wrist. It was warm and encompassing as a muff – Mrs Lawrence had once given her a muff made of rabbit skin – which Prue found reassuring. She had vaguely imagined there might be a tussle. But there was not so much as a peck on the cheek. Barry merely said that if it suited her they could go out again some time. Plainly, as Prue told her mother next morning, he was a gentleman.

For several months they went out once or twice a week, to different pubs that all suffered from the same lighting and smoke. Champagne was not offered again, but Barry urged Prue to try various cocktails. Proud of his cocktail knowledge, he would give strict instructions to the barman, whose pursed lips indicated instructions were not necessary, he knew his job – and Prue grew to love White Ladies. The first cocktail would lull her into a mood of rather odd contentment. Barry Morton was not an exciting man, but he was easy to be with – Prue simply had to ask a question about his rise in the world and she could sit back for an hour or so while he described his progress in unsparing detail. It did not occur to her to be offended by his lack of reciprocal interest: it was a relief. She felt no inclination to talk about herself. There were no jokes, as there had been with Barry One. No laughter, except when Barry came to a part of his story in which some woman had behaved so badly that he had been obliged to give her a comeuppance she was unlikely to forget. At these parts of the story – and there were quite a few – Barry growled with laughter, but he laughed alone.

The outings always ended in the same way: a decorous goodnight in the porch, the muff-grip of his hand on one wrist.

'I can't think what he gets from our evenings out,' Prue said to her mother. 'He doesn't fancy me, that's plain.'

'I wonder what he's up to?' Mrs Lumley had kept this question to herself for several weeks. 'Perhaps he just wants companionship.'

'No man in his right mind just wants companionship,' said Prue. 'Most of them don't want companionship even after they've had their way.'

'Dare say you know best,' replied her mother, who had always secretly wondered whether her daughter had clung to her virginity during her days as a land girl.

'What do you mean by that?' Prue assumed a look of such total innocence that Mrs Lumley quickly chided herself for ever having thought badly of her daughter. They both laughed for their different reasons.

The evenings had begun to lighten. One Saturday, as Prue climbed into the passenger seat of the Daimler (the grasp of its huge front seat was by now wonderfully familiar) Barry Morton looked at her and frowned. 'Not that blue again,' he said. 'You've worn it every time. I'm not partial to blue, though I've kept it to myself. Haven't you anything else?'

Prue tilted up her head, caught his eye in a defiant glare. 'It's my best dress,' she said. 'I wore it at the Palace. And no, I haven't anything else that's suitable. I mean, what if one evening you decided to take me somewhere posh?'

Inadvertently she had delivered a punch below the belt. Barry blew out his cheeks, amazed to discover what had been going on in Prue's mind. All these weeks she'd seemed to be quite happy, now she was confessing she'd been hoping he'd take her somewhere better. Why hadn't the thought occurred to him? He had no idea. But he was full of remorse. His hand searched for her wrist and took it in the usual soft grasp. 'I'm sorry. I really am. I never thought – well, I thought we were quite happy having a drink, chatting, getting to know each other . . .'

'Oh, we've been quite happy. It's been good going out with you . . . just a bit different. But then I've never been out with an older man before.'

This new blow – he had never thought of himself as an older man – caused Barry to reach for his wallet. He took out a five-pound note, the huge piece of fragile white paper folded into crisp edges, its black script a beautiful pattern scrawled across it. 'Here, take this,' he said. 'Get yourself a couple of new dresses and we'll go somewhere grand. Bright lights, pancakes set alight, crapes they call them—'

'I can't take money from you. Thanks all the same.' Prue handed back the note.

Barry pushed it away impatiently. 'I want you to.' Prue heard the truth of this in his voice. She resisted no more – too much resistance, she had learnt, meant you could miss out on valuable things. She put the note in her bag. Never having been in possession of so much money in her life, she felt light-headed.

'You treat yourself,' Barry was saying. 'If you need more, you only have to say the word.' There was a catch in his voice, a softness she had not detected before. Had kindness or nefarious intent spurred such generosity? Prue wondered. It was the last time she wore the blue dress.

The following week Barry arrived in a tie that shone like beaten gold, and Prue wore a new dress of amber crêpe that fluttered round her legs like a breeze. It had taken most of her saved coupons and was, her mother assured her, a wonder. Barry's look was complimentary. 'That's better,' he said. 'That makes a change.'

They drove to a large hotel in the centre of Manchester where Prue went round the glass entry doors several times. She had never been to such a place before and the view of red carpets, pillars and posts with golden edges made her laugh.

'You're quite a child sometimes,' Barry said, when she had finished merry-go-rounding. 'You need looking after. You could do with a firm hand.' Prue laughed again. She was used to his slight criticisms. They didn't offend. She gave him her wrist – a little nervous of all the red carpet – and they went into an enormous white dining room where a waiter at the entrance gave what Prue supposed was a bow. He showed them to a round table so dazzling with white napery that Prue rubbed her eyes in the way people do when caught out by snow. There was a confusion of cutlery, too – which knife or fork or spoon should she choose first? Such a collection of silver was unnerving. In a tall thin vase a single rosebud stood at attention. It would never open, Prue thought, though she chose not to mention this to Barry in case he took it as a reproach. In the great white lake of the place a few other diners sat at far-apart tables like people stranded on islands. Their mouths moved, but there was no sound.

Barry guided Prue through the short menu with some delicacy. Not a French speaker himself, a decade of studying menus had left him with a certain ability to understand culinary language, made easier, these days, by the paucity of post-war choice. Prue was impressed and agreed to all his recommendations. She was further impressed by his exchange with the wine waiter, mentioning names and vintages that meant nothing to her.

As they ate their miniature cutlets, almost hidden beneath paper ruffles, and Barry spoke of the childhood love affair with cars from which his present business had begun, Prue studied his face. She had never seen it before in such a good light: the pubs had all been so gloomy. Here, the dark eyes sparkled, the pockmarked nose shone. The thin line of his top lip was less noticeable when he smiled: a smile also reduced the heaviness of his long jaw. Not exactly handsome, thought Prue, though from a distance he might be considered quite passable-looking. But she was aware of being used to his face, fond of it. She regarded him as a kindly uncle. She was grateful to him for taking her out in his amazing car, buying her as many drinks as she wanted, and now bringing her to this place. Most of all she was grateful that he had not tried any hanky-panky, and it looked as though he never would.

Three elderly musicians entered in an orderly line, crossed the small dance-floor and took up their positions. They wore dinner jackets whose shoulders were uniformly bronzed with wear. Prue did not see a look pass between them, but when the pianist gave a slight nod they started to play a somnolent version of 'Pack Up Your Troubles'. Barry jumped up so fast he knocked over his wine. Red surged over white. From behind pillars several waiters ran to deal with the emergency. 'Dance, Prue?' he said, holding out his arms.

Here goes, she thought, embarrassed by all the fuss at the table, such tall strong rather handsome men dealing with a mere glass of spilt wine. Here goes, Mum's wish come true: fox-trotting.

In her high heels, Prue was only an inch shorter than Barry. He led her through the maze of tables to the floor. One other couple had got there first. Married, they looked, as they gently rocked like an old boat at low tide. Barry put one hand round Prue's waist: he held her hand very high, as if clutching a long skirt to avoid a wet street. He moved, tilting his head fractionally toward her.

Barry was a dancer whose enthusiasm outreached his talent. As they traversed the floor Prue was aware that, while his feet kept in time, his body lacked the essential rhythm to match her own. She longed for him to be livelier, but that was plainly beyond him. His Brylcreemed head bent lower towards hers: to avoid it, she was forced to bend her neck into a painful position. 'Gee, it's great to be walking back late, walking my baby back home,' slurped the music.

Prue shut her eyes and thought of the party she had gone to with the girls and Joe: a big hall somewhere, cold, chairs that squeaked on the floor, a buffet of bridge rolls and jellies in primary colours. It was there that Stella had been pursued by a tiny wing commander who danced like an angel. So brilliant was their dancing that others moved away from the floor and watched them perform like professionals who had danced together all their lives. At the end, Joe had stood up and clapped. Prue herself had paid less attention than she might to Stella, for she had caught sight of the flight lieutenant with whom she had recently exchanged glances in a teashop. She had made her way across to him and they danced – not like Stella and the wing commander, but with something flaring so hard between them that the edges of her legs, her arms, her body felt blurred, the flesh made soft. Unwisely she had accepted the flight lieutenant's offer of several more drinks, and vaguely remembered being supported to the car. When they had got back Joe had carried her into the house, but she was long past being excited by Joe.

That evening was the beginning of her real love for Barry One. Barry One the brave airman with his crinkling eyes and floppy hair who had made her feel there was nothing she had to explain. Their language had been almost devoid of words, though their laughter always seemed to come together. Even when they had realized they loved each other they had made few declarations, both nervous of failing to choose the right words. '"I love you" is the hardest line to say,' Barry One had ventured not long before he was shot down – thereby conveying his feelings in a way that made Prue love him all the more. That first evening, when Prue's dignity had flown and Barry One didn't seem to mind, had been very different from the staid time she was now having with Barry Two, she thought, as she released her hand to rub her aching neck.

She was aware of the present Barry's stomach pressing against her, and his quickened breathing. The band lurched into 'I'm In The Mood For Love'. Oh, cripes, she thought. Here goes.

But Barry restrained himself. He didn't speak in the car and didn't grasp her wrist as they walked up the front path. In the porch he put a hand up and briefly touched her hair. 'You're a good girl, Prue,' he said. 'I hope you enjoyed this evening.'

Prue nodded.

'And next time . . . next time, do you know where I'm going to take you?' Prue shook her head, dreading the answer, but curious. 'I'm going to take you to my house. I want you to see it. You've waited long enough.' He said this with solemn conviction, as if he had no doubt that seeing his house was just what Prue had been longing for. 'I'll pick you up at the usual time.'

He twirled round, surprisingly nimbly for one who had drunk a good deal of his favourite vintage, and headed back to his car. Barry Morton plainly had plans and she would have to think about them very carefully.

In bed, her own head quite clear, she began to weigh things up, an art she had never completely acquired. By dawn she was laughing silently at herself: she was running ahead in a foolish way. It was unlikely Barry Morton saw her as marriage material.

It was quite possible he had no serious intentions whatsoever. He was simply biding his time, waiting for her to give in. Then the laughter turned almost to tears when she thought of how she had felt after that other, wartime, dance, with the other Barry, the proper one.

The Larches, as Barry's house was called, stood very upright in a wide street on the outskirts of the city. It had been built in the era when builders aspired to fashionable mock-Tudor, and its neighbours were similar in appearance. The Daimler swooshed into a drive of deep gravel. The light in the porch was a lantern of stained glass. The front-door knocker was a brass lion's head.

'I was dazzled even before I got out of the car,' Prue wrote later to both Stella and Ag, 'but also a little uneasy. I had no experience of rich men's houses.'

Barry led her through a thickly carpeted hall to what he called the front room. It was all he had promised. Three-piece leather suite, low velvet armchairs, indistinct pictures, a very grand mirror over the fireplace – a dark room, but when your eyes grew accustomed to its umber light it was possible to see that someone with an eye for rich colours had been in charge of the decorating. Prue was intrigued by the fire – gas, she thought, though it was hard to tell, so skilfully depicted were the imitation logs piled into a neat mound. Imitation flames flickered against the iron back, not quite the random colours of real flames but pretty good.

'What a clever fire,' she said at last.

Barry shrugged. 'Like it all, do you?'

'It's amazing. Beautiful.'

'You wait till you see the rest.'

On a low table by the fire there was a plate of sandwiches and two fragile glasses. Prue wondered if Barry had arranged all this himself – he didn't strike her as a sandwich-making man. Perhaps there was some invisible servant who lived in the back of the house. The centre of each sandwich was decorated with a minute sprig of parsley. Surely Barry . . .

'Shall we celebrate with some bubbly?' he asked.

'Celebrate what?' The question had sprung from her inadvertently. 'I mean—'

'Celebrate the fact you're here at last, sweetheart,' Barry said. 'I'll just fetch it. Won't be a mo.'

Alone in the room, Prue was able to observe that every piece of furniture, every ornament, the carpets, the tall silk curtains, must have cost unimaginable amounts of money. Barry Morton was obviously a very rich man indeed. Prue sighed.

In front of the fire that never died down, they drank the first bottle of champagne, and a second. They ate the fish-paste sandwiches. Prue longed for a bowl of soup, fish and chips, anything to calm her swirling head, but no suggestions of proper dinner were forthcoming. Was Barry Morton up to something? Prue giggled. 'Are you up to something?' she asked.

'Up to something? What do you have in mind?'

'Well, I don't know. It's all so surprising, this.'

'There are more surprises.' Barry walked over to Prue, put his muff-hand round her wrist, pulled her up. They stood facing each other, very close. Prue would have moved away had not her legs felt so unsteady. Her eyes had become a little out of focus, but she was able to see the piercing intent in his.

'Now, my sweet Prue, I've something to tell you. I've been thinking about it very hard these months we've known each other, and I've made up my mind. I want you to be my wife. How about that?'

Prue fell backwards onto a chair. One leg tipped up, knocking the low table. Two champagne bottles, two glasses and the empty plate fell to the floor, silenced by the carpet. Her cheeks blazed. Behind Barry's patient smile she saw a ghostly look of annoyance.

'I'm so sorry.'

'Don't worry.' In a trice Barry had picked up the fallen things and returned them to the table. He could see that this small, irritating accident had taken the edge off Prue's answer, but he was a patient man. He wouldn't alarm her by pressing her. He could wait. 'I think you should see the rest of the house.'

'Right.'

They went side by side up the staircase, its banisters of dark oak so thick they would have prevented an army from falling into the hall. Prue felt very much as she had on the night of the dance when the girls had had to support her to the car: everything swirled.

They went through a dark and silent door to the bedroom. In her unclear state Prue had a slippery picture of an enormous bed, shining satin eiderdown, dark drawn curtains, acres of carpeted floor, lampshades the colour of peaches. She crossed the room, knowing she was going to fall and not wanting to drop ignominiously to the floor. She let herself flop onto the end of the bed. Barry stood looking down at her, very serious.

'What do you want?' she heard herself say.

'What do you think I want, sweetheart?' An icicle of sweat ran down one of his cheeks. 'What do you think I've been waiting for?'

He ripped at his gold tie with one hand, pulled up her pretty skirt with the other. Then he was hammering into her, groaning. It was all over very quickly.

Later in the night, while Barry Morton snored quietly beside her, Prue reflected it had not been like any other shag she had ever known – and she'd known quite a few. But, to be realistic, it seemed Barry was no better a lover than he was a dancer. Sex, however, Prue told herself, was not everything, and again she began to try to weigh things up. Here was the rich man she had always longed for, who could give her everything. There'd be no money worries as there always had been at home. He was solid, safe, agreeable, kind – wasn't he? They could make a life. Be married, have children. She'd be better off than millions of girls in search of a husband. The shortage of men, after the war, was a disaster. If she didn't say yes to Barry she might never have another chance. Prue turned, studied his thick shoulders in a chink of early light spearing the curtains, and made her decision.

When she woke Barry had gone. She was wondering what to do, how to make the long journey to work, when he came out of the bathroom. He wore a short towelling dressing-gown so that she was able to observe the peculiarities of his short legs. The shins were covered with black hair: the calves were hairless round balls that tapered to thin ankles. Prue swallowed.

Barry sat on the bed, took her hand. 'Thought I'd let you sleep on a while,' he said. 'It's six thirty.'

'Thank you.'

He bent down, kissed her cheek. There was a strong smell of toothpaste and potent cologne. Then he crossed the room, calves trembling like jellies, to draw back the curtains. Nebulous light filled the room. The orange satin eiderdown made a frivolous patch of colour among the dark furniture. Barry returned to the bed. 'Was it all right, last night?' he asked.

Prue paused. She wished she'd had more time, this morning, to think about life with Barry Morton. 'Course it was,' she said, reaching for a smile.

Barry took her wrist. 'And did you manage to think of an answer to my question?' There was a pause. 'Marriage? You and me, man and wife?'

'Yes . . .' Prue's answer was so quiet Barry had trouble hearing it. But he gave a broad smile and kissed her cheek again. He made to get up, but was restrained by Prue's hand on his arm. It had suddenly occurred to her that there was something she ought to know. 'Why do you want to marry me?'

'Well, obvious, isn't it, sweetheart? A man needs a wife.'

'But does love come into it at all? Do you love me?'

'Course I love you.' He sniffed. Glanced at his watch. 'Breakfast on the table at seven, then I'll drive you to work.'

'I can still carry on helping Mum in the salon, can't I?'

'Don't be daft, sweetheart. Not once we've tied the knot. I'm not going to have my wife working. I'm a very rich man and you can have anything you want. Why would you want to spend your days in a hairdresser's? You can tell your mum this morning. Give in your notice.' He laughed, stood up and tightened the sash of his dressing-gown so that a roll of flesh bulged both above and below his waist.

They met again downstairs in the small dining room that overlooked a bare garden. The table was laid with a professional neatness that Prue found unnerving: Mrs Lawrence used to dump honey, jam and toast randomly on the kitchen table. She wondered again about the invisible servant who had produced tea, coffee, egg cups on matching plates, napkins in silver holders.

'There's a Mrs Morley, Bertha, who looks after me,' said Barry. 'She's a wonder. Does everything. Been here some years. You'll meet her.'

But Bertha didn't appear before they left. In the car arrangements were discussed. They would carry on 'as normal', Barry said, until the wedding in a few weeks time, when the weather was better. After that, of course, she would move in. Prue found nothing wrong with the idea. She felt bruised, crushed, sore: was not impatient for another night of Barry's inept lovemaking.

In the salon she found her mother. 'I was so worried! Where were you?'

'You must have known.'

'Well, I suppose I guessed. You look ever so pale, Prue. Here, I'll put the kettle on.'

'Mum.' Prue put an arm round her shoulders. 'Barry asked me to marry him.'

Indignation flared briefly across Mrs Lumley's face. 'Well I never. What did you say?'

'I said yes. You'll never have to worry again, mum. Everything'll be taken care of.'

'Well . . . He's an older man, isn't he? But age never got in the way of true love, did it?' She did up her pinafore, patted her hair. Tears came into her eyes. 'I'm so pleased for you, Prue. You deserve the best. You've had some bad times with men.'

Prue giggled. 'Not so bad,' she said. They hugged each other, then drew apart to embark on a normal day of permanent waves.

Barry gave Prue a large square diamond ring and the weeks before the wedding passed with alarming speed. During that time, when Prue was not making lists or comparing florists, she made herself think with great care about the forthcoming event. Not an introvert by nature – her mother's advice had always been to get on with life rather than think about it – she found this exercise tedious and her concentration frayed quickly. But she knew she had finally to convince herself that Barry was the man for her.

'Course I love you,' he had said when she had asked if he loved her. What did that mean? Did it indicate he was suffused with the kind of love that might well be everlasting? Or did it mean he loved her a *bit* – just enough to take her as his wife? She remembered she had never said, 'Course I love you,' back – but, then, he had never asked her to measure her own love for him. The difficulty was to work out what, exactly, their love was made of. Certainly not the same thing as her love for Barry One, which had been so overpowering there had been no need to question it. Certainly not what she had felt for Joe, a high-spirited passion that had electrified her body through the long days of hard work at Hallows Farm.

Her love for Barry Morton was, she supposed, closer to affection and gratitude than to an exhilarating feeling of wanting constantly to be together. The thought of him did not keep her awake at night. When he was absent during the day she did not long for his return, though she was always pleased to see him. They simply got on in a friendly way, exchanging snatches of news or reflecting on their particular interests – cars and farming. That was probably good enough, Prue told herself. Besides, love sometimes grows. There was a chance it would expand beyond her imaginings. And it was impossible to back away now – the cake, the hat, the flowers were all ordered. So while in her heart there were doubts and worries (surely normal in all brides-to-be?) she reckoned Barry was a pretty good bet. That was as far as her ruminations went. They ended, each time, as they had begun: she had made her decision and she would go through with it. The fact that she sometimes secretly cried at the thought of the more positive love she had once known would not deter her. Total love probably did not happen more than once in a lifetime. It was foolish to hope for it again. She would settle for a different kind, lucky to be Barry's wife.

They were married on a windy day in a register office. Prue wore a felt hat shaped like a plate that kept slipping down over one eye, and on her left breast a corsage of velvet roses. Her mother and Barry's showroom manager were the witnesses, and joined them for lunch in the posh hotel where they had recently danced. Neither Stella nor Ag nor any of the Lawrences was able to come. They all sent cards, and good wishes, and hoped to meet Barry very soon: but Ag was off to Egypt with her husband, Stella could not leave Philip who was ill again, and the Lawrences had to deal with some farming crisis in Yorkshire. Prue cried one last time in her bed at home on the night before the wedding, but she also felt a strange sense of relief. She was not entirely sure what the people she loved most would think of Barry. She wanted their approval but could not be certain it would be forthcoming.

After the wedding Mr and Mrs Barry Morton took various trains to Brighton where they were to stay at a hotel on the front. From their bedroom window they could see the pier. Room service provided their first dinner – very small helpings of fish and chips – and they talked of Prue learning to drive. They drank a bottle of champagne and soon the the outlines of the room, and Barry, began to dissolve: Prue realized this was the beginning of the kind of life she had always longed for. A woozy sort of gratitude to her husband rose in her, but she was very tired. The wedding hadn't been as she imagined – no white dress, large church, choir – but Barry had been quite right to insist on nothing too showy in these hard post-war times. Barry, she appreciated, was a wise man. A wise, kind, very rich man. She undressed in the marble bathroom and slipped into the large bed still in her dressing-gown.

Barry did not look up when she came in: he was reading the car-sales pages of the evening paper. When he had finished it he glanced over to his wife and saw that she was already asleep. This was not, he reflected with a smile, how the average wife would behave on the first night of the honeymoon, but he saw no point in waking her.

# Chapter 2

In the first months of their marriage Prue struggled to find things to occupy the days. Barry had forbidden her to carry on working, which was no hardship for she was not a keen hairdresser, but she did want to see her mother regularly. Several times a week she took the long bus ride into the city and they would meet for a sandwich in the lunch-hour. Barry showed no sign of issuing an invitation for his mother-in-law to visit the house, but Prue assured her it would not be long in coming.

She did not try to keep secret her visits to the salon. She did not mention them only because Barry, at the end of his busy days, did not question her about how she had spent hers. When she happened to say one evening that she had seen her mother – and, yes, she had gone there on the bus – Barry had been oddly annoyed. 'No more going on a bus for you, my girl. I'm not having my wife travelling by bus. No. We'll get you driving lessons, buy you a car. Then you'll be free to go all over.'

Prue was grateful for the lessons. They took up an hour or so of the day and Rod, her instructor, was a good-looking young man, keen for a laugh. She found herself putting on mascara on lesson mornings, and taking care over her lipstick. She enjoyed the driving, found it easy.

'You're a talented young lady,' said Rod one day. They had pulled up in a quiet road to discuss the art of double-declutching. 'There's not many get the hang of it this well in so few lessons.'

'Well, I drove a tractor for three years.' Prue was warmed by his flattery. 'As a matter of fact, though I shouldn't say this, I was the best driver of us three girls. I could do a big field in a morning. Furrows straight as a die.'

'Could you, now? I'm impressed.' He turned to Prue, smiled. She fluttered her heavily-encrusted lashes, thinking that for her next lesson she would wear one of the bows in her hair that had caused the Lawrences' disapproval until they had grown used to them. Prue put one hand, for half a second, on his thigh. 'Thing is, you're a great teacher.'

'Thanks.' There was a flash between them so powerful that Prue blushed and Rod, as if short of air, wound down his window. 'I think we'll do the double-declutching next week,' he said. 'Time's up.'

A few moments later when he drove away from the front door – ten minutes before their time was really up, Prue noticed – she blew him a kiss. The rest of the day, quite without guilt, she spent wondering. Funny to think a strange young man could still fancy her.

Barry left home at seven every morning in the Daimler, returning in time for dinner. At least once a week he would bring her a present: there had been a gold watch, a scarf he swore was from Paris, a fountain pen with a gold nib, a leather, silk-lined case, which he called a 'vanity case', a name Prue failed to understand but did not like to ask – and a ruby brooch. They would come, these presents, in grand boxes and tissue paper. After dinner Prue and Barry would move into the sitting room, light the gas fire, switch on the Light Programme and there would be a ceremony of giving and receiving.

The slower the unwrapping the better, Barry thought. He enjoyed watching his wife's pink-cheeked delight, her struggle to find more and yet more adjectives to describe her wonder, amazement, gratitude. One evening the gift was a wallet of scarlet leather. It held five new five-pound notes. Prue burst into tears. 'I can't go on taking all these things from you,' she said. 'And as for all this money – I've never seen so much in my life. What can I do with it?'

'You can spend, spend, spend, sweetheart,' Barry said. His satisfaction at her response was faintly alarming in a way Prue could not explain to herself. 'What better way for me to spend my money than on my wife?'

'Well . . .' A hidden part of Prue agreed. What she had always wanted she was now getting in abundance. It was both exciting and a little alarming.

Once the present was unwrapped, and the last dregs of amazement plucked from it, Barry would say he had to be getting to bed for he had an early start. By the time she reached the bedroom, half an hour after him, Barry was asleep. Saturday nights were the exception. Prue dreaded Saturday nights. It was then Barry would ask her to undress completely, but throw her new scarf round her neck or hold up her new brooch to her chest. He then required her to walk across the room to where he lay on the bed. He would put on his glasses, scrutinize her, as if she was some kind of specimen, hold out a hand to her wrist and pull her down on top of him. The next part of the ritual was always very quick, but uncomfortable and passionless. His lovemaking bore no resemblance to anything Prue had ever known before: it simply had to be endured. He seemed to have no desire to ensure Prue's enjoyment. His own fast satisfaction was his only aim.

At first Prue, willing to be a good sport, found Saturday night requirements bearable but disappointing. They soon became boring. Once she tried hurrying across the room, instead of progressing at a languid pace. But that had caused a cry of impatient fury: 'Go back and come here again,' Barry shouted, maroon in the face, 'slower.'

'At least he doesn't tie me up or thrash me,' Prue wrote to Ag, some time later, 'but I think he's a bit weird. Still, perhaps it's a small price to pay for all this . . . stuff.'

To her own amazement she grew less enchanted by the presents, too. She begged Barry to stop buying her things, but he impatiently waved away her protest. 'You're a good wife,' he said. 'You deserve a lot.'

'Not every week, Barry, please.'

'Whenever I want. Up to me.'

'It's almost as if they were a substitute for – well, love.'

'Is that what you think?' Prue could not tell whether his look was one of surprise or indignation. 'Why don't you just say to yourself, sweetheart, that you're lucky enough to be married to a very generous man?' This was a melancholy voice Prue had not heard before.

'Oh, I am,' said Prue, quickly. She felt there was a kind of madness in the stuffy air of the room, silence only frazzled by the hiss of the gas fire. She wanted to run across Lower Pasture, meet Barry One in the wood on a summer evening: not kneel on the floor admiring three pairs of kid gloves she would never wear.

When it wasn't one of his very early starts, Barry liked Prue to be at breakfast with him, and sometimes she joined him. It was a simple way of pleasing him, though she failed to see exactly how her presence was rewarding. He read the paper while he ate his porridge. Bowl empty, he would light his first cigar of the day, then run from the room in unfailing hurry. Sometimes Prue wondered where he went, and how his day was spent. His answers to her questions were always perfunctory. She could never imagine what he was doing, or how he was, when he was gone.

One morning after he had left the dining room Prue went to the window and opened it. She hated the smell of cigars. The open window drew out a single thread of smoke, but years of it had blighted the air in a way that was impossible entirely to extinguish. Prue looked at the large, bleak square of lawn surrounded by dark bushes and ivy-covered brick walls. It occurred to her that bulbs should be showing, trees blossoming. But there wasn't a single tree in this part of the garden, not a single flower. So dispiriting was this realization that Prue went into the kitchen to ask Bertha if she knew if Barry had any plans for planting.

Prue had not been able to make friends with Bertha. She had run the house satisfactorily for several years and did not want any interference. In a taciturn way she made it clear she would rather Prue did not visit the kitchen and, no, she had no need of help of any kind. Prue had offered to iron, to shop, to clear away: all such offers were almost politely rejected. Bertha lived in a flat over the garage. As far as Prue could make out she spent all her time there when she was not engaged in cooking and cleaning in the house. She was something of a mystery, Bertha, but when Prue asked Barry about her, he gave one of his reticent responses. She'd had a hard life, he said, and he'd been able to rescue her. No other details were forthcoming and Prue knew better than to press him with questions he did not want to answer.

On this particular morning Bertha was standing at the kitchen table polishing silver spoons. She looked up as Prue came in. Just perceptibly, her mouth tightened. 'Good morning, Mrs Morton,' she said, concentrating on a spoon.

'Good morning, Bertha.' Prue regarded the thin, tense woman in her wrap-over pinafore, hair in a single roll round her neck a little in the fashion of Mrs Lawrence's. She wore carpet slippers and a thin gold band on her wedding finger. She was both hostile and sad, bitter but resigned. Prue did not know how to begin. 'You've got a wonderful kitchen,' she said at last. 'All these modern things. At the farmhouse where I was billeted as a land girl there was nothing like this. It was very rough. Vegetables and dead pigeons scattered about . . . You know.'

'Really.' Bertha picked up another spoon. 'And no, I don't know and I'm not that much interested.'

Prue joined the silence. She was determined not to leave the room before she had asked about the garden. Bertha was not going to intimidate her. 'I'm sorry to disturb you,' she said at last, 'but I just wanted to ask if you knew whether my husband has any plans for the garden.'

Bertha gave Prue a look that suggested some kind of mark had been overstepped. Such inquisitiveness was an affront.

'I mean, it's a nice big garden, isn't it? It cries out for – well, I don't know. Trees and flowers and things . . .'

'Mr Morton has never made any mention to me of plans for the garden,' Bertha said, this time with a trace of triumph. 'I'm sure I've no idea what he has in mind. It's not my place to ask.'

'No.' Prue managed to give a small laugh. 'Well, I won't disturb you any more. By the way, the fish last night was lovely,' she lied.

'I should hope so. Mr Morton likes his fish.' Bertha turned to put the spoons in a drawer, her thin shoulders hunched with general indignation.

Prue ran upstairs to put on her mascara. It was a driving-lesson morning. She hoped concentrating on her three-point turn would deflect her from the encounter with Bertha, which had left her with shaking knees.

That morning Rod was very silent, his usual friendliness evaporated. He gave her brief instructions, but no praise when she got something right. When finally they parked in their usual quiet street, Prue turned to him. She liked his profile. 'What's the matter, Rod?'

He stared through the windscreen. 'Nothing.'

'I don't believe you.'

'No, really.'

'Come on, out with it.'

Rod turned to her. His eyes were the colour of slate. 'If you really want to know, I feel a bit topsy-turvy. I was in half a mind to send another instructor.'

'Why?'

'Can't quite put my finger on it. But you know how it is. Sometimes out of the blue, something hits you. You're knocked off your perch. All you want . . . and I'm not a womanizer. Don't see many girls except the plain bunch who want to learn to drive. First thing we're warned in our training, of course, is never to get involved with one of our pupils. Never.'

'Of course not.' It was all Prue could do not to put a hand on his arm or his cheek.

'So, this is no good. I'm going to have to pass you on to another instructor.'

'No!' Prue gave a small shriek. 'Please don't. I love our lessons. You're a wonderful teacher.'

'I love them too. That's the trouble.' Rod smiled. 'Just my luck I get a beautiful young married woman. Happy as they come, I dare say. Socking great house, everything . . .'

Their eyes locked in the moment before unexpected tears burst upon Prue. The encounter with Bertha must have shaken her more than she had realized, she thought, and now this handsome young man being sympathetic. She heard herself howling. As she rubbed at her cheeks she could imagine the ragged black mess her mascara must have made of them. The thought turned the tears to laughter.

Rod took out a handkerchief, dabbed at her face. Then he ran a finger along her top lip. 'You are a surprise,' he said. 'What's the matter?'

Prue sniffed, and blew her nose on his handkerchief. 'It's all just so odd,' she said.

'I'm sorry.' He tried for a light note. 'That's why I don't go for marriage. It's always struck me as a weird business.' He took back his handkerchief. They both laughed in a minor way. 'Think our time's up,' he said. 'Let's see if you can reverse into the road.'

When they got back to the house Rod shook her hand. 'Good luck with the test,' he said. 'I'm sure you'll do fine.'

It was only once he had driven away that it occurred to Prue his wishes for success meant he had definitely decided it would be better to cease being her instructor.

Despite driving lessons three times a week, now with an old and uncharismatic instructor, Prue was finding her days long and empty. Sometimes she went into the city on a bus – it took up time – to spend one of the five-pound notes, but there was little in the shops and nothing she wanted among the gloomy clothes. Sometimes she went to the salon, but felt herself in the way now she no longer worked there. She made lists of things she would like planted in the garden, and of the few friends she had had in Manchester before the war.

But one small excitement, two months into her marriage, was finding the telephone – a heavy, dusty black thing with a long tangled brown lead – under a table in the hall. She had never known Barry to use it and she had never heard it ring. She spent an afternoon trying to get through to two girlfriends with whom she'd been at school. They had both moved away. No one knew where they were. It then occurred to Prue, who had never written more than a postcard in her life, that she could ring Stella and Ag. God, how she wanted to hear their voices, know about their lives. Since leaving the Lawrences the three had kept up their arrangement of lunching in London once a year, and it was six months since they had last met. Time to make another plan.

Stella, who lived by the sea in Norfolk, was full of apologies for not having been able to come to the wedding.

'Oh, that. It wasn't much of a wedding,' said Prue. 'Very quiet.'

'And Barry – your second Barry – what's he like?'

'Kind. Generous. Tons of presents. Huge house.'

'All the things you wanted, then.'

'Almost. Not quite. I'm learning to drive. Nearly there, though it's not as much fun as the tractor.'

'No.'

Prue, sitting comfortably on the carpeted stairs, wanted to go on talking to Stella for ever. Her soft, comforting voice, her way of indicating she knew what was going on even if nothing was said. 'Once I've passed my driving test,' she said, 'perhaps I could come and see you.'

'Please, please do. I can't leave here often. Philip needs a lot of looking after. He's so brave and uncomplaining, but he keeps getting infections. Come and see us long before we next meet in London.'

'I will, I promise.' Cheered by the thought of a visit to look forward to – Barry One used to say everyone should have something to look forward to – Prue then telephoned Ag. She and Desmond lived in Devon.

'I thought you'd never ring,' said Ag. She was in high spirits. 'We've just moved into our new home. I'm over the moon.'

'Crikey, Ag! Wonderful. When I can drive I'll come and see you.'

'We'd love that. You'd like it here – all much smaller than Hallows Farm, but I've a good orchard full of Mrs Lawrence's plums and we're about to buy some cattle. Lots of hens, of course.'

'Hens? Gosh.'

'And you, Prue, what's your news?'

'I'm a very respectable, grown-up married lady. My husband's a little older than me, very rich, very generous. I've a diamond ring, jewels, a fur hat, kid gloves and all that stuff . . . And, well, that's the sort of thing I wanted, didn't I?'

Ag hesitated. 'Gold taps?'

'Almost,' said Prue. They both laughed.

Two visits to look forward to: Prue's spirits lifted, though she continued to sit on the stairs, remembering. Two ideas began to form an inchoate shape in her mind: pregnancy and chickens. If she had a baby, and half a dozen laying birds, she could be busy again. Work hard. It was the idleness in this dark, rich, bleak house that was so depressing.

A few weeks later Prue passed her driving test. She couldn't think who would be pleased for her. She rang her mother – by now she made frequent use of the telephone – who congratulated her, but plainly underestimated the scale of the achievement. She thought Barry would not be much interested, though perhaps it might spur him on to buy her a very small Austin.

Prue was wrong. Barry's delight seemed out of all proportion to the news. First, laying aside his cigar, he hugged her – something he had never done before. Apart from the times he bashed roughly into her, he never touched her other than to guide her with a hand on her wrist to their table in the hotel dining room on the occasions he took her out for dinner. His arms round her were so tight that Prue felt the breath squeezed out of her and gave a little cry. Barry released her, apologetic, and took up his cigar again. Then he suggested they celebrate – a word Prue had come to dread, with its usual connotations. They would be off in the Daimler for a slap-up dinner, champagne. She was to wear one of her new dresses, her new scent. They'd have a good time.

Barry's excitement, so much greater than Prue's own, was puzzling. She felt once again that she didn't begin to understand her husband, so oddly delighted by her small achievement of passing a driving test yet so completely uninterested in her barren days. What did he imagine she did? Read romantic novels, eating fudge? Perhaps, she thought, she should take advantage of his sudden liveliness. She decided to interrupt his usual stories of his past, and mention chickens. Or the possibility of a baby. Or perhaps both.

They sat at their usual table, had their usual miniature cutlets and mashed potato forked into a pattern that reminded Prue of the permanent waves her mother was so skilful at conjuring in elderly hair. She giggled.

'What's up, sweetheart?'

'Nothing. I was just thinking.'

'You know what? You've the greenest, prettiest eyes I've ever seen on a girl.' The compliment left him as surprised as it did Prue. With a hitch of his shoulders he had braced himself to deliver it. Now he sank back against the chair, deflated.

'Barry! You've never said anything so nice!'

'Nonsense, sweetheart. I've often thought it.'

Perhaps, reflected Prue, finishing her wine very quickly, this is where I start to love Barry Morton, for all his funny ways, and it really could be happy-ever-after.

Strawberry ice cream arrived. Prue pushed hers aside, clasped her hands as if in prayer and she leant towards her husband. 'Barry,' she said, 'you're the most generous husband in the world, and I know how lucky I am, but . . . there's just one thing.'

'Out with it.' Barry's frog eyes narrowed.

'I haven't much to do all day.'

'What? You've time to yourself, sweetheart. Nothing more precious than that. Total luxury. You can do anything you want. What are you saying?'

'I'm saying . . . Well, I've always loved working hard. I'd like to work hard at something again.'

Barry pushed his ice cream to join Prue's and lit a cigar. 'Far be it from me to stop you.' His previous softness, almost loving, was suddenly gone. He spoke like someone in a meeting. 'You've got the world at your feet, all the money you want, and you're complaining.' He was slightly frightening.

42

'Not complaining, honestly.' Prue sighed, smiled, uncertain which way to go. 'I was thinking that perhaps with so much time on my hands . . .'

'You could always work for charity, visit old people, that sort of thing. Make yourself useful. Help those a great deal less fortunate than yourself.' He was scornful now.

'I could. But what I had in mind – I don't know how you'll take this, Barry – but what I had in mind was that perhaps we should try for . . . a baby.'

There was a very long silence. When she and Barry One had first mentioned the possibility of a child – a spring day in the woods – they had hugged and declared it would be the most exciting thing in the world. Now here was her husband pursing his lips and tapping his cigar, weighing up all his boring doubts like some financial adviser. 'That hadn't occurred to me,' he said. And again there was a sudden, unexpected shift in his demeanour. His mouth edged into a half-smile. His free hand tapped Prue's wrist. 'That's something to think about, any road,' he said. 'I rather fancy a son with your green eyes. My brain,' he added with a laugh. 'We could put that plan into action, sweetheart. We could start tonight. We can keep at it. That's a good idea.'

Prue inwardly quailed as her husband's eyes trawled her exposed chest and the small rounds of her breasts. If his intention was to work at conceiving like some kind of business plan, she hoped it would happen very fast and that once she was pregnant she would be spared his hammering.

Barry asked for the bill. He seemed to be in a hurry to get home. Prue put aside her idea of suggesting chickens. Two major possibilities at once might be too much for him. Chickens would have to wait.

All the way home Barry drove with one hand on the steering-wheel, the other on her knee. 'That's a good idea, love, that baby plan,' he said several times. 'I like the idea of green eyes, handsome little bugger.'

Despite Barry's apparent enthusiasm to get going straight away on the baby plan, the first attempt did not take place that night. When Prue obligingly walked from the bathroom, naked, to the bed, Barry impatiently told her to cover herself up. 'No jiggery-pokery tonight, sweetheart,' he said. 'I'm all for getting going soon as possible, like I said, but I'm knackered. Lot of stuff on my mind at work. Don't worry. Won't be long till you're tripping round with a stomach like a balloon. Only we're not going to make it happen tonight.'

There was a hint of apology in this, and Prue could see he did look unusually tired. So with mixed feelings she got into bed and turned out the light. A baby, she knew, would be the answer to everything. But curiously, for all Barry's initial enthusiasm, his threat 'to keep at it' did not come about. The old routine of Saturday nights only carried on, and there was no sign of Prue conceiving.

There was serious deflection from this disappointment. Within a few days of Prue passing her driving test, a scarlet Sunbeam Talbot was delivered to the driveway of The Larches.

She sat in the pale leather driving seat overawed. She felt sudden tears blur her eyes. 'This is the most beautiful car I've ever—'

'It's so you can do what you like, sweetheart. Go where you like, drive all over. Keep you happy.' Barry stood beside the open car window, chomping on his cigar.

'Thank you, Barry. How ever can I say thank you enough?'

'I like to keep you happy.'

'I'm going for a first short drive. Can't wait to try her out. Want to come?'

'Best you go alone. I've got things to do.'

Prue waved, wound up the window and started the engine, which made the most thrilling music she had ever heard.

She spent many days driving about in her car – not far, at first, but once she had grown used to it she bought a map and began to explore the country beyond Manchester. Several times she went to Derbyshire, which she loved. Often, when she parked at the roadside to study the view, she consciously thought: I'm happy now. Quite happy. She made a plan to go to Yorkshire, once she was a more confident driver, to visit Mr and Mrs Lawrence.

One afternoon, on returning from an outing to the city where with long-saved coupons she had bought a pair of irresistible pre-war red shoes, she found a man standing in the porch, his hand on the knocker. He turned to her as she got out of the car. 'Whew! Quite some car.'

He was tall and thin, with the kind of quirky face that was attractive. He had red hair – a ruddy amber rather than carrot, Prue judged, but red enough for him to have been teased at school. He reminded her a little of Robert, and of George, a man she had met on a bus soon after she had returned to Manchester just after the war. He had got off at the same stop as her, said he'd walk her home. She had asked him in for a cup of tea – her mother was still at work – and they had had a long talk about the breeding of rabbits. Then they'd rogered themselves to a standstill in her virgin bed, and he had slipped out just before Mrs Lumley arrived home. He also reminded her, this stranger waving a letter in his hand, of a sweet looking sub-lieutenant who had once sat beside her in a cinema and added hugely to the pleasure of the film.

'Sorry to disturb you,' said the man. 'I'm looking for Barry Morton. I'm Johnny Norse.'

'Prue. His wife.' They shook hands.

'Nice to meet you. I'm one of Barry's tenants, as I expect you know.'

Prue smiled. She had never met any of Barry's tenants, had no idea how many there were. 'He should be back in an hour or so. Would you like to come in?'

'I don't want to bother you.' He waved the letter again. 'Just want a word about the tenancy agreement, that sort of thing. As a matter of fact, I wanted to ask about . . .' He trailed off.

'Come on. I'm not exactly busy.' Prue liked the way his eyes screwed up when he gave even a minor smile. She opened the front door. The early-evening light was flung over the heavy furniture, the elaborate mirror, the grim pictures of unknown ancestors, certainly not Barry's.

'Blow me down,' said Johnny. 'It's not at all like this next door, my place.'

They stood awkwardly in the hall – awkwardly because, as Prue explained on the telephone to Ag the next day, she had suddenly found herself in a social dilemma. Her instinct was to go to the kitchen, put on the kettle, settle down at the table. But she knew that was not possible in this house. The kitchen was out of bounds. To take a visitor there and start finding tea and biscuits was not something Bertha, so fierce in her silent way, would tolerate. Prue knew the housekeeper was capable of being rude in her disapproval, and she did not wish anyone to be rude to this friendly man, who had turned out to be the next-door neighbour. The alternative was to go alone to the kitchen and ask Bertha if she would mind bringing a tray of tea into the sitting room. But in the shadow-packed hall Prue's courage left her. Even if Bertha agreed, her grim disapproval would shade, rather than ease, the atmosphere. Nothing for it but to go and sit down and make conversation. She led the way not into the front room but to the smaller sitting room that overlooked the garden.

Johnny immediately went over to the window and stood staring out, his back to Prue. 'Same shape garden as mine,' he said, 'but otherwise different altogether. You could do a lot to this

– lots of potential.' He turned round. 'Have you and Barry got plans? Because I know a lot of plants people . . . I could put you in touch.'

'I'm not sure Barry's a very keen gardener,' said Prue. 'Won't you sit?' She asked this so primly she made herself giggle. 'I'm sorry I can't offer you—'

'Oh, don't worry about that sort of thing. I only wanted to deliver this.' He smoothed the envelope with a swirl of his long fingers. There was a faintly expectant silence, as if each of them was waiting for the other to suggest the next move. Prue uncrossed her ankles, gave a high kick with one leg and crossed it over the other.

Johnny did not smile, or compliment her on the prettiness of her legs, but seemed deep in thought. 'You know what?' he said at last. 'All that grass? Chickens would make all the difference.'

'Chickens?' Funny they should both have the same thought. Prue felt almost faint with excited possibility.

'Chickens. I've got a couple of dozen Rhode Island Reds, fresh eggs every day in the laying season. It's a bonus, I can tell you. They've got a good run, and a house at the end of the garden. I've camouflaged it with a few bushes. They've made a real difference to the place.'

'I can imagine.' Prue now chose to uncross her legs, put her elbows on her knees and cup her chin in her hands. Suddenly reckless, she felt like trying out all her poses, see if she could get anywhere with this man. At least they had one thing in common: chickens. Not a bad beginning. She fluttered her eyelashes, furious with herself for not having bothered to put on her mascara. 'On the farm where I was a land girl, there were dozens of chickens, and bantams. In fact . . .' Prue now screwed up her eyes, wondering whether to confess the small incident to this stranger. '. . . the day we arrived we were greeted by all these birds running all over the place, and I was stupid enough to say I'd never seen such small chickens. The posh girl, Ag, she soon put me down. "I think you'll find it's a bantam," she said, in her lah-di-dah voice. Snubbed me, all right, but we were soon friends. And, I mean, I'd never seen a live bird before, just the dead one at Christmas for roasting.'

Johnny laughed politely. 'You were a land girl?'

'I was.'

'Well, good for you. Congratulations.' He nodded, full of respect. Prue felt herself blush. 'I don't know what we'd have done without you girls. How was it?'

'Best time of my life,' Prue said quietly.

'Never be anything like it again. When it comes to history, land girls will take their place.'

'Maybe.'

'But to get back to chickens.' Johnny returned to the window, scanned the bare lawn. 'I don't mean to be impertinent, but here's an idea. Why don't you suggest to Barry you have a chicken run at the bottom of your garden, too? I could get you half a dozen layers to start you off. I could even build them a house – I do carpentry in my spare time.'

'I might suggest it.' Prue went to join him at the window. She stood close to him, but not close enough to make him think she was standing close.'

Johnny handed over the envelope. 'Will you give him this? I just want his permission to extend my own chicken run.'

'I'm sure he wouldn't mind. I'm sorry he's not back.' She took the envelope, wanting to detain him for a few moments longer. 'Do you work in Manchester?'

The question produced a very large smile: the slight raise of the amber eyebrows indicated self-deprecation. 'If you can call it work. At home, not in an office. I sit at my desk looking at my chickens, writing what I like to call poetry. But I'm also thinking of starting a market garden some miles from the city. Not a good time, of course, but I'll persevere. During the war I ran an allotment, gave the stuff to people who were having a hard time – sold it just for what it cost me.' He moved away from the window. Prue sensed a slipstream of chill replace the brief warmth. 'I must go and shut up the birds for the night.' Prue went with him to the front door. 'Let me know if Barry agrees to the chicken idea. We could go off and buy the first batch.' He nodded towards the Sunbeam Talbot. 'It'd be a good excuse for a ride in your swanky car.'

Prue laughed.

When Johnny had gone a sense of anti-climax swarmed through her, but beneath it simmered nebulous anticipation. With Johnny the chicken-lover next door, perhaps there would be new ways of filling the days. She had enjoyed his interest in her days as a land girl.

Prue returned to the hall. She decided on a long bath, in which to think about things. Then she would put on one of her new dresses in which to approach Barry about the chicken idea, guessing that he would not take to it as eagerly as he had to the possibility of a baby, so she would be spared another celebratory dinner in the posh hotel. As she began to climb the stairs, Bertha appeared from the kitchen. Prue hesitated, looking down at the housekeeper whose jagged line of top teeth dug into her scant bottom lip.

'Visitor?'

Prue nodded, blushing, even though she could not see any reason for her to be either guilty or ashamed. 'Just the man from next door,' she said, 'with something for Barry.' She moved on up the stairs, curiously put out.

An hour later, having made a great effort with her appearance, she came down again expecting to find Barry, as usual, sitting by the gas fire with the evening paper and a cigar. But there was no sign of him. She went to the front door, looked out. No sign of the car either. She switched on the porch light and saw, on the step, a box of six eggs. She picked it up, opened the lid. No message, but they were obviously from Johnny to encourage Barry. Prue smiled. The large brown eggs glowed like discreet lamps. She touched each one with a cautious finger, remembering the chill feel of shell. Then, determined not to hand them over to Bertha, she took them into the sitting room.

Barry came home an hour late that evening, no explanation. Preoccupied by some business matter, he did not notice Prue's efforts to look particularly alluring. Over anaemic sausages and mash Prue gently put her idea to him. 'Think, we could have eggs like this all the time,' she ended, and pushed the open box towards him.

'Where did they come from?'

Prue gave an edited story of Johnny's visit and suggestion. Barry waved a hand, uninterested. 'You go ahead, sweetheart, do whatever you like. Set it up. I'll give you the money. Get that Johnny fellow to help you.'

Prue got up from the table, went round to Barry and kissed him on the temple.

'Thank you,' she said. 'You won't regret it. Eggs . . .'

Barry patted her stomach with a cuffed hand. 'Pregnant yet, are we?'

'Not yet, no.'

'Can't for the life of me think why not.'

'It takes a bit of time.'

'So it does, too. I must get to my desk, try to sort out this business.'

Left alone for the rest of the evening, Prue wrote a short note to Johnny thanking him for the eggs and telling him of Barry's agreement. Then she ran up the stairs, one finger skittering up the grim old banister as if in a lively dance.

# Chapter 3

It was a late-autumn afternoon. Through the mullioned windows of the sitting room the sky was white as paste, thick, cheerless. Prue threw the magazines she had been trying to read onto the floor. Once again she allowed herself to glance at Johnny who was still there, fiddling with something on the roof of the chicken shed. He had told her not to come out till he gave the sign.

It had taken just two weeks to make, this habitat for future hens. There had been several expeditions in Johnny's van to fetch wood, wire-netting, tins of creosote. Prue's main contribution had been encouragement and praise. She had been amazed by his skill in measuring, sawing, nailing, heaving it all together. The work had been an agreeable interruption to the days. Time had gone faster. Prue had a project, a point, two things she had been missing. Now it was finished.

At last Johnny turned and beckoned to her. Prue ran down the garden to join him. They stood side by side, looking at the completed work – a chicken house and run identical to Johnny's on the other side of the wall. 'Not bad, what?' he said.

'I think it's wonderful.'

'Now for the chickens and the feed.'

'When can we get them?'

Her impatience made him laugh. 'Dare say it could be tomorrow.'

As Prue waited for Johnny's van to park at the gate next morning, she remembered feeling like this on some mornings at Hallows Farm: cold mornings when, after the milking, she and Joe would have the chance of a word, a look, to confirm the fun they'd had the night before, or would have again shortly. At the beginning of the Barry One time, she remembered feeling so excited every new day that her clumsy fingers had trembled on the cold udders, making arcs of milk squirt onto the floor. Even in the early days of Robert, who had been a pastime rather than a romance, she had felt twittery, as she had described it to the others, when she struggled out of bed at dawn. And now here she was, feeling twittery again – a feeling that had never assailed her during her courtship with her husband – because the man next door was taking her to buy some chickens. Daft, she thought.

They drove slowly through dense fog to a poultry farm some miles from Manchester. Six coops, holding two Rhode Island Reds each, were waiting for them. Johnny piled them into the back of the van. Prue handed over one of her huge white fivers and was given a handful of change.

All the way back the stutter of the engine was ameliorated by the hens' indignant clucking. There was a smell of chicken shit and damp feathers. It was bitterly cold – there was no heating in the van.

'Much better', said Prue, 'than travelling in the Daimler.' Johnny laughed. It was easy to make him laugh.

They lugged the coops to the run and set the birds free to shake themselves and scurry about exploring their new territory. They watched them try the water in the drinking trough, begin pecking at the pristine grass. The fog still hovered low on the ground, giving an ethereal quality to their fat bird-shapes. Johnny put an arm round Prue's shoulders. But only for a moment.

For the second time Prue was faced with a dilemma. Again, she would have liked to ask Johnny into a kitchen she felt was hers and make him a cup of tea. But again she was thwarted by the very thought of Bertha's jealous guarding of her territory, the outrage she would incur if she entertained a visitor there. 'I don't know how to thank you,' she said. 'I wish I could ask you in—'

'Sounds to me as though that housekeeper woman's tyrannizing you.' Johnny's immediate understanding of the situation, and his not requiring any further explanation, was a relief.

'Not really. I'm just not welcomed. I keep my distance.'

'There's no reason, though, why you shouldn't come and have a cup of tea with me.'

Prue hesitated only for a moment. 'No,' she said, with a last look at the birds who were already at home in the run.

Johnny's flat was on the first floor of the next-door house – a house identical in proportion and some detail to Prue and Barry's. They went into a large room that incorporated an unruly kitchen and a collection of armchairs and tables covered with papers and files. Johnny looked for clean cups. Prue went over to the window and could see that on a clear day there would be a good view of both gardens and chicken runs.

'You know what?' Johnny was saying. 'I'll be able to look out and see you, morning and night, carrying buckets of chicken feed. Even better, collecting the eggs. It'll give a rhythm to the day.'

'I'm sorry – all this chicken business has taken up so much of your time,' said Prue, 'kept you from your poetry.' She turned to look at him putting spoonfuls of tea into a pot the colour of liver. The china was overlaid with a silvery sheen, like the bloom of grapes in a picture she had once seen by some old master. Identical, it was, to the teapot at Hallows Farm. Prue felt her heart give a downward beat.

'Don't worry about that. Nothing takes me from my poetry. It's in my head all the time.'

'Goodness, is it?' said Prue. 'I don't really understand about poetry.'

'I'll read you some one day. Here.' He handed her a cup painted with such delicate roses that the suspicion of a wife occurred to her. Surely he couldn't have chosen such prissy china himself. 'Why don't you sit on one of my battered armchairs?'

Prue chose one by the window, a morose but comfortable-looking piece of furniture. On the ledge beside her was the single frivolous object in the room: an empty vodka bottle in which was propped a child's windmill on a stem. She wondered whether, when the window was open, a breeze would power the paper arms. She flicked the bottle with a finger.

'Is there something significant here I'm missing?'

'No. Just a silly moment of a minor triumph,' Johnny said gruffly, and lowered himself onto a stool opposite her.

The thing about Johnny, thought Prue, was that he never seemed to think that talking instantly was necessary and he wasn't one for explanations. He'd leave you to marinate in silence for a few moments, which indicated he was thinking seriously about whatever you had last said. Though probably he wasn't.

As she shuffled about in the chair during one of these silences, Prue studied his slightly out-of-kilter face in which the air of cheekiness seemed too young for it. He wasn't the kind of man she would have looked at twice a few years ago: too thin, a touch too tall, altogether too indeterminate. But now she was older – more mature, she reckoned – she found his outward melancholy rather appealing. And the really intriguing thing was that she had no idea whether or not he fancied her. Usually she could tell in an instant. One flick of her curls, one *moue* of her scarlet lipstick and men (so many) could hardly contain themselves. It had all been easy. But Johnny – did he even register that she was a pretty girl? They had seen each other most days in the past two weeks, bonded by their project, but there hadn't been the smallest signal that he had anything on his mind other than completing the chicken run. Ridiculous, thought Prue. Or perhaps she was losing her touch.

She put the cup of tea on the window-ledge, then leant back into the unstable arms of the chair, which creaked as she moved, and bent one leg up onto the seat. She gave a shake of her head, a pat to her hair, the fraction of a smile. If he was inwardly on fire with lust for her, Johnny gave no sign of it.

'Shall I put the lights on?' he said.

'Shouldn't bother.' Prue changed her position, now crossing her legs. 'It's nice in here, all grey.'

Her movement stirred in Johnny a look that Prue interpreted as a first positive reaction, almost interest. She blinked at him slowly, aware of the weight of her black-encrusted eyelashes.

'You know something funny?' he said. 'I always wanted to meet a land girl. I had this feeling they weren't quite real. I used to look at pictures of them in *Picture Post* – those sexy breeches and tight jerseys. Have you kept yours?'

So odd, the extraordinary impression that land girls' breeches seemed to have made on the men of the British nation. 'I have.' Prue felt a flicker of apprehension. 'We weren't meant to – we were only allowed to keep our coats. But somehow I had two pairs so I kept one.' Surely nice reticent Johnny wasn't some kind of creep who wanted . . .

'You must put them on for me one day.'

'Not on your life!' Her answer was a squawk.

'I was only joking.' They smiled at each other, and the moment of awkwardness evaporated. But it was then that Prue decided she was not going to make any attempt to seduce him. She liked to think that had she tried she would have succeeded just as easily as she had with all the others. But she wasn't going to. Because somewhere deep within her lay the morals taught in childhood: a girl could have as many boyfriends as she liked (this being her mother's teaching rather than that of the Church) but once married, no matter how difficult, you remained faithful. She liked to think she would remain faithful to Barry because he was – well, he provided many things she had always wanted, and he was kind and tranquil. He just wasn't *there*.

'Are you married?' she asked suddenly, studying her cup and saucer with its prim roses.

'Was once. Briefly.' Johnny shook his head. 'Pretty much of a disaster. Nothing in common. The wife was cursed with a vicious tongue and a pretty mean streak, though none of that was apparent before we married. Or perhaps I was blind. Strange how you can be taken in, wanting to believe. What I thought, though, and luckily she agreed, was that having made a mistake we should undo it as quickly as possible. No hanging about hoping for things to get better. She had money of her own and I had none so there were no financial fights. She's married to a man in Las Vegas now.'

His large hands were clasped tightly round his cup, as if for comfort against the thought of a past wife. They trembled slightly. Then, Prue noticed, a small pulse in his jaw began a regular beat. She began to think that here was a neurotic neighbour, a touch highly strung, nervous. She'd have to take care to avoid any minefields. Not mention the wife again. But then he looked at her with such a disarming, happy smile that she thought she must have been mistaken. 'Can't say I ever think of her,' he said. 'But Barry? Your Barry? I scarcely know him. We have occasional landlord-tenant conversations, but that's all.'

Prue tipped up her head. (There was a way in which a head could be tipped that signalled nothing more than polite interest.) 'He's a good man, Barry. I don't see much of him. His work. But he's generous.' She held out her wrist, tapped the gold watch.

'He is. Are you happy?'

'What a question!' Prue giggled, caught off guard. 'Course I'm happy. I wouldn't have married him if I hadn't thought we'd be happy – though I have to admit we're a bit chalk and cheese. But there's no saying what makes a good marriage. Sometimes the most unlikely—'

'Quite.' It was almost completely dark by now. 'Really is time to put on a light,' said Johnny, getting up and taking Prue's empty cup.

'And time for me to be getting home. Barry'll be wondering,' she added, knowing that this was unlikely.

Now that Prue had taken her decision not even to flirt with Johnny, she felt unconstrained, able to make gestures that she knew were innocent and assumed Johnny would see as innocent too. She moved to face him, standing close. 'I don't know how to thank you,' she began. 'You've taken so much time and trouble. They'll change my life, those hens. Isn't there something I can do for you in return?'

Johnny frowned. There was a pause while he gave thought to the question, plainly not seeing in it a devious signal. Then he smiled. 'Well, there is, come to think of it. Your car . . . I'll never afford one even half as beautiful. I'd love a ride in it. Would that be possible?'

'Of course.'

'We needn't go far. And I'll bring a can of petrol. I've stored a bit.'

'But I've only just learnt—'

'I'll drive, if you let me. I'll show you its paces. I know a good straight trunk road.' He put his hands on her shoulders and swivelled her gently to face him. Then he kissed her forehead. 'It'll be fun,' he said. 'I'll look forward to it.'

When Prue arrived home she found that the Daimler was not in the garage and the house was in darkness. She let herself into the hall, switched on the light. From the passage that led to the kitchen Bertha appeared. She moved to the point where the passage widened into the hall, stopped and stared at Prue who gave a nervous laugh. 'Johnny Norse has finished the chicken run. The hens are all there. Perhaps you've seen them?' she said.

'I haven't looked,' said Bertha. 'I'm not that interested in hens.'

'But there'll be the eggs,' Prue floundered. 'Do you know when Barry's coming home?'

Their eyes met. Bertha folded her arms across her hollow chest. 'I don't,' she said. 'How should I know? It's not my place to know, is it?'

Prue hated her. 'Well, I'm going to shut up the chickens,' she said, picking up the torch from the hall table. 'It'll be my nightly duty from now on.' She tried for a carefree voice – no intention of acknowledging Bertha's powers of intimidation.

'Very good.' Bertha turned away, strode back down the passage, her shoulders lifted so high they touched the mean little roll of hair at her neck. Her posture, Prue supposed, was meant to indicate triumph. Bugger her, she thought. Witchy old cow. She's not going to lord it over me.

It took her longer than she had imagined to round up the hens in the dark. They skittered about, avoiding the beam of the torch. Sometimes one gave an uncanny squawk as she ran hither and thither. Prue was half entertained by their silly lack of direction, then remembered the place was new to them: they would take a while to become familiar with the geography of their house and run. She was also impatient – not a born chicken lover, like Ag – but she'd get used to them.

When she had finally shut the door on every bird, Prue looked over to the house next door, Johnny's lighted window, undrawn curtains – actually, she remembered, there hadn't been any curtains. He was standing at the window. He waved. She waved back, and turned towards the house.

The kitchen light was on, the curtains there, too, not drawn. Prue turned off her torch and walked down the lawn keeping close to the wall. Something compelled her to study Bertha on her own. To spy, she supposed.

But Bertha wasn't on her own. Barry was there, too. He stood, hands in the pockets of his overcoat, at the opposite side of the table. He seemed to be listening intently to Bertha, who gave an occasional stiff movement of her arm. Then suddenly he put both hands on the table, leant over and shouted. Prue couldn't hear what he was saying, but it was plain he was angry, or threatening. Bertha now wiped floury hands on her pinafore and put them over her ears. Barry turned away and quickly left the room, taking a cigar from its case as he did so. He slammed the door behind him. Bertha picked up a tea-towel and dabbed at her eyes.

Prue felt the battering of her heart, a kind of unexplained guilt. She could think of nothing she had done wrong, but guessed she was the reason for the row between her husband and the housekeeper, and felt uneasy.

Barry was sitting by the gas fire, a balloon glass of brandy by his side, cigar lighted. He looked up when Prue came in, gave one of his wider smiles. 'Hello, sweetheart.'

'Barry.' Prue went over to him, bent to kiss his temple. It shone a little with recent sweat and left a trace of salt on her lips. This evening greeting had become a ritual.

'I hear the whole chicken business is up and going,' he said.

'It is. Johnny and I went to fetch a dozen Rhode Island Reds this afternoon. They seem quite happy. I've just shut them up for the night.'

'Good, good.' Barry stared at the peach flames of the gas fire. 'I hear you went over to his place for a visit.'

As far as Prue could tell this wasn't an accusation: his voice was light. 'I did. He asked me in for a cup of tea. Well, I mean, I couldn't very well ask him here, could I?'

'No.' Suddenly Barry stirred, shifted. 'I mean, why not? It's your house. You can ask who you like here, right?'

'I had the feeling Bertha wouldn't much like that, using her kitchen. I thought I couldn't very well ask her to bring us a tray in here.'

Barry looked at his wife very hard, a look she couldn't fathom. Then he spoke loudly, close to anger. 'Listen to me, sweetheart. Bertha is the housekeeper. She's in my employ. I pay her good wages. I give her a roof over her head. If my wife wants to bring the next-door neighbour in for a cup of tea, a man who's given his time and trouble to set up your chicken thing, then that's fine by me and it's bloody well going to be fine by Bertha. I'll see to that.'

'Right,' said Prue, confused. She watched Barry visibly calm down and sink back into the chair.

'Here,' he said at last, and held out his hand. Prue gave him her wrist. 'Sweetheart, sweetheart,' he said quietly. 'I know we're a funny mixture, but we're all right.'

Blimey, thought Prue. What's got into him? Not a man for declarations, but he could surprise.

He let go of her wrist, gave her a fond look. 'That Johnny Norse is a good tenant,' he went on. 'Good neighbour, though I don't see much of him. He helped with a leak upstairs once. Seems he's a good carpenter. Writes a bit, too, I gather. Any road, if you want Johnny Norse as your friend, me away so much of the day, that's fine by me and you ignore Bertha's cheeky disapproval. She's probably jealous. I saw her giving him a look once – he was walking down the road, she was polishing the front door. I happened to mention what a nice young man he was, and she bit her lip, near to tears, I thought. I scarpered, as you can imagine.' He laughed his growling laugh, stood up. 'Let's go and eat, sweetheart,' he said, and in that moment Prue was near to loving him.

It was customary for Bertha, at supper, to bring in two plates of whatever unappetizing food she had cooked and put it down in front of them – Barry always first. This evening they saw a change in her habit. She had left two slivers of cod in a dish on the hotplate. There were boiled potatoes but no other vegetables.

'She knows how to send a message, Bertha does,' said Barry, and again he laughed.

A few days later Prue invited Johnny to try out the Sunbeam Talbot as she had promised. He sat for several minutes without moving in the driving seat before he started the engine. Then he coaxed it into an exciting roar, something she had never achieved, and moved off with confident swoops of the steering-wheel.

The fog that had lingered for a week had lifted. It was a sunny morning and soon they were on a clear road. Johnny drove more slowly than Prue had expected, but she said nothing. Impatient for speed herself, she supposed he was getting used to the car before putting his foot down. They seemed very quickly to leave the suburbs of the city: the country suddenly swept upwards from each side of the road. Johnny accelerated, smiling. 'This is more like it,' he said. 'What a car.'

But the burst of speed was short. At the top of a hill, he parked in a clearing cut out in the verge.

'Just thought you'd like to take a look,' he said.

Prue glanced down at a wide valley and giggled. 'Funny thing is,' she said, 'whenever people get to the top of a hill and look down they say the view's wonderful. Course, it often isn't.'

'True. But you have to admit it's pretty good here.'

'Suppose so.'

'I'll have to try you out on a few of my other favourite views.'

'OK.'

'But not today. We'll have a cup of coffee then go back.' Johnny stretched over to the back seat and brought out a string bag in which he'd put a Thermos and two cups.

'Gosh, you think of everything,' said Prue. She had a strange sensation that the moments were slipping away very fast. If she didn't think of something quickly, this outing would be over and there would be no firm promise of another. She couldn't rely on his mentioning journeys to see other views. She sipped the hot, sweet coffee, staring through the windscreen. 'Thanks for this.'

Then she opened the passenger door, got out and went to lean against the bonnet. Johnny followed her. He folded his arms, let his eyes clamber over a cluster of elms, a slanting field darkly ploughed, a carthorse whose ears were flattened against its sadly lowered head.

'The reason I can't go on living in the city', said Prue, surprising herself, because the thought had only just come to her and it was one of those unimportant thoughts not really worth passing on, 'is because there's no sky. I'm starved of sky. All the nearby houses, and other people's trees, break into it, leaving just little jigsaw bits. That's no good for me. I need big skies, like we had at Hallows Farm. They came right down to the hedges . . .'

'Is that so? I know what you mean.' There was a pause. 'So what are you going to do about it? Your husband lives in Manchester.'

Prue shrugged, giggled again. 'I'm being stupid. I didn't mean to say that. There's nothing I can do, is there?'

Johnny turned to look her. 'Don't suppose there is. You'll just have to get used to living in the city.'

'Never. I never could. Not for always. I'll have to get Barry to do something. He's always saying, "What do you want?" One day I'll say I want to live in the country. I can't imagine why I didn't think about that more carefully before I agreed to get married. I suppose I just thought I'd get used to living in gloomy old Manchester in the end – I was brought up there. But I can't.'

'Doubt you'll get Barry to change. I hardly know him but he looks to me like a city man through and through. We must be getting back.' Johnny moved to open the passenger door for Prue. 'I've got to work.'

'Lucky you.'

'Tell you what, on the way home we'll get up a bit of speed.' For the first time that day Johnny smiled.

'Good.'

They roared back to Manchester. The car skidded so fast into the driveway of The Larches that the gravel spun about, screeching. Bertha was at the kitchen window breathing disapproval onto the panes.

'Silly bloody bitch. Wizened-up old baggage!' shouted Prue. Further to annoy Bertha she slipped round to Johnny and kissed him on both cheeks. 'That was fun. You're a good driver. Thanks.'

'We'll do it again. Go somewhere else. Promise.'

Johnny kept his promise. Several times he and Prue drove out into the country, sometimes fast, sometimes slow, sometimes stopping at a pub for a drink or fish and chips. They were both reticent in the matter of exposing their hearts. Only with the greatest delicacy did Prue hint at the oddness, the loneliness of her marriage. Johnny, equally, kept all but an outline of his desires to himself. They gave each other signals, but did not colour them in. It was best like that, thought Prue, for they were friends, not lovers, never would be lovers when more secret things could be exchanged in bed. And she was hugely grateful for Johnny's friendship. She missed Stella and Ag – their wisdom, their laughter, their strength. She had no girlfriends in the city and felt disinclined to go out looking for any. So Johnny's proximity, his waves from his window as she fed the hens, his insistence on lending her books of Wordsworth's poems – 'Blimey, Johnny, expect me to get through all this stuff?' – were a comfort. The time to meet Stella and Ag for their annual lunch in London was a long way off, and all the while Bertha's hostility increased, making life in the house uneasy. 'What the heck do I do?' Prue asked herself.

The chickens were a help in breaking up the day, though her initial interest in them soon waned. It was often a nuisance to have to go and shut them up on a wet night. Still, there were the eggs. Barry liked the eggs. The thing that would really change her life, of course, was a child. By devious means she sometimes persuaded Barry into his crude act of lovemaking more than once a week. He did not protest, but he did not share her enthusiasm. Quite a business, he grumbled, this getting a baby going. Perhaps there was something not right with Prue, he suggested. Perhaps she should see a doctor.

Prue did not take up this suggestion, and almost two years after their marriage she was still not pregnant.

The spring after the arrival of the chickens Prue and Johnny began to go for longer drives. Prue never kept them secret from Barry: she found that describing to him exactly where they had been, the state of the narrow lanes, the number of farms they passed, was a help with conversation at supper. Barry seemed pleased she had found 'a pastime', as he called it, that she enjoyed. He was also pleased that his present of the car was such a success.

'If ever there's a problem with petrol, sweetheart,' he said one night, 'let me know. There are ways and means.' Barry was proud of his skills in negotiating the black market, but as he handed over petrol coupons or boxes of chocolates, he had the grace to look faintly ashamed. Prue always accepted these 'small aids in difficult times', as Barry called them, rather than cause offence by refusing them. The Lawrences, she knew, would have been appalled. She didn't like to think of that.

She was pushing globs of Bird's custard among a gathering of tinned pears. Custard was one of the things that induced intense nostalgia: Mrs Lawrence used to make real custard with real eggs and vanilla. Bertha's stuff was not the same at all, though Barry liked it at least three times a week.

'If it's fine tomorrow we're planning a slightly longer trip than usual – over towards Bakewell,' she said, 'but Johnny can't leave till after lunch, so if we're a wee bit late don't worry. Get Bertha to leave something in the oven for me.'

'That should be a nice drive,' said Barry. Then, after a long pause: 'Good thing I'm the trusting husband.'

Prue laughed. 'You've every reason to be. I wouldn't lay a finger on Johnny, would I? Or he on me. You know that. He's just a good friend. Someone to talk to, or drive with sometimes. They're long days here, you away so much.' She tried to say this lightly so that Barry wouldn't take it as an accusation.

'It's a good arrangement you've got.' He lighted a cigar, although Prue hadn't finished her pudding. He had never noticed she hated the smoke. 'Up towards Bakewell – that'll be a good drive.'

The day didn't turn out as Prue had hoped. There was a light rain that smudged the views, and Johnny seemed to have something on his mind.

'Got a poem coming on?' Prue asked, to deflect the tension that wrapped round him like barbed wire. Johnny ignored her question. Realizing she had struck the wrong note, Prue joined his silence. He drove rather too fast, hands gripping the steering-wheel in the same fierce way they had gripped the cup when he was speaking of his ex-wife, as if to halt a distinct trembling. The sharp knuckles were horribly white and again a pulse had started to beat, this time in his cheek. Perhaps he was fighting some inner demon, thought Prue, but she had no intention of asking what troubled him. He was the kind of man to be frightened off by sympathetic interest.

The tyres hissed and skidded round corners. Eventually – Prue had no idea where they were and didn't like to ask – he came to a stop. 'I wanted to show you this,' he said. 'An amazing valley. But it's not the day for it. Sorry.'

'That doesn't matter. There'll be other chances.' Prue was puzzled that the disappointment had little effect on her. Come to think about it, the drives to look at views were beginning to pall. She was as keen on nature as Johnny, as she often told him, but didn't see the point of just looking, admiring. What she liked was working the land: digging, ploughing, hedging, looking after the animals, doing something useful. So when he suggested they might as well find somewhere to eat, then return home early, Prue agreed almost eagerly.

They drove a longer way home in case the mist lifted and there was a chance to see more of the landscape. Prue assumed false sorrow as the rain fell harder and they failed to see any views. She was impatient to get home, shut up the hens – whose requirements by now had become a daily irritant – and have a bath. Johnny dropped her at the front door at five o'clock. They said goodbye with a kiss on the cheek, both feeling the day had gone wrong somewhere.

'Probably just the weather,' Johnny said.

Surprisingly, the Daimler was in the garage. Barry was never normally home so early. Prue let herself into the front hall and stood for a moment, taking in the ugly dark shapes of the furniture and pictures as if for the first time. What has all this got to do with me? she asked herself. There was no answer in the silence.

Then, from the passage that led off the back of the hall came a squawk like a frightened pigeon's. Round the corner dashed Bertha – her knees rising high, Prue noticed: usually she glided as if on wheels. Bertha's neat roll of hair had come loose. Strands trickled down her rough neck. There was a scarlet patch on each of her cheeks, bright as sealing-wax. Her eyes rolled. Her long front teeth dug into her bottom lip. When she saw Prue she screamed. Then she clamped a hand over her mouth, and her fingers, smeared with blood, skittered to the bodice of her grim beige dress. Without looking down she fumbled to do up the two top buttons. 'You're back early!' she shouted.

'Do you mind?' Prue turned to shut the front door.

When she turned back again Bertha was shouting towards the kitchen. 'Don't come out here, Barry.' But she was too late. Barry was now at the back of the hall, tieless, doing up his cuff-links.

'What's all this kerfuffle, sweetheart?' he asked, ignoring Bertha. Prue shrugged. 'I came in and found Bertha screaming.'

Bertha, now a deadly white and clutching clumps of her skirt, was shifting from one shoeless foot to the other. 'She came back early,' she whimpered. Then she turned on Barry and screamed. 'You told me this would never happen! You said you'd make sure she'd never know! You lied to me . . .' The scream trailed away.

'I think you'd better leave us,' Barry said quietly. His cuff-links in place, he pulled a maroon tie from his trouser pocket and slung it round his neck. Bertha fled. Barry kept his eyes fixed on Prue, as if she was a mirror, while he knotted his tie. Then he said, 'I think you're due an explanation.'

Prue nodded. What on earth had Barry and Bertha been getting up to in the kitchen to cause such disarray? In the chaos of her mind there was no answer to this question. Perhaps there had been another row between them and Barry, God forbid, had hit her.

In the sitting room Barry turned on the gas fire, poured himself a glass of whisky and lit a cigar. Then he sat back in his usual chair, knees apart, the pin-stripe material of his trousers pulling into uneasy ridges and furrows about his thighs. Prue took her usual place on the sofa opposite. The furniture, so familiar, moved strangely: the pictures were askew on the walls. Prue had always found that when unexpected happenings, either joyous or tragic occurred, the stable things of every day began to dance, making normality unrecognizable. It was a kind of magic that had always alarmed her.

'I expect you're wondering what all the carry-on was about. Well, I'll tell you. You deserve to know.' Barry drew on his cigar with some pleasure, as if he was ready to enjoy the explanation. Then he exhaled a swirl of smoke that hurt Prue's eyes. 'Bertha, you must understand, sweetheart, is a very complicated woman. Unloved, pathetic.' He paused to reflect on this judgement, tipping back his head.

Again it occurred to Prue that, half lit by the small table lamp, he could be mistaken for almost handsome in a fat sort of way. 'Oh yes?' she said.

Her lack of acute interest spurred him. 'Oh yes. Definitely one of life's unfortunates.' Another pause. 'I've tried to do what I can for her – not always very rewarding. But I feel sorry for her – who wouldn't?'

'How did she come into your life?'

'Ah, there's the story, you see. There's the story.' He gave a small laugh. 'Funny thing was . . . same way as you and your mother came into my life. Wet Manchester night, sirens, no one about. I passed this pathetic woman at a bus stop where I knew there wouldn't be a bus till morning. Drenched, she was. I stopped and asked where she was going. She was too frightened to answer at first. I think she thought I was a murderer.' At the thought, Barry gave another bout of laughter. 'I told her to get in. She had trouble climbing into the seat. I asked her where she wanted to go. She said she had to get to Liverpool where she had a cousin, her only living relative, who might put her up while she sorted herself out. But he had four children and only two rooms, and she didn't know how to get to Liverpool at that time of night . . . Didn't sound promising. She began to sob and shake and fall towards me. I pushed her up again.' He lowered his eyelids, remembering. Prue had never before noticed their plumpness, faintly repellent. ' "Well," I said, "I can't leave you at the bus stop, can I?" She shook her head, swayed about, sobbing harder. I explained I had a nice staff flat over my garage where she could stay for the night, and I'd take her back to the city in the morning, try to find some charity to help her. That seemed to cheer her up. So I drove her here, the room over the garage.'

Prue sighed. She wondered where this story was leading. Half her mind was on one of the chickens, which was limping badly. She'd have to ask Johnny . . .

'When I got down to the kitchen in the morning,' Barry went on, after one of his longer pauses, 'my usual time, she was there. Table laid, toast in the rack. She'd tidied herself up a bit, smiled. I could see that once – no, believe me – she could have been . . . not pretty, heavens, no, but not too bad. She was plumper, then. Bosom, hips, all that. She came right out with it, bold as you please, not at all like the woman of the night before. Could she stay and cook for me? She'd worked in the kitchen in some big house before the war, learnt a lot from the cook there. Well, you know me, soft-hearted to a fault. I said I'd give her a month's trial – I needed someone. She's been here ever since. Keeps the place clean and tidy, as you may have noticed. Does the ironing, whatever's necessary.'

'And?'

Barry tapped his cigar into an ashtray, pushing the stump of ash around as if prodding out some delicate specimen. 'And? Well, it's here we come to the twist in the story. Inevitable, I suppose. You know yourself, sweetheart – desperate people become obsessed with completely unsuitable others—'

'What do you mean, I know myself?' Prue was alert now.

'All those men you serviced in the war. The ones you told me about. The whole lot of others I don't know about.'

He was smiling a little, clocking up points against her should they be needed, Prue reckoned. 'It wasn't like that! I wasn't servicing them, as you so crudely call it. I was having a good time here and there. One or two were more than sex. One, I loved.' She kneaded her fingers, suddenly tense, affronted.

Barry was unmoved by her offence. He waved his cigar in the air, increasing the smoke left from the last wave. 'Well, whatever you say, sweetheart. Anyway, Bertha declared herself. Said she loved me, all that. She was pathetic, irritating in her efforts to make me feel the same. I avoided her as much as I could, tried to laugh her out of it. Then one evening I came home to find her gone – well, gone from the house. Nothing cooking in the kitchen. I went up to her room, found her sobbing on the bed. When I came in she just stood up, opened her dressing-gown, let it drop to the ground. What could I do? What would any man have done?' He paused. 'She's no Rita Hayworth, never has been, but there was something nice about her—'

'You can spare me the details,' said Prue, lightly. Fascinated, she was trying to picture the unlikely scene.

'All that was a mistake, of course. Next day I said she had a choice. She could either stop pestering me for love, which I was never going to give her, or go. Naturally she stayed. And I have to admit, sweetheart, occasionally I was obliged to give her what she wanted. About once every three months seemed to be all she asked.'

'Really? And does that arrangement still continue? Has it carried on since we were married?' Prue was intrigued by the unwavering formality of her own voice.

'Well, here we go.' Barry shifted his thighs, crossed one over the other. 'I always thought it would never come to this . . . There was big trouble, of course, when I told her I'd found a wife. She went haggard overnight. Face completely dropped, changed, hair suddenly screwed up. I told her, "never again" . . . But you know how it is. A man feels sorry for a sad woman, likes to cheer her up. And it has to be said, it's the plain ones who're often the most grateful. Don't get so many chances, do they? Know what I mean?' He paused, then went on quietly. 'So, yes, I have to admit, from time to time, there's been a lapse. Don't think it meant anything, sweetheart. It was only ever a quick roger to keep her happy.'

'I see,' said Prue. She sighed, as a child does at the end of a story. 'And what's the plan now?'

'Well, obviously it's finished for good. Over. I'll give her notice tomorrow morning. We can get someone younger, nearer your age, company for you . . .'

'I don't think you should sack her,' Prue heard herself saying. 'Poor old thing. Nowhere to go. She does all right for us. Spares me all the boring bits. No, don't sack her.'

Barry was shaking his head. 'What can that mean?' he asked. 'Wife suggests husband keeps his bit on the side. Does that mean you don't care?'

'Don't care? What do you mean?'

'Does it mean you care for me so little, sweetheart, that my small infidelities mean nothing to you?'

Prue tipped up her chin, working out an answer. 'Of course I care. I just don't think the whole Bertha thing is terribly important. You're like all men. Plenty of qualities, plenty of weaknesses. Women know they've got to put up with all that. Thing is, to weigh up whether it's worth sacking a pathetic woman just because she's screwed the boss. I don't think so. Please, Barry, let her stay.'

Barry swerved his damp lips from side to side as he tapped off more ash. 'Very well,' he said, after only a second's hesitation, 'if it's all the same to you. Save all the bother of finding someone new. But I promise you—'

'Fine. I believe you till the next time. And please tell her it meant nothing to me. I wouldn't want her to think I was put out by the whole business.'

Again, amazement clouded Barry's half-shut eyes. 'You've taken this very well, sweetheart,' he said. 'You're more grown-up than I thought. You're quite a mature woman. Here.' He put out a hand. Prue got up, went to him, gave him her wrist. She wondered if he could hear the battering of her heart. 'Am I forgiven?'

'Of course.' She bent down and kissed his temple. It tasted of cigar.

'What we need, to put the seal on things, is a child.' He pulled her further down, quite roughly. 'Perhaps we should go at it a bit harder.'

'Perhaps.' Prue pulled herself away from him, moved to the door. 'I'm going up for a bath,' she said.

'I'll follow you soon.' His chuckle froze Prue's innards. 'We'll lie down, rest a while, then I'll take you out to dinner. Don't suppose Bertha'll be up to much *haute cuisine* tonight.'

Prue climbed the stairs two at a time, heaving herself up with the kind of spring she used to employ to jump on to the back of Noble, the great shire horse at Hallows Farm. Only two thoughts pushed for space in her mind: she must see Stella or Ag as soon as possible, find out what she should do. Meantime a sense of freedom flared through her, so powerful she could have jumped high enough to reach the ceiling. Whatever happens, she thought, I'm free now. Lummy, I'm absolutely free.

# Chapter 4

As Prue made her way to bed late, buoyed by her new sense of freedom, she was puzzled that she felt nothing else: no outrage or sense of betrayal, no despising Barry for his treachery, no fury against the pathetic Bertha. Instead, a curious, benign understanding lapped within her. Of course she could see why things had come about between Barry and his housekeeper. And she didn't care. Married life could carry on, materially provided for. She and Bertha could continue in their mutual ignoring. It was up to Barry whether he continued to pleasure the house-keeper from time old time, ugly old cow, and once she, Prue, was pregnant, sex could be whittled down till it was almost non-existent.

Loveless marriage, with extravagant compensations, was not so bad. Prue had never supposed she would be blessed with the kind of loving union had by Mr and Mrs Lawrence. She had done nothing to deserve that. But she was lucky to be married at all, she thought. There were thousands of young women whose boyfriends had been killed, thousands of young widows. So given that she was married and, now, free, she would avail herself of everything she could get: the security of Barry, the freedom to look around. Somewhere behind these nebulous thoughts lurked a faint melancholy, though she guessed it was nothing to do with tonight's revelations. It was more a kind of disappointment: she was disappointed in herself. When she was a working land girl, she remembered, when a field of straight furrows was finished or the whole herd of Friesians milked single-handed, she had sometimes experienced a sense of satisfaction that never came to her now. Stella and Ag, she was sure, would have good advice, but it was still some months till their next London reunion, and both lived too far away for a spontaneous visit. Petrol coupons would have to be saved.

Her longing for a reunion with the others was fulfilled surprisingly quickly, well before the annual meeting. Ag sent a telegram to say Mrs Lawrence had died of a sudden heart-attack, and Mr Lawrence very much hoped the girls would be able to get to Yorkshire for the funeral in three days' time. They could stay in the farmhouse. Prue looked up cross-country trains, and asked Barry's permission to leave for a few days. He seemed relieved to give it to her. It occurred to Prue that in his fleeting visits to the kitchen he was being berated by the livid Bertha, who now managed to avoid addressing any word at all to her. Since Confession Day, as Prue called it, Barry had had the air of a man deflated: relieved to have confessed his guilt, but caught up in the aspic of confusion as to how, now, he should play his part. Up to him, thought Prue. She didn't really care.

Barry drove her to the station, gave her money for a first-class ticket. A porter carried her Louis Vuitton case – a birthday present – to an empty carriage and touched his cap when she gave him a shilling. Despite the sad reason for this journey, there was something exciting about setting off on her own, leaving the stifling house. She sat by the window, head against the spotless antimacassar, the back of her knees brushed gently by the fuzzy stuff of the seat. A sepia photograph of a Dorset village not far from Hinton Half Moon hung opposite.

By the time the train had left the station tears ran jerkily from her eyes. She sniffed, imagining the mess scrawled across her cheeks. But she couldn't help it. The evocative photograph had brought it all back: most of all Mrs Lawrence, who had become a kind of surrogate mother, with all the strength and wisdom and dignity that her own mother lacked. Prue shut her eyes, remembered. Mrs Lawrence . . . her kindly face, hard of bone but soft round the edges when she smiled: voice either hard and cracked with fatigue or disapproval, or gentle as a mourning dove when she had time to feel her happiness. Mrs Lawrence: her stringy arms, honed from a lifetime of kneading bread, rolling pastry, milking cows, smoothing her men's shirts with an iron that weighed a ton. Her food, so good it was hard ever to imagine there was a war. Her generosity, her concern always for others, her sudden flare of incomprehensible temper when she came across something that, innocent to others, displeased her. What on earth would Mr Lawrence do without his wife? Much of his huge strength came from her. They communicated more in being than in words, and it had worked so well. They understood each other without ever having to spell things out. Oh, to find such understanding. Once, the night they had gone to some dance, Mrs Lawrence had come up to the attic to help the girls dress. The place was a warm litter of slung-down clothes and scattered makeup, the air thick with the scent of Prue's Nuits de Paris. Mrs Lawrence's cheeks had turned pink with vicarious excitement, yet Prue had seen a wistful shadow in her eyes – thinking back to her own youth, perhaps, when she had prepared for just such an evening out. And when the girls rollicked down the stairs, Mrs Lawrence behind them, Prue had seen Mr Lawrence, waiting below to chauffeur them, give his wife an almost invisible nod and smile, acknowledging her feelings.

Mr Lawrence came so sharply to her mind, too: tall and lean and gruff, wise and silent – he'd do anything for anyone, would Mr Lawrence. Only incompetence or laziness made him angry. There was some sadness, obviously, that his son Joe was not fit to fight. But he was proud of him, you could see that. He was proud of the way Joe rose above his own disappointment, put everything into the farm. Joe, Joe ... Such a good way, he had been, to start life as a land girl. And once their flaming had died down he had remained a good friend, their friendship burnished by the knowledge of lovers. No wonder poor Stella had loved him so much ...

Prue put up a hand to stop fresh tears. Her cheeks were cold. Her fingers came away smeared with black. Better clean myself up before the station, she thought, and held up a small mirror to assess the damage. She saw that she was wearing the old red spotted bow in her hair, the one that had always brought her good luck with ploughing. Ashamed that she could have been so thoughtless as to wear it on arrival, she pulled it off and stuffed it into her bag. From her coat pocket she drew out a black one and fixed it into her curls. She could, she thought, go without a bow altogether, but that would be out of character. The others would be surprised. A black bow, she reckoned, they would judge as custom rather than frivolity. But why, at this time, was she thinking about bows?

Looking out of the window, Prue saw nothing to cheer her spirits. They passed outskirts of industrial towns where bomb damage had still not been cleared, and weeds tall as ripe wheat sprouted through rubble and broken stone. There were houses that had been cut in half, leaving parts of rooms where paper curled away from cracked walls, and a few pieces of smashed furniture still stubbornly kept their place on the remaining planks of floor. These ruined houses, their private tastes still exposed to all who passed, perhaps never to be rebuilt, filled Prue with renewed gratitude for having spent the war in deep country away from most of the bombing. How lucky they had all been: only one bomb and no one killed but poor old Nancy, the cow.

Once the desolate townscapes gave way to the swoops of Yorkshire hills and dales Prue looked out with a farmer's interest. But still there was little to cheer her in the landscape. While the fields themselves were in good order – mostly due to her fellow land girls, Prue thought, with a sudden smile – the farmhouses and villages were much in need of repair. A whole row of cottages was deserted, the roofs caved in, slates still scattered over the weeds of front gardens. Plainly, random parts of the country had not escaped attack. Here, as in Dorset, a German on his way home must have chosen to drop his excess bombs.

Prue wondered where she was. The train chuntered slowly, parallel to small roads, but there were no signposts. Perhaps returning them was not a priority for those who had to put things back. The locals knew their way: who cared if strangers were confused? And there didn't seem to be many people about – the occasional woman on a cumbersome bike, a rare car eking out its petrol ration by driving at twenty miles an hour. In one farmyard, only a few yards from the train, Prue saw an old man backing a cob into the shafts of an ancient cart while in an upstairs window his frail wife was hitching black material to one side of the frame, perhaps too exhausted to replace the years of blackout with the original curtains. Protected by her narrow, privileged married life in Manchester, Prue realized she had not been aware of the slow process of Britain's recovery. Now, on this journey to Yorkshire, she was aware of a sense of inertia. It was hard to imagine the return to normal, a distant time of incalculable years.

The station, cloudy with smoke and steam through which very weak lights made a pathetic attempt to brighten the place, was crowded with people in shabby clothes of uniform dullness. With a strange feeling of impatience, Prue wondered how long it would take before there was brightness on the streets and in public places again. And when clothes rationing came to an end, would people want brightness after so many years of dreary dressing? Would beautiful colours start to appear in the shops?

Prue took a taxi from the station to the Lawrences' farm, a half-hour ride through unfamiliar country: wide views, no hedged-in narrow lanes, villages scattered beside the Dales. The house itself was much smaller than Hallows Farm, its cracked face a little lopsided, its window small and lustreless. The farmyard was to one side, and a small barn housing a Fordson tractor. No sign of any animals: no pigsty for Sly's grandchildren, no stable for a replacement Noble.

Prue walked up the narrow front path squeezed between a painted fence plainly not homemade. This made her smile. The idea of a fenced front path at Hallows Farm would have been risible. Mr Lawrence's brother, from whom this house was inherited, must have had very different ideas from Faith and Tom, whose aim was always practicality rather than neatness. In the patch of garden opposite the farmyard, a washing-line had been slung between two trees. Mrs Lawrence's sage-coloured cotton dress, which she must have worn a thousand times, was pegged to it. Puffed up by the breeze, it blew about, only star of the washing-line. How on earth could that old dress still exist? thought Prue. None of her own clothes had more than a few months of life. At the thought of Mrs Lawrence's parsimony, and seeing the thin cotton in its last dance, she felt tears pressing again. Quickly she turned away.

Prue had never knocked on the Lawrences' door and decided not to do so now. Inside, she saw an open door off the dark passage. She made her way there, wondering whom she should find, where everybody was. She looked through the door, went no further.

Mr Lawrence was sitting at the table – the old table, the old chairs, but how clumsy they looked in this strange, much smaller kitchen. He had an open newspaper before him but he was not reading. The toll on him of his wife's death was rampant in his face. The ravines that ran from his nose to his chin had become deep enough to sharpen a knife. The whites of his eyes were confused with red veins, and the lids, previously so taut in their hollows, were now swollen. He moved his hands together in the shape of a spire, the rough fingers quivering. The familiarity of those hands – seen so often helping with an udder, showing how to hold a chopper or skin a rabbit – made Prue want to cry out loud this time, but she controlled herself. 'Mr Lawrence,' she said quietly.

He raised his head. 'Oh, Prue.' He stood up. 'I'm mighty glad you've come, all of you.'

Briefly, they embraced. He smelt the same: hay, root vegetables, sharp tobacco.

'I'm so sorry. I wish I could say something to let you know how sorry I am.' For all her effort, her voice had cracked.

'It was very quick, thank the Lord. She had a good last day. No notion of what was to come, I don't think . . . Heart-attack in the night. Didn't even wake me.'

'Always so considerate,' Prue dared say, and it worked. Mr Lawrence gave the faintest smile.

'Best way to go. Though she was getting used to this place. We never stopped missing Hallows, but we were carrying on with life.' He gave a brief wave, a wooden gesture, to indicate the newness of the place that was still not home. 'The others arrived a couple of hours ago. They're up in the attic – not quite the old attic, but all right for a night or two.'

'And Joe?'

Mr Lawrence gave her a look she knew well. She cursed herself for having asked the question.

'Joe's on his way. Janet's not long till she gives birth again. Shall I take your bag?' Prue shook her head. 'Very well. I'll put the kettle on. Up the stairs, left turn and up the next flight.'

While climbing the steep and narrow stairs, Prue heard the girls' voices: muted, familiar. What is it about familiarity, after a spell of absence, that is so affecting? She pushed open the low door and there they were, Stella and Ag, sitting on low beds, shoes kicked off, knees together, shins splayed, their old end-of-the-day positions. Ag's shoulders were hunched against a small casement window, Stella's chin was cupped in her hands. At first, in the poor light of the room, Prue could only make out shapes, no detail.

'Crikey,' she said, not knowing what else to say, 'not the same, is it? But at least we're all here.' There were brief hugs, steps taken back to observe each other. Stella was thinner, pale. She looked tired. Ag was more rounded, her Madonna-shaped face and beautiful cheekbones pronounced against scraped-back hair.

'I said to Ag you'd get yourself a black bow.' Stella was almost laughing.

'And I said you'd be in swanky mourning clothes and diamonds. You said you get diamonds every week!' said Ag.

'Bit of an exaggeration.' Prue tried to laugh but realized their attempts at lightness had evaporated. The three girls in the small, unadorned room were lost for the next move in their reunion.

Stella came to the rescue. 'We'd best be getting down, find something to eat,' she said. 'I've brought a basket of stuff.'

'Me too,' said Ag.

'I brought Mr Lawrence's favourite whisky and a bottle of Barry's best wine.' By now, Prue reckoned, the moment for teasing her about her riches had passed. She felt no guilt about bringing such drink.

They clattered down the stairs.

'Joe's on his way,' said Prue.

'I know,' said Stella.

Mr Lawrence was ambling about as if he neither knew nor cared which way he traversed the kitchen. He carried a frying-pan, letting it swing at his side.

'Here, you sit down, Mr Lawrence,' Stella said. 'We've brought things. We'll do it all.'

Mr Lawrence took his old place at the table, let his eyes wander among the three girls as they rummaged for plates and knives and forks. Stella took the frying-pan from him and set it on the range. There was an air of busyness, and almost at once the smell of coffee and frying eggs and bacon.

'Good to have you girls back,' said Mr Lawrence. 'Good of you all to come so far.' He spoke as if he was not entirely sure they were there.

They laid a place for Joe, but he did not turn up for lunch. They talked quietly as they ate. Mr Lawrence, still with the air of one who is uncertain of where he is or why he is there, allowed himself to remember some of the incidents at Hallows Farm. Then, gathering strength – from the girls' presence, perhaps – he was able to speak in the customary dry way they remembered so well. The girls followed up his recollections with some of their own, striving for lightness. The knowledge that their memories overlapped gave warmth to the chill of the occasion. 'But for the strangeness of it all,' as Ag said later, 'it was almost ordinary. Almost as if Mrs Lawrence would come in any minute.'

Prue looked at every detail of the kitchen. She guessed that Mrs Lawrence, tired out by the war, had not had the energy to make much effort here. The walls, a sour mint green, plainly had not been painted for years. There was a battered linoleum floor, cracked tiles of municipal white on the wall behind the range, two bare light bulbs hanging from the ceiling. Above all, there was no warmth: this was not a kitchen smouldering with work – cooking, kneading, scrubbing. Perhaps Mrs Lawrence had ceased to care once they had left Hallows Farm. Prue knew none of them could ever ask why: they would never know. And the dogs – where were they?

She held up her bottle of whisky towards Mr Lawrence. He gave a slight nod. She poured him a quarter of a glass. 'What happened to the dogs?' she asked.

He sighed, swung the liquid in the smeared glass. 'They came to an end,' he said. 'They'd had their time. Still, Faith and I were thinking of getting a new collie. But I don't know, now.'

'You should,' said Ag. 'You need a dog.'

'Probably do. I'll think about it after the funeral. It's all arranged, you know. Eleven tomorrow, church down the road. All Faith's favourite hymns. Pity Ratty's not here – he could ring a good funeral bell. He liked the sad sound better than the merry one, if you ask me. Now, if you girls don't mind, I'm going to take a rest. You could go for a walk, see what you think of the place. And make a pot of tea when Joe arrives.'

He left the room, a little unsteady, glass in hand.

'I can't believe it,' said Ag. 'I remember that time at Hallows Farm when Mrs Lawrence was ill. We were all so surprised. She wasn't the sort of woman to be ill, was she? I looked after her. The thought of her dying never occurred to me.'

'She was probably completely exhausted by the war,' said Stella. 'Once it was over, perhaps the fight just went out of her.'

'I'm sure it didn't. I'm sure if they hadn't had to move she would still—' said Prue.

'She probably wouldn't,' said Ag. 'She had a bad heart, remember?'

They had come to a bridge they did not know how to cross. The old ease was muddied by death, absence. With one accord they got up from the table, wanting to leave the strange room.

'Let's go and explore Yorkshire,' said Stella. They put on the battered land-girl boots they had all thought to bring with them, and began to walk towards the distant Dales.

On their return they found a small Austin parked in front of the house, but no sign of Joe. In the kitchen Mr Lawrence was making some attempt to set tea as it had always been: a pile of bread and butter on a plate in the middle, the huge glossy teapot beside it with its old partner the cracked blue jug of milk. The pathos of his efforts struck the girls, who at once helped with additional things found in cupboards, but they made no comment.

Mr Lawrence sat down, relieved to have them taking charge. 'How did you find it, the land up here?' The question was to Stella, the one land girl who had caused him deeply disturbing sensations, though he had succeeded in hiding them.

'Very different,' Stella answered.

'Different, all right. But we were lucky to have somewhere.' He turned now to face her and said quietly: 'Joe arrived when you were out. Devil of a long journey. He'll be down.' Stella smiled at him, a silent thanks for the moment he had given her in which to compose herself.

They were spreading Mrs Lawrence's homemade plum jam on their bread when Joe came into the room. The three girls looked up at him with one accord, noted the newness of his tweed jacket, the shadows under his eyes. Superimposed over his physical presence were the private visions it produced in each of them.

Ag: that single night in a cottage in the woods when he had so kindly, so gently, relieved her of her virginity at her request.

Prue: that first morning in the milking shed, trying to decipher if his lust flamed as hard as hers . . . and discovering it did on the night she fell from the beam in the barn, and the many nights in his narrow bed till they had to give up from exhaustion.

Stella: oh, Joe. The time it had taken for mutual discovery of love – that terrifying day of the bomb falling on the haystack, Joe taking her in his arms and saying all he cared about was that she was safe. The time they had sat up through the lambing night. The time she had had to tell him that honour meant she must marry Philip, and his terrible, silent pain that matched her own. Then the journey she and Joe had taken round Normandy, soon after they had all left Hallows Farm – miles of shattered country seen through the windscreen on the old Wolseley which Mr Lawrence had willingly lent them, as if he understood . . . and when it was over Joe saying, as they faced the white cliffs of Dover, 'At least we've had a week of our lives . . .'

'So good you could all come,' Joe said, looking at none of them directly. He sat in the empty chair next to Ag. They pushed bread and honey and jam towards him and laughed when there was a clash of plates.

Mr Lawrence eased himself higher in his chair, as he often did when he was about to make an announcement. 'I was wondering,' he said, his voice almost at its old strength, 'if by any chance you girls have brought your uniforms?'

They shook their heads.

'We no longer have them,' said Ag. 'They were taken back. Such a mean gesture . . .'

'I didn't know that. It's just that . . . Faith was so proud of the three of you, so proud to have played some part in your wartime work. I think she would have liked you to be at her funeral dressed as land girls . . .'

'I'm so sorry,' said Stella.

'No matter.' He paused. His shoulders rose, indicating the next effort he had to make. 'Well . . . I'm going to take Joe round the place, show him our so-called progress here, then walk down to the church. If you girls could manage supper . . .'

It was while they were preparing it, chopping, peeling, shifting things in saucepans, just as they used to for Mrs Lawrence, that they questioned each other about their lives. They always did this at their annual lunches in London, but preparing supper in the Lawrences' house somehow made it easier.

Ag had little news: settled on a Devon farm with Desmond, she more or less carried on with her land-girl work, she said, and loved it. She had become famous in the community for her hedging, she modestly admitted when Prue pressed her to say exactly what work she did on the land.

Stella, in a cottage on the Norfolk coast – Philip insisted on being by the sea – could do little beyond look after him, bound to his wheelchair, and their son James. It was hard to get help and sometimes, Stella said, she was so tired she could lie on the floor and sleep. But they wanted another child – hoped for a girl. 'What keeps me going,' she said, 'are long walks on the vast empty beach, all weathers. The skies . . . Sometimes I wheel Philip down to the marshes, but I don't think he sees it all as I do. He feels the cold so. Turns up the collar of his coat after a moment or two, wants to go home almost at once.' She sighed, picked up her bag, rummaged for her wallet. 'Want to see a picture of James?' She took out a photograph of a small boy, lock of hair falling over one eye – such an exact image of Joe that Ag and Prue gasped.

'Has Joe seen this?' Prue asked.

'No. But I'll show him one day, perhaps.'

Ag studied the photograph carefully. 'Does he know?'

'I think he's probably guessed. I mean, I'm sure he knows. I knew I was pregnant soon after we were back from France, before Philip and I were married. I wrote to Janet and Joe when James was born. He wrote back a note saying . . .' Stella turned away, pushed her fist into her eyes. 'The main thing is that Philip is in no doubt James is his – keeps saying their foreheads are so alike. Amazing how people can see what they want to see.' She turned back to the table. 'But, Prue, what's your news? Is your millionaire husband still the man of your dreams?'

Prue giggled. She sat down, pulled a chopping board of parsnips and a knife towards her. 'He's very rich, just as I wanted,' she said.

'And?'

'He's very generous.' She lifted the hand with the diamond ring and tapped the gold watch on her wrist.

'Good.' Stella was brusque. 'And are you happy?'

Prue felt herself blush. 'I'm fine,' she said.

'Happy?' persisted Ag.

Prue giggled again. 'Course I'm happy. I mean, I don't suppose any of us – except you, Ag – has found the actual man of our dreams. There's always got to be something wrong, hasn't there? You can't expect a hundred per cent, can you? Barry isn't exactly what I'd imagined, but we get along fine in a funny sort of way. He's got a wizened old housekeeper who doesn't fancy me, and he's out a lot of the time so I haven't much to do. He let me buy some chickens – I think of you every time I collect the eggs, Ag – and one of his tenants, a carpenter who says he's a poet and lives next door, Johnny, built a lovely house and run for them. But chickens aren't much company, are they?'

Her question wasn't answered. Stella, frying at the stove, said: 'And what about this Johnny carpenter-poet?'

'Oh, Johnny. He likes driving me about in my Sunbeam Talbot. He shows me Derbyshire, talks about poetry – a bit above my head as you can imagine. He's all right. Nothing to make the heart race.'

'That's good.' Stella smiled at her, motherly.

'Don't you worry, I'm not up to my old tricks. I know bloody well how lucky I am being married at all. I'm not going to risk messing that up. All I want is to find something to do, something useful. I'm not used to a lazy life. I mean, crikey, I'm glad I no longer have to get up at four in the morning to pick a field of frozen sprouts . . . but I'd like to be doing something.'

'Quite,' said Stella.

Supper was a muted occasion. Joe barely spoke. Mr Lawrence's repertoire of memories, so bravely conjured to ease lunch, had run out. The girls did their best, but everyone was relieved when it was time to listen to the news on the Home Service in the sitting room. It was another cheerless room despite the familiar furniture. Pictures were still stacked against a wall, and there was still blackout at the windows, which awaited curtains. On the seat of the chair by the fire – Mrs Lawrence's old chair – lay a bundle of knitting speared by two long needles, each full of stitches, suggesting that the unfinished scarf, trailing on the floor, had been quickly abandoned. Perhaps Mrs Lawrence, on her last night, had felt a strange desire to hurry upstairs to bed, Prue thought. And it was suddenly unbearable. With no excuse she left from the room, intending to go up to the attic to shed private tears, but Joe, who had not followed the others into the sitting room, was ahead of her. With no plan in mind, she followed him to the kitchen. He went out through the back door. She followed him again, knowing he was unaware of her, watched him make for the barn. There, from a distance, she saw him lean up against one wing of the new-looking Fordson and light a cigarette.

Prue crept into the barn, a dark and husky place, no feeling of husbandry there had been in the barn at Hallows Farm. A few bales of hay and the unfamiliar tractor were the only furniture.

'Joe,' she said.

He looked up, surprised. 'Oh, Prue,' he said.

She moved nearer to him. If Mrs Lawrence hadn't died she would have flung her arms round his neck and kissed him in the old, thrilling way, telling herself it was for old times' sake. It would all have been innocent, the kind of innocent gesture neither Stella nor Janet would have minded. As it was, she had no plan in mind. She just wanted to be close to him, to feel . . . what? She couldn't say. Comfort from Mrs Lawrence's son, perhaps. She stood with her arms by her sides. 'I just wanted to say how dreadfully sorry—'

'Yes, well.'

'None of us can believe it, really.'

'It's hard to believe, Mum not there.'

'Not there . . . Your dad seems to be coping.'

'He's in shock at the moment.' He glanced at her, his eyes two shards of pure silver as the moon moved from behind a cloud.

Prue took a step nearer. 'I often think Stella and Ag and I will remember our year at the farm as the best time of our lives.'

'Perhaps,' said Joe, dragging on his cigarette. 'How's life with you? Married woman.'

'It's OK. It's fine.'

'Good.'

'And you and Janet?'

'What about me and Janet?'

'Are you . . . ?'

'We're fine, too. We'll be coming up here in a few months' time. Taking over. Looking after Dad.'

'That's good.' So slowly she might have been playing a private game of Grandmother's Footsteps, Prue moved even nearer to Joe. 'Do you remember all those times, Joe?' she said.

'Course I remember all those times,' Joe snapped, 'but I don't think about them often. I'm not thinking about them now.'

'No. Nor you should. Quite right. It must be odd, seeing us all again.'

'You're the one who hasn't changed,' said Joe, reverting to a milder tone. 'You're exactly as you ever were, you minx.' He suddenly laughed. Prue saw that as the signal. With no thought of betrayal to Stella, who really loved him, or to his wife, who probably did too, she threw her arms round his neck. She felt him rock against the tractor bumper, and clamped her mouth to his. For an infinitesimal moment she knew that in another time, another place, he might have responded. But now he was shocked, angry. He pushed her roughly away, bent down to pick up the butt of his fallen cigarette.

Desolate at having done the wrong thing, Prue cursed herself for not having thought hard enough about how Joe might respond to her act of 'comfort'. Most of the mistakes she made, she remembered in the sharpness of the moment, were due to her thoughtless spontaneity. 'I'm so sorry,' she whimpered. 'I didn't mean . . . It's just all the sadness. I thought—'

'You thought – what? You'd be a comfort? My mother dead? A quick kiss in the barn for old times' sake? Honestly Prue. Your sense of timing. Your rotten judgement. Go on. Get back to the house.'

Prue turned from him and ran. In the house she sped up the stairs, mortified. The others were already in their narrow beds. A lighted oil lamp made soft shadows creep out of the real darkness.

'You been seducing Joe?' Ag asked, laughing.

'Don't be silly,' said Stella. 'Even you wouldn't go that far, would you Prue? Not on this occasion.' She laughed, too. Their trust in Prue's honour was almost unbearable. She got into the empty bed by the window, cold under two thin blankets, wondering why the beams she knew so well in the attic at Hallows Farm were not holding up this ceiling. Ag turned down the lamp. The three girls struggled in silence with their own thoughts. Then Stella said: 'Prue, I've been thinking. I've an idea. What you should do is get a job on a farm.'

The thought of that possibility deflected Prue's agonizing over her shameful behaviour, but it was a long night of little sleep for all of them.

Next morning the girls, once breakfast was finished, continued to sit round the table, unsure what to do. There was an hour until the hearse arrived and they were to walk to the church. Ag looked out of the window. Dark ribbons of cloud chased across a sky pale as a wheatfield: sometimes they clustered together, then divided again to swoop off in another direction, like flocks of starlings uncertain of which way to go. 'What a frivolous sky for a funeral,' she said.

'What on earth?' Prue giggled. 'Trust you to come up with some fancy observation, Ag.' Though Ag smiled, Prue could see that once again she had said the wrong thing. It was not the moment to scoff at her old friend. 'Sorry, Ag. But you still say the sort of things that would never come into my head in a million years. I like that.' She stood up, scraping her chair with a hideous note across the floor. 'I'm going to change. My black . . .'

Mr Lawrence came in. He wore a newly ironed white shirt – perhaps the last shirt his wife had ironed for him – and a black tie that hung thinly down its front, the knot tight as a small fist.

'Shall I cook you something?' Stella asked.

Mr Lawrence paused, trying to understand the question.

'Not this morning, thank you, Stella. Joe and I had a pot of tea earlier. That will do.' He paused again, working something out. 'Mary from the village will be coming up with something to eat after the . . . service.'

Half an hour later Stella and Ag came downstairs in quiet black dresses. They found Joe in the hall sitting on an upright chair by the grandfather clock. He was still in his new-looking tweed jacket. His black tie was as narrow as his father's. He got up and they stood there, the three of them, in silence.

'Prue ready, is she?' he asked at last.

'I'm coming,' she shouted from the top of the stairs, and hurried down. Her long, full black skirt, gathered from a tiny waist, thrashed round her legs. She joined the group, looked from one to another. 'The New Look,' she said quietly, desperate to explain in case they thought it inappropriate. 'Mum ran it up for me from some blackout stuff. We couldn't get anything else. Hope it's—'

'Car's here,' Mr Lawrence shouted from outside, where he had been waiting for the arrival of the hearse. He opened the front door. Sun had scattered the last of Ag's frivolous clouds. It beat into the hall, outlining everything with a dazzle of gold. The hearse was parked at the bottom of the garden path. There were just three bunches of white flowers on the coffin: one each from husband and son, one from the three girls, which Ag had organized through a florist.

Prue let Stella and Ag go ahead, one each side of Mr Lawrence, each holding an arm. She took her chance. 'I'm so sorry, Joe,' she said. 'I made a mistake. I misjudged – I didn't think. Please forgive me.'

'Don't give it another thought. We're not ourselves. None of us.' He said it kindly enough, but his mind was not on Prue's apology. She could see that anything he had felt for her in the past had long since evaporated. She was of no concern to him. Her clumsy kiss had been a mere irritant: he was surprised – shocked – that she could have behaved so carelessly, but not angered because his mind had been on his dead mother rather than a scatty land girl he had fucked for a few weeks long ago.

'Come on,' he said, and hurried ahead of her down the path.

Prue followed him more slowly, disentangling her legs from the frolicking skirt, wishing she hadn't been so insistent on the New Look. Her sadness about Mrs Lawrence was added to, now, by the way that Joe had made it clear that all he wanted was to be rid of her. Perhaps she had destroyed his friendship completely by acting in such thoughtless haste. In future reunions with the past, she vowed, she would curb expectations, hopes. It was foolish of her to have supposed that sensations that were once alive still burned with the kind of flame that could be reignited.

There were a dozen or so people in the church, villagers who had come to know the Lawrences in the last three years. No one from Hinton Half Moon. Mr Lawrence would not have expected any of them to travel so far. He stood very upright, arms folded, his eyes avoiding the coffin. Joe, beside his father, also kept his eyes fixed on the altar where two candles were lighted. Their flames, against the rods of sun that came through the stained-glass window, were deathly pale. The girls sat in the front row opposite Jo and Mr Lawrence. They sang loudly to make up for the lack of male voices, and kept their tears in check until the coffin was borne out to the graveyard.

After the burial they returned to the farmhouse where sandwiches and a coffee sponge were laid on the kitchen table. The kindly Mary bustled about making tea, relieving the girls of any responsibility. Mr Lawrence sat in his upright wooden armchair, hands hanging over the arms as if they were weighted. Joe was the one who, knowing his mother would have had little patience with gloom, suddenly felt the need to invest the occasion with a little merriment. He began to reminisce, with stories of the land girls when they had worked at the farm, and there was relieved laughter.

By supper Mr Lawrence had unbent a little, though he looked exhausted. He went early to bed. Joe remained downstairs to tell the girls his plan was to stay for a few days to make sure his father was all right – 'which he will be' – and that he and Janet would be moving in as soon as they had sold their house. Prue noticed that while he and Stella glanced in each other's direction they made sure their eyes never met.

In bed, for all their efforts to cast aside melancholy, there was an air of disbelief, which each one knew would take a long time to fade. By now they were too tired to try to be cheerful, and they knew each other too well to pretend they had accepted the death of a woman who had meant so much to them.

'It's unbelievable,' Prue said several times. 'I mean even though Mrs Lawrence was far away, we knew she was always there.'

'And however often you say it's unbelievable, it doesn't help to make it more believable,' said Ag.

They turned out the lights, lay down in the dark room that was not their attic. Restless with their varied thoughts, there was no more to say. But each one knew of the others' disturbed night, and shared the dread of leaving Mr Lawrence, his wife in her grave, the next morning.

# Chapter 5

Their farewells to Mr Lawrence were brief, constrained, for there was nothing left to say, nothing that could be of comfort. He gave each girl a peck on the cheek. His skin was scratchy, unshaven, his breath rank with tobacco, his eyes focused far from the present scene of departure.

Joe was to drive them to the station in the old Wolseley. When he opened the passenger door, it was Stella who chose to get in. Prue saw them exchange a barely visible smile. She and Ag got into the back. Mr Lawrence gave a brief wave, then moved towards the barn.

'Dad's going to the market, luckily,' said Joe. 'He'll keep himself busy, make the most of the smallholding. When Janet and I move in we'll probably increase the stock . . .' He spoke in a flat and weary voice. The journey continued in silence.

When he dropped them off at the station he got out of the car, came round and opened both front and back doors but, unlike last night, kept his eyes on Stella. One of his hands was shaking. He hugged Ag and Prue, then turned to Stella. She stood a yard or so away, waiting her turn, her suitcase at her feet. Joe moved the short distance to her like a man with poor sight, stumbling. They faced each other, eyes locked. Then he bent to give her a kiss so light and swift it would only have registered on the most sensitive skin. They dare not hug, thought Prue. She turned to Ag, who, having the same thought, nodded. Stella took a step backwards. Joe's kiss had whipped every trace of colour from her face. Then he was gone, muttering something about letting them know when Janet gave birth, but not even trying to produce any sort of coherent farewell.

The three girls turned into the station. Ag and Prue each took one of Stella's arms. 'Better than nothing, I suppose,' she said. 'The occasional meeting. Seeing him.' Tears were pouring down her cheeks.

On the journey home Prue was aware of a sense of rising desolation. There was nothing to look forward to beyond her monotonous, empty life with Barry. Stella and Ag were far away: Mrs Lawrence was dead. Prue said the word out loud to herself several times. Dead, dead, dead: but still it did not convince. She tried to shift her mind to some happy prospect – the chickens, perhaps. The chickens! A young, rich, still pretty wife with nothing to look forward to apart from her reunion with the chickens. It was ridiculous, pathetic. She laughed, self-mocking. Then she thought of Johnny: he was not exciting or very fanciable, but at least he was a friend – her only friend in Manchester.

It was a muzzy October evening, the light low behind the ugly trees that guarded The Larches from the road. Prue had come to hate the monkey puzzle, with its great muscular arms. Next time Barry said he'd like to grant her a wish, she'd ask if it could be cut down. There were no lights on in the house, no sign of either Bertha or him. She dumped her case in the hall and made her way into the garden to see to the chickens.

Johnny was in the run, a basket over his arm, collecting eggs. She felt a moment of gratitude. He smiled. 'You're back,' he said. 'How was it?'

'Sad. Thanks so much for looking after the hens.'

'They've been fine. I've put quite a few eggs in the kitchen for Barry's breakfast.'

'Thanks.'

Johnny left the chicken run, came over and stood by her. 'I've looked out of my window each morning, expecting to wave at you, but you weren't there. It could be said I missed you.' Prue gave a fraction of a smile. Johnny put an arm round her shoulders. 'Hey, you're shivering,' he said. 'You're cold.'

'Not cold. Just ... back.' They stood for a few moments without speaking.

'Go in and light the fire,' Johnny said. 'I'll walk to the house with you.' At the door, he handed her the basket of eggs but refused to come in. 'Let me know if there's anything I can do – any help ...'

'As a matter of fact there is.' Prue paused. 'Stella came up with the brilliant suggestion that I should go and work on a farm. I must do something and farming is what I know and love best. Can you think of anyone in need of a farm worker?'

'I might be able to – it's a very good idea.' Johnny took his arm from her shoulders. He looked serious. 'In fact, I do have one instant idea.'

'What's that?'

'Leave it with me for a few days. And there's something else I've been meaning to put to you. How would you like it if we drove to Hallows Farm one day? I'd love to see it, having heard so much ...'

'Lawks! I'd love that. But it's a very long way. Petrol ...'

'I'll take care of that – ways and means. Come round tomorrow morning and we'll make a plan. But now go in – go on. You're icy cold.' He kissed her cheek, a kiss fractionally longer than his usual greeting. Had Prue been less anxious to get to the fire, and less sad, she might have responded with a tilt of her head that invited more. As it was, she went inside and shut the door behind her.

An hour later, warmed by the gas fire, she heard Barry's voice. He hurried into the room – not his normal gait – followed by Prue's mother. Astonished, Prue jumped up. Her mother had only been to the house a few times, usually when Barry was out – Prue had always had the impression he was not keen on visits from her, so mother and daughter continued to meet in Manchester.

Elsie Lumley was prancing about, exclaiming at the wonder of almost everything in the room. Once or twice, to tone down her astonishment, she clamped a hand over her mouth, but a roar of approval could still be heard. She had a new and complicated hairstyle, inspired by film stars of the day, and a dress that she must have embellished herself. It was crystallized with odd bits of tinsel. What on earth . . .? Prue wondered.

'Imagine, Prue: Barry here rang me at the salon – I was all of a dither, kirby-grips in my mouth – said it was high time I came over and why not tonight, to cheer him up, him being all alone. You away . . . Wasn't that a lovely idea?' She skittered over to her daughter and hugged her. 'But you're not away. Better still.' Her voice had a dying fall.

'What happened? Barry was pouring himself a whisky and soda. He glanced at his wife. 'I thought you were coming back tomorrow.'

'Today, I said.'

'I must have misheard. Anyhow, here you are.' He lumbered over to Prue and kissed her cheek. 'Very nice. I thought it was high time your mother came over. How was it up north?'

Prue was aware of the vast distance between what had happened to Mrs Lawrence, the miserable business of the funeral, the land girls meeting again, and Barry's ability to understand any of it. 'It was fine,' she said.

'What will it be?' Barry asked Mrs Lumley.

'Gin and orange, if you please, Barry.'

'Gin and orange it shall be. Prue?'

'Nothing, thanks.' The whole scene and its possible implications were casting a feeling of disbelief over Prue that was making her physically weak. She wanted to run from the room – anywhere, but to leave all this, this weird threesome.

'I thought I'd show your mother round the house,' Barry was saying, 'take advantage of her designer's eye, then go out for a slap-up dinner. So, now you can join us. It'll be all the better for that, won't it, Elsie?'

She smiled and agreed.

'Actually, Barry, it's been a long day. We didn't have much sleep. I think I'll just go to bed,' said Prue.

'Oh, Prue . . .' Her mother sounded genuinely disappointed.

Barry shrugged. 'Up to you. Dare say Elsie and I'll manage to get by . . .'

'That's what you arranged in the first place,' Prue heard herself snap, unusually fierce. 'Dare say it won't be a hardship.' She saw her mother wince, swallow her gin and orange in one gulp.

Barry gave her a look. 'We'll be off, then, Elsie, shall we?' Her mother scurried about, suddenly nervous, looking for the coat she had dropped on the floor. 'You have a good sleep, Prue. I won't be late.' In his haste to leave, Barry clumsily helped Mrs Lumley put her coat round her shoulders and crossed the room to the door faster than Prue had ever before seen him move. His plan to show his mother-in-law the house seemed to have been forgotten. 'Sleep well, sweetheart,' he said.

Prue had more important things to think about than her mother's date with her husband: the possibility of working on the land, a job with animals. The idea was exciting. She quickly fell asleep. And Barry kept his word: he was in bed beside her by eleven, waking Prue with his customary heaving about under the blankets, treating them as if they were his sole property. 'Sorry you didn't come,' he said. 'We had a good time. It was nice to be able to give your mum a treat. She was dazzled by the hotel.'

'Good.'

'She's wonderful company. A bundle of laughs. There's nothing I don't know about her clients.'

'I can imagine.'

'You aren't cross? Put out?'

'Why should I be?'

'I suppose I must have felt a bit lonely, you away. I thought, Well, at least Prue can't be put out if I take her mother – it's not as if I'd asked some young—'

'No, of course not. Barry, I want to go back to sleep.' Their voices were inharmonious in the dark. And the dark was the best place, she suddenly thought, to venture the important question. 'Would you mind, Barry, if I took a little job?' There was a long silence. 'I need to do something. I need to work. I appreciate you keep me so well, but I need—'

'Course you do.' She heard a long, heavy sigh. 'I'm not the sort of man who'd like to see his wife go out to work. I like to feel I can provide everything for her and she can sit back and relax. Have a good time. But then again I'm not the sort of man so firmly stuck in his opinions that he can't change them, if there's good reason, every now and again.'

'That's right.' Prue smiled to herself.

'What sort of job do you have in mind?'

'Farm work. It's what I'm best at. It's what I love.'

'Why not, sweetheart? You find yourself a nice farm, and I'll be proud of you. If you buy me a pair of boots I'll come and see it one day.' He laughed at the unlikeliness of his own threat. Then, surprisingly, he added, 'I've sometimes wondered if you weren't wasting your talents with not much to do here. It'd be nice, land-girl work again. Nice. But only till we have a child, of course.'

'Of course.'

Then Barry thrust back the bedclothes, heaved himself onto her and squashed the breath out of her so that she had to scream for him to shift his weight. For the second time that week, an attempt at conception was made very quickly. Then Prue went back to thinking about the furtive look she had seen between Joe and Stella, and the meaning of real love.

The next morning, soon after Barry had left the house, the telephone rang. Its old black body was misted by neglect, for it was against Bertha's principles to clean what she saw as unnecessary objects. On the rare occasions it rang Prue was always filled with alarm, fearing bad news. She would never forget the call at Hallows Farm one evening for Stella, who was told of Philip's wounds . . . This morning there was no bad news, but much cheerfulness.

'Prue? Mum here. Couldn't wait to tell you. Such a lovely evening I had. You're a lucky girl to have found a husband like that. You mind you keep him.'

'Of course, Mum. I'm glad you enjoyed it.'

'He told me you had such a happy life, you and him.'

'Did he?'

'I don't wonder. House like that. No money worries.'

'Quite.'

'You must both come to supper here one day, if Barry wouldn't mind such a small house. I could do a rabbit stew. Does he like rabbit, do you know?'

'I don't know, Mum.'

'What did you think of my dress?'

'Very glamorous.'

'Barry paid me a lovely compliment. He said he could see where his wife got her looks.'

'I must go now, Mum. Feed the hens.'

'You and your hens!' Mrs Lumley laughed merrily. 'Ooh, and I never gave you my condolences – poor Mrs Lawrence and all that.'

'Thanks.'

'Well, I'd better be going too. I like to get to the butcher before work, though even then there are queues. Queues, queues, queues everywhere, every day. And what do you get when it's your turn? A scraggy little piece of offal if they've not sold out. Though last week I was offered a scrawny-looking pigeon – a pigeon! I mean, what would I have done with a pigeon, Prue?'

'Quite.'

'But between you and me, when I told Barry that, he said he had ways and means of getting me a decent piece of meat if I wanted it. Wasn't that nice of him?'

'It was, Mum.'

'Come and see me very soon, Prue.'

'I will. Tomorrow.'

'Love you very much, darling.'

'Love you too, Mum.'

Prue went over to Johnny's flat as she had said she would and found the door ajar. He was at his desk, drawing. There were a few moments before he became aware of her presence in the doorway.

'You all right?' he asked at last, looking up. His anxious face told Prue he knew she had had a turbulent night and was exhausted. She nodded, said she was fine. Her concern was for him: he was red-eyed, haggard. She wondered whether he had some illness he did not want to mention. One day she would ask. But now he braced himself, managed a smile. 'I've news for you,' he said. I talked to these people who farm about ten miles from here, nothing very grand, couple of hundred acres, mixed crops, a few pigs—'

'Pigs? Wow! I love pigs.'

'I made a shed for them a few years back. Seems they'd be grateful for help two or three days a week. Loved the fact that you're an experienced farm worker. I said we'd go over and meet them next week. Come on in, sit down. I'll make you a cup of coffee.'

Prue sat in her usual chair by the window, the sun warm on her lap. She felt at ease here, in Johnny's untidy room. She felt, again, a profound sense of gratitude, both for his intuition and his kindness. 'Thanks so much.' She cupped her hands round the mug. Johnny went back to the table. There was no need for Prue to think of anything to say. She was grateful that he was the sort of man who could cope with long silences, didn't see in them anything suspicious or accusatory. Prue was grateful for that, too.

Eventually he pushed aside his papers, turned to her. 'Also,' he said, I thought we might drive down to Hallows Farm at the end of the week. We could start very early.'

'That would be wonderful.'

'I'll wait till I see Barry's car has gone . . . then off we'll go.'

Prue was puzzled by the note of conspiracy but did not query it. As Barry seemed not to mind what she did while he was working – it held no interest for him – she would feel no guilt at spending a long day out with Johnny. But perhaps he was right – it would be better not to mention their plan.

'I look forward to that, though it might be . . .' Prue decided not to add the word 'difficult'.

'People say you shouldn't go back to somewhere you loved,' Johnny went on. 'But it can lay to rest the memory.' Prue gave a very small laugh. 'I hate to see you so sad, Mrs Lawrence dying. We'll try to have a good day.'

'We will. Thanks, Johnny. You're the kindest man . . .'

On the day they planned to go to Hallows Farm Barry left the house soon after six for he had to catch a train to London. As soon as he had driven off in the Daimler Prue parked the Sunbeam in the road to avoid curious glances from Bertha. It was half an hour before Johnny had said he would be 'concealed' by a neighbouring tree but, to Prue's surprise, there he was already, waiting. As he got into the passenger seat she giggled at the slightly nefarious nature of their rendezvous. Her spirits lifted. 'You're early,' she said.

'I had a hunch Barry might leave earlier than usual.'

'You're either uncannily intuitive or very peculiar,' said Prue.

'I've been awake for ages. Rather looking forward to it all. And it means we've got a good start, clear roads,' said Johnny, 'so you can put your foot down, see what it's like. I don't think you've ever done over forty in your own car, have you?'

They drove through semi-darkness, which gradually gave way to a spread of pure, colourless light in which the rising sun spread its trails of amber. Once on the trunk road Prue accelerated obediently, and loved the speed. The long journey flashed by. When they came to the familiar country near Hinton Half Moon she slowed down, stopped. She asked Johnny to take over.

'I just want to concentrate on looking,' she said. They drove to the farm, parked in the lane outside the yard. 'Best if we go and introduce ourselves to whoever,' she said. 'I'm sure they won't mind if we look around, walk over the fields.'

The farmyard was now an empty place: no steaming dung heap, no rank smells, no hens running amok. The cobbles were swept, Sly's old pigsty was empty. Not a sign of farming life.

'Cripes,' said Prue, frowning at the new blue paint on the window frames. 'I'm glad the Lawrences can't see this.'

She knocked on the back door – there had never been a bell – dreading the moment the new owner appeared.

A middle-aged woman with an angry mouth opened the door. 'Yes?' In the single word she managed to convey her distaste for people who dropped by uninvited.

Prue gave her a charming smile. 'I was one of the land girls billeted here in the war,' she said, 'when the Lawrences owned the place. My friend and I were nearby, and wondered if you would mind if we just looked around, went for a walk . . .?'

The woman allowed pure scorn to move her face. 'You were a land girl?'

'I was.'

'We all know what they got up to.'

Prue giggled. 'We had to work extremely hard, but it was a wonderful job.'

'I'm sure.' The woman's defensive stance melted a little. She didn't go so far as to ask them in – and had she done so Prue would have refused. She did not want to see what abominations had appeared in the kitchen. With a look of extravagant condescension the woman agreed to their looking round the place. 'Mind you shut the gates,' she said, in case Prue had forgotten a prime rule. 'We've got a lot of sheep.'

'You didn't keep the Friesians?'

'We couldn't run to cows, no. We're not cattle people. We're going to pull down the old milking sheds next year.' With a tilt of her head she indicated the sheds across the yard, lest Prue had forgotten, too, their whereabouts.

'Gosh,' said Prue. 'Well, sorry to have bothered you and we'll be sure to shut the gates.' She hoped her note of sarcasm was appreciated.

The woman backed into the kitchen. Prue saw a flash of hideous new paint and shut her eyes. Then she and Johnny made their way back across the yard.

'The trouble with that old bat,' said Johnny, 'is that she missed what she thought the land girls got up to.' They both laughed.

At Sly's old pigsty Prue stopped, leant on the wall and looked at the bare concrete floor.

'I suppose they're going to pull this down, too,' she said. 'Can't think why they bothered to buy a farm.'

'Why don't you take me on a guided tour of the land?' Johnny asked. 'I'd like to know some of the things that happened in some of the places.'

His interest, reckoned Prue, wasn't just kindness: it was genuine, and she warmed to him for that. On the other hand he seemed . . . out of place: a northern poet-carpenter in thin clean trousers and a tweed jacket. Prue disliked him for not being Joe, or Barry One, or even Robert, and berated herself for such thoughts. They began to walk down the lane, stopping at gates to look into some of the fields where Prue had spent so many days ploughing, or picking up potatoes, or harvesting. They came to the huge hedge where Ag had earned her colours in Mr Lawrence's eyes: he had nominated her the best female hedger he had ever known. Now it was shaggy, uncared-for, its high branches adrift.

'Good work not kept up,' said Prue. 'Everything goes to ruin.'

At that moment a bird fluttered out of the lower branches of the hedge and rose into the sky. Prue clutched Johnny's arm, excited. 'Look at that! I do believe it's a stormcock. Mr Lawrence would have loved to see it. Ag taught him its Latin name. She said he was so pleased she'd reminded him.'

'*Turdus viscivorus*, isn't it?' said Johnny, quietly, moving his arm from Prue's hand.

'You know what? Ag would have liked you. She' s a real scholar, too. I remember the evening of the day they saw the *Turdus*-whatsit. At supper that night Mr Lawrence taught us all the other names for a stormcock. He said we should learn about birds. So I wrote all the names down and tried really hard just to show them I wasn't a completely stupid hairdresser.' She frowned a little, patted the red spotted bow in her hair. 'Shrite, skite, gawthrush, mistle thrush, garthrush, jercock . . . and one more. What was it?'

She looked up at Johnny.

'Could be syecock?'

'That's it! Syecock. So you know more than just about chickens.'

'A little. I'm glad we saw the stormcock.'

Suddenly Prue did not dislike him any more, though she could not be reconciled to his trousers.

They began to walk. They walked a long way, through all the fields so familiar to Prue that past and present were an inextricable jumble in her sight. Long Meadow, Lower Pasture, the place where Ratty's mad wife had thrown the scalding tea at the harvest gathering . . . They pushed their way through dozens of sheep, who paused from eating to look at them with their indignant yellow eyes: sheep, but not the Lawrences' sheep. Prue used to know the habits of every animal in the flock. But not these, not one did she recognize.

They came to the field where ploughing, on a steep slope, had always been hazardous. At the top Johnny suggested they have a rest. He laid his jacket on the ground, produced a Thermos of tea from a pocket.

They sat without talking, looking down on the fields and the trees which were just beginning to turn. By now the sky was a blue very like that of her Buckingham Palace dress, thought Prue, untrammelled by cloud. The occasional bleat from a sheep or the call of a skylark were the only sounds that chipped the huge silence.

'Think we'd better go back,' she said, when the tea was finished. The truth was she could not be sure that she would not cry if she went on taking in all this for much longer. Memories could be dangerous, as Stella had said at one of their annual lunches, thinking of Joe. Just when you thought you were doing fine, they could suddenly flay you.

On the long walk back, the weather had one of those swift changes of mood that had often surprised Prue in the past. She would go off on the tractor on a sunny morning, only to be drenched by a downpour a couple of hours later. The blue gave way to bruised sky and dark clouds. It began to rain. Prue did not care: she liked rain, and was pleased to see that the admirably quiet Johnny did not put on his jacket again.

They passed the coppice, Prue's constant meeting place and most loved corner of the Lawrences' acreage. She looked up at the yellowing leaves of the elms, which guarded the dense mass of evergreens of the inner wood, with its complicated tracks among the undergrowth and mossy banks.

'Lovely-looking wood,' said Johnny. 'Shall we go in? Shelter from the rain?'

'I'd rather not,' said Prue, and they walked on. That he did not insist earned him further high marks in her appraisal.

Back at the farmyard the owner's car had gone and there were no lights on in the house. Prue suggested they had a quick look at the barn before returning home. By now it was raining hard. Their clothes were dark and clinging to them.

There was a grainy light in the barn. It took Prue's eyes a few moments to adjust. She saw that here, at least, nothing had changed. Bales of hay were piled high. The old tractor – her tractor – was still in its usual place in the corner. There were sacks of meal, some leaking beige trails thin as rats' tails, and bags of pig food Sly had not eaten before she was slaughtered. Plainly the new farmer did not consider the barn a priority and Prue was glad. She went over to the tractor, put a hand on one of its mudguards. Then she climbed up onto its seat, remembering the exact curves of the iron, so well designed – especially, she used to think – to support the shape of her bottom. Looking down on Johnny, she laughed. 'You realize this is a great privilege, Johnny, do you? You're seeing the Land Army's best ever plougher actually sitting on her tractor. Cor, what I wouldn't do to start the engine, drive off . . .'

'In this rain?' Johnny mimicked her light note.

'Best in the rain, I often thought. Lovely getting into your eyes, your mouth, though it didn't do much for these.' She touched the sodden bow that had flopped in her wet hair, then climbed down. Johnny was looking up at the rafters, peering around. Prue imagined he was seeing just some untidy old barn. It would be impossible ever to explain to him what this place had meant to her and the others: the things that had gone on there. She had no intention of trying.

'Is that the rafter you walked along?' he asked.

Prue nodded. 'It is. It's quite high, isn't it?'

'It certainly is.' He gave her a look. 'Would you dare to try it again?'

'What? Now?' For an infinitesimal moment Prue contemplated the idea, then dismissed it as absurd. 'No,' she said. 'That was then. Some things can't be repeated.'

She moved towards the stack of hay bales, began to climb. It was as easy as she remembered. She sat on the highest one, looked down. Johnny had judged her feat as a challenge and was following her surprisingly fast: she had not thought of him as athletic. He sat beside her, looked up at the rafters, some six feet above their heads, then down at the lowest spread of bales.

'Quite some way to fall.'

'It was. Though I didn't fall to the bottom. I—' She stopped. What had happened next was private, nothing to do with Johnny. As it was, she felt a rising of the resentment that had come and gone all day. What was he doing here, trying to share her past?

The rain was harder now. Noisy gusts hit the roof with a sound of spilt nails. In her soaked shirt, Prue felt cold. She rather envied Johnny's tweed jacket, which he had brought up here with him and laid over the hay. But she resisted picking it up and putting it over her shoulders.

'That rain,' said Johnny. 'It sounds like barrels of rice tipped onto iron.'

Prue looked at him with utter scorn. 'No, it doesn't,' she said, 'it sounds like rain on a corrugated roof, which is what it is. But then of course you're a poet, so I can't squabble with your fancy ideas.' She had no idea why she was so cross. Johnny had spent the day doing his best to be sympathetic, and all she could do was snub him.

'You're quite difficult, you know. Hard to please,' he said.

'Sorry.'

Johnny pulled the jacket towards him, took a Mars Bar from the pocket. He tore off the paper, and passed it to her.

Prue burst into tears. No wonder, she thought. This is the Lawrences' barn and I'm here with Johnny, not Joe. I'm in the place Joe and I first made love, and he gave me a Mars Bar. And now *Johnny* is doing the same thing.

'This is unbearable,' she sobbed, shaking her head as Johnny passed her the chocolate. 'No, I don't want it. This whole thing is an utter mistake. We should never have come here. Why are we here?'

Johnny could scarcely understand her protest, so fraught were her sobs. 'I don't understand what's happened – what's the matter? Why's a Mars Bar set you off?'

'I can't explain – I can't ever explain.'

'No, well, OK, but put this round you. You're shivering.' He fumbled to put the jacket round her shoulders.

'I don't want your bloody jacket. I want . . . I don't know what I want.'

His jacket rejected, Johnny put an arm round her shoulders with a sudden firmness of purpose. He pulled her close to him and kissed her cheeks, which were awash with salt tears. Prue resisted for no more than a moment. Exhausted, despairing, not caring, she lay back on the bale. She could feel the strange, light weight of him, and the rasping of their two sodden shirts. She heard him saying things, but couldn't be sure what they were.

A few moments later Prue was able to sit up. She was no longer crying. She knew her cheeks were black and her lipstick was all over the place, and the rain was still drumming in her ears. Johnny was on his back beside her.

'Oh God,' he said. 'I don't know how that came about. I—'

'Let's not talk about it.' On one of the nearby bales Johnny's wet but well ironed, prissy trousers lay neatly folded. When had he had time to fold them up? It had all been so hurried. Prue felt sick. 'We'd better be getting back,' she said. 'Long way to go.'

Johnny bent his long thin legs: his shoes had gone but green socks were held up by suspenders. Droopy underpants were askew round his thighs. He sat, stood, reached for the trousers. Repelled, appalled, Prue looked away.

They slid down the bales, dashed out into the bare yard cross-hatched with rain – a place that seemed unrecognizable, as things often seemed to Prue when they were touched by unusual events. They hurried to the car in the lane. Johnny got into the driver's seat. Prue, glancing at his grim profile, could not decide whether he was full of fury or afraid of her own wrath.

Half an hour later Prue patted her wet hair. 'Must have left my bow in the hay,' she said. 'When the new people come across it one day, they'll wonder.'

After that, neither of them spoke till they reached The Larches.

# Chapter 6

For three days after their visit to Hallows Farm Prue did not see Johnny. Each morning when she went to feed the chickens she looked up at his window, but there was no sign of him. On the fourth day he was at his usual place, and waved. Then he beckoned. For a moment Prue wondered whether or not to go to his flat. She was not sure what she felt. The anger that had struck her in the barn had long since disappeared. What had taken place there had not been rape, but apathy on her part. It had been a one-off, and there had been many of those. It had meant nothing to her. But she wondered, as she had constantly wondered since they had got back, what Johnny was thinking. Was he apologetic, pleased he'd had his way, ashamed? Eager to find out, Prue abandoned the thought of ignoring him, and knocked on the door of his flat.

'Oh there you are,' he said, and immediately turned from her, a slight flush rearing up his neck, and made for the kettle.

'You haven't been around, at least not at your window,' said Prue. She took her usual place in the arthritic chair by the window.

'No.' A few silent moments later he handed her a cup of coffee. 'The Ganders are looking forward to meeting you,' he said. 'I thought we might go over this afternoon, if that's convenient.' There was a trace of sarcasm in his voice that Prue had never heard before. He was indicating that he knew her afternoon, like most of her afternoons, would be empty.

'The Ganders? You mean the farmer I might work for?'

'That's right.'

'Well. Fine. That would be OK – this afternoon.' Prue concentrated on her coffee. She was determined not to be the one to bring up the subject of the incident in the barn.

'I suppose we'd better get the matter of . . . the other day cleared up,' Johnny said after a while. 'Then I hope we'll be back to normal.'

'I hope so.'

'I'm sorry. I don't know what came over me. At least, I do. I was suddenly gripped by the longing to comfort you. You seemed so sad, so overcome, back in your barn.'

'You don't have to explain,' said Prue. She was troubled by the harshness of his voice and the regret in his eyes.

'But I want to. I don't want you to think I'd planned to take you to the barn at Hallows Farm on purpose to seduce you.'

'I didn't think that.'

'It was completely spontaneous. What I had in mind was . . . just a hug, brotherly, sisterly. But it went wrong. Got out of hand. I mean, you're not exactly resistible.' He gave the faintest grim smile. 'And somehow, weakness of the flesh and all that, my planned brief hug turned into—'

'Quite.'

'What happened was a misjudgement.'

Having heard this word from Joe so recently, Prue flinched. 'Heavens, Johnny,' she said, as lightly as she could, 'we all misjudge all the time.'

'Are you angry with me?'

'Not any more.'

'Thank God for that.' He came and sat down on the chair opposite her. 'I hope you don't think I'm the kind of man bent on seducing other men's wives.'

'Of course not. I've never had any such thought.'

Johnny now gave a wider smile, almost back to his usual demeanour. 'You have to admit, when we first met, I didn't respond with so much as a flicker to your flirting.'

'My flirting?' Prue was shrill with mock-indignation.

'There was the odd cock of the head, the odd look, the occasional positioning yourself close enough for me to ease an arm round your shoulders had I felt inclined – wasn't there?'

Prue laughed, really laughed. 'Honestly, Johnny, I'm surprised you noticed. You call that flirting? I know when I was younger I was a bit wild, but I'm a married woman now, aren't I? And I behave with – what's the word Ag was always using? – decorum. That's it. I behave with "the utmost decorum".' She said this in what she liked to think was a grand, prim voice.

Johnny laughed too. 'What I'd like to suggest . . .' He clasped his hands, perhaps to stop their slight shaking, perhaps to assist his thoughts. 'What I'd like is that we put all this behind us. No need to mention it again. Go back to being straight and narrow friends. I'd hate to lose you. There aren't many people here—'

'Agreed,' said Prue. 'Let's just carry on as before.' She felt the small thrust of a tear behind one eye, and quickly stood up.

'I'll pick you up at two,' said Johnny. 'I think we'd better go in my van. Mr Gander might be unnerved by the Sunbeam Talbot. It might make him think you're not the sort of girl he's looking for.'

'Fine. I like your van.'

Johnny held the door open for her. Recently, on meeting and parting, they had exchanged a quick peck on the cheek. Now Johnny made no move to approach her for their customary farewell. Prue shrugged. The tear continued to threaten. She wondered if their friendship could ever be quite the same again, or if its innocence was shadowed for good.

The Ganders' farm was only a twenty-minute drive away, an oddly rustic place so near to Manchester. Johnny explained that Steve Gander was a widower. He lived with his daughter, Dawn, and son-in-law Bert, a printer, who worked in the city.

'Dawn's a bit of an odd one,' he said. 'Chippy. You want to mind your words there. Just keep asking about her is the best thing. She won't want to know about you.'

'Right.' Prue, looking out at the unkempt hedges, was wondering whether this was going to be the job of her dreams, after all. The van bumped down an uneven track to a clear area of rough land on which the farmhouse stood. 'Farmhouse?' said Prue. 'It's the most hideous bungalow I've ever seen.'

'Well, you won't be in it much. And I do promise you the view from the other side is a surprise. Wonderful oaks, elms, ash, chestnut. Must have been someone's carefully planned wood in the past. When the Ganders bought the land they just chopped down half of it to build the bungalow.'

They parked in a corner beside a large farm building made of corrugated iron. Prue, glancing inside, was pleased to see a jumble of farm tools, an old tractor and a large stack of pig feed.

'Wow, Prue,' she heard Johnny say. 'I've only just noticed.' He looked her up and down, fighting natural appraisal. 'Your land-girl gear?'

'Just the breeches.' Prue blushed. 'OK, do you think?'

'Fine.'

'I mean, I'll wear them when I work here. Why not?'

'Why not?' Johnny laughed. 'There's Steve. Come and meet him.'

A small bent man was hobbling towards them. He wore gaiters and a cap whose tweed shone greasily with age. A pipe hung from his mouth. When they were close enough to shake hands he removed the pipe to a place between his ear and the cap. The smoke stood up like a feather. Prue had to control her smile.

'Welcome, my dear,' said Steve Gander, gathering Prue's hand in both of his. The hard roughness of his skin felt unnervingly familiar: farmer's hands, Mr Lawrence's hands. His eyes flicked up and down Prue. He gave a thrilled wail. 'Well I never! Well I be dashed! You a land girl, were you? I believe Johnny mentioned it.' Prue nodded. 'I'm proud to meet you. I want to shake you by the hand again.' This he did, squeezing her fingers till they hurt. 'What would we have done without you? I always wanted our Dawn to join the Land Army, but it wasn't for her, she said. She's never been one to get up early. So my wife did the milking, Dawn did her best at the stove.'

'Do you still have cows?' Prue withdrew her hand.

'That we don't. We had a fine herd of Herefords before the war, but had to turn over to arable like everyone else. Once it was over I hadn't the heart to start again.' He turned towards the bungalow, retrieved his pipe and waved it about. 'As you can see, things have gone downhill a bit. Amy gone, it's not the same. But I was hoping you might help us get it together again, few hours a week.'

'I'd love to try,' said Prue.

'Let's go into house. Dawn'll maybe get us a cup of tea.'

Johnny and Prue followed his rocking progress to the front door of the bungalow, a building of rough grey concrete and window-panes in rusting frames. The old man had some trouble pushing open the front door, obviously not often used. 'Don't usually go in this way,' he said, 'but I'd like you to see . . .'

Prue was expecting a dark passage, in keeping with the outside, and it *was* dark, painted a sour brown – but the paint was scarcely visible between the dozens of glass boxes of butterflies on the walls. Steve turned on a switch. Strings of small bulbs lit up in the cases. The colours were brilliant in the dusky light of the corridor. Prue went from case to case, enchanted by the fragile wings so carefully preserved.

'Used to be my hobby, butterflies,' he said. 'When I was a lad I went all over, collecting. I was in the Merchant Navy so I had the opportunity – all over the world. Very fine specimens I was lucky enough to find. They've done me well. I spend a lot of time here, just looking. Dawn, now – well, it could be said Dawn doesn't see the point of butterflies the way I do.'

He turned off the lights. In the instant gloom the creatures' colours were lowered into a minor key, but still they glowed magically.

Steve led them to the kitchen, a room so crowded with furniture, boxes, piles of old newspaper and general detritus that it was hard to weave through the junk to chairs at a chaotic table. A very tall, bony woman was pouring tea. 'Dawn,' he said. 'This is my daughter Dawn. Looks after me. Dawn, this is Prue, coming to help us out. You know Johnny.'

By way of acknowledgement Dawn blinked lashless eyes in Prue's direction. She gave a reluctant smile that was hampered by a pair of exceptionally long front teeth. 'Hello,' she said. 'What – you the land girl?'

'I was once,' said Prue.

Dawn banged the teapot onto the table. 'If you ask me, they didn't know how to behave,' she said.

'No one's asking your opinion,' her father quietly chided.

'I've got a friend who knew a land girl,' Dawn went on. 'You'd be shocked if I told you what they got up to.' Prue and Johnny exchanged a glance.

'They weren't all the same, Dawn,' said Steve. 'And it's good for us we've found someone who knows about farm work.'

'Maybe,' said Dawn, and left the room.

Over the horribly strong tea Steve began to explain the kind of job he would want Prue to do. 'The pigs,' he said. 'They're in a field down the hill, round the other side.'

'I love pigs,' said Prue.

Steve clattered at his teeth with the stem of his pipe. 'Some of them can be right buggers,' he said. 'You'll have to mind your step.'

Dawn came storming back into the room. 'The main thing for you to take over,' she said, sitting down next to Prue, 'is my job.'

'What's that?'

'Exercising my horse. Jack the Lad.'

As she showed no sign of explaining any further, Steve braced himself, with a long suck on his pipe, to enlighten Prue. 'See, before the war we bred Shires. Amy loved them. Suffolk Punches, Clydesdales – won a lot of prizes. We kept three for the field work in the war, but then . . . they went the same way as the cows. Great pity.'

'But we kept Jack the Lad,' Dawn suddenly offered, with a liveliness she had not previously displayed, 'because he's my horse. He's a bloody great stallion. Marvellous. I love Jack.'

Prue saw Johnny had turned away from the table and was concentrating hard on the view from the window. His mouth twitched as he fought a smile.

'It was like this,' Steve went on. 'He was a fine stallion. We'd this idea of keeping him, getting another mare one day. But that wasn't to be. And he became – how can I put it? – restless. Dangerous, sometimes. He'd go for people.'

'Not for me.' Dawn banged the table.

'Not for you, Dawn, no. But in he end there was nothing for it. We had to have him cut.'

'I've never forgiven my father for that.' Dawn banged the table harder.

'No. But he's a lovely quiet horse, now, docile as a lamb. He can live out his days here, far as I'm concerned.' Steve averted his eyes from his furious daughter, turned to Prue. 'Thing is, there's not much for him to do. Bit of harrowing, that's all. So he's bored. He needs a bit of exercise.'

'So I walk him on a leading rein,' said Dawn, 'but I've not really the time for that.'

'No,' said her father, uncertainly.

'So that's what you'll be doing.' Dawn's front teeth flashed nastily at Prue.

'Fine,' she said.

'We should be going,' Johnny said. Steve leapt up to guide them through the clutter on the floor.

'Let's see you here first thing Monday morning,' he said. 'You'll be most welcome.' He grinned at her breeches.

In the van, once they were out of the gate, she and Johnny were able to laugh at last.

'What do you think?' asked Johnny.

'I'll give it a go,' said Prue.

When she turned up for work at seven o'clock the following Monday morning, there was no sign of Steve Gander or Dawn. She parked the Sunbeam among some buildings behind the large shed, sensing it would be better if her employers came across it later, rather than were immediately affronted by its scarlet presence next to the bungalow.

As she got out of the car, wearing her land-girl breeches in defiance of Dawn's hostility, she saw a figure emerge from the corrugated building. It was the tall, bony Dawn, in baggy dungarees, her hair sticking out in awkward wisps. From a distance she might have been a scarecrow.

Prue drew herself up, summoned an enthusiastic smile. She was ready and keen to start work and anxious to convey her enthusiasm. The two women walked towards each other.

'So,' said Dawn, her eyes on the bow in Prue's hair – carefully chosen, a very modest affair of dark green with a paler stripe, 'your first morning. Down to it, that's what I say. In at the deep end. The pigs need mucking out. They're in a field at the back of the house, down the hill.'

'Right,' said Prue. 'Just tell me where to find a wheelbarrow and a fork.'

Dawn threw her a look of considerable scorn. 'You'll come across them if you use your eyes. But before that you'd better meet Jack. He needs his walk. He's the most important animal on the farm, as you'll see.' She turned away.

Prue followed her skeletal employer behind the shed and round a corner, where the scarlet Sunbeam glared in the sunlight. Dawn stopped, turned. 'This thing yours?'

Prue nodded.

'Some people,' Dawn said, and carried on, her shoulders raised huffily. From behind the car three geese rushed towards her with mysterious enthusiasm, their greeting a sea-hiss, necks fully stretched. Prue, who hated geese, was pleased they ignored her.

They came to a block of run-down loose boxes. Dawn gave Prue her horrible rabbit smile, plainly enjoying the surprise she had in store. Prue moved to her side and looked into the stable, which was almost entirely taken up by the most enormous horse she had ever seen. Its head seemed the size of a beer barrel, its hoofs were larger than elephants' feet. The circumference of a single knee was larger than her own waist. The horse turned as carefully as a liner easing its way in a small harbour and thrust its vast head over the half-door.

'Jack, my lad,' whispered Dawn. She stroked the grey nose, then placed her mouth on the top lip, which instantly rolled back. For a moment Dawn's mouth was on the horse's grimace of giant teeth. Then the great head gave a shake and turned away from the pressing kiss. Evidently he'd had enough, though from the look in Dawn's eyes she could have carried on the embrace much

119

longer. 'Our morning kiss,' she explained breathily. 'Every morning. We'd never miss it, would we, Jack?'

'Cripes,' said Prue.

'What's on your mind?' snapped Dawn. Her dreamy eyes gave way to a look of sharp suspicion.

'I was just thinking . . . how would I reach to put on Jack's head-collar? I mean, you're much taller than me.'

The question caused a superior laugh – a sound somewhere between a bark and a snarl.

'There are ladders,' she said. Then a flicker of charity entered her dark soul. 'But just for once, first time, I'll do it.'

'Gosh, thanks,' said Prue.

Dawn fetched a head-collar. Prue observed that it weighed down the skinny little arm that held it, but its weight seemed to be giving pleasure rather than pain, judging by the look on Dawn's face. With some awe Prue watched the process of Dawn's stretching up to put the head-collar over Jack's ears. As she stretched up to do up the chin-strap, her shirt rode up and frothed over the waist of her dungarees. For a moment there was a flash of greying vest. Then Dawn led her horse out: it moved with a few huge, gentle steps, then stopped. Dawn handed the leading rein to Prue. 'Just go down through the fields, anywhere, it doesn't matter. Jack'll lead you. He has his favourite ways. Go on.'

Prue met the challenge with a toss of her head: land girls had always been up for anything. Taking the leading rein, she moved close to the horse. She came to an inch or so above its shoulder. Uncertain how to behave in front of Dawn, she gave Jack's neck a firm pat. Dawn reacted swiftly. She, too, patted the horse, but on the withers, which Prue could barely reach. Then she tangled a few strands of its mane between her fingers, which Prue thought horribly spooky. Finally Dawn darted back to Jack's head, kissed him once more, on the nose this time. 'Goodbye, my darling,' she whispered, like an actress in a third-rate romance. 'You'll be back with your Dawn soon.'

Prue was relieved to see their love was not entirely mutual. Jack seemed eager to be off. They moved away, Prue keen to be out of range of Dawn's critical look.

'Cripes,' she heard herself say. 'It's like taking a tractor for a walk.'

Dawn, busily rummaging with the mess of her vest and shirt, either ignored or did not hear the comparison. Clothes reassembled, she wiped an eye. Prue was reminded of newsreel pictures of wives saying farewell to their soldier husbands as they left for a long spell of fighting abroad.

Prue, nervous at first, soon found Jack an easy companion and, as Dawn said, he knew the way. They went along paths through the woods that were thick at the back of the farm buildings, as Johnny had said, occasionally turning into grassland or a lane. Every now and then Jack would toss his head and give a long, snorting sigh, which flattened the stinging nettles as they passed. This reminded her of Noble. She reached up to pat the horse's shoulder. But mostly she kept her eyes on the way ahead: to look back at the mountain she was leading was unnerving.

They came to the field in which some dozen or so pigs rootled in the mud. Their accommodation was bridge-shaped shelters made from the ubiquitous corrugated iron. Prue could see that inside these shelters the soaked and rotten bedding was an insult to any pig. She understood why one of her priorities would be mucking out and giving the wretched animals beds of clean straw. Mr Lawrence would never have stood for such inconsideration to what were, he always insisted, naturally clean animals.

By the time they got back Prue reckoned she and Jack had walked some three or four miles. She returned him to his stable where, obligingly, he lowered his great head so that she could slip off the head-collar with no difficulty. Then she made her way to the bungalow to ask what her next job should be.

Steve Gander was standing at the door, waiting for her. He touched his cap. 'All well?' he asked. 'Dawn was worried.'

'Oh? She didn't tell me how long she wanted me to be.'

'No – well, she usually takes him just down the lane and back. Not much of a walk. He'll have enjoyed going further.' He ushered her through the door and into the kitchen. There was a strong smell of bones boiling in a great pot on the stove. 'Normally,' said Steve, stumbling across the littered floor to the kettle, 'Dawn doesn't allow a morning break, coffee, tea. Says it's an indulgence. But seeing she's not here, why don't we treat ourselves? Amy and I used to love a sit-down, mid-morning, one of her oatmeal biscuits . . . None of that now.' His voice dropped into a minor key. 'And with our daughter Dawn, a strong-minded lass, it's easiest to do as she says.'

But ten minutes later they were caught out. Dawn charged into the room, red-faced, elbows juddering, shirt askew again. She turned on Prue. 'And where were you?' she screeched. 'I've been out looking for you everywhere.'

'I'm sorry,' began Prue. 'I thought—'

'She gave Jack a nice long walk,' said Steve.

Dawn sat down, glared at the teapot. 'This isn't our normal routine,' she said, anger waning as quickly as it had come. 'We don't indulge, Dad and I, in fancy tea-breaks, elevenses.'

'I know,' said Prue. 'I understand.'

'And what you should get going on this afternoon is the pigs. Dad'll show you where the pig feed is.'

'Fine.'

Silence fell. Ask her about herself, Johnny had advised. He'd obviously discovered how to deal with the grumpy old bat. Prue turned to Dawn, whose fingers played scales on her ruddy cheeks, with a smile as sweet as she could make it. 'And what about your husband?' she asked. 'Does he have time to help on the farm?'

Dawn appeared stumped by this flash of genuine interest. 'Help on the farm? Bert?' She gave one of her honking laughs. 'Bert doesn't have time for anything but his business. He runs a printing firm. Comes home stinking of ink. It's printing, printing, morning, noon and night, isn't it, Dad?' Steve revved himself up to give a nod of assent, then decided against it at the last moment. 'So we don't see much of him, do we, Dad? Just comes home evenings, wants the meal on the table.' Her hands now flickered through her wild thin hair, agitated. 'Still, I've got Jack, haven't I, Dad?'

This time her father nodded firmly. 'You've got Jack all right,' he said.

Prue spent the afternoon crouched uncomfortably in two of the pig shelters. So deep and dense was the muck she had to clear that there was no time to attend to more. To begin with the stench of powerful, aged pig urine was almost stifling – she felt nostalgic for Sly's milder-smelling bedding – but soon she became used to it. As she tossed the sodden bedding into the wheelbarrow she felt the old, familiar pull on her shoulder muscles: they had been bad when she had started work at Hallows Farm, but soon hardened and caused no more trouble. She knew that, after a day or so, physical labour would no longer be painful, and she would enjoy surprising Dawn with the speed and efficiency of her work.

She drove home at five, pleased with herself. She looked forward to recounting to Barry the madness of the day, the place, the neurotic Dawn, all so utterly different from Hallows Farm. But she had no thought of leaving. Walking a horse and cleaning out the pigs didn't seem to be an entirely normal way of farming, but then there had been little that seemed normal at the Gander farm, a place of various kinds of unhappiness. She hoped when she recounted it all to Barry she could make him laugh. And tomorrow she would describe it to Johnny, and telephone Stella and Ag. They would be astounded.

When Prue drove through the gates of The Larches she found a very large green Humber parked by the front door and was put out to think some visitor had arrived: her stories would have to wait.

But there was no visitor. Hurrying into the sitting room, she found Barry alone in his usual chair, fidgeting with his usual cigar. He sniffed as she came in. 'Sweetheart,' he said, with a tolerant look that showed he could be a tolerant husband, 'you stink.'

'Sorry,' said Prue. 'I'll go and have a bath. But I just want to tell you—'

Barry raised a hand to stop her. She knew there was no point in challenging it.

'I've news for you. Big news. You saw that car outside? That Humber?' Prue nodded. Barry gave his widest ever smile. 'Well, sweetheart, it's ours. Yours and mine. Our first Humber. I got it at a price. What do you think?'

Prue swallowed. She had no idea what she thought. 'Wonderful,' she said. 'Are you going to sell the Daimler?'

'Not on your life. I'm going to get a grand collection of cars. Be worth a fortune, one day.'

'I can imagine,' said Prue, who could not imagine any such thing. By now she was aware of the pig smell that was all over her. She wanted to run her bath, but knew Barry hated to let her go before she produced a full measure of wonder and appreciation concerning his news. 'I look forward to a ride.'

'You go and have your bath, sweetheart, and we'll make a plan.' Let off lightly, Prue flung him a smile and fled upstairs.

Except for a few brief enquiries about her day, talk of the Humber occupied the whole evening. Prue realized it was not the moment to entertain her husband with stories about her new farm life. After supper they moved back to the sitting room, the fire, the cigar. Barry tipped his head back on the chair and kept on smiling. Prue, stiff and a little weary, went to kiss him on the cheek before she went up to bed.

'Night, sweetheart.' He opened one eye. Flicked her stomach with the cigarless hand. 'Any luck?'

'Not yet.' Prue moved back. She hated both the manner of the enquiry and his curiosity.

'Have to be patient. You get off to bed. I'm just going to spend a few minutes thinking about the Humber.' He closed the eye again. 'And I tell you what, how about this for an idea? How about we do a little run down to Devon, Dorset, wherever it was you worked – trial run in the car?'

'That would be . . .'

'I knew you'd like that idea. Now you get off to bed. I'm just going to spend a few minutes here having a nice think . . .'

Cripes, thought Prue, and ran from the room.

'It's not a proper farming job,' she told Johnny a few days later. 'It's not even a proper farm. Steve seems to care for it, but does little more than moan that things are no longer like they were in the war, when his wife was alive to run the place. As for Dawn, she's scatty, desperate, angry, more than slightly peculiar. She's jealous of my relationship with her horse, yet she's bored by taking him for walks herself. She never used to go further than some old woman with a Pekingese in a park.' Johnny laughed. 'But you're going to stick at it?'

'Oh yes. It'll fill three days a week. And I think that if I go carefully I might be able to show them a more efficient way of managing things – selling the pigs and so on, which they haven't bothered to do for ages.'

'Steve'll be grateful,' said Johnny. 'I know he hates to see the place slowly disintegrating, but he seems incapable of doing anything about it.'

'It's just a matter of negotiating with Dawn. I can't get on with her. She's the problem.'

'I've an idea there. I happen to know she loves cars. Have you seen the piles of car magazines in the kitchen? Why don't you . . . one day, offer her a ride in the Sunbeam?'

'I'll think about it,' said Prue, after a while.

'You might win her over like that.'

'How do you know how well she drives?'

'Might be worth taking that risk.'

Prue was grading Johnny's eggs at the table in his kitchen. The sun made the room warm. She liked handling the eggs. Johnny, his hands always shaking, was inclined to break them. She felt happy, useful. 'Have you noticed the huge great Humber in the drive?' she asked.

'What's that all about?'

Prue smiled. 'Barry's new acquisition. Apparently he's going to collect a whole lot of cars that will be very valuable in about fifty years' time. The bad news is he's suggested we do a run in it to Hallows Farm.'

'You're not going to mention our visit?'

'Of course not. I'm just going to suggest we look at a few fields, the village, Ratty's house – just glance at the farmhouse from afar and not go anywhere near the barn.'

'Right.' At the mention of the barn Johnny's mouth had tightened.

Prue filled the stack of egg boxes and piled them neatly on the table. Her job finished, she left to go back to The Larches for the grim ceremony of Sunday lunch alone with Barry – tepid shepherd's pie, tinned plums, two cigars. At his door Johnny gave a very slight movement of his hand, not quite a wave: this was his new goodbye. Since the visit to Hallows Farm he had never once kissed her on the cheek, or looked as if he wanted to. Even as they sometimes gathered eggs together he seemed to avoid being near her.

Prue sighed deeply as she let herself into the stale hallway of The Larches. She was determined today to make Barry shut up about his wretched Humber and listen to her own news.

Over the next few weeks Prue made a routine for herself at the farm. In truth, there was not enough for her to do. Once she had thoroughly mucked out the pig shelters she had merely to lay clean straw once a week, a job she could do in a morning. This surprised Steve. He told her it used to take him a week.

She tidied the large shed, cut down nettles, chopped wood and took Jack for longer and longer walks. She had established good relations with him: there was give and take. Prue would let him stop every now and then when he was particularly keen to try a patch of tempting grass. In return, he lowered his head when he saw her coming so that there was no problem putting on his head-collar. His size no longer alarmed her. Sometimes, when he paused to graze, she would lean against him, enjoying the warmth of his great body. She always hoped they would not run into Dawn on their return for, confused by her feelings of relief and jealousy, Dawn would invariably snarl some criticism then storm off in angry silence.

One day, on their return to the stable, they found Dawn waiting for them with an unusual smile on her face. She came right up to them, patted Jack on the withers, which she knew Prue found hard to reach – the gesture seemed to be designed for point scoring.

'We need some more pig feed,' she said, in a small girl's voice Prue had never heard before. 'The van's playing up. I wondered if I could ask—'

'Of course,' said Prue, remembering Johnny's advice. 'I'll drive over and get some now.'

Dawn continued to smile. Her face had gone rigid with the effort. 'I don't want to put you to that bother,' she said. 'Perhaps, I was thinking, you might let me run down in the Sunbeam. I mean, I'm a good driver. I like driving. If I had a decent car I'd drive all over, like the wind.'

Prue laughed. She handed Dawn the keys. 'Here you are. Don't drive like the wind, though. Put the stuff in the boot.'

'Oh my goodness. What a treat.' Dawn hurried off, forgetting her usual backward glance at Jack.

Prue went to the bungalow to join Steve, engaged in the football pools, for a cup of tea. Whenever Dawn was safely out of the way they indulged in this practice, made all the more enjoyable by its secret nature. Steve enjoyed Prue's company: he liked to hear stories of her days as a land girl, and she his stories of his past farming glories and the pleasure of breeding prize-winning Shires.

The pig-feed suppliers were only a ten-minute drive away, but Dawn did not return for an hour. Prue waited, anxious, by the large shed where it was to be stored. When the car eventually roared along the track and pulled up with a show-off swirl, she showed no flicker of the worry she had suffered. That would have been too pleasing for Dawn. The car, apart from being heavily mud-splattered, seemed undamaged.

Dawn, back to her normal scowl, leapt out of the driving seat, opened the boot and picked up a large bag of meal as if it weighed nothing.

'That was grand,' she said, with difficulty. 'Lovely little engine.' She could not bring herself to say thank you – Prue had not expected thanks – but something in Dawn's exuberant carrying of the sack indicated gratitude for the loan of the car. Goodness knew where she had gone, or how fast she had driven – Prue was determined not to ask.

'You must drive it when you want to,' she said. Dawn sniffed, tried but failed to smile and went off to the shed with another bag.

On her way home, driving very slowly down the lanes as she always did, Prue suddenly tasted Steve's strong tea in her mouth.

She was not used to tea in the morning so was not surprised when its bitter taste returned to her. But suddenly it filled her mouth – strong liquid that seemed to fountain up from her stomach. She made an emergency stop, flung herself onto the verge and was violently sick in the ditch. No more elevenses, she told herself. The sickness over, she thought no more of it.

A week later she and Barry drove to Hallows Farm where she managed to stop him visiting both the barn and the house. They merely looked over a few gates into the fields, and as Barry showed no interest in knowing what part they had played in his wife's work as a land girl, she did not trouble him with the kind of anecdote that had entertained Johnny a few weeks before.

On the way back, in the comfort of the Humber's front seat, she felt not positively sick, but queasy.

'You look pale, sweetheart,' Barry said, once they were home.

'It was a long drive. I'm fine.'

'Lovely, the car.'

'Lovely.' Prue realized she must be extraordinarily pale for Barry to have noticed. She went upstairs to the bathroom, took one look at herself in the mirror and was sick again.

In the sitting room Barry was pacing, fiddling as usual with his cigar. 'You still look pale,' he said. 'Sure you're not coming down with something?' It was the first time she had ever seen him worried.

'Sure. I think it was . . . well, you know. Beautifully sprung cars do make some people feel sick.'

'No! Not a Humber. You could travel round the world and back and not feel sick in a Humber.'

'Perhaps some people could.' By now, spurred by the cigar smoke, Prue was feeling a new surge of nausea. 'But I don't think I could face fish-paste sandwiches. I might go to bed.'

Barry gave her a long, hard look. 'You do that. That'd be best. I'll get Bertha to open me a tin of pilchards.' He sat down heavily in his usual chair, confused in a no man's land of irritation that his wife was going to leave him for the evening, but knowing that, if she was feeling as wretched as she looked, he had to do encourage her to lie down. She was wrong on one count, though: it was nothing to do with the Humber – a Humber had never made anyone feel sick as far as Barry knew, and Prue was going to have to get used to it. They couldn't always take the Daimler . . .

Prue confessed to Jack, on their next walk, what she was going to do. She spoke of her plan out loud to him, and felt a surge of relief at having made her decision. On one of their stops for Jack to graze, she leant her entire weight against him and felt herself shudder. Then she saw that mysterious tears had clotted a small part of his coat.

The next day she booked an appointment with her mother's doctor in Manchester. Within the week he confirmed it: she was pregnant.

# Chapter 7

For two months Prue kept the news to herself. Only Jack the Lad, had he known about human pregnancy, would have been aware of her condition for often when he stopped to graze Prue was sick beside him. She was aware that she looked wretched – unusually pale, and patches of grey skin that had swelled slightly under her eyes. She brushed rouge thickly over her cheeks and hoped Barry noticed nothing. From time to time she saw Bertha give her acute, prying looks, but that was not unusual.

Impatiently she waited for the joy of pregnancy to consume her, but she waited in vain. Perhaps, she thought, once she felt better, the anticipated happiness would arrive. Behind this hope snarled the desolate thought that her old dream of having a child by a man she loved was not going to happen, and pregnancy was no consolation for all that was missing in her marriage. So she continued to keep her silence. There was a particularly wretched morning when the smell of a bucket of chicken feed made her retch into a hedge by the chicken run and Johnny, from his window, pointed to her white cheeks. She was tempted to run to his flat, tell him, seek comfort. Instead she waved back, smiling.

One evening, pregnant for almost four months, her secret was blasted by a stodge of rice pudding produced by Bertha for supper. Topped with a blob of seedless raspberry jam, Prue saw it as one of the housekeeper's challenges. She always forced herself to eat even the most unappetizing of the woman's food, for to leave it, she felt, would mean triumph on Bertha's part. But as she crushed the jam into the loathsome mess, she felt her gorge rise: strange, for she usually felt fine in the evenings. She rose, ran from the room, no time to explain to Barry, and upstairs to the bathroom.

When she had rinsed her mouth, and washed her face with cold water, she felt able calmly to return. Barry had left the dining room. He had moved his own helping of pudding to one side of his plate – a rare gesture. Prue had always guessed that he liked Bertha's cooking no more than she did but was nervous of causing offence.

Prue moved to the sitting room. Barry was in his chair, cigar already lighted, smoke moving blowsily above his head. 'Ah, sweetheart,' he said. 'What was the trouble?'

'That rice, Barry. I'm sorry. I just couldn't—'

'It was little thick,' Barry agreed.

Prue took a seat opposite him, rested her chin on clasped hands. 'But also,' she added, 'I've not much appetite, these days. I feel queasy quite often. I mean, in the mornings.' She did not want to use the word 'pregnant' herself. She wanted Barry, sometimes a dim idiot, to guess.

'Anything wrong? Are you ill?'

Prue hesitated. 'I'm pregnant. Having a baby.'

There was complete silence. Barry waved away a scarf of smoke from his face. Prue could see a dull glitter, more like a second skin than tears, appear in his eyes. He shifted in his seat, changed his cigar from his right hand to his left. Then, as if enlightened, he stubbed it out in the ashtray. 'You won't want smoke around you,' he said at last, trying to control an emotional voice. 'I'll give up smoking in the house . . .' A very small smile cracked his mouth, then stretched into a bigger one. There was a flash of his gold tooth. He heaved himself out of the chair, stood up, patted his trouser pockets with cupped hands. It was plain he was undecided how to act. The smile still intact, he moved towards Prue, took both her wrists, pulled her to her feet. 'This is the happiest day of my life, sweetheart. Me, a father! Imagine! You a mother! How about that? Are you excited?'

'I'll be more excited when the sickness is over.' Prue managed a smile.

Barry kissed her on both cheeks, then laid a hand on her stomach. 'Is it kicking? Don't they kick quite early?'

'Not just yet. It's only a few months.'

'You'll have the best private care, of course. And we'll get a room done up however you want it, a nursery.' He said the word with great care, for it was not one he had previously had reason to use. 'Oh my goodness, sweetheart. This is the news we've been waiting for. Trying for. Haven't we? You must take such care of yourself. You'll have to give up all that farm work. You can't carry on heaving things about. It's not even necessary. You can lie back reading magazines all day, thinking about the colour of the nursery.'

'I don't heave things about,' Prue interrupted. 'Mostly I just walk with the horse.'

Barry, noticing her indignation, decided not to pursue his point. 'Well, we'll see.' He moved his hand from her stomach. 'And now you're having a baby I won't have to bother you any more. I've heard it said sex can be dangerous during pregnancy. We wouldn't want to take any risks, would we?'

'Of course not.' Prue hoped the lightness of her reply concealed the depth of her relief at his plan.

Barry returned to his chair. For a moment he looked with longing at the cigar stub. A hand automatically went to his inside pocket, home of his cigar case. Then, with a small, pathetic laugh, he forced his strength of will to triumph. His hand returned to his knee, gripped the stuff of his trousers. 'Silly me,' he said. Then he frowned. 'Who else knows?' The question was a swift change from mellow to sharp.

'No one. Of course you're the first to know.'

'I'm glad, sweetheart. It's wonderful. You can't know how my heart's bursting.' He was gentle again. A real tear escaped from one eye.

'It *is* wonderful,' said Prue. He deserved the pleasure of her agreement. She would not want him to guess at her honest, muddled sensations. 'I might go to bed. Early start tomorrow . . .'

'Course. You go. Get as much sleep as you can. Is there anything I can do for you?' Barry's unaccustomed solicitude was making his voice unsteady. He seemed to be ungrounded by approaching fatherhood.

'Nothing at all, thanks.' Prue moved to the door, turned back for a moment to blow him a kiss. He sat beached on his chair, knees apart, a man too stunned to know how to regiment his body. He clapped his fingers silently together and apart; one knee began to jiggle violently. A moment of fondness speared through Prue. She blew him another kiss but, engaged in his own paternal thoughts, he was too preoccupied to notice.

'I tell you what,' he muttered, so quietly Prue had to strain to hear his words, 'this baby of ours, he's going to want for nothing money can buy.'

'He?' said Prue.

'My son. I'm telling you, sweetheart, it's going to be a boy.'

Prue did not hear Barry coming to bed, leaving next morning. She left the house earlier than usual in a wakeful state, though for once she did not feel sick.

When she arrived at the farm she found an Austin 7 parked outside the bungalow. Then a man came out of the large shed. He was small and narrow, in an ill-fitting suit. Spikes of oily hair stood up on his head and his face was contorted with anger. Prue guessed him to be Bert, Dawn's husband, who usually left for work long before she arrived. He moved fast towards the car. 'All I ask is that a man should have a decent breakfast before setting off for work, earning the only proper wages round here, and where's Dawn? Where's my so-called wife? Saying her bloody prayers, that's what.' His mouth twisted to one side, as if he was about to spit.

'I'm sorry,' said Prue. She had no idea how to react to this outburst . 'Would you like me to cook you something?'

Bert was by now standing right by the Sunbeam. He put out a hand, touched the bonnet. 'No, I would not. I'll manage. You the land girl I hear so much about?' Prue nodded. 'A land girl with a Sunbeam Talbot? That's a first if ever I heard one.' He turned away, stumped off to his Austin 7. A moment later the small box of a car was seething down the driveway, its owner's rage urging it to a speed quite out of keeping with its horse power.

For a moment Prue leant on the Sunbeam, wondering whether to go into the bungalow and discuss the day's plans with Steve – they were always the same, but the farmer liked a routine discussion – or whether to find out what had so enraged Dawn's husband. She decided on that, and went quickly to the shed.

Bert had been right. Dawn appeared to be saying her prayers. She was kneeling on a bag of pig feed, hands clasped at her chest, mouth moving, eyes scanning the corrugated roof. Every now and then she gave a small groan in which the words 'Oh, Lord' were so distorted they were almost indistinguishable. Then, abruptly, she rose from her knees very fast, swung round and faced Prue before she could back out of sight. But Dawn seemed unabashed to have been caught in her devotions. 'I was saying my prayers for you this morning,' she said. 'You'll need them.'

'Thank you.' Prue nodded.

'Though I was saying them more for your baby,' added Dawn, coming to stand close Prue and bringing with her a strong smell of toothpaste.

'My baby? How did you know I was . . .?'

'Ah!' Dawn gave a triumphant laugh, then smiled down at her. 'I can see things others can't. Always have done. I've known for weeks there's been a bun in your oven.' Prue winced at the description. 'Yes, a child in your womb, a baby to be born . . .' She trailed off, her creepy smile clamouring right through her cheeks.

Prue, shaken, felt a nausea different from that caused by rice pudding. There was something about toothpasty Dawn, in the early light, that was deeply unsavoury. 'I say my prayers in the shed because it's the best place for me to pray. I see things here. I'm close to Jesus. He's close to me. He's all about us. Can't you feel His presence?' Her frantic eyes flung over the bags of pig feed. 'You should believe me.'

'I do,' said Prue, feebly. All she wanted was to get away from the demented Dawn.

'Bert and Dad say I've got a screw loose. They can't understand anything if it's not black and white. But they'll discover one day, things I've seen. One day they'll learn I'm telling the truth, seeing things that come to me.'

'Quite. Well, thanks for your prayers, Dawn.' Prue smiled, stifling the laugh that rose in her. 'I must get in to your father, see what he wants me to do.'

All the way to the bungalow she knew Dawn's eyes were on her, but she did not look back. It wasn't till an hour later, walking Jack in the woods, that she felt calm again. Dawn was mentally unbalanced, she knew, but even the half-mad could be terrifyingly accurate in their visions. What she most hated was the thought that Dawn had known about the baby before she herself had known. The uncanniness of that chilled her, despite the high sun that had come out from earlier clouds.

Now that her pregnancy was no longer a secret, Prue decided the time had come to tell Stella and Ag, her mother and Johnny. The girls, as she had known they would be, were delighted for her, but they did not go overboard in their congratulations. Mrs Lumley was a different matter.

Not wanting to break the news on the telephone, Prue drove to her mother's salon one afternoon. There were no clients. Mrs Lumley was sitting in one of the chairs in front of the mirror reading a magazine. She looked up to see the reflection of her daughter coming through the door. She turned, shouted, rushed to leap onto Prue with a hug that nearly knocked both of them over. 'Oh my darling! You look so happy. I can tell. I can tell you've got news for me. Haven't you?' She released her grip on Prue's neck, stood back to scan her face.

'I have, as a matter of fact, Mum—'

'That's wonderful, wonderful, wonderful, isn't it? When? Quickly, tell me. When?'

'About another five months. I'm not absolutely sure.'

Mrs Lumley's overwhelming joy caused her to laugh, cry and make curious twisting movements. She would bend, straighten and bend again, like a demented ballet dancer. In need of a paper handkerchief to wipe the mascara that had run amok on her cheeks, she aimed for the shelf that held bottles of dye and other potions. But so overcome was her excited hand that it swiped everything onto the floor. Suddenly streams of liquid were blurring into each other on the linoleum. With a scream of horror she bent to pick up a bottle, she slipped and fell. Prue put out a hand to heave her up. Her mother shouted that on no account was she to lift anything in her condition. So Prue obediently left her groping among the chairs, trying to find some purchase among their legs, which would help her to her feet. At last she stood, shaking, her feet adrift in slime, but smiling again. 'Oh dear, silly me. I'm so over-excited, darling. Barry said you were trying. Hard,' she added.

'When did he tell you that?' A flicker of annoyance rose within her. What was Barry doing, telling . . .? 'You rang him, did you? You didn't think that was prying?'

'Oh no. I don't like the telephone, do I?'

'So he came round here?'

Her mother hesitated. 'I don't believe he did. I believe he stopped off at the house one evening on his way back from work.'

'I see.'

'No need to be so huffy, Prue. I think he knew you hadn't told me your plans and thought I had a right to know.'

'Quite.'

At that moment a tall woman with a puny crest of hair came through the door. She looked on the scene with some amazement. 'Is everything all right?' she asked.

'I'll leave you to it, Mum,' said Prue, and made a dash across the slippery floor to the door.

Last to be told was Johnny. When she returned from the salon, and saw a light in his window, she made her way over to his flat.

'Just come to tell you I'm pregnant – having a baby,' she said, with no preamble. Johnny looked at her unsmiling. When, after a long silence, he failed to congratulate her, she shrugged. 'Aren't you going to say anything?'

Johnny stirred himself from a minor reverie. 'Of course. Sorry. Well done. That's good. What does one say to pregnant friends?'

'That'll do.'

'You'll be very preoccupied. I won't see so much of you – or at least without a pram.'

'Dare say.'

'Want a drink? Tea? Anything?'

Prue shook her head. 'I've got to get back. Barry likes me to be there when he gets home.'

'Bet he's delighted.'

'Seems to be.'

Johnny opened the door for her. 'I've got to go up to Bakewell next week,' he said, more gently. 'I'm making an elaborate gate for someone. Like to come? There's a good pub. We could have lunch.'

'Why not? We could go in the Sunbeam,' Prue said.

At last Johnny smiled. 'That'd be lovely.' He stooped and kissed her forehead, then patted her shoulder with a rigid hand. 'Well done – the baby thing. Take care of yourself.'

As she walked back to The Larches, through a hurrying dusk that weighed down the laurels in the drive, it occurred to Prue that since the incident, as she thought of it, things had changed between her and Johnny despite their agreement that all would remain the same. Pity. He had been a kind and easy friend. Now it was as if she had disappointed him in some way, or offended him. She hoped that one day their friendship would return to its old ease, but relations with Johnny were not currently the most important thing on her mind. Barry, she knew, was set for an argument about her work, and she was determined not to be beaten.

He left it till after the jam roll. Then he moved to the sitting room and took his usual seat by the gas fire. For a while the soft putt-putting of its small blue flames, which danced like periwinkles in a breeze, was the only sound. Then he gave a deep sigh and slapped both fat hands onto both fat knees. 'This business,' he said. 'This business of the baby – wonderful . . . wonderful, sweetheart.' It was a feeling he expressed most evenings.

'Yes,' said Prue.

'Now you'd never call me a fussy man, even a cautious man. I know when it's the right time to take a risk. But I'd never take a risk when a risk isn't advisable.' A little unsteadied by his own profundity, he went on: 'And in the case of pregnancy, well, obviously not the slightest risk should be taken. All caution on board. My – our – son will be the most precious creature on earth. We have to do everything we can to make sure no risks come anywhere near him.'

'Quite,' said Prue.

Barry's hand went automatically to the inside pocket of his jacket, previous home of his cigar case. Then he withdrew it with an impatient jerk of his head. 'So that means, sweetheart, no more farm work for you. I'm not having you sweating your guts out heaving bales of hay or . . . whatever it is you do. You don't need the few shillings they pay you. You don't need a job. I can see it's good to be out in the open when you're used to fields and that, but the time has come to stop. So I'm asking you to give in your notice.'

Prue raised her shoulders and looked up at the ceiling. 'I don't think you understand,' she said at last. 'I'm not working as I would on a normal farm – it isn't a normal farm. It's a sad old horse who needs to be taken for walks, a few pigs and six geese. That's all. I lead the horse about like a dog. I muck out the pigs twice a week, and make cups of tea for Steve when his batty daughter's out. So you see I don't think I'll come to any harm – there's no risk of that – and I'd like to stay on till, say, a month or so before the baby's born.'

Barry raised an eyebrow. 'Sounds like a weird place,' he said.

'It is. I thought at first I might be able to help them get it into better shape, be a bit more business-like. But they're not really interested. They've no energy, little knowledge. I think that when Steve's wife died – she ran the place well, apparently – the fight went out of him. I just do what they want me to do. Steve took me on because he liked the idea of a land girl, but there was never a real job.'

'No.' Barry, who had braced himself for a tough argument, was melting under Prue's simple logic. 'I'm rethinking,' he said, 'something I'm never able to do very fast, sweetheart.' He gave her a small, self-deprecating smile that Prue realized was endearing. He could surprise her sometimes. She smiled back. 'So, this is what I think. You stay on at this so-called farm for a while longer. Carry on taking the horse for a walk like a Pekingese, and making the farmer's tea, but give up mucking out the pigs. I ask you that. Lifting pitchforks of sodden straw would be daft.'

'It would,' said Prue, warm from winning the greater part of her argument, which had turned out to be hardly an argument at all. 'You're quite right. I promise to give up the pigs.'

'Thank you, sweetheart.' Barry tipped his head onto the back of his chair and closed his eyes. Suffering from the weariness peculiar to easy compromise, he laced his fingers over his stomach and appeared to fall asleep. She crept out of the room, not wanting to wake him.

Prue kept her promise to Barry. She explained to Steve that she could carry on exercising Jack but would no longer undertake anything else. Naturally, she said, she wouldn't want to be paid for walking Jack. It was a pleasure.

'Of course I understand the position,' said Steve. 'I just pity the pigs. I'm not up to them, though I'll have to have a go. Dawn hates them, won't go near them.'

'Why don't you sell them?' Prue suggested.

'Not a bad idea.' Steve stared out of the window as if puzzled that the solution hadn't occurred to him before. But anything to do with his farm, Prue had noticed of late, seemed to strike him with an unaccountable lack of enthusiasm. 'I might put that into motion. But then again I might not,' he added.

In the next few months there were no signs of his slight intention materializing. As she walked with Jack past the pig field

Prue observed that the bedding in their shelters was thick, sodden. The stench permeated the whole field. She pitied those animals: during her spell as pig-manager they had been clean. Looking down at her swollen stomach she wished she could help. But she had given her word and wasn't going to break it. She also noticed on her walks that the hedges of the pig field – as everywhere else on the farm – were in a very bad state. Ag and Mr Lawrence would have been shocked, she thought. They could have put them right in a few days. But there was no one on this so-called farm who knew a thing about hedging, or seemed to care that the whole place was going to ruin.

By the time Prue was seven months pregnant she was feeling extraordinarily well. The sickness long past, most of her old energy had returned and she was thrilled whenever she felt the baby kicking.

One morning she arrived at the farm to find that neither the Ganders' car nor the trailer was there. A message was pinned to the door. Steve and Dawn had taken Jack to be shod, and would then be going on to the market – perhaps to check the price of pigs, thought Prue, with a smile.

It was a morning of pallid sun and cool breeze. Prue had no heart to return home. She liked the routine of leaving the claustrophobia of The Larches for three days a week to come to the farm and spend the day outside. She decided to wait for Jack to come back, go for a walk before returning to the bungalow to look at yesterday's *Daily Mirror*. She set off for the woods.

The bare winter trees, the colour of smoke, were tugged by the breeze and the undergrowth sparkled from last night's rainfall. Prue loved such winter mornings. At Hallows Farm, when she and the others had had to be out in the fields at five in the morning, she had loved the sharpness of the air, the sudden frosty chill on her cheeks. She walked fast along the path that dipped down into the valley, then left the wood to go along the side of the pigs' field.

A few yards ahead she saw a huge and bad-tempered old Middle White sow standing in the path, foraging in the earth outside her field. Prue moved slowly towards her. She came to the large hole in the hedge through which the pig had evidently escaped, and cursed herself for not mentioning it to Steve. Still, to usher the pig back into its own field and block the exit with a fallen branch would not be difficult.

As she came nearer to the sow it raised its head, grunted. It stared at her, its veined ears, hostile, menacing. Prue was alarmed by its threatening air. She would have to be careful.

Slowly she moved past it, turned. Her plan was to whack it on the buttocks – just hard enough to make it understand it should go back through the hole in the hedge. She bent to pick up a small stick lying on the ground. As she did so she felt the baby give a thumping kick. She brought down the stick on the pig's hindquarters, not very hard, shouting orders as she used to at Sly.

But the sow, furious at being discovered and disturbed, had no intention of returning to its own muddy pasture. With an ear-piercing squeal she leapt forward and began to lumber towards the wood. Prue, amazed by the speed of so gross an animal, watched her in horror. There was a path out of the wood that led to the road. If the pig . . . Prue reflected no further. She began to run after it.

But to get ahead of the sow and turn her back would mean she had to run very fast. She was naturally a good sprinter but the size of her belly, now, was an impediment. She increased her speed. Running, just running, she thought, can't do any harm.

And it didn't. In the wood she followed the pig's tracks, the grunts and squeals, and came upon her snuffling at the root of an oak tree. Prue picked up a large fallen branch, gave the animal orders in what she judged was a persuasive voice. By lucky chance the sow, enfeebled by the spurt of exercise, decided to co-operate. With a defeated grunt she trotted back to the gap in the hedge, eased her way through and made for her friends on the brow of the hill. Prue, bending awkwardly, followed. She pulled some stray branches across the gap. Steve would have to arrange something more secure when he got back.

The incident now over, Prue felt a sudden weariness. It must be due to the anxiety of the near-disaster, she thought. She began to climb the hill. Her feet were heavy: the churned-up mud grasped her boots. The stench from the shelters came in waves on the breeze, sickening, eye-watering. Suddenly she felt a strong, hot pain in her lower back.

Prue stopped, arched her spine, rubbed it. It persisted. Nothing to do with the baby, she thought. Labour pains were surely in the stomach. She set off again, very slowly, bending as she went to ease the pain. But there was no ease. The pain increased. And then she felt wetness on the legs of her winter dungarees. She saw dark stains gushing through the corduroy, clotting its pile.

Prue told herself not to panic, to keep going. When she reached the bungalow Steve would run her to the hospital, just in case something was wrong.

Somehow she made her mud-heavy boots plod on. She placed both hands on her stomach to stop their shaking. It felt taut and hard as iron. Sometimes the scorching pain stopped for a moment, then returned with greater strength. By the time she reached the top of the field, and was in sight of the farm buildings, she was groaning out loud. The pigs raised their heads and looked at her. Tears were pouring down her cheeks. The Ganders and Jack the Lad had not returned.

The gate from the field to the farmyard was heavy and stiff – always an effort to open it. In her panic, and with only a filament of energy left, it took Prue several moments. With no time to try to shut it behind her, she turned to make for the shed. No longer able to run, she hobbled, bent almost double now. A chorus of squeals from the pigs made her glance back at the field: they were surging through the open gate, lumbering about the farmyard in celebration of their freedom. Prue didn't care. There was nothing she could do.

As she made her way to the shed she could feel the baby pushing down. The pain was grotesque. In the shed at last she made her way to a single layer of sacks of pig feed. She longed for bales of hay, the comfort of Hallows Farm's barn. But there was no hay, no straw. Shaking, she pulled off her jacket, laid it over a sack. She knew there was no hope of pulling off her boots. So she tore down her dungarees and pants to below her knees, and threw herself on the bed of pig feed. She could hear her own screams, a kind of torn, blue noise that curdled with the ghastly sound of the pigs' hysterical squealing. She opened her eyes to see the shed's corrugated roof: its striated lines seemed to quiver.

Minutes later – it might have been ten, or eternity – she felt a scalding sensation that she thought would rip her apart. Then something slid between her legs. The pain stopped.

Prue heaved herself into a sitting position. Between her thighs lay a pink and blue baby. It wriggled. It looked very small, but Prue had no idea of the size of a new-born baby. The umbilical cord glinted in a wisp of sunlight that had appeared in the shed. Prue kept looking, unable to believe what she saw. The baby was a boy. Barry would be pleased. She noticed her son had thin, definitely amber-coloured hair.

Prue knew little about babies. It had been her plan to study the intricacies of childbirth in the last two months of her pregnancy. She vaguely remembered hearing they had to be smacked as soon as they were born. Strong with relief that the pain had ceased, Prue acted instinctively. She picked up the bloody little creature, who slithered about in her grasp. She felt oddly proud. With a shaking hand she thumped him gently on the back. He whimpered for a moment, then began to yell.

It was cold in the shed. The earlier fragment of sun – which, in her spinning mind, Prue fancied had come to congratulate her – had gone. She knew she had to get the baby to hospital as soon as possible. But how? No one was here. The nearest ambulance was miles away – if, indeed, she could get into the bungalow to use the telephone.

There was a sudden, second expulsion from between her legs. For a horrified moment Prue thought it might be another baby. Then she realized it must be the afterbirth. She had heard of that but had had no idea what to expect, or what should be done with it. It was attached to the umbilical cord, which was attached to the baby. Prue was surprised that she could look on the alarming products of her womb with some detachment. From outside the barn, the pigs' screams were louder. In the terrifying wonder of the birth, she had forgotten about them.

Prue pulled the blood-sodden jacket from beneath her and dumped the scarlet mess of baby and attachments into it. She wrapped them as well as she could. Then, standing shakily, she pulled up her sodden dungarees, but could not waste time on the buttons. She picked up the whole bloody parcel, cradled it in her arms, and turned to move outside. Her legs were unsteady. She had trouble in keeping her balance.

Just before she reached the opening of the shed a pig appeared, its head back, sniffing, grunting, squealing, excited by the smell of her and the baby. Then another, and another. In a moment a crowd of pigs was barring her way. Some of them nudged her legs with flared, wet nostrils. Others, in their excitement at the smell of blood, made a heavy, hopeless attempt at jumping up to reach the baby she held. Prue shouted abuse at them. With a surge of adrenalin, she barged through the obscene animals, feeling their scratchy warmth on her legs, to the Sunbeam. They followed her, squealing louder. Prue flung open the passenger door, threw the jacket and its extraordinary contents onto the seat. The straps of the dungarees were slipping off her shoulders: the entire rank garment was descending, impeding every movement.

Once in the car, the warmth of its leather seats rose up to her like a balm, but the baby was screaming again. 'God, help me,' she cried out loud. 'Don't let him die.' Her bloody finger kept slipping on the starter button.

God granted her wish. The engine started. She could hear the pigs still clamouring round the car, snuffling furiously at its sides. Prue banged the horn. A few pigs jumped away, the baby screamed louder. She put her foot on the accelerator and lurched forward, hitting some of the animals, she was sure. But she didn't care. She was aware that the adrenalin was still there to help her. Suddenly completely in control, she found herself driving faster than she had ever driven down the rutted track to the road. She could see everything as clearly as in a nightmare: the frill of new sun round the edge of a black cloud, the shadow patterns of bare trees on the mercifully empty roads to Manchester. She swerved too fast round corners with no thought of danger.

The baby's screams died down to a whimper. She glanced at his face above the blood-sodden lapel of her jacket. A minute hand wavered across his forehead. Tears came to Prue's eyes, blurring her vision. She saw blood oozing through the jacket and was terrified lest any part of its contents slipped onto the floor. But she knew that in a matter of moments, now, someone else would take charge of the whole business. Safe in the hospital she would be able to start again. She would be able to think. The comfort of this idea made her smile through her tears.

Prue concentrated on a last tyre-screeching turn into the hospital grounds. She slammed on the brakes outside Casualty. In the distance a nurse was walking towards her. She wore a cloak and a frilly white cap, which seemed to be a halo, worn by someone who would know what to do. 'Thank God,' Prue whispered. She opened the door and screamed for help. The baby twitched violently at the sound. The nurse appeared not to be getting any nearer, though her legs were moving, like those of a figure in a bad dream. Prue yelled again. The word 'help' was lost in an abstract scream. Then the nurse, her kindly face out of focus, was bending down into the car, enquiring, smiling, calmer than anyone Prue had ever seen.

Prue felt the cut of a stiff sheet against her cheek. She moved her thighs together. They were dry. She opened her eyes. Thin flowered curtains were drawn across a small window. The walls of a narrow room were painted blue, but not a blue she recognized. She felt too drowsy to concentrate, and wondered what they had given her.

In the absolute silence, threads of the morning's events began to weave across her empty mind. Pictures were outlined in red – the baby, the bags of pig feed, her jacket, the car seat, the baby. Her son. Where was he? Prue glanced at each side of the bed for a cradle. There was nothing. Why not? She thought mothers had their babies beside them in hospital. What had happened since she had arrived and called out to a nurse with a kindly face? She couldn't remember.

The silence was broken by raised voices. The door opened. Barry flung in carrying a bunch of chrysanthemums so large it hid the top half of his body. He dropped it onto the end of the bed. 'Where's a vase?' He turned to a nurse who had followed him in. 'We need a vase, water.' The nurse, lips gripped into a single line, left the room. Barry looked at Prue with something near to reluctance. He bent over her, kissed her hair. The heaviness of his body was painful on her breasts. She wondered vaguely how the hospital had got hold of him, but she didn't care.

'Sweetheart!' he shouted. 'I've seen him. My son.' The crumpled skin beneath his eyes was damp. 'What a thing to happen,' he said. 'What you've been through. Terrible for you. Terrible. I told you you should have given up all that bloody stupid farm work. Still, the main thing is Alfred's all right. He's fine.'

'Alfred?'

'Didn't I tell you he has to be called Alfred? After my Sheffield uncle, the one who encouraged me. It's always been my dream to have a son called Alfred.'

'I see.' Prue heaved herself up on the pillows. Nothing in the room was quite still.

Barry sat on the bed. 'Haven't they brought him in to you?'

'No.' In her drowsiness Prue felt no sense of urgency about seeing her son. She loathed the name Alfred.

'Maybe, if you don't like Alfred, we could call him plain Fred. Though Alfred would be on the birth certificate. I'll attend to all that, sweetheart.'

'Right.'

'Would you like me to take you to see him? He's in – what do you call it? The place where they put the babies in those incubator things.'

'Later,' said Prue. 'I'm a bit tired.'

'Of course.' Barry sighed. 'They say he'll pull through. They say he'll be fine in a while.'

'Is there something wrong?'

'Looks pretty good to me. He's very small, of course. But a mighty fine little fellow, I'm telling you. He's got a good punch on him. Raised his fist at me . . .' Barry gave a half-smile, lifted his arm with a clenched fist, punched the air. Prue managed a smile. Barry took her wrist. 'I'm so sorry, sweetheart. It wasn't meant to be like this. Must have been a terrible shock, and then you managed so bravely, driving yourself here, they told me.' A splay of fat fingers went up to each eye in turn, wiped it. 'I can't wait for you to have a look at him. He looks like me, I'd say. Though he does have rust-coloured hair – auburn, you could call it. But then I had a great-aunt who was a redhead. At least, everybody thought she was a redhead till one day she couldn't get to the hairdresser in time and her secret was out . . .' His shoulders rose in his effort to make Prue smile. But when she simply looked towards the window and asked him to draw the curtains, he turned his attention to his watch. 'Better be getting back, sweetheart. Things to organize. Got to get the little fellow's room done. Painters and so on. Any colour you'd like?'

Prue shook her head. No one could get bluebell blue, the Buckingham Palace dress blue, so there was no point in trying.

'I'll get all that under way, then, and come back this evening.' He kissed her again, this time on the forehead. 'Anything I can bring you?'

Prue shook her head.

When he had gone she lay down again. Barry and his son did not exist. She herself did not exist – at least, not as the person she had been this morning. All she knew was that she was in an alien place after strange events where there were no feelings whatsoever. Not even curiosity.

The door opened again and the nurse came in with the flowers in an enormous jug. She put them on the table by the bed. Prue averted her eyes from their forest of hideous curry colours, but their smell, of damp earth, evoked the autumn jugs of chrysanthemums that Mrs Lawrence had always put on the dresser. That memory was the best thing about the day so far.

'Your mother's outside,' the nurse said. 'She seems a little upset. Can I bring her in?'

Prue heaved herself up again. 'I suppose so. Tell her I need to rest and she mustn't stay long.'

A moment later Mrs Lumley shunted into the room, carrying another vast bunch of flowers. Prue didn't know what they were, but shuddered as a barrage balloon of multi-coloured petals moved towards her bed. On top of it rested the tearful face of her mother. 'Prue!' she shrieked. 'I'm in shock. I'm telling you, darling, I'm in shock . . .' Her arms fell to her sides. The flowers dropped to the floor. The dull linoleum was now a chaos of orange, yellow, scarlet, purple, pink, blue, more orange, more yellow . . . 'Look what I've gone and done now. And I'm telling you, darling, those flowers cost me all of half a crown . . .'

Prue shut her eyes.

It was decided that she should stay in the hospital for a few days. After her first night's sleep the drowsiness receded and between visits from Barry and her mother – who both brought her small pots of Shippam's salmon paste and reminded her they were quite a luxury – it was a peaceful time. She visited her son – she could not bring herself to think of him as Alfred – every morning and evening. He was in a primitive-looking incubator: naked, small, pale. Sometimes his tiny fist punched the air, just as Barry had imitated. Sometimes he lay completely still. The paediatrician said he would not be able to go home for a while. As Barry's arrangements for the nursery were apparently not progressing fast, Prue was not disturbed by this news. She wanted everything to be ready for him when they arrived home.

On her last night in the hospital Barry came later than usual, and stayed for a long time talking about Alfred's future: he would go to public school, university, then into the army, perhaps, a good regiment – all the things that had been Barry's own unaccomplished dreams. 'So much ahead, so much to look forward to, sweetheart,' he said, when he got up to leave. 'I'll tell you something: I'm the happiest man alive.'

When he had gone Prue got out of bed and went to the room where the incubators were gathered. A nurse was adjusting a tube that ran from her son's nose. Prue thought she looked a touch concerned, but there was reason for constant anxiety in this room of ill babies.

'He's very still,' said Prue.

'End of the day,' the nurse replied briskly. 'Babies this size don't have much energy.'

'But he's a good colour, isn't he?'

The nurse glanced at her. 'He is,' she said.

Prue put two fingers to her lips, eased her hand into the incubator. With a butterfly touch she transferred the kiss to the baby's forehead. 'Night, little one,' she said, and went back to bed.

Each morning in hospital Prue woke very early. The thinness of the ugly curtains meant the dawn sky turned the blue walls to a cloudy silver before the arrival of denser November daylight. On the morning she was to go home – Barry had been in a dither about whether to fetch her in the Daimler or the Humber – Prue looked at her clock and saw it was four thirty. She shut her eyes, but knew there was no hope of further sleep.

She was woken by someone opening the door. It was the nurse who had rushed to help when Prue arrived. She crept in.

Prue sat up. Alert. 'So?' she said. 'You on night duty?'

The nurse nodded and sat on the bed. A small pulse twitched under one eye. 'I wanted to be the one to tell you,' she said. 'Your son passed away in the night.'

Prue wished she could have said 'died'. 'Oh? Why?' Her own voice was so tight she thought it might snap.

'These premature babies . . . it's always touch and go. His lungs – in Alfred it was his lungs. Under-developed. There's not much to be done when that's the case. Some hang on, and the lungs gradually mature. Others . . . don't make it.'

'No.' Prue sighed. There was a long silence.

'Are you all right?' the nurse asked. 'Is there anything I can get you?' Prue shook her head. 'I'm so sorry. So very sorry. But still, you're very young. Plenty of chance for . . .'

Prue gave her an incredulous look. The nurse tried to take her hand, but she snatched it away.

'You musn't try to be brave,' she went on. 'Cry, scream, yell, let it all out. Don't bottle it up. Everyone understands.'

Prue stretched her dry mouth into an approximate smile. 'I'm not bottling anything up,' she snapped. 'I'm fine. My son was never real. Barry was never real. None of it. None of it's been real. So I'm fine. On, on . . . I'll just get on with the unreal life till one day, perhaps . . .'

'Of course.' The nurse was frowning.

'It must be very difficult, your job,' Prue's voice was unusually high, but steady. 'I mean, breaking the news to parents that their baby has died.'

'It's not easy.'

'No.' Prue slid further down into the bed. 'Can't be. Could someone ring my husband at six? He's always awake by then.'

'Of course.'

At last the nurse stood up. Automatically she tweaked the bedclothes, ran a hand over a crumpled area of blanket.

'Thank you for all your help when I arrived,' Prue said. Her longing to be left alone pulsed through her.

'You'd had a bad time. You were very courageous. Now, if you want anything just ring the bell.'

'Thanks.'

At last the nurse and all her kindness were gone.

Barry arrived just after seven. His grey unshaven cheeks sagged. His tie was askew. In one hand he held his cigar case. He stood at the end of the bed. 'Sweetheart,' he said, 'I've brought the Daimler.'

'Right.'

'I've come to take you home.'

'I know.'

'This is the worst day of my life. My son. Alfred. Come and gone. Just like that. Two days on earth. Two days.' He held up two shaking fingers.

Prue nodded.

Barry gripped the iron bed end with his free hand. 'I need to see him, last time. Then we'll go. Are you coming with me?'

Prue shook her head.

'Don't you want to say goodbye?'

'No. I want to remember him alive.'

'Very well.' Barry shuffled out of the room. Prue got out of bed. Somehow there was a pile of clean clothes on the chair. She put them on, imagining Barry staring at his dead son.

Some time later he returned. He did not seem to know what to do next. Prue took his arm. 'Where's the car?' she asked.

They moved in awkward tandem down long, chipped passages of gloomy beige, rank with the smell of disinfectant and tinned soup. At last, in wonderfully cold air, they came to the parked car. Barry's trauma was momentarily obliterated by surprise. 'I don't understand,' he said. 'It's the Humber . . . I thought I'd brought the Daimler.'

'Never mind. Get in – go on. Let's go home.' Prue opened the door for her bemused husband and they began the journey through the city. Barry, who knew the streets so well, drove like a man who had lost his way.

# Chapter 8

After the funeral Barry began to leave the house even earlier than usual each morning, and came back only in time for one cigar before supper. Eating was now always in near silence. Once Prue said, 'I do wish the baby's coffin hadn't looked so like a shoebox,' and Barry did not reply. Another time it was he who broke the silence, with the news that he was going to move into a different bedroom.

'Now it's all over, sweetheart, there's no point in trying any more. I know you don't like it. So I won't bother you again.' He gave her an expectant look, perhaps hoping she would disagree and ask him to stay.

She nodded. 'Very well,' she said.

She wrote a long letter of apology and explanation to Steve Gander and said she would not be going back to the job. She had neither the heart nor the energy to spend further time on a non-job, and she never wanted to see a mob of pigs again. She telephoned Ag and Stella, both of whom asked her to come and stay. She said she would, once she had made sure Barry was resettled. On several occasions she had heard terrible sobs coming from the small room he called his office. Previously he had scarcely ever used it. Now he often shut himself in there after supper to deal with his devastation undisturbed.

For some reason that was not clear to her, she was nervous of telling Johnny. But one morning he appeared at her chicken run with a basket of eggs he had gathered but failed to deliver. 'I heard,' he said. 'Barry rang and told me when you were in hospital. Asked me to look after your birds. Then he rang me again once you were home.'

'Really?' Prue frowned at this unexpected news.

'I'm so sorry.' Johnny turned away from her, fiddled with the eggs.

'Well. It happens.' Prue shrugged.

Johnny turned back to her, his face clenched. A pulse was wildly beating in his cheek. 'Barry said the boy – Alfred, he said – looked just like him, except for the colour of his hair.' There was a long pause.

'He did think that, yes.' Prue moved a little away from him, stared at the grovelling birds through the wire netting. 'Thing is, Johnny, I'm going to go away for a while. Both Stella and Ag have asked me to stay, have a break. After that, I don't know . . . I haven't made any plans but I think I might . . .'

'Of course I'll look after the hens. You know I enjoy it.'

Prue suddenly smiled at him. 'What I'd really like is for you to have them. I want to give them to you.'

'I don't know about that.' Johnny looked touched, but uncertain.

'Please. You've done so much for me.' She stopped, feeling the break in her voice. 'The least I can do is give you my chickens.'

'Well, if you're sure.' Johnny ruffled his hair, reflecting. 'I won't move them in with mine till I've extended the run. If it's OK with you I'll keep them here for a while.'

'That's absolutely fine.'

'And thank you.' He moved over to Prue, touched her cheek with the back of his hand. 'You look pale. I'm glad you're going away. Let me know as soon as you're back and we'll go off for the day in the Sunbeam. Bakewell, perhaps. Take care of yourself.'

For the first time in weeks he gave her a light kiss on the cheek, then walked quickly away, the basket of eggs over his arm, still undelivered.

That evening, sitting by the gas fire in a haze of cigar smoke, Barry looked particularly wretched. He had not touched the sliver of cod at supper, or even his favourite junket. Prue sat on the other side of the fire, worried. She wondered how and when this period of his abject misery would end.

Barry stubbed out his barely smoked cigar, stood up. 'I've things so crushing on my mind, sweetheart, that I have to tell you. I'm sorry . . . but I have to.' He flapped his arms up and down against his sides, reminding Prue so strongly of an anxious penguin that she felt a surge of untoward laughter. She could see that, without a cigar between his fingers, he felt at a loss, yet for her sake he resisted lighting another.

'What I have to tell you is this. I've made a big mistake. You've made a big mistake. We, together, have made a big mistake. We married.' He spoke slowly and quietly. He sighed, long and deep. Then he began to waddle about the room, in and out of the chairs and tables. Prue had to keep turning her head to follow his random progress.

'Thing is, sweetheart, and perhaps I wasn't so sure of this then as I am now, I married you without care or real thought of proper love. I married you for the wrong reasons. And it wasn't long before I could see you married me for the wrong reasons, too. You wanted security, a roof over your head, a child, company, above all the safety of money. No?' He waited for Prue to nod very slightly. 'I wanted a wife. I most definitely wanted a wife. I found you by chance, waiting at a bus stop one rainy night. Chance meetings so often end in mistakes, don't they? They bring a special kind of hope, a feeling that Fate itself has made them happen. But marriage, like anything else, should be researched

157

before entering. Rather like buying a new car . . .' His sad mouth rose briefly into a smile. 'And we didn't research each other, did we? We just plunged in, hoping but not convincing even ourselves, didn't we? I'd found this very pretty land girl with lots of life and spark and spirit. But very soon here at The Larches the gaiety began to go out of you, even when you got the chickens and that daft job . . . I didn't know what to do. I didn't know how to ask you what to do. Money's only a temporary balm, I've always believed. I knew the presents would soon lose their novelty and I felt I was losing my way. And then came the news of the baby – happiest day of my life.'

He stopped by the fireplace, put a hand on it, moved it over the grain of the stone. 'But that wasn't to be, was it? Alfred came and went so fast it was scarcely believable. Worst time of my life – but probably the same for you, too, sweetheart.' Their eyes met but Prue made no sign of acknowledgement.

Barry launched himself back across the room, arms flapping more strongly, the sound of flesh against baggy clothes ruffling the quiet. He reached a large mirror on the wall, glanced at it. Prue was able to see his reflection: a tightening in his face muscles as he braced himself to go on.

'Don't suppose I've ever spoken for so long outside a board meeting in my whole life . . . Anyway, now I've started, I must go on. There's another confession I have to make.' Clumsily he spun round to face Prue. 'No man could hope for a prettier, sweeter girl,' he said, 'but the fact is . . . I'm not interested in smooth youth. What appeals to me – and I understand if you think this is peculiar, or even perverted – is the older woman. The well-worn skin, the friendly wrinkles, the comforting sense of someone who has seen much more of life . . . I don't know. I don't understand it myself. But I feel at a loss with the young. I'm not sure how to behave. I'm sure if ever young girls deigned to show an interest in me, it would be only for my money. You, sweetheart, were very interested in money, but you put up a good show of being kind, easy. I appreciate that. But I know I'm not the husband for you, any more than you're the wife for me.'

Prue looked down at her clasped hands. Barry gave a small laugh.

'When I picked you up that night, you know what? I looked at your mother, who jumped quickly in beside me, you remember, and I thought, Here's an attractive older woman. Good deal older than me, she must be. I thought a lot about what to do before I sent those flowers. But I convinced myself the answer was to marry you, the young one, have children. Win you over, best as I could. Very quickly I knew I'd snared you, and that you were strong enough to say no if you didn't want me. But you didn't do that. You went along with it. We both went along with the mistake.'

With an air of exhaustion Barry took to his chair again and at last allowed himself to light a new cigar. Once he had drawn on it, he exhaled deeply. He had managed his long, pent-up speech without breaking down, and that had brought relief and strength.

'There's just one more confession, sweetheart, though I suppose by now you've worked it out. The Bertha business. I didn't tell you at the time, but I suppose it's my funny liking of older women, particularly indigent older women, that led me into all that foolish nonsense. I'll never forget how understanding you were about all that.'

Prue, who did not like to ask the meaning of 'indigent', nodded. 'I didn't mind,' she said.

'I know you didn't. And the reason you didn't was because you were never in love with me.'

'I'm sorry.'

'So, sweetheart – and this is almost over, I promise – let me tell you my plan. When a mistake is made the best thing is to find a remedy as soon as possible. Now there's no Alfred, there isn't anything to keep us together. It wouldn't matter how much we tried, we'd never have more in common. Pulling in different directions would lead to terrible resentment, unhappiness. So what I thought was this: we should go our separate ways.'

Prue's eyebrows flicked up, then down. 'How could I—'

'You'd have nothing in the world to worry about. When you've made up your mind where you'd like to go, what you'd like to do, I will take care of everything. Buy you a house, a flat, whatever you want. Give you an allowance for the rest of your life – give you whatever you need. You'll always be able to count on me, always.' He stopped, his voice breaking. 'I think we should set sail towards the next era as soon as possible.'

Prue nodded, unable to speak. This was a Barry she had never known existed, and for whom she had never thought of looking. Life unprotected by the claustrophobia of The Larches was an alarming prospect. But Barry was right: it was what she wanted, and he was keen to replace her with some wrinkled old woman. 'I don't know what to think.'

Barry moved over to the window. His back to the light, his expression was unclear. 'You've been so brave about Alfred,' he said quietly. 'Much stronger than me. No weeping. No collapsing. And yet you must be feeling . . .?'

Prue shrugged. 'Oh, I've been *feeling*. What mother wouldn't, when her baby dies? But I don't see there's any point in trying to describe those feelings. I couldn't find the right words. I could say I'm traumatized, devastated, but what would that mean to anyone? It wouldn't give a picture of what's going on in my heart and of course' – she gave a faint smile – 'it isn't really my heart that's hurting, is it? It's just battering away, while it's my stomach, my innards, that are churning about . . . There, you see. No good. Can't do it. Difficult feelings need a poet, like Johnny, to explain. I'm sorry. But I tell you this.' She paused, made an effort to control her voice. 'I'll never forget Alfred. I don't suppose a day will go by when I don't think of him.'

Barry, a fist damming the tear that came from one eye, went back to his favourite chair. 'You're a strong girl, Prue,' he said at last. 'God knows, I wish things hadn't turned out like this. But you must go away now, to your friends. Make plans. Take their advice, sweetheart. Come back and tell me what to do.'

Prue felt herself hurrying to his side. She knelt down, put her head on one of his knees. 'You're so generous,' she said. 'I'd never have guessed you could be so wise.' She felt his fingers weaving through the strands of her hair.

'There you go, then,' he said. 'I've surprised you. I've surprised myself.' He managed a smile. 'Time for bed. Off you go.'

'Thank you for everything, really.' From the door Prue blew him a kiss. But Barry's eyes were shut against more threatening tears. A tremulous cigar made its way towards his mouth.

Prue's first visit was to Ag and Desmond. As soon as she arrived she observed that they moved very slowly, which perhaps accounted for the peaceful air of their cottage. They filtered round the huge kitchen table one after the other: Ag collected plates to be washed, Desmond collected knives and forks that had not been used. Ag sauntered to the sink at the window, Desmond moved as if on wheels to the drawer in the dresser. Within a couple of days of staying in their cottage Prue found herself in awe of their unspoken marital harmony. They did not seem to need to communicate about mundane matters: one simply observed the other and got down to whatever was the next job that needed to be done. This, she thought, was a proper marriage.

Ag was almost as tall as Desmond. Both of them, standing upright, came within an inch or two of the low ceiling. Ag had lost none of her somewhat fierce beauty – which, when they had first met, had intimidated Prue. Her own flirtatious instinct did not exist in Ag's being. She was serious – how they had teased her for her brains – and strong and kind. And patient. She'd waited so long for Desmond. She'd almost given up hope of ever seeing him again when they had met by chance in the National Gallery. Desmond himself, Prue reckoned, with her critical eye for looks, was almost good-looking, but not quite. His nose was lopsided and his eyebrows too wild. But when he smiled his whole body reverberated with pleasure, and the person on whom he smiled felt the strength of that delight.

When Ag and Desmond had re-met after the long absence, Ag had just finished her degree in law and was planning to practise at the Bar. But given the choice of working in London or a country life in Devon, there was no hesitation in her decision. They had found a run-down cottage on the edge of a village not far from Exeter: with it came an apple orchard and some decaying milking sheds. Within weeks of moving in they had bought two Jersey cows and a dozen hens, and Ag was attending to the hedges even before she had begun on the interior of the cottage. Desmond worked for a firm of long-established solicitors in Exeter. The plan, when they had managed to save some money, was to buy more land, extend the cottage, find a herd of Hereford cattle and settle down to serious farming.

It was early January, a colourless morning. Outside the window the bare apple trees made a complicated sketch in the sky and the two Jersey cows stood head to tail, disinclined to graze on the frosty grass. Earlier, Prue had gone out with Ag to milk them. They had led them into the rickety shed, sat on stools, balanced buckets between their knees and pulled at the cold teats. When the first familiar sizzle of milk against tin sounded, Prue laughed so much she almost fell off her stool. 'This is the life!' she shouted. 'This is what I've been missing, Ag. This is what I want to get back to. Chickens in a Manchester garden, walking a giant horse round the fields – rubbish. This is the real thing. You're so lucky.'

'Not so lucky milking at dawn in freezing weather, rain coming through the roof.' Ag lifted her head from the russet flank of her cow. Prue could see her smiling. 'One day, perhaps, we'll have milking machines for our herd.'

Their post-breakfast chores finished, Desmond kissed his wife on both cheeks and left for work. Ag picked up the pot of coffee he had left for them on the stove. She sat at the end of the table, pouring it into old mugs. Prue's fingers gripped the edge of the table. This was the third morning of her Devon stay and time was racing in an alarming way. The length of her visit had not been discussed. Dreading her return to Manchester, she hoped they would not mind if she stayed for at least a week. She loved the cottage, despite the cold, though in the kitchen, with its log fire, it was warm. Her bedroom under the eaves was icy, but with a hot-water bottle each night and plenty of blankets, she had slept better than she had for months. Each morning she had woken at dawn, looked out of the small window onto the orchard and the ruddy Devon earth of the rising fields beyond, and her heart had contracted. This was where she was meant to be, she thought – this sort of place.

It reminded her of Hallows Farm in so many ways, especially the kitchen. Mrs Lawrence's way of doing things had brushed off on Ag: the random arrangement of objects, pictures of pre-war prize cows on the wall, mugs hanging on the dresser among faded plates from local markets. And somehow the smells were the same: the coffee, the slow-cooking stew, the sharpness of wet earth clinging to carrots waiting to be scraped.

'Crikey, Ag,' said Prue. 'It's all wonderful here, utterly wonderful.'

'It's going to take a long time to get it into shape,' said Ag, 'but we like that. Slow progress has its own pleasures.'

Prue had recounted a detailed story of the birth of her son the night she arrived – she had wanted it out of the way – and also told them of Barry's suggestion that they separate. She had made light of this, even made them laugh with her descriptions of Barry and his cigars, his flapping hands. They had understood the seriousness of the decision she had to make, but come up with no immediate solutions.

'What do you think I should do, Ag?' Prue now asked.

'I think you should probably live on your own for a while. Solitude's nothing to be afraid of as long as you don't indulge in too much rumination.'

'I've never tried it. Dare say I could manage it. But where? Where would I go? I couldn't ever live in a city again. But if I was somewhere miles from everywhere, like here, wonderful though it is, who would I find to have a laugh with in a pub? Where could I go dancing?'

Ag laughed. 'There are plenty of young farmers back from the war. If you found somewhere with a pub and a village hall you'd have no problem at all – knowing you.'

Prue giggled.

'Talking of which . . .' Ag got up and took a small leg of lamb from the fridge – swapped with a neighbouring farmer for two dozen eggs: she explained that there was much happy bartering in the village. She pulled a jar of honey out of a cupboard and, with a knife, began to spread it over the meat. Then she shook powdered ginger over it. Prue watched her in amazement. She was so competent, Ag. Whatever she put her hand to, she did well.

'Talking of which,' Ag went on, now pulling spikes of rosemary from their stalks, 'Desmond and I are aware you'll have a very quiet time here. It's far from a giddy life. We don't know many people, yet, and those we do aren't the sort of people you'd be naturally drawn to.'

'Oh, Ag, don't be silly. I don't want entertainment, meeting people. It's just wonderful to be with you both in this perfect cottage, catching up, getting your advice . . .'

'But we've managed to lay on one man for you—'

'A man?'

'A very unalarming man, doesn't know what flirting is.'

'There's a challenge! Listen, Ag, I don't want another man of any kind for a very, very long time. What's he called? What's he like? What does he do?'

'He's called Paul Simmons. He's a kind of low-key charmer, sublimely sympathetic . . .' Prue laughed.

'Is he a young farmer?'

Ag took some time arranging the lamb in a roasting tin and covering it with a dishcloth, then took it to the fridge. Her back to Prue, she finally answered the question. 'He's our vicar.'

'A *vicar*? Don't be utterly daft, Ag. How would I cope with a vicar? What vicar would want anything to do with me, bursting with sins?'

'He's only coming to supper.'

'I don't know how to talk about God.'

'He doesn't talk much about God over supper.'

Prue sighed with relief. 'How old is he?'

'Possibly thirty, possibly not. Hard to tell.'

'Oh, lawks, another older man.'

Ag laughed. 'He's rather nice, honestly. He lives in an enormous cold vicarage near here, looked after by his sister. She's a bit – unusual. We haven't asked her. Once was enough.'

'I'm used to unusual,' said Prue. 'You should've seen Dawn Gander.'

Ag returned to sit at the table. She opened a tin of homemade biscuits. 'These were Mr Lawrence's favourite. Remember?'

'What shall I wear?' Prue asked.

'Honestly, Prue, don't give clothes a thought. I mean, just keep on your dungarees. There's no dressing up here.'

'OK,' said Prue, a touch disappointed. 'I'll just put on my spotted bow and a flick of mascara.'

'You haven't changed, thank goodness,' said Ag, smiling.

That evening, soon after Prue and Ag had shut up the chickens and checked the cows, Desmond arrived home with three bottles of wine. He brought with him a flurry of cold air, a touch of frost that cut into the thick warmth of the kitchen. He piled more logs on the fire and a new flare of heat was added to the old.

Prue asked how she could help. Ag suggested she lay the table. 'I'm just off up to my room,' she said. 'Then I promise I'll do it.'

In the cold of her bedroom she sat huddled under several cardigans contemplating what to wear. She had given her word that she would not appear overdressed, but was determined to change out of dungarees that smelt of hens and cows. She opened the small wardrobe where the 'few' things she had chosen to bring were jammed together. After much contemplation she chose a soft violet jumper with a dipping neck and a scattering of diamanté leaves – she'd seen a picture of Rita Hayworth in something similar. She put on a black skirt and judged it needed cheering up so chose her scarlet patent shoes with ankle straps. Finally, she fixed her best satin bow – scarlet with white spots – in her hair. In the poor light it was hard to be accurate with her makeup but she did her best to plaster her long eyelashes with mascara – she loved the routine of spitting on the brush and scraping at the black stuff in the small box – then made her mouth a perfect bow with a fiery red lipstick. Had she overdone it for a vicar in a kitchen? Probably, but she didn't care. She wanted Ag to see she hadn't given up trying.

She went cautiously down the steep stairs and into the kitchen. The table was already laid, candles lighted.

'Crikey, I'm guilty,' she said to Desmond. 'You've beaten me to it.'

He smiled at her. 'My job,' he said.

Ag, whose only concession to sartorial change was the rolling up of her sleeves, turned from stirring something on the stove.

'Have I gone over the top?' Prue asked.

With a straight face Ag looked her up and down. 'I don't suppose you have,' she said, 'by your standards.'

'You look fantastic,' put in Desmond, quickly. 'Paul will be dazzled.'

The compliment had a deliquescent effect on Prue: it was a very long time since anybody had remarked on how she looked. She didn't give a fig about Ag's disapproval. Ag had always had her prissy moments.

Desmond handed her a glass of wine.

'Gosh, you two are so kind having me here,' she said. She had wanted to choose better words, but they came in a rush, no time to think. 'I love it here so much. Thank you.'

She tottered over to Ag, high heels uncertain on the rough stone floor, put her arms round her. They stood locked for a moment, arms about each other. Ag made no comment about her friend's sparkly jersey, more suitable for a nightclub than a vicar. Prue moved on to Desmond. She felt his skin on her cheek, the momentary pressure of his huge hand on her back, and a flicker of mercury went through her. Quickly she backed away. Not for anything in the world would she try it on with Desmond. But if they were left alone on a desert island, she reckoned, they wouldn't ignore the opportunity.

The doorbell rang. Desmond went to answer it. Prue pushed down the floppy wool neck of her film-star jersey.

Paul Simmons followed Desmond into the kitchen. He carried a bottle of sherry and was smiling a smile that looked as if it had been arranged for some time and was cracking at the edges. He was extraordinarily pale, with a wide, weak face framed by tufts of prematurely greying hair. From a distance, Prue thought, he might be mistaken for handsome. But there was something – not quite detectable – spoilt the first impression. And he was not exactly manly, like Desmond. Tall and thin, concave chest, bony fingers fashioned to pray, Prue supposed. You couldn't really ask him to pick up a heavy suitcase or a dead sheep. They were introduced, shook hands. 'Crikey!' squealed Prue. 'A dog collar! You really are a vicar.'

The smile fell from the Reverend's face. 'I'm afraid I am,' he said. Then, guilty of disloyalty to his beliefs, he added, 'Though before my calling I was in the navy.'

'You fought in the war?'

Paul Simmons blushed. 'Unfortunately not. On account of asthma. It took a turn for the worse just as Germany invaded Poland.'

'Crumbs,' said Prue.

Ag, wary of this first encounter, was eager for everyone to sit down at the table. She produced her triumphant Greek lamb, deep in its sea of cider and rosemary, and dishes of bright vegetables. Prue sat opposite Paul and was quickly aware he found it difficult to turn his opal eyes away from her. She flashed her eyelashes at him, to encourage him just a little, and listened to his story about one of his parishioners, who had run off with the chairman of the parish council, with an air of intense interest.

As Ag had promised, Paul did not talk much about God. Hardly a mention. After a good many glasses of wine he became bolder, and dared make a few jokes. Not a natural humourist, they were funny enough to make everybody laugh slightly and, yes, thought Prue, Ag had been right. The vicar had a certain charm, not least in his self-deprecating stories. Luckily nothing went wrong in church, he said, but in the real world everything conspired against him. His car had a habit of breaking down on the way to funerals, his surplice was ruined at the cleaner's, his paperwork was in such a state of chaos you'd have thought some pernicious spirit had been at it in the night. Once, on the occasion of a visit from the local bishop, he had found himself in the pulpit without his sermon. 'All I could do was ask God's blessing,' he said. 'And, well, though I say it myself, words miraculously came to me. The bishop congratulated me on a certain . . . freshness.'

'Brilliant,' said Prue.

'But oh my goodness, what a time.' He was filling his glass again.

Prue, who found his language funnier than his stories, laughed encouragingly. He looked a little surprised, though grateful that his contribution to the evening was so appreciated by Ag's friend.

After they'd finished the Sussex Pond Pudding, Mrs Lawrence's recipe, they sat round the kitchen table drinking till almost midnight, when Ag said she had to go to bed if she was to be up at five. Desmond, having dealt with the washing up, said he must join her. Paul claimed he was about to walk home: the night air would clear his head.

When they were left on their own, Prue filled his glass again. 'Know something?' she said. 'I've never, ever met a vicar before.'

'And I've never met a girl like you before. Glorious, glorious, glorious,' he added. 'A free spirit. A true wonder.' He gave a small, almost soundless laugh.

If laughs were animals, Prue reflected, this one would have been a snail. She blushed, and giggled. She, too, was feeling the effects of more wine than she usually drank.

'Get away with you, Vicar,' she said. 'I was worried you were going to talk about God all evening.'

He gave a small frown. 'No point talking about God when it's inappropriate,' he said. 'I'm always thinking about our Maker, mind. He's always with me, every moment of the day.'

'Gosh, golly, gosh,' said Prue.

'But I leave Him alone until I feel called upon to ponder on Him. This evening wasn't that sort of occasion.'

'I can see that. Mr and Mrs Lawrence, whose farm Ag and I worked on in the war, they were believers, but they kept quiet about it. I found that rather inspiring.'

'Quite. For God to be appreciated, He must fit in appropriately – though that's not something I learnt in my training. Well, I'd say I've had more than enough to drink ... Think I'd better be going.' He stood up, wavered a little. 'How long are you here for?'

'Not sure. A week, perhaps.'

'Then I hope you'll wander over to the vicarage, let me show you the church.'

'I'd love to.' Prue managed this with conviction.

She followed him to the front door. An oil lamp was lighted in the hallway. It made long umber shadows that cut into the small space. Prue put a hand on the latch. She could feel Paul standing very close behind her, his wine breath strong. With what she imagined was a fierce expression that would deter him from any hanky-panky, as her mother called it, she turned to face him. Startled – so the expression must have been successful – he took a step backwards. Then he raised one hand slowly, as if it was a heavy weight, and held up two fingers in a V. Prue was puzzled as to whether he was copying Winston Churchill's famous victory sign, or whether it was something rude. The fingers made an uncertain flight to her shoulder, where they alighted for just a moment, then moved to her cheek. Prue allowed them two seconds' rest before she flicked them away with a toss of her head.

'I've been wanting to do that all evening,' he whispered.

If that was all he'd been wanting, Prue thought, then she was happy to oblige for a moment, despite the danger of one thing leading to another. 'You are a one,' she said.

'Yes, I am a one.' The vicar sighed. 'You could say that. I am indeed a one. But then it's not very often that living in this rural place a one has the opportunity of running into anyone as . . . delicious as you.'

'Suppose not,' agreed Prue. The word 'delicious' seemed odd, coming from a vicar. Not something she'd ever been called before. She wanted to hurry along with the weird farewell now. Go to bed.

Paul aimed the V towards his dog collar. When his fingers reached it, and tapped to make sure of its certainty, the small click of his nails chipped the silence. 'Well, I really must be on my way, difficult though that is. My whole being wants to stay a while longer, but that would be untoward, would it not?'

Prue considered the question not worth a reply. She opened the door. A blast of night air flew in.

'God bless you, dear Prue.'

'Good night, Vicar.'

'I trust you'll come and see my church?'

'I might.'

'Dear Prue . . .' He wavered down the path shaking his head, his gait that of a much older man.

'Cripes,' said Prue to herself, and shut the door.

Prue's habit of early rising was broken next morning. She woke with a headache at ten o'clock and came down to the kitchen in her pyjamas. There was no trace of last night's supper: everything was orderly, the cat asleep on the window-sill, breakfast laid just for her.

'Christ, I'm sorry, Ag,' she said. 'I meant to help with the milking.'

'Desmond's here on Saturdays. He did it. He likes it. He's getting quite good.' Ag smiled, poured coffee. 'Anyhow, you cast your spell as usual. I've had Paul on the telephone already. He wants you to "take tea", as he calls it, at the vicarage. He's dying to show you the church.'

'OK, OK.' Prue rubbed her forehead. 'Have you got an aspirin?'

Ag handed her a bottle from the dresser. 'You don't normally drink that much,' she said.

'Not often, no. Though you remember the dance? When Joe carried me home? But I've given up most of my wicked ways. Barry's not a keen drinker, though he likes champagne. He flashed a lot of it when we were courting – if you can call it that.'

Desmond came through the back door carrying a large cabbage and a knife. He wore an ancient weatherproof jacket that cracked as he moved. His eyes went at once to his wife. 'Everything all right?'

'Fine,' said Ag.

Desmond put the cabbage on the table. 'Got a touch of frost, but it's OK.' Again he looked anxiously at Ag. 'You're not feeling . . .?'

'No. I'm fine.'

A look swift as light passed between the three of them. Desmond moved to Ag, put a hand on her shoulder. Despite her muzzy, aching head, Prue quickly guessed the reason for his unease. Perhaps he and Ag had agreed not to mention babies – hers or theirs. She conjured a smile. 'It's such good news,' she said, 'your baby. It's wonderful. I'm so pleased. How much longer?'

'Six months.'

'I wouldn't mind being a godmother.' Prue got up, went to Ag. They hugged.

When she returned to the table Desmond took his turn in embracing Ag. He looked over her shoulder to Prue. 'She's been feeling so wretched,' he said. 'I automatically check up on her every day.'

'We decided on no baby talk,' said Ag, 'but I suppose that would have been unnatural.'

'It would.' Prue managed a small laugh. 'Anyway, I'm absolutely fine. And I'm thrilled for you.'

Ag and Desmond drew apart, but their eyes remained linked as if by invisible cobwebs.

'I haven't collected the eggs yet,' Desmond said. 'Coming?'

Ag nodded and took a duffel coat from the back of the door.

'Can you remember how to cut up a cabbage, Prue?' Desmond asked. He handed her a huge knife. 'It'll make your hands cold but it's one of the nicer chores.' He opened the back door for Ag, put a hand on her shoulder. They went out.

All that day Prue watched her hosts very carefully. She was mesmerized by the deep, almost tangible link between them.

Their oneness, she supposed it must be. Their absolute rightness for each other. Their certainty of life together, their profound happiness, their quiet humour, their constant but unspoken awareness of the other's feelings. Ag only had to glance at Desmond and he seemed to know what she was thinking, and vice versa. Much of their communication seemed not to be put into words: their silences were easy. And they seemed utterly content with their lot: a smallholding, a few animals, fruit trees, hedges, a vegetable patch. They conveyed no longing for nights out at posh hotels, foreign travel or any kind of exotic life. The fact that they had finally found each other, and the war was over, and they had their small patch of land was all they asked. One day, when their child or children were old enough, Ag said, she would consider going back to the Bar, but for the present she had no plans to further her career. She was utterly content, moving in her stately way from stove to table to garden to chicken shed, waiting only for Desmond's return each evening. Cripes, thought Prue, cutting into the noisy block of icy blue cabbage, that's what I want one day.

Later that morning, as Ag ironed Desmond's shirts at one end of the kitchen table, Prue ventured to explain the wonder she was feeling in their cottage. 'Your happiness – you and Desmond,' she said. 'It sort of rubs off. It's extraordinary.'

Ag smiled. 'There's always the risk of complacency,' she said, 'but I think we're lucky enough to be blessed with *eudaimonia* – an Ancient Greek word.'

'You and your scholarship,' giggled Prue. 'What the hell does that mean?'

'It's difficult to translate, but something along the lines of flourishing happiness, well-being.'

'Well, I hope some of it comes my way.' Prue piled up a few folded shirts. 'That's what I'm after.'

'You'd be bored by our sort of quiet life.'

'Not if I was with someone I really loved. It could have been with Barry One. Maybe I'll be lucky again one day.' She smiled at Ag. 'But I tell you what: the man of my dreams doesn't live next to the church. Can't really see myself as a vicar's wife, can you?'

'No,' said Ag, 'but be careful. He's a vulnerable soul, not used to dazzling girls. He could lose his heart.'

'Rubbish,' said Prue, who was thinking she would wear her dullest bow for tea at the vicarage.

Her headache gone, the navy striped bow in her hair, Prue arrived at four-thirty. It was a bitterly cold afternoon. The short walk from the cottage had left her shivering. Paul Simmons, who had been standing on guard at the front door for half an hour, observed how cold she was as soon as she appeared through the gate at the end of his long front path. By the time she reached him, shoulders hunched, lips blue, he had decided on a quick change of plan: tea before a tour of the church. The beautiful but thin girl needed warming up.

The vicarage, a large red-brick Victorian house, was a sullen-looking building, uncared for. Paul led Prue down a long dark passage that smelt of boiled fish and rotting apples. From behind one of the many closed doors there was the sound of loud banging, then wailing.

'My sister isn't the most domestic woman on earth,' he explained. 'She's probably having trouble with the kettle. Still, I'm fortunate to have someone for company.'

He opened a door and ushered Prue into his study. He gave a small bow as she passed him. 'This is where my parishioners come with their grievances.' He pointed to a desk piled with papers, some of which had fallen onto the floor. 'I write my sermons here, too.'

It was a room of such utter cheerlessness that Prue could find no words. The walls were painted the yellow-green of elderly

174

toenails, while the threadbare carpet and two armchairs on spindle legs matched exactly the colour of the dung heap at Hallows Farm. Jesus, appropriately, was the only agreeable presence in the room: in a picture above the fireplace He smiled down at them. His shirt – well, sort of shirt – was drawn back to show a glowing red heart from which spurted yellow and orange flames.

Prue kept her arms folded beneath her breasts. She had no intention of abandoning her jacket. Paul indicated she should take a chair to one side of the two-bar electric fire. 'It'll soon warm up,' he said. 'I only put it on . . .' He couldn't quite remember when he had taken this precaution, but Prue was faintly endeared to him by his optimistic hope of imminent warmth. 'One day,' he added, suddenly misty-eyed, 'the Church Commissioners might afford us central heating. Until then, well, I just pile on the jerseys. You get used to it.'

'You're very – stalwart,' Prue said, not altogether sure that that was the word she wanted.

'Oh yes, that's me. Stalwart. But, you see, I love the place. Been in the village all my life. My uncle was the vicar before me.' He looked up at the dun ceiling, its centre light covered with a mesh of cobwebs. 'I don't suppose, looking round, you can see why I hold the house in such affection.'

'No,' said Prue, because he was expecting an answer, and she didn't like to lie to a vicar.

'People often find it difficult to see what others see . . . Especially about houses . . .' He trailed off. 'But that's how it is. I understand from Ag that you all loved the farm where you worked as land girls, though that, too, was cold and rather dark.'

'We did,' said Prue. A silence stretched between them.

A line of red was rising above the his dog collar and jersey and creeping up over his jaw. He was about to pronounce something important. 'I feel I owe you an apology, dear Prue,' he said. 'That little gesture last night – it was untoward. I should never have touched you. God forgive me, I fear I had imbibed a little too much of Desmond's excellent wine.'

'Didn't matter at all,' said Prue. She giggled. 'I love the way you talk. Such funny old-fashioned language. I could listen to you for hours, though I don't understand half the words.'

'Really?' His relief that he had not caused offence with his inebriated behaviour, and his delight in her odd praise, sent the wash of red scuttling back down his neck. 'Well, I love the English language and all it's whirligigs of expression. We shouldn't let it go. We should do our best to keep its intricacies alive, no matter how we're scoffed at. Don't you think? Now, Liz will bring us a pot of tea. Then we might venture out to the church.'

At that moment there was a loud, peevish ring from the telephone buried under the papers on the desk. Scowling, Paul got up and went over to it, scattering more papers onto the floor as he rummaged to find the receiver.

'Dash and blow,' he said. 'Tell you what, if you could nip down the passage to the third door on the right, you'll find Liz. She'll hand over the tray. So sorry about this.'

The ringing telephone had put him into a considerable dither. He lifted the earpiece to one ear, changed it to the other, signalled with a waving hand to the door, finally made contact with the caller. 'My dear Mrs Spooner,' he said.

Prue went out in search of the right door, opened it, and moved into a kitchen even colder than the vicar's study. There was someone at the sink, back to her, running a tap. At first Prue thought it was very short, fat man: cropped hair, man's trousers, long baggy jersey. The tap was snapped off. The figure turned. Large ungainly breasts now revealed it was a woman.

'Sorry to bother you,' Prue began.

'Oh, it's no bother.' There was a sneer in her voice. 'I'm Liz, the sister. You must be the girlfriend.'

Prue felt herself blush. 'Not exactly. I only met Paul last night. He's going to show me the church.'

'Ah.' Liz moved to the table, dumped a few rock cakes from a tin onto an empty plate. 'He's always got the excuse of the church, hasn't he? You mustn't mind that.'

Prue frowned, puzzled, uneasy. 'Why should I mind that?'

'Well, darling, my brother's in search of a wife. He tries it on, here and there. Doesn't get very far. Though I have to say he hasn't come up with something like you before. It's usually the older spinster.'

She now smiled, a smile of dark and chipped teeth, her eyes hard on Prue's face before they scoured her body. It was the most terrifying smile Prue had ever seen, a rape of a smile. A surge of cold sweat swept over her. She was sickened, giddy, and put one hand on the table for support. In a trice Liz lowered one of her own hands on top of it, squeezed. 'If it's comfort and fun you're looking for, dear, I'm always here.' She smiled again, then limped heavily to the boiling kettle, her laugh almost smothering its hiss. 'I've something of a reputation in this village, so I don't go out much.'

Prue was sidling towards the open door.

Liz, having filled the pot, shuffled things onto the tray. 'Don't worry, darling. I'm not going to hurt you. But it's always worth a try. I might get lucky one day.' She handed Prue the tray.

Prue hurried back to the study. Paul was sitting in his chair again. His surprise at her entrance made him raise both hands – it was as if he had not expected her to return. 'Oh, very good, lovely, wonderful, excellent, thank you so much,' he said in a rush. 'Put it down here.' He glanced at Prue, noticed her state. 'Are you all right? I hope my sister did nothing to offend. She has her funny ways.'

'I'm fine,' said Prue. She dreaded the rock cakes.

Surprisingly, tea with the vicar was less of an ordeal than she had thought it might be. Paul made her laugh from time to time, more by his archaic use of language than his meagre jokes, and she saw what Ag meant about his mild charm. He was not entirely to be dismissed, she thought, though she could not imagine in what way they might continue an acquaintance.

An hour passed quickly. It was suddenly dark. Paul got up to draw the grim curtains.

'Bit late to see the church,' said Prue. 'I could come back tomorrow.'

'Oh, do.' He clapped his hands and gave a sort of skip back to his chair. He looked up at the picture of Jesus over the fire. 'Are you a churchgoer?'

'Not really. Christmas, weddings, that sort of thing. I like the hymns.'

'You sound like the average British Christian,' Paul replied, with a smile that Prue took to be pitying, 'but I hope you're at least in touch with God.'

'In touch? How do you mean?'

'Well, He's everywhere, all the time, to put it in the simplest terms.'

'You mean He's in this room? With us?' Prue glanced up at the picture. She didn't like it.

'He is indeed.' Paul gave a long, inward sigh, then exhaled silently as he pushed his hands against each other to make a steeple.' I can feel Him beside us.'

'Well I can't.' Prue, close to giggling, looked down at the clerical shoes. They were enough to make anyone stop laughing.

'Oh dear, oh dear. I don't know where to begin. I'm always stumped by semi-believers. But at least I must urge you to walk and talk with God. That's not a bad beginning.'

'Walk and talk? What would I say? I'd feel a bit daft talking to someone who's not there.'

'You could start by saying thank you. Most people pray to God only when they want something—'

'I prayed when I thought my premature son was going to die. I admit that. I think I shouted at God.'

'And did He hear you?'

'No.'

'Well, He works in mysterious ways. You may find there was good reason for your son to die. But you've plenty to give thanks for, haven't you?'

'I suppose I have.' Prue wriggled in her chair, tugging at her jacket, signalling she was about to leave. 'I'm a little bit intrigued, I have to admit, Vicar, about all your God stuff.'

'Good, good. We could talk some more.'

Prue stood up. Paul went to open the door for her.

At the front door, looking out on to a clump of yew trees, their darkness just touched by moonlight, she shivered. 'Tell you what, I'll try talking to God on the way back, shall I? He might show me the way. I haven't got a torch.'

'I think you're teasing me, Prue.'

'Course I am. But I will try. It might be easier in the dark.'

'Come back tomorrow and we really will go round the church before it gets dark.' He put a brief hand on her shoulder.

'OK. And thanks for the tea.'

Prue set off down the path, knowing he watched her until she was out of sight. She looked forward to recounting her afternoon to Ag and Desmond. For some reason she decided to leave out the God bit. In a funny way, it had felt private.

The next afternoon Prue returned to the vicarage. Paul gave her a brief history of the church, which wasn't nearly as boring as she'd expected. The oldest part was fourteenth century: no wonder it was even colder than the house. What most fascinated her was the tomb on which a young couple lay, each with marble hands pressed together and legs stretched out very straight. The woman, who was as po-faced as the woman in the corner shop down the road at home, wore a long dress of many cold and dusty pleats and ruffles. On the side of one of her legs a dog was stuck, limpet-like: very unrealistic, Prue reflected. If it hadn't been marble it would have fallen off. And she couldn't work out what sort of dog it was – either a very young puppy, or some miniature breed. She didn't like it. And the couple's feet, neatly together pointing towards the ceiling, were completely flat. Their shoes had no heels. Prue moved to study their faces. She wanted to see if they looked happy. Their marble eyelids were at half mast, no expression in them. They looked as if they had never been able to see, as if they had had no memories.

'They don't look as if they'd been hard at it, exactly, do they?' she asked Paul.

'I suppose they don't, no.' The vicar blushed. 'I think they're just sleeping the sleep of the innocent.'

'Glad I didn't live then,' Prue mused. 'All those heavy skirts. Be so difficult—'

'Quite,' interjected Paul. 'I know what you mean.'

Prue doubted this, but decided it was time to leave speculation about the effigies' sex lives. She asked to go round the graveyard.

There, she wandered away from the vicar who was pinning up something in the porch. She went from grave to grave, touching the leaning tombstones smothered in brambles and moss, their inscriptions powdery with age. Some of the names she loved: Dora, Agnes, Violet, Edwin, Sage. She came upon a small headstone: one Hamish, who had lived for three months, born and died before the Great War. Prue knelt down, put a hand on the small mound of turf. She wished she could find flowers to put on the grave, but she could see none. She stayed on her knees for a long time.

Then a flock of rooks rose from the tops of bare elms to one side of the graveyard and cawed their way into the dense grey sky, startling her. She got up, turned to look back at the church. The vicar was still in the porch, regarding her.

Prue waved. They walked towards each other, then made their way back to the vicarage for more bitter tea and rock cakes. This time there was no sign of Liz, which was a great relief.

To her surprise, Prue found herself visiting Paul every afternoon for the next five days. Once, there were digestive biscuits instead of the rock cakes: he explained they very rarely appeared in the village shop, but he'd happened on some this morning and pounced upon them. As they sat by the pallid fire Prue talked a little of her own life. She confessed to the breakdown of her marriage, which Paul had heard about from Ag, but did not mention the baby. The vicar talked of his love for the village, for Devon, but was not forthcoming about his private life – well, he probably didn't have much of one, Prue guessed. With some diffidence she did ask his advice on what she should do once she left Manchester.

'Go and live somewhere in the country, work on a proper farm. There's lots of work to be had, now, as the farmers return from arable to dairy. Live on your own. I recommend it. God will be with you.'

'Oh, Him,' said Prue, a touch petulant. 'I knew whatever your suggestion was that it would include God.'

'I'm sorry, then. I haven't been helpful.' He clasped his hands, looked down at them.

'Sorry, Paul. I didn't mean to snap. But life on my own . . . I've got to think hard. God might not be there to guide me, whatever you say.'

'O ye of little faith.' The vicar smiled. He was used to people having no faith in his suggestions.

'I'd better be getting back, helping with the supper,' said Prue. She stood up, which meant the scant warmth from the electric fire fled from the top half of her body.

'Of course. I mustn't detain you. How much longer are you staying?'

'I go home – home! – the day after tomorrow. Ag said I could stay as long as I liked, but I think it's time to go, make plans.'

'Quite. And, well, it's been such a pleasure . . .'

'Been nice meeting you, too. My mum'll be over the moon when she hears I've been having serious talks with a man of God.'

Paul smiled again, very faintly. What Mrs Lawrence used to call an under-smile. Joe used to give Prue under-smiles sometimes.

On Prue's last night Ag and Desmond had to go to Exeter for a business dinner. They could neither put it off nor include Prue. She declared herself more than happy to be by herself, listening to *ITMA*. But once they had left the house, Ag's *eudaimonia* – she had learnt how to pronounce it – which Prue had felt ever since she arrived, evaporated. She began to fret. What now? Both Ag and the vicar had suggested a solitary life. But where? She didn't much fancy the idea too far from any gaiety, and yet she could never live in a city again.

Prue went into the sitting room – not much used: they had spent most of their time in the kitchen. And not warm. But it housed the huge radiogram, in its walnut cabinet, that Desmond had given Ag for Christmas. Prue began to go through the pile of records. There was a lot of jazz, some twenties and thirties singers. The rest was classical, but she had no idea whether to go for Bach, Beethoven or Mozart so she plumped for Glenn Miller. That, she knew, would take her back to those wartime dances in Dorset.

She turned the volume so high she could hear the music in the kitchen, where she ate the bowl of soup Ag had left for her and drank a half-bottle of wine. Beneath the table her feet skittered in time with the thump of the music. When it ended she returned to the sitting room to choose another record, this time Ruth Etting, whom she had never heard but Stella had once told her she played 'Harvest Moon' every night on her old wind-up gramophone, and it always made her cry.

Ruth Etting made Prue cry, too. Not sob, but she was aware of self-pitying tears running down her cheeks. She had no idea why she pitied herself, so much better off than millions of others in many ways. Perhaps, she thought, she was confusing self-pity with straight fear of the future. Or perhaps it was just the wine. She wiped her mascaraed cheeks and cut into a piece of cheese. The kitchen sailed round her, a strange geometry of comforting shapes, colours and cooking smells. She was, she knew, slightly drunk.

The bell rang. Man of my dreams, she said to herself, and wavered to the front door.

The vicar stood there, his pale face wide with anticipation. He carried a bottle of wine.

'Oh, my God,' said Prue.

He looked taken aback. 'Just me,' he said. 'I knew it was your last night and I wanted to say goodbye.' He held up the bottle of wine.

'You'd better come in.' Prue had failed to sound enthusiastic, but she pulled the door wider. 'Desmond and Ag had to go out. I'm here alone.'

He followed her to the kitchen. Prue fetched another wine glass. He opened the bottle, poured. It was, Prue woozily thought, like a minuet between two strangers who had no idea what the other would do next. She was faintly intrigued. They sat down.

'Lovely voice,' said the vicar at last. 'Pure melancholy. Ruth Etting, isn't it?'

Prue was impressed. As far as she knew, no one besides Stella and Ag knew about Ruth Etting. They clicked their glasses together.

'Well, here's to . . .' said the vicar.

'Here's to what?'

'All manner of things. Your future. Your happiness. Your success. Your finding whatever it is you're searching for.'

'Thanks,' said Prue. She was disconcerted by his earnestness.

'Your visit, if I may say so, has given us all so much pleasure. It's not often such a bright spark lands among us here in Devon. It's not often the bright spark finds her way five days running to the vicarage for a utility tea . . .' They both laughed. 'I have a fantasy about taking you to London one day. We'd go to Westminster Abbey, then have tea at Gunter's.'

'Really? What's Gunter's?'

'Best strawberry ice cream in the world.'

'What I'd really like, if ever I go to London, is tea at Lyons Corner House.'

'Not beyond possibility,' replied the vicar with a small shudder.

'But then I dare say visits to London will never happen.'

'Probably not.'

They had been drinking quickly: the vicar's bottle of wine was running out. As he poured Prue a third glass she noticed a spot of red high on each cheek. She knew from past experience that red spots were usually followed either by declarations or attempts at seduction. Wanting to clear her head a little, to be prepared for any advance, Prue pushed away her glass. The vicar sipped at his.

After a while he said: 'Prue, I'm going to put my cards on the table.'

For all her attempts to be clear-headed, Prue's thoughts remained indistinct. She vaguely wondered in which pocket he had brought his pack . . . What he actually put on the table were his hands, placing them slowly and gently as if they were very precious. They were flat and pale, the fingers splayed out. Exotic fish came to Prue's unsteady mind – they reminded her of exotic fish she had seen in biology books at school.

'I've been thinking. I've been talking to our good Lord – no, don't sneer at me.'

Prue looked up at him. She was unaware she appeared to be sneering. But some kind of explosion was kindling within her.

'I've been thinking a lot about you, Prue. This last week, a great many of my thoughts have been associated, tied up, indeed entangled with you . . .'

'Lawks,' said Prue. 'What've you been thinking?' She wasn't sure she wanted to know. The question came from the politeness her mother had always insisted upon.

'Well, many things.' The fish hands rose for a moment, as if coming up for air. 'First, how fortunate I am to have met a girl like you. You're extraordinary, Prue. There's a kind of . . . magic about you.' Having found the right word, the fish dived down again. 'And this I have to confess: your charms have quite thrown me off balance.'

'Cripes,' said Prue. 'You don't half have a funny way of putting things.'

The vicar attempted a laugh. 'My theological training, no doubt,' he said. 'Or maybe a lifelong reading of Trollope.'

'Who?'

He did not answer this but wound in the fish and clasped his fingers as if in prayer. Despite her good intentions to keep a clear head, Prue took another gulp of wine. The inward explosion was gathering pace. Paul was gearing up to make some declaration she did not want to hear: she did not want some pale old vicar blathering on about how he'd lost his heart to her, how he could imagine whatever. The last thing she could imagine was him touching her, let alone—

He unfurled his hands, stretched one out to cover Prue's. She flinched. But the politeness had set rock hard. It kept her from snatching her hand away from his. The vicar's troubled, hopeful eyes were on her scarlet cheeks.

'As I was saying, I have been very much in touch with our Maker over this. And it seemed to me He was definitely guiding me in a certain direction.' His voice had become soft, soppy. For a moment Prue tried to see him as she had most liked him, not

185

at all soppy but making quite good jokes over the rock cake at the vicarage. But that picture was now superseded by the vicar as a man changed by desire – a state, as Prue well knew, that often obliterated the charms of a man whose mind happened temporarily not to be on sex. If he had been fighting carnal thoughts all through the rock cakes, he had disguised his battle very well.

'And what I think I understood from our Lord was that . . . however unlikely it may seem, there might be hope for you and me, Prue, to make a life together.'

Prue looked at him, astounded. It wasn't just sex he wanted. It was marriage, life. Permanent life in the ghastly vicarage. Jesus Christ. 'I'm flattered,' she said quietly, 'but I don't think you're on the right path, Vicar.'

Her instant dismissal turned him into a fiercer being. 'What I'm saying, Prue, is that the message I've received from God is to ask you to come with me – bodily, spiritually. Be with me, be mine – be committed to me as I want to be to you.' His voice was now loud, ugly. 'That is what God said to me.'

Prue felt a raging heat rise up through her body. She banged the table. 'It's not God telling you!' she screamed. 'It's your under-used, over-excited cock telling you, Vicar!'

Against her own voice she heard the wail of his chair on the floor as he leapt up, looked down on her with twisted face – the whitest face she had ever seen – spittle drooping from the corners of his mouth.

'I have never, ever been spoken to – *thus*,' he half shouted. His hands shook on the back of his chair.

There was complete silence. Prue shrugged, sniffed. The mist in her head flew away. Suddenly everything was wonderfully clear: the whimpering vicar with his daft desire, her own fury, which, having exploded, was now retreating.

'Well, I suppose I'm sorry,' she said at last, 'but surely, as a man of God, you should be able to read people a bit. I mean, what on earth made you think I'd ever be interested in anything but tea with you?'

The vicar was wiping one eye with a large unlaundered handkerchief. 'You certainly know how to cut to the quick,' he said. 'We all live in pathetic hope. I'm sorry if I offended you. I ask your forgiveness. But I was putting to you serious things. It was no flash of nefarious desire, I do assure you.'

'Oh, no offence. Honest.' Prue stood up. She wanted him to go, fast. 'One day – you know what? – the woman of your dreams, or prayers, will turn up at the vicarage and you'll live happily ever after. Question of patience. What you don't want is to take on someone who isn't right ... like I did.' Paul's eyebrows raised slightly. Prue remembered telling him one afternoon that she was a free woman now. Perhaps he had thought she meant divorced. 'And I'll tell you another thing, Vicar. Not in a million years would I be the right girl for you. Either God was mistaken, or you misheard Him. I'm a scatty ex-land girl full of romance and rubbish. Probably not right for anyone.'

The vicar put away his handkerchief, ran a finger round his neck where the dog collar, as usual, had made a red rim. 'I'd better be going,' he said. 'And despite this evening, these misunderstandings, it's been such a pleasure of a week.' He gave a difficult smile.

Prue followed him to the front door. 'I dare say I drank too quickly,' she said.

'Perhaps we both did. I'm an infrequent drinker.'

'I'm not normally so beastly.'

'Of course you aren't. You weren't beastly. You were outraged. I got my timing wrong, but the evening was running out. I messed up everything, didn't I?'

'I'm sorry I—'

'No need to apologize. All is forgiven,' he said. 'God be with you, dear Prue.' He opened the door, went out, shutting it behind him. Prue stood watching his brisk departure, curious about her own ability to cause such hurt to so innocent a man. He would, of course, one day become a funny story to recount to some handsome young boyfriend who would never dream of using words like all the vicar's – dashing and blowing and thus-ing . . . For now, she had to admit to herself, he had behaved rather well in the face of her rudeness: presumably God had urged him to keep his hair on, and he'd managed it.

'Thus,' said Prue out loud, making herself laugh. What God needed to tell him now, and she presumed He would in one of their conversations, was to forget her as soon as possible.

Prue left for Manchester the next morning without mentioning most of the events of the past evening. She had a feeling Paul would not be recounting the story, so her own silence might go towards making amends – not that the vicar would ever discover her contrition.

She left Ag and Desmond with great sadness. They had shown her the kind of married life she would like to aspire to, though she doubted she would ever achieve it.

# Chapter 9

Prue did not know exactly what time she would leave Devon so she did not tell Barry when she would be home. She arrived at four, noticed that Bertha's bicycle was not in the garage and remembered it was her day off.

She let herself into the house. There was a strange smell of cleaning stuff scented with some vile artificial flower and – a new addition – an arrangement of imitation pansies very similar to one her mother had had for years at home. All the pleasure that had seeped into Prue on her visit to Ag flew away. Still, she wouldn't be here for much longer.

She went to the sitting room to light the fire. There was a strong smell of cigars. Barry had plainly been making up for the temporary ban on smoking with which he had struggled while Prue was pregnant.

On the table a tray was laid for tea: two cups and saucers, and a plate covered with a napkin. There was a pile of Shippam's salmon-paste sandwiches, not quite as usual – as Prue saw when she picked one up and pulled it apart – for there was slice of cucumber on top of the smear of fish-paste. Also surprising was the bunch of parsley on the side of the plate. Altogether grander sandwiches than usual. Prue was curious.

The front-door bell rang. Prue went to answer it. Her mother stood in the porch. Her look of anticipation gave way to one of shock. 'I wasn't expecting you, darling. I thought you were down with Ag.'

'I was. But I'm back. Come on in.'

Mrs Lumley had taken the precaution of dressing carefully for tea with her son-in-law. She wore a fox fur round her shoulders – an old dead fox with glass eyes, its mouth made into a clip to hold its tail. Floppy legs drooped down over her blouse of olive artificial silk. Prue had always hated the fox, but her mother said it had been handed down through generations of her family, it was of sentimental value and not for anything would she get rid of it. She also wore a hat shaped like a saucer balanced on one side of her head, and a new magenta lipstick. Thick blue eye shadow detracted from her green eyes.

She stepped into the hall, cast her eyes round the darkness. 'The pansies look nice,' she said. 'I thought the hall could do with a bit of brightening up so I brought them round last Thursday.'

She trotted ahead of Prue to the sitting room with the air of one to whom the geography of the house had become familiar. Prue followed her, went to light the fire.

'Barry said he'd be here at four.' Her mother unclipped the fur stole, slung it over the back of a sofa. Fox limbs now straggled over a cushion. It glared at Prue with an unreal light in its eyes. She had seen enough dead animals to know the clouding of the eyeballs that, in reality, death instantly inflicts. But realism in fox stoles wouldn't attract many buyers, she thought, and took a seat as far from it as possible.

'I expect you're wondering why I'm here, darling. Truth is, not long after you'd gone Barry asked me over to tell me your news – the parting. The end of the marriage, I mean.'

'I'm sorry I didn't have time to tell you before I went.'

'No – well . . . Besides, it's difficult to break that sort of news. I feel very sorry for you both.' She took a handkerchief from the old leather handbag Prue had known all her life. 'We got to talking, and I told Barry all about the salon.'

'What about it?'

'If the truth be known, its heyday's over, Prue. People just aren't coming. It's never really got back to how it was before the war – you remember? The place jammed every day. Rushed off my feet, I was.' She paused to blow her nose and to dab at one bright eye. 'And the other thing is, there's competition just down the road. Some fancy place with a French name. I've seen people going there. To be honest, I'm not sure I can struggle on. I'm thinking of closing.'

'Mum—'

'I told Barry all that. He was most sympathetic. And then this morning he telephoned me and asked me round to tea. He said an idea had come to him. That's why I'm here.' She stood up, adjusted her hat, which had lurched over the tearless eye. 'Tell you what, I'll run into the kitchen, bring us a pot of tea. Barry shouldn't be long.'

By the time she returned she seemed to be in better spirits.

'So you get along with Bertha, then?' said Prue. 'I was never welcome in the kitchen.'

'Oh, Bertha and I get along all right. We understand each other.'

Prue wondered how many visits it had taken for this understanding to take place. It was all faintly puzzling but, also, she didn't much care, felt no eagerness to know the answer. She watched her mother, with the definite air of the hostess, peel back the napkin from the sandwiches.

'The other day I told Barry how to brighten up a sandwich,' she said. 'He was ever so grateful. He said he would never have thought of cucumber and parsley on the side, what a difference they'd make.' She smiled, pleased with herself. The hat slipped down again. 'It's good to see you, Prue. I hope you're going to be all right. Barry said he'll take good care of you. You'll not want for money. You're a bright girl, can turn your hand to anything. I'm sure you'll find—'

'I'll be fine, Mum.'

Barry walked into the room. On seeing Prue he paused quickly to adjust his surprise to pleasure. 'I didn't know you'd be here, sweetheart.'

'I didn't know what time I'd—'

'I thought you'd be back later.'

'I was surprised, too, Barry, finding Prue here,' said her mother.

Barry went to his wife and kissed her on the cheek. Then the three of them sat in a triangle round the low table on which the tea tray glowed with its rose-strewn, gold-rimmed cups and the pile of imaginative sandwiches.

'Well, it's good you're here together,' said Barry, 'because now I can put to both of you the plan that's been going through my mind.' He turned to Prue. 'Your mother has told me the salon's not doing well and she's thinking of calling it a day. Well, it's to be expected. Not so many people after the war with money to spare on permanent waves.' Mrs Lumley nodded. She smiled at Barry, grateful for his understanding. 'So what I've been thinking is this, ladies. I'm in need of a new housekeeper.'

Mrs Lumley gave a small start which dislodged, her hat once more. She put out a hand to Prue, who held it.

'What about Bertha?' Prue asked.

'Ah, Bertha.' Barry put down his cup of tea, leant back in his chair. He felt in his inside pocket for his cigar case, and gave Prue a look. 'I think Bertha and I have come to the end of our run. She seems to have gone off the job, doesn't make much effort any more, though she's taken to brushing her hair. I've a feeling she's met someone, might want to be off to pastures new.' He laughed. 'Anyhow, I thought I'd put the idea to you, Elsie. If it appealed to you, I'd give Bertha her marching orders – see she was all right, of course.'

Mrs Lumley sighed audibly. She took her hand from Prue, leant over to pat one of Barry's knees. 'I don't think I've ever heard anything so kind, Barry,' she said. 'What do you think, Prue?'

'It's a wonderful idea, Mum.'

'I know you like cooking, I've enjoyed your cooking, you're a good cook,' said Barry. 'I'd be in clover and you'd have a decent job. You could stay in your house, come daily.' He paused. 'Or move in.'

'Oh, I'd keep my house for the time being. See how it all goes. Don't you think, Prue?'

'Whatever's best for you, Mum.'

'You could start in a couple of weeks, if that suits. Or whenever you've made arrangements about the salon.'

'If that suits,' mimicked Mrs Lumley, a trembling hand lifting her cup to her lips. 'Tell you what, Barry, it's the best news I've had in years.'

Barry stood up and went to the window to light his cigar. Prue sensed he wanted her mother to go now. Mrs Lumley herself received no such signals, but when Barry said he'd run her home, either in the Daimler or the Humber, whichever took her fancy, she stood up, smiles flickering to and fro across her face. She went up to her new employer, tapped him on the shoulder. 'Well, there'll be a choice of cars once I'm here, won't there?' she said, with a skittishness that made Prue blush. 'So what I'd really like to do today, maybe my last chance, is get my daughter to give me a ride in her Sunbeam . . .'

'You buzz along with her, then. I'll sit down and work out some kind of formal arrangement.' Barry dabbed at her arm, avoiding a fox leg.

'Oh, you're a marvellous man, Barry.' She made as if to kiss his cheek. Then, thinking better of it, she skipped away from him, child-like. Prue hadn't seen her mother so happy for years.

In the time she had lived at The Larches Prue had learnt to judge Bertha's mood from the food she produced. By some instinct the housekeeper knew what she liked, or didn't like, and frequently produced the things she most disliked. From time to time she served up dishes Barry disliked, too, as if challenging him to complain. He loathed the sliminess of tinned peaches and assured Bertha he was willing to pay anything for fresh ones from France – he knew how to get hold of them from some (probably dubious) source. Bertha ignored this repeated offer and continued her praise of peaches in a tin. The peach disputes were the only times that boss and housekeeper clashed in front of Prue, though often she heard raised voices coming from the kitchen.

That evening Bertha had left a plate of cold, mottled meats and baked potatoes. For pudding there was strawberry blancmange from a packet, a delicacy that Prue could scarcely swallow. This choice of menu was plainly the sort of welcome home Bertha felt her employer's wife deserved.

But the food was not important on this occasion: Prue was too intrigued by Barry's news.

'I'm extending into a new world at last, sweetheart,' he said. 'Cinemas.' He paused to take in her reaction.

'You mean you're going to have something to do with making films?' For a moment Prue saw a new chance on the horizon: film star. A Rank starlet, perhaps.

'Actual cinemas. I'm going to start buying them up – have a whole chain in a few year's time. I completed a deal on the first one a couple of days ago. Brighton – well, on the outskirts, overlooking the sea, a lovely site. Pretty run down, but that'll be seen to. What do you think of the idea?'

Prue, who could summon no thoughts about it at all, agreed it was good. Barry pushed away his scarcely touched blancmange, so Prue did the same.

'Be quite different when your mother's working here,' he said. 'Supper will be something to look forward to. Now, here's the next piece of news.' He took his cigar case from his pocket, chose one of the two cigars, ran through the whole rigmarole of pre-lighting preparations. 'Don't worry, sweetheart. I won't light up in here.'

'Oh, do if you want to.' End of the marriage: why should she care where he lit his cigar? With a grateful look, Barry struck a match and puffed away till at last a wisp of smoke brought him relief. But for the scrape of the match and the exertion of his breath, there was silence between them.

'Yes,' he said at last. 'So it happens this lovely old cinema has a little flat above it. One day the manager might like to be installed there. It's fully furnished – nothing very grand, but perfectly comfortable, all included in the purchase price. I was just wondering if it might be the answer to where you could go while you're . . . deciding what you want to do. Where you want to live.'

Prue looked at him but he did not meet her eye. The fingers of his free hand were doing a five-finger exercise on the table. 'Well,' said Prue, 'yes. It might be just the thing, mightn't it? Flat by the sea, and I can't swim. Don't know a soul on the south coast. It might be just the thing.'

'I'm only suggesting temporary,' said Barry. 'You could try it. If it didn't work out you'd only have to wave the flag and I'd send a driver with the Daimler for you.'

'I'm sure you would,' said Prue.

'And another thing. I know you don't want to hang around here much longer, now we've come to our agreement. And I'm sure going back to your mother wouldn't work. So I thought, well, sweetheart, you could move in soon as you like. I'd make all the arrangements for you.'

Prue looked down, swallowed. The whole idea was so preposterous she could think of no words with which to respond. Finally she said: 'I'm going to stay with Stella and Philip next week.'

'So you are!' By now Barry's head was in a swirl of smoke. He batted it away, but his expression was still hard to decipher. 'You could make arrangements, then, as soon as you get back.'

Prue gave an unplanned nod of acquiescence. It was suddenly clear that Barry wanted to be rid of her as soon as possible. Considering that her desire to end the marriage was strong as his, Prue was puzzled why his suggestion for her imminent departure was unsettling. She had imagined she could take her time. Stay at The Larches while she looked around for somewhere to live – where to begin, she had no idea. But, she told herself, in so many ways Barry had been good to her: it was only fair not to make a fuss when he had so quickly found her somewhere to go. She stood up, went to the door. 'OK,' she said. 'I'll go to Brighton. Try it out.'

'If it doesn't work, sweetheart, you can always . . . I mean, I'll always provide a roof over your head.'

'Thanks.' She turned the door handle.

'Just one more thing. When you were away your friend Johnny rang a couple of times. He wanted you to get in touch soon as possible.' He looked at his watch. 'Why don't you ring him now? See what he wants.'

Prue went into the hall, sat on the dark oak chair by the dark oak table, picked up the receiver and asked for Johnny's number. On hearing her voice, he sounded cheerful, as he used to before the incident in the barn had put constraint between them.

'I've news for you,' he said, 'but it'll keep till we meet.'

'That's good,' said Prue. 'I've had enough news for one night. My head's spinning. So: I hope your news is good.'

'It could be,' said Johnny.

They ate cottage pie made from tinned mince and reconstituted potato at a pub in Bakewell.

'When you think,' said Prue, 'how many potatoes I dug up . . . There must still be some. Why give us this muck?'

'Easier,' said Johnny. 'There are still lots of places where the scrambled egg is powdered. Probably will be for years. Last time I came here, with my father – well, I suppose it was a year or two before the war – the food was wonderful. Sorry about the decline.'

The poor quality of the food did not stop them having a merry lunch. Prue, with a lightness of touch she liked to employ for serious matters, told Johnny a little about the decision to end the marriage, and Barry's suggestion she should move to a flat in Brighton. Johnny grimaced, but made no comment other than to say he was sorry. Then, over blood-red jelly topped with imitation cream, which made them both laugh, Johnny broke the news to Prue that he, too, was soon to leave Manchester. It seemed he had a childless uncle who lived in a cottage in Wiltshire and was emigrating to Australia. He had offered to let Johnny have the cottage for a peppercorn rent on the condition he kept it and the garden in good order. There was a large shed in the garden where, Johnny said, he could set up a proper carpentry business, take on an apprentice. His idea was to make furniture from local wood, particularly elm, which he loved best of all woods.

'That all sounds pretty good,' said Prue. 'But what about the poetry?'

'A poet has to live. I'll keep writing. There'll be plenty of room for the chickens. I'll sell the eggs.'

'When will you move?'

'Soon as Barry can get a new tenant for my flat.'

'And is this cottage far from Brighton?'

'Yes. Miles. But you can have my number if there's a telephone. You'd be welcome any time.' He poured pale coffee from a pot into their two cups. 'As a matter of fact, it had occurred to me that . . . the cottage might be a solution for you.'

'How do you mean?'

'I mean, we could live there together.'

'What – as—'

'As friends. Platonic friends.'

'I see. Can platonic friends live under one roof?'

'I believe they can. Men don't only want sex, you know.'

'Most of the ones I've met did. It's a kind thought, but it could be difficult. I mean, the woman of your dreams might turn up to order a table or something, and then you'd have to chuck me out.'

Johnny gave a wry smile. 'Doubt it,' he said.

'I've said I'll try out the Brighton flat. Might as well. I've nowhere else to go. I hate the sea, what I've seen of it, but I dare say there'll be pubs nearby. Maybe I'll run into some friendly young things, find some boring job, make a life.'

Johnny asked for the bill, spent a long time counting out coins. His face had closed again. 'Chickens'll have to do better,' he said, with a wry smile. Prue considered taking the bill from him, but resisted. Johnny would be affronted. He stood up, left sixpence on the table and went to the bar to pay. 'The offer will always stand,' he said. 'Now I'm going to take you up into the Dales. We'll go for a walk.'

'And I've got a story to tell you,' said Prue. 'Staying with Ag, I met this vicar. But wait till we're walking.'

The story lasted all the way up a steep, wooded rise. At the top they sat on a bench and looked down over a soft, open landscape. Groups of Derbyshire's grand trees flared on the horizon. Others gathered, less darkly, nearby. Johnny began to laugh.

'What's so funny?' Prue asked.

'You're incorrigible. I feel for that poor vicar.'

'He'll survive. He's got God to talk to.'

'I sometimes think you've no idea what you're capable of doing to men. Your stories – you slay them. But you don't finally want them.'

'No. Not yet. Not till I find the right one. Then I'll be the best wife.'

Johnny folded his arms, stared ahead. 'I would have done anything to see his face when you accused him in your unGod-like language.'

Prue, encouraged by Johnny's appreciation of her story, added some details about the Incident of the Spurning of the Man of God, as she called it. Some of these suddenly remembered details were not entirely accurate but kept them laughing all the way back down a track through the woods to the car.

When Prue left for her visit to Stella and Philip in Norfolk she drove very slowly to save petrol. She chose cross-country roads and stopped every now and then to consult her map and select a diversion that looked interesting. Late morning she parked in a field to eat a sandwich she had made for herself, and drink a flask of tea. As she drew nearer to the east coast she marvelled at the swelling of the sky: the vast arc of thin blue, darned with cloud, that exercised her eyes, stretching them as she could never before remember such stretching, such filling of vision.

It was early spring: the hedges were just beginning to turn – strange hedges in East Anglia, she thought: there was a clump of hawthorn, then a gap, another clump, another gap. From afar they looked like loosely strung necklaces. The huge fields reminded her that this had been arable country before the war. There were no cows, but patches of just visible green crops, a thin fuzz scattered over dark earth.

Prue paused for a moment at the top of a hill – cripes, a steep one at that, she'd thought Norfolk was meant to be flat – for her first sight of the sea. It was a silver thread tacked to the hem of the sky, whose misted blue gave Prue a moment of regret: if she had found that colour when she was looking for her Buckingham Palace dress, she would have thought it even more appealing than the bluebell blue she had chosen.

A church spire rose from the flat land at the bottom of the hill. There was a gathering of red-brick cottages, thick trees. Beyond them, marshes stretched towards dunes. Beneath the vast sky, in which clouds scarcely bothered to move across the blue, everything in the landscape looked small enough to gather up in your hand and throw into a basket.

Prue followed Stella's written instructions through the village and down a wooded track. She came to a bungalow of no great beauty, but it faced the marsh, the dunes, the distant sea and the overwhelming sky. She got out of the car, leant against it, saw and heard a skylark high above her. A feeling of utter safety warmed her: for a week or so she would have to make no decisions, no plans. She could just be here quietly with Stella, and get to know Philip.

But the peace she had imagined would greet her was not altogether forthcoming. She saw Stella at the door, arms folded under her breasts, smiling – not quite the old smile, a pinch of anxiety at its corners. They hugged, went inside.

Stella's kitchen had less of Mrs Lawrence's influence than Ag's: there was a feeling that not much effort to make it welcoming had gone into it – but then Stella was so constantly busy looking after her husband that anything beyond that priority was probably neglected. There were two big wooden armchairs at the table in the large window, a jug of sea gorse on the table.

'That view,' Prue said.

'Aren't we lucky?' Stella took coffee from the stove, carried it to the table. 'It never stales. Every morning when I come in here and look out, no matter what the weather, I think how lucky we are.'

Stella, Stella, beautiful Stella . . . what has happened to you? wondered Prue. Even since Mrs Lawrence's funeral, there had been a change. There were shadows under her cheekbones, shadows under her eyes. Her thick hair had lost its shine. Her hands seemed to have aged: there were small blue dips between the knuckles. Her shirt was not ironed – and Stella had always been first into the laundry room at Hallows Farm, usually to press not only her own things but the others' as well.

'Philip will be here in a moment,' she said, glancing at the clock. 'It's a long process, his getting up every morning. Still, we've got a pretty good routine.' She smiled. 'It's just a matter of patience and organization. Though he hasn't been too well lately, which has meant . . .'

Prue guessed at troubled nights, hence Stella's look of exhaustion. 'Can't you get any help?' she asked.

'Oh, we can. A bit. But Philip, poor love, isn't easy. Really he only likes me to look after him. Though he didn't complain when I left for the funeral, which was nice of him. But what about you? I want to hear about this vicar you mentioned.'

Before Prue could begin her story Philip, in a cumbersome wheelchair, came into the room. He, too, was pale, but smiling: Prue remembered his blunt good looks, the kind of face that is at its best under the peaked cap of some uniform, as it had been in the photograph by her bed in the attic that Stella used to kiss every night. He edged himself close to the table. Prue got up and went to kiss him on the cheek.

'So, so glad you're here,' he said. 'Stella's been talking of nothing else for days. Afraid we haven't laid on any parties for you – we lead a pretty quiet life – but you and Stella will be able to go for walks, see the seals, catch up a bit.'

'Perfect,' said Prue. 'That's all I want.' She noticed that when he picked up the mug of coffee Stella had put before him, his hand was shaking, as was his lower lip. With his free hand he supported the one that was taking the weight of the mug.

In Devon Prue had been instantly aware of the deep affection between Ag and Desmond, and was lulled by the slow pace of their contentment. Here, in the Norfolk bungalow, she quickly sensed an air of anxiety between the couple. Stella's eyes constantly flicked towards Philip, alert to any sign that he might need something. He smiled a lot in her direction, occasionally moved to pat her hand.

'She's a saint, my wife,' he said quietly, when Stella had moved away to grill kippers. 'Don't know what I . . . I'm the luckiest . . .' He cleared his throat. 'As for this place, don't know how much longer I've got, but whatever it is, I said to Stella, it must be by the sea. Inland, I'd frizzle up and die very quickly. I think Stella loves it here, too – don't you, darling?'

'I do.' Stella returned to the table, arranged knives and forks. And over lunch – Mrs Lawrence's homemade bread (Stella had practised her recipe) with the kippers – Prue told the vicar story with such relish and liveliness that her hosts laughed throughout. The atmosphere lightened. When they had finished Philip said he was going to have a rest. 'Every afternoon, I'm afraid. I rest every day. What from? I ask myself. Life's one bloody long rest.' His arms jerking sharply on the wheels of his chair, he went skilfully out of the narrow doorway.

'In fact,' said Stella, when he had gone, 'he's decided to write about his childhood and his war. Doubt he'll get it published, but it'll give him an aim, a discipline.'

'Just what we all need,' said Prue. 'And where's James? I'm longing to see him.'

'Gone to his grandmother in Cromer. He loves it there and I'm afraid . . . we only have the two bedrooms. You'll be in his, if that's OK.'

'Of course.' Prue smiled, looked out of the window again.

'I'm sorry he's not here. I would have loved you to see him. He cheers Philip up enormously. He sits on his knee and gets read to for hours.'

'And Philip still has no idea?'

'Not a clue. I'm sure of that. And he never will know.'

'And Joe?'

'Joe said it was the price we had to pay, but my having his child is some compensation for having to lead our lives apart. At the funeral I managed to show him a small snapshot. Perhaps I shouldn't have done that. He went a deadly white. He said, "Stella – oh, God, Stella, why did it have to be like this?"' She shrugged. 'We both knew why it had to be like this, but I know neither of us regrets James and one day we'll tell him about his real father. Not possible to do that now. It would kill Philip to think James wasn't his son. He's a marvellous father . . .'

Prue told Stella about the birth of her own son. Stella, horrified by the pigs' terrifying aggression, suggested the whole thing had been traumatizing.

'It wasn't, really,' said Prue. 'I know that sounds odd but I felt it was more a waste of time than a devastating event. By the time I became pregnant I knew the so-called marriage was on the rocks, and my ambition to have a baby by a man I love was not to be. So I was really surprised when the disaster had very little effect on me.'

'And Barry?'

'Barry was broken-hearted. The baby's death was the moment he realized, I think, that there was no use struggling on. He would have loved a son. I sometimes think what life might have been like, in the claustrophobia of The Larches, confined by looking after a baby, Barry endlessly telling me how it ought to be done . . .' Prue paused. 'Besides, as the child grew up he might have noticed his son hadn't inherited anything of his dark looks.'

'You mean . . .'

'I'm not absolutely sure.'

'Oh Prue, what have you been up to? What muddles we get into when timing goes awry.'

'We do. But there's no point not hoping.'

They walked along a dyke that curved round fields on one side, marshland on the other. At some point the marsh melded with the waters of the staithe, where small boats quivered, their sails down. The distant sea seemed never to get any nearer. The horizon played its usual trick of dallying with the water so that it was unclear where one ended and the other began. The sky, here the colour of sea gorse, was disturbed every now and then by flighting geese. But there were no raucous calls of gulls, just an arched canopy of silence.

'I didn't know Norfolk at all,' said Stella, 'but I do love it here. It must be one of the quietest places in England. I love the fact that the villagers have lived here for generations and the shop, where there's always a run on Oxo cubes, probably hasn't changed for fifty years. Even in the summer there are few people on the beach. Visitors go to Cromer, where there are ice creams and amusement arcades. We're lucky to be here now. One day it'll all be discovered, changed, overrun. I don't like to imagine it.'

'But don't you sometimes long for a bit of fun?' Prue asked. 'You can't live for ever on scenery.'

'Philip's a whole-time job. He does his best, but there's so much he can't do himself. And the "scenery", as you call it, makes up for everything. I go for a walk every day on my own. I could never miss that, though I always wonder if I'm going to return to some disaster.'

'Has Joe ever been here?'

'Not as far as I know. I can't think of anything I'd love more than for him to come. But after our French trip, when I came back to Philip and he to Janet, we've never been in touch. We can't be. It wouldn't be fair. The only time I've seen him was at Mrs Lawrence's funeral, and the shock of that – the shock of realizing nothing had changed – is still with me. In a silly way I still hope that one day . . . Well, what can I hope for? Janet's still young and healthy and they'll have more children. As for Philip . . . I can't ever leave him. I can't wish him dead. I do love him in a way that you can love a good man, and yet not . . . When we left Hallows Farm and I told him I was off to France for a week with Joe, he was magnanimous. I didn't ask him. I told him. "A week of your life with the man you love isn't much," he said. "You go and enjoy yourselves. I'll never be able to give you that." What it cost him, I'll never know. Neither of us has ever mentioned it since. He didn't even ask if Joe had been at the funeral when I got back from Yorkshire. I don't think he can bear to mention his name.'

'What about Janet? How did she take your week away?'

'She was pretty hysterical, Mrs Lawrence said. But Joe gave her no choice. I think she thought that if she didn't agree to the plan he might never marry her. But of course once they were married Joe, being the honourable man he is, behaved – still does behave, I imagine – like a good husband. Though you only have to see him, as we did in Yorkshire, to know that—'

'Quite,' said Prue.

Stella shrugged, her eyes full of sky and tears, and they turned back.

When they arrived at the bungalow they found Philip looking pleased with himself. He had laid the table for tea, a job, Prue realized, that would have cost him many journeys of twisting and turning round the kitchen in his chair as he fetched plates and jams and everything needed for proper tea. On the table beside him he had the local paper, and was studying a notice he had marked with a red pencil.

'Found something that may be of interest here,' he said. 'We're very quiet in Norfolk, but sometimes we burst into parties. It's not going to be as dull as you thought, Prue.' He smiled at her.

'Don't be silly. I never thought it would be dull – how could it be with you and Stella? I've been longing for it.'

'Well, anyway, tomorrow night there's a dance at the air base. Big band. Beer. Sausage rolls and so on. How about that?'

Almost imperceptibly, as she poured the tea, Stella brightened. 'If Prue wants to go,' she said, 'I'm game.'

'Course I want to go, if it's OK with you.' Prue's least exciting clothes, which she had brought thinking them suitable for Norfolk, were reeling through her mind. Perhaps her red daisies might do—

'And actually,' said Philip, 'you'll be surprised to hear I'm coming too. Used to love dancing, didn't I, Stella?' He turned to Prue. 'Oh yes, Stella and I used to dance.' He swivelled his head to his wife. 'Didn't we, darling?'

'We did,' said Stella. 'We did. Philip was a good dancer.'

The next day it rained. Rather than join Stella on her daily walk, Prue stayed in her bedroom, rummaging through half a dozen dresses, pairs of shoes and most of her hair bows. She sat on the bed surrounded by stuffed animals belonging to James. A wire mobile hung with shells, made by Philip, swung from the ceiling: when the wind rattled the windows the shells made an empty, chinking sound, less musical than bells. Prue smiled. She was in a state of excited hope: surely among a whole camp of American servicemen there would be one . . . A single possibility was all she asked. An evening of fun. Something she hadn't had for a long time.

That evening they gathered in the kitchen, the three of them, united in their expectations. Though what could Philip hope for? Prue wondered. He wore a beautiful silk scarf in the open neck of his shirt, and had Brylcreemed his hair so that it was a flat and shining helmet. Stella was transformed, almost the Stella of Joe days at Hallows Farm. She had disguised the patches under her eyes with swipes of Max Factor foundation, and resuscitated her beautiful mouth with a deep red lipstick. Her hair, loosened from its band, swung about her shoulders. She was almost exactly as the picture Prue would always hold in her mind. The thought of such a creature stuck here for years and years, with a man who couldn't dance, brought tears to her eyes. Then when she remembered the amount of mascara she had applied, they vanished.

They went out into the wind and rain to the car, floral skirts whipping about the skinniness of their thighs, hair everywhere. Prue offered to help, but her help was not needed. Getting into the car was a routine Philip and Stella had perfected. Prue marvelled at Stella's patience as she lifted each of Philip's feet into the footwell. It was all so slow. Prue herself couldn't imagine putting up with such slowness for a single day. Observing the laborious process, even this one time, fired her impatience. She was both ashamed of herself and longing to be off. Stella, she thought, was a saint.

As they entered the large hall where the dance was to be held it occurred to Prue that the organizers of all such gatherings, wherever they took place, had the same idea about decorating, and what food to provide: for this East Anglian hall was almost identical to the one where Stella had danced with the wing commander so brilliantly that everyone else had stood back to watch – and where Prue had overdone the gin and lime and could scarcely stand upright for the national anthem. She looked round, smiling, past and present clashing and swerving in her mind. The same paper chains were pinned to the curtains, a sprinkling of tinsel randomly scattered among them. The old blackout stuff had not been taken down but enlivened with a few cotton-wool snowflakes. 'Very early winter, here,' she whispered to Stella who, with blazing eyes, laughed. They both remembered. God, how they remembered.

Stella pushed Philip's wheelchair through the crowds, who parted as they advanced, towards an empty table near the stage. On one side of the hall there was a long table rich in post-war party food, which seemed not to have improved a jot in the last four years: more bridge rolls, more jellies scattered with silver balls, plates of Spam arranged on dying lettuce leaves, a few shavings of gherkin to add interest.

'Blimey,' said Prue. 'Nothing's changed.' Then she looked down on Philip's shining head and remembered how wrong she was.

They sat at the free table near the stage. A quartet of musicians were rumbling through hits of the day without much energy, but rows of metal chairs behind them promised that the big band would appear later. Philip offered to go to the bar for drinks.

'I'll go,' said Prue at once.

'No, no. Let me.' Philip quickly swivelled his chair away from the table.

'Let him,' said Stella.

'Gin and lime, is it, Prue?'

'No thanks. Just a lager.' Tonight she wanted to keep her head.

The thump of the music so close to them meant that Stella and Prue saw little point in trying to talk. In any case Prue had no interest in conversation. She wanted to see what was on offer.

A large crowd of tall American pilots was gathered at the far end of the hall by the bar. Some of them gently punched each other. There was much laughter. They, too, seemed bent on finding out what the evening might hold.

Prue was glad to see that among the girls there wasn't much serious competition. Many of them, corralled into giggling groups, had not benefited from mothers who had Mrs Lumley's skill with her needle and bits of pre-war material. There was a single blonde in a dress of orange poppies – brighter than all the rest, but not a dress you could admire. The rest were a dowdy lot who had concentrated on the lipstick and overdone the permanent waves. Prue flicked at the skirt of her expensive daisy dress, pushed the short sleeves higher, and tugged at the sweetheart neck to lower it enough to expose her shallow cleavage.

Stella was amused. 'Don't worry, you're the star. They'll be fighting for you.'

Prue shook her head, blushed. Not at Stella's words but because she was aware that every pilot in the distant crowd had turned with one accord and was staring across the hall at her and Stella. She slipped off her wedding ring, handed it across the table. 'Keep this for me,' she said.

Philip returned to the table. The drinks had been put on a tray, which was balanced across the arms of the wheelchair.

'Well done, and thanks,' said Prue, with the kind of exuberance that comes from knowing that something exciting might be about to happen.

'I can still be useful on occasion,' said Philip, with a twist of his mouth.

The music above them plodded on. The three of them drank, looking about but not talking. Eventually the weary trio wandered off, instruments slack in their hands. Then, with a great surge of energy, a group of some twenty musicians hurried onto the stage and took their places on the chairs. Prue's heart pounded as she made a plan. She saw a few of the pilots take a step or two forward, as if to cross the vast floor and approach their table, but then think better of it and step back to much jeering. She smiled, glanced up at the stage. Several of the musicians were worth a second look, too. Then, they were off. With an uproarious boom they launched into 'In The Mood'. Prue could contain herself no longer. She stood up. Stella and Philip laughed at her. Philip reached for one of Stella's hands.

With a toss of her head Prue spraunced off towards the group of cowardly servicemen, hips flicking so that the daisy hem of her dress flirted round her knees. As she got nearer, aware that every single one of them was watching her progress, she tried to distinguish between the mass of smiling, mostly handsome faces. Then she was among them.

'Hiya, doll,' said one, and touched her arm. 'Shall we dance?'

Prue took in a narrow face and narrow shoulders, as a pilot edged towards her with a narrow smile. Then, too quickly for her to be sure what had happened, a very tall man stepped forward, put a hand round her waist, and she found they moved to the dance-floor. The music seemed to come both up from the floor and down from the ceiling – pounding, enveloping, demanding.

Prue, flung about by her tall partner, was just aware of stares from the other girls, and the general move forward by the rest of the Americans as they chose partners and moved onto the floor. In a moment it was crowded with dancers. Stella and Philip, at their table, hands still clasped, watched.

When the music came to an end, Prue and her partner were hemmed in by dancers in the middle of the floor. Prue was panting. Her breasts rose quickly up and down. Her partner was looking down at her, solemn-faced. 'Why, thank you, ma'am,' he said. He gave a small bow. 'If there's just time to introduce ourselves – I'm Rudolph. Rudolph Vincent Basie Junior.'

'I'm Prue.'

'I guess that must be Prudence – my grandmother's name.'

The music started again, a jitterbug. Rudolph Vincent Basie Junior did not bother to ask Prue for this dance: with a smile of the whitest teeth she had ever seen, he simply took hold of her and they jitterbugged as if they'd been partners for life, continued for three more dances, never speaking.

Finally, when the band paused for a drink, Rudolph moved his hand to Prue's waist and guided her to the bar. He bought two glasses of lager. 'Not much place to sit down,' he said.

'My friend Stella and her husband are at a table by the stage. We could go and join them.' An idea came to her. Although she had known Rudolph for less than an hour, she felt she could put it to him. 'My friend Stella,' she said, 'is a marvellous dancer. Once at a party we went to she was picked up by a very small wing commander, a professional dancer, and they gave such a great show that all the other dancers came off the floor. But her husband was wounded in the Navy. Wheelchair for life. I was wondering . . . I know how much she'd love . . .' Rudolph nodded. He understood at once.

They made their way to the table. The music started before they sat down. Prue quickly introduced Rudolph and immediately he turned to Stella. 'I hear you're something of a dancer,' he said. 'Would you care to have a go at this one with me? I'd be honoured.'

Stella glanced at Philip.

'Go on, darling,' he said. Stella pushed back her hair, stood very upright facing Rudolph. Her beauty, returned tonight in abundance, caused a lurch in Prue's heart. As she watched them push their way into the crowd and begin to dance, conflicting sensations gripped her.

'It's going to happen again,' said Philip, with a wry smile. 'Just look.'

'You're right,' agreed Prue. Already dancers near to them were turning their heads, moving back to leave more space. Others followed their example. Soon there were only three couples left, then none but Rudolph and Stella.

Prue's eyes never left them. She was thrilled by Stella's obvious excitement at this public display of sensational dancing, but she also would have liked it to be her and Rudolph who won the acclaim. When she glanced briefly away from the whirling couple, she saw Philip's downturned mouth. A muscle flicked in his cheek

– though when he saw Prue's face he smiled. She could not bear the melancholy in his eyes, the knowing what he must be feeling.

The band was enjoying the solo as much as the dancers. They played on for a long time. When finally they stopped everyone applauded. Prue stood up – secretly, meanly, glad the exhibition had come to an end. She climbed onto the table and clapped harder than anyone. For a moment, as Rudolph led Stella back, she was on a level with him, which made him smile his white smile again.

'You were marvellous, darling,' said Philip at once to Stella. 'Haven't lost your touch.'

Stella's breasts were heaving, her cheeks were scarlet. She sat down, took Philip's hand again.

'Thank you, ma'am,' Rudolph said to her. 'That was wonderful. A great pleasure. There's not many who can dance like you.'

The band now slid into a slow number. Rudolph looked at Prue swinging her hips on the table. He put out both hands, lifted her down and guided her back onto the floor. Prue was aware of people glancing at her, perhaps wondering if she was going to put on a show like Stella's. But she and Rudolph moved very slowly – hardly moved at all.

'I'm in the mood for love', was playing. It was the kind of tune that gave hope to so many strangers. Prue could feel Rudolph's large hand covering most of her back. She leant against his chest, shut her eyes. His chin rested lightly on her head. Unless something went dreadfully wrong in the next few hours, she had found her man.

Nothing did go wrong. They danced, danced, almost without stopping. Sometimes they jitterbugged, flinging about, parting, meeting. Sometimes they were so close Prue could feel the drumming of Rudolph's heart.

Then it was 'God Save the King'. Rudolph stood very straight, eyes ahead, solemn with duty, a ramrod in his spine. Prue tried to imitate his stance, but kept glancing at him to check he did not move until the last chord had died.

People began to leave very quickly. Rudolph took Prue's hand, led her towards Stella and Philip's table. At the sight of them Philip, previously tired, bored, suddenly revived. Rudolph sat down beside him.

'You're not by any chance a chess player?' Philip asked. 'I don't seem able to find one anywhere along the coast.'

'Well now, there's a thing.' Rudolph smiled. 'I've been chess-starved, too.'

'Come over tomorrow, please do,' Philip said.

'Sure will.' Rudolph shook Philip's hand. It was a deal. Stella stood up and moved to push the wheelchair. She, too, her few moments of exhilaration over, looked tired. Rudolph took the handles from her. 'Let me,' he said. 'My grandfather's been in a wheelchair for years. I'm a pretty good navigator.'

Prue and Stella watched as he sped across the emptying hall, effortlessly avoiding empty chairs and tables.

'The sort of occasion,' said Prue, 'when I suppose you could believe in God. He must have been looking down and put the idea of chess into Philip's mind and it so happened—'

'Or you could call it happy coincidence,' said Stella.

'Anyway, it's the solution. I was wondering what was going to happen next. Time's against us. But now at least Rudolph and I will meet again in your kitchen.'

'And you can stay as long as you like. We love having you. I must go and get the car.'

While Stella was lifting Philip into the passenger seat, Prue and Rudolph stood looking on, a foot apart, light from a full moon scattered over them.

'Blimey,' said Prue, with a small shudder. Rudolph turned to her and smiled a half-moon of electric white against the dark. Then he went to help Stella put the wheelchair into the boot of the car.

From her place in the back seat Prue waved to him as they drove away. He had given no sign of wanting to give her a polite kiss on the cheek. But that was OK for a while, she thought. She would try not to be in a hurry. Best not to appear too eager, as her mother often said, though she did not often take her own advice.

'There's a gentleman if ever there was one,' said Philip.

Prue was about to agree when Stella, in her heart-wrenching voice, began to sing 'They Can't Black Out The Moon'. It was the song – as Prue knew, but Philip did not – that she had sung on the night in the pub when Joe had fallen in love with her.

# Chapter 10

Prue could not sleep. Her restless limbs seemed to be filled with shards – shards of wonder, she supposed them to be. She thought back to when she had met Barry One. The sensations were similar, but not exactly the same. Whatever this was, it was stronger. She had a feeling it might be something to do with conviction: Rudolph Vincent Basie Junior might be the right man at last.

Was there any way she could be sure? All they had done was dance for three hours, scarcely speaking. But it had seemed to Prue that the quality of their closeness was extraordinary. She now knew what people meant when they said they had met someone, very briefly, whom they felt they had known all their life. Words were unnecessary: communication was through magic waves. All the same, thought Prue, it would be nice to talk to Rudolph soon. But when? No plans had been made beyond a promise of a game of chess with Philip. She tossed about in the narrow bed, horribly awake, goaded by speculation.

At five o'clock it was almost light. From James's narrow bed Prue could now clearly distinguish the toys on the high shelf on the opposite wall. There were several wooden trains, a windmill, a whole menagerie of stuffed animals. A monkey with a leering smile looked down on her, scoffing at her foolish thoughts. She shut her eyes, longing for it to be time to get up.

Prue was already in the kitchen when Stella and Philip appeared, apologizing for their lateness.

'We're not used to such giddy hours,' said Philip, 'and we had your young pilot on the telephone at eight, ringing before he went on duty. Plan is, he's coming round for tea.'

The agonized worries of Prue's night fell away. The wonder remained.

After lunch she went for a walk along the marsh path: anything to hurry the hours till tea. A strong breeze bent the reeds and made a rush-hour of clouds in the sky: normally they would have filled her with delight, but they scarcely registered. In her mind she was still dancing, Rudolph's huge warm hand on her waist.

When she arrived back at the bungalow an official military car stood in the driveway. Rudolph was at the kitchen table absorbed in a game of chess with Philip. He barely glanced up when she came in. 'Hi, Prudence,' he said. 'I got off an hour early.'

'Hi.' Prue, never normally afflicted by shyness, felt a sudden longing to be invisible. She realized that Rudolph would not notice if she disappeared to check her appearance and choose a brighter bow, so she slipped off to her bedroom. Her hand shook so hard as she put on her mascara that she made a sooty mess of her cheeks and had to start again several times. When she returned half an hour later the game was still in progress. Stella was turning out scones from a tin. She smiled at Prue and asked her to find the strawberry jam. In a daze that rendered her completely inefficient, Prue began opening cupboards and searching among the jars with unseeing eyes.

Stella laughed. 'You,' she said quietly.

The game went on all through tea and continued as the light began to fade. When eventually it came to an end Philip, a touch reluctantly, observed that Rudolph was a skilled player. 'And an interesting challenge,' he added.

'Haven't had so much fun for a long time,' said Rudolph. Neither Prue nor Stella knew who had won. They didn't understand chess, and neither enquired. 'Hope we can do it again.'

'Come over as often as you like, any time,' said Philip.

'Why don't you stay for supper?' Stella was at the stove, throwing bay leaves into a stew. 'I mean, it's almost time . . .'

'Why, a great pleasure that would be, ma'am.' Rudolph stood up and directed one of his minor bows in Stella's direction. Then, at last, he looked at Prue. 'Should you and I take a breath of fresh air, walk a while? I don't know this part of the coast. You could show me the beach.' He gave her one of his astonishing white smiles.

'Love to,' said Prue, in a minuscule voice. 'Is that OK, Stella?'

'Of course. Go on.'

'I'll help when I get back.' Looking at Rudolph, magnificent in his uniform, Prue felt herself stumble as she moved to the door.

They walked down the marsh road to the beach, then turned up onto the dunes. By now the sky was the thundery purple that comes in early spring before complete dark. The moon was a small curve, pith white.

'Cripes,' said Prue at last. She had thought of no words to break the silence between them on the road. 'Looks like we've got lucky. Moon, no rain, no wind, sound of the sea. Wow.'

Rudolph laughed. He took her a hand and pulled her up through the marram grass. At the top of the dunes they found a shallow nest of soft sand, still just warm from the day's sun, and sat down. Behind them the marsh was a stretch of muddy dykes: the reeds bowed towards a gathering of distant dormant sailing boats that awaited the incoming tide. Ahead, the beach was deserted. Light from the moon was a pale imprint on the sea.

Rudolph pointed to an angular structure that rose above the water some way out. 'Looks like a wreck,' he said.

'It is a wreck. Stella told me it was used for target practice in the war.'

'Right.' Rudolph's interest in the wreck was quickly spent. He put an arm round Prue's shoulders. She was shivering. He kissed her.

If kisses were yards of fabric, she told Stella later, it would have been velvet. She had never been kissed so velvetly. Then he had pulled back, though his arm remained round her shoulders. 'I'm not a man for hurrying things in the normal way,' he said, after a pause into which Prue fitted a dozen guesses as to what he was going to say, 'but I get the feeling time's against us. I've a few day's leave. Perhaps we could get together a little. Go places. How would that be?'

Prue was enchanted by his accent, the softness of his voice, the way he made each word linger. She asked where he came from in the States.

'Savannah, Georgia. Few miles north. My folks have a farm there. That is, my dad. My mom died last year.' He shifted his position, stroked Prue's neck with a finger. 'You know something? There's an eighteen-mile avenue of azaleas leads into Savannah. What I wouldn't do to show you that when they're all out. Dazzle the eyes, they do.'

Prue giggled. She had never seen an azalea so was not able to imagine the avenue. She wanted to return to kissing. 'It's good you've got some leave,' she said. 'Let's do things, yes. I'm here for as long as I like.'

'Sure will.' Rudolph kissed her again, less velvetly, rougher. Then once more he pulled back, surprising Prue. She had thought he felt as if he wanted to carry on for ever, as she did. 'Pity the stars are missing tonight,' he said. 'I think we should wait for stars.'

'Oh, I don't know.' Prue was feeling cold. She shivered again. 'Are stars that important?'

'They are to me. They remind me I'm no more than a grain of sand and won't be here long.' He gave Prue a hand. 'I think we should be getting back, help your friend Stella with the supper.' Prue considered saying that Stella had no need of any help, but decided against it. She was aware of a slight dip in her expectations: a jab of impatience. Why wait? If time was against them, if they were the grains of sand he liked to imagine, soon to be swept away by some tide – Prue felt pleased she could carry on thinking in his funny way – then all the more reason to waste not a moment.

On the way back she put her arm through Rudolph's. He began to describe his English teacher at high school, a man who was determined that his pupils should acquire rich vocabularies. 'So each vacation he would give us a list of words, some unusual, which we had to learn and try to use when appropriate. When I left school I often got ribbed for my use of words, but I didn't care. I was glad of them.' He laughed. 'One of the first ones I learnt came back to me tonight: "deliquescent".'

'What on earth does that mean?' In truth Prue didn't care. She wasn't under the moon for an English lesson. But when Rudolph stopped and bent to kiss her again, she forgave him.

'It means turning to liquid, melting. It's how you can sometimes feel. How someone can make you feel. I felt you were melting in the dunes. I know I was. You could say we were both kinda melting . . .' He removed her arm from his, took her hand, laughed a little. 'I think maybe we still are. And you know what? Though perhaps I shouldn't tell you this, when I looked across that hall last night and I saw you . . . well, my heart stopped. Every cliché hit me right here in the solar plexus. I just didn't know what to do, how to play it.'

'You did all right,' said Prue. Her spirits had risen again. They found themselves walking more slowly, not wanting to arrive.

'You're the most ravishing creature I ever . . . God knows what you could do to a man.'

Rudolph had spoken so quietly that Prue could hardly hear him. They reached the back door of the bungalow. She giggled. 'Well I don't ever seem to get it right,' she said. 'There've been disasters, disappointments, dashed hopes, all that sort of thing. Doesn't seem easy just to find a good man, love him and be loved back. But I shan't give up trying.'

They kissed once more, then pulled apart, slow and reluctant as tangled netting. Prue knew that Stella would understand, from one glance at her burning cheeks, the nature of the walk to the beach. She didn't care. She had her man now, didn't she? If she played her cards right, maybe he would ask her to go back to America with him. They could drive along the azalea avenue, if that was what Rudolph wanted, though for her that would not be a top priority. Rudolph went to his car to fetch a bottle of wine.

At supper Stella broke the news that James was returning tomorrow. He'd had enough of his Cromer grandparents and wanted to come home.

'That doesn't mean you have to go, of course,' said Stella to Prue, 'so long as you don't mind sleeping on the sofa. James is a bit small for that.'

'Of course not. The sofa's fine. I'm so glad he's coming back. I'm longing to see him.' She looked at Rudolph.

'I think maybe I have a solution,' he said unexpectedly. 'I've a few days' leave and I'd like to take Prue to . . . I don't know. We could explore a bit. Find some small hotels, grilled fish, take a boat out to the seals . . .' His voice petered out, uncertain. There was a long silence.

Then Stella said, not looking at Prue, 'I think that's a lovely idea.'

'Same here,' said Philip, firmly, 'so long as you promise me a return match, Rudolph, when you come back.'

'Sure,' said Rudolph. 'I look forward to that.'

Prue slept deeply that night. She dreamt she and Rudolph were dancing on a deserted beach. They had an audience of seals who were balancing on their tails, applauding with their flippers.

The next morning Stella drove to fetch James, a three-year-old so identical to Joe that Prue only just stopped herself from remarking on this. He seemed pleased to be home. He rushed to sit on Philip's knee, produced a paper bag of shells to show him.

'His father's son,' observed Philip. 'When I was a child I was forever collecting shells and forcing them upon my parents.' Prue dared not look at Stella.

They played with James for only a short while before Rudolph arrived. Although off duty, he was still in his olive-drab uniform, which in Prue's opinion added to his handsomeness. They set off in the Sunbeam, having decided it would be more fun than the official car that Rudolph was allowed to use. Along the coast road they drove, then turned inland. A sort of mutual impatience was upon them: they could not be bothered to consult the map. Every now and then Rudolph would put his hand on Prue's thigh and smile one of his half-smiles. She looked down at her twitching feet in their red shoes with ankle straps and shiny buckles. Driving in the Sunbeam with Johnny had not felt like this . . .

Rudolph extended his leave from four days to six. Exploring Norfolk was not their chief priority, although they travelled along most of the coast, and paused in villages to look at small, cold churches set in graveyards where sheep grazed and mourning doves chimed in nearby woods. They concentrated on places to stop. By night there were spartan chilly rooms above pubs or small hotels. By day they chose woods, remote fields, places in the dunes to which they supposed no one would come except in high summer. Rudolph had brought rugs, tins of frankfurters and jars of potted meats from the base. Some days he would add Californian tins of fruit salad, bright with flabby cherries. He always seemed equipped with a flask of coffee and stacks of milk-chocolate Hershey bars, with or without nuts. In the evenings they would take an early supper in a pub, often fish and chips, and steamed puddings with Bird's custard: Rudolph had developed a passion for that English symbol, which the war had done nothing to destroy, though Prue assured him he would have gone even crazier over Mrs Lawrence's homemade version.

The first time they made love was just an hour after leaving Stella and Philip. They parked on a high drift of land, where a crop of wheat was just beginning to green the earth; and found a hidden dell screened by hawthorn. Beech, elm and ash soared above them into a loose blue sky that threatened rain. Through chinks in the bushes they could see the far-off sea, melding so closely with the sky that only the smallest shiver of light indicated water, waves, tides.

It was cold. They lay on one of Rudolph's rugs and pulled the other over them. As they struggled out of their clothes, they could feel the chill on their limbs as the top rug ran amok and the sharp air assailed them. Then suddenly they were warm, hot: there was sweat on Rudolph's temples. There was a brief shower. The raindrops that fell on them were thinly scattered, but they cooled their new heat. They found themselves laughing, but were uncertain why. A memory came to Prue of being a child in a boat-shaped swing at a fair. She was alone, clutching the scratchy ropes in her hands, thrust into the sky then returned, thrust and returned. With each rising she felt she had penetrated the arc of blue, seen something on its other side. She had the same feeling now.

Prue, still lying down, watched as Rudolph sat up, wiped the rain from his face with his green uniform shirt and put the shirt back on. 'Hope you're going to put your tie on, too,' she said.

'What? Here? Is that right? Do I need to? You'd like my garrison cap, too? Should I salute you?'

Prue laughed. 'I like your uniform. It's the best I ever saw, apart from the land girls'.'

Rudolph obediently slung the khaki cotton tie round his neck, urged it under his pristine collar and quickly made a neat knot with his long, agile fingers. 'To your liking?'

'Perfect.' Prue sat up, stretched for her yellow bow, which had flown a few feet away from the rug.

'I like your different-coloured bows,' said Rudolph. 'Do they have a message?'

'Of course,' she said, though she had not thought of this before. It was a good idea. 'I'll keep you guessing.' She retrieved her red shoes, bent over to do up the buckles. Then, rather than struggle to put on her clothes under the rug, she suddenly rose and faced Rudolph, who was still sitting on the ground. She stood in front of him, hands on hips, which she jutted forwards.

'Why, Prudence,' he said, 'could be I'll never forget this sight. I'll be able to tell my grandchildren. There was this time, this place, a long time ago. There was this naked girl in red shoes and a yellow bow in her hair, trees all round us, distant sea, rain falling from the leaves making her sparkle . . .' He said all this in his soft, slow, teasing way, as if he dared not be serious. His voice made stars shoot through every part of Prue's being.

'Cripes,' she said. Rudolph leant forward and kissed each of her knees in turn. Then, spurred by a sudden hard gust of rain, he rose higher on his knees. Prue put one of her hands on top of the other, and laid them both on his head.

* * *

Later he produced the flask of coffee, much needed now the heat of their bodies was spent. And somehow they found themselves dozing between the two rugs, listening to the rain which sometimes came in sharp bursts, sometimes drifted softly. In one of the trees above them a bird was shuffling around, trying out sharp-edged notes that added up to a cheerful song.

'All that time in the Land Army and I still don't know which bird is which,' said Prue. 'Only chickens.' Rudolph laughed. As Prue said to Stella later, they did not talk much. There seemed little need. The important things, the excitement and the understanding, could not possibly have been further enhanced by words.

In the next few days they made love across a swathe of Norfolk: the edge of cabbage fields, in barns, haystacks, on the dunes, the beach.

'You get to learn about the land this way,' Prue said once, brushing ploughed earth from her skirt. At night they slept little in their various hard beds, in small dark rooms with sloping ceilings and ugly furniture, smells from pub kitchens rising through wooden floors. They were constantly ravenous. One day they found a fisherman who sold them two lobsters. They persuaded the old cook in some dying pub to boil them – a variation on fish and chips. Gradually, in the slivers of time between their lovemaking, they exchanged parts of their own histories. Rudolph assured Prue that the plan to part from Barry was a wise move – she did not mention the baby – and he was entertained by her stories of the men who had played a part in her life. He tried to describe what it was like to fly an aircraft of inconceivable power and speed, scorching through an empty sky. Exhilaration was mixed with terror, he admitted. 'And I'll tell you something else,' he said. 'I'm a member of the Three Minute Egg Club.'

'What on earth is that?'

'Well, after long missions over enemy territory some of us often returned to base with only enough gas left in the tank for a few minutes. Often some didn't make it. The lucky ones among us became club members.'

'Scary,' said Prue. 'I could never imagine—'

'No, well. Staring at an appalling death, each moment as long as a year, does something to you.' He seemed shaken. She took his hand.

To deflect his thoughts, she decided to descend from the horrific to the mundane. She began to describe her mother. 'I'd like to meet her one day,' Rudolph said, cheerful again. They were sitting at the bar of a pub near the staithe, drinking ginger beer.

Prue gave one of her loud squawks. 'Oh no you wouldn't,' she said, as fishermen's heads turned. 'Not my mother. If I brought home a black boyfriend she'd have hysterics. Hysterics. She wouldn't let you into the house. She'd threaten never to speak to me again. She says black skin gives her the creeps, though she's happy to entertain some of the most revolting white skin you've ever seen . . . She's just totally prejudiced. I'm afraid she thinks Negroes are the lowest form of life.'

Rudolph stared down into his drink. 'A lot of people over here feel that way,' he said. 'That's perhaps why I wear my uniform most of the time. Men in the services are less of a threat. In fact they were pretty popular when the war was on and the husbands were away fighting. They left behind a lot of American babies.'

'Mum was appalled by all that. I hate her for it, but she won't change,' said Prue.

'Maybe it would be all right if you didn't say I was your boyfriend. You could say I was just a friend.'

'It wouldn't work. Honestly. She wouldn't let you through the door,'

'OK. I'll give up on that one.' He shook his head, then turned to Prue and smiled. 'Do you suppose I am your boyfriend? Is that how you think of me?'

Prue paused, thinking as seriously as she was able. 'Thing is, we've been so ... busy there hasn't been much time for thinking.'

'No.'

'And we haven't exactly declared what we feel for each other , have we?'

'No. But it's usually best not to, too soon.'

'Even when it's more or less obvious?'

'I'd say so.'

'But time's running out.' Prue heard a very slightly frantic note in her voice. She understood that Rudolph was a man haunted by the shortage of time, something so many fighters in the war, he said, had discovered. So perhaps he would understand her impatience.

'Possibly,' said Rudolph. He looked at her, his black eyes more serious than she had ever seen. 'But possibly it isn't.'

Just as the meeting of Norfolk sky and sea was indistinct, so the days bled into each other with no firm line of demarcation. The inevitable end was a thought Prue successfully kept at bay. She was determined to live only in the present moment. So when Rudolph announced, on Sunday morning, that it was his last day of leave, he had to return to work on Monday, Prue was shocked, disbelieving. Time played so many unkind tricks. It had run through her fingers with no warning of its imminent end.

It was a fine day, that Sunday. They decided to go and see the seals. They took a bag of food, the sandy rugs, and coats against the chill breezes that blew without warning from the sea.

The enormous beach was almost empty: they passed just one old man and his bucket, digging for cockles. They walked barefoot on sand hardened into ruffles by a million tides. They walked side by side, not touching, not speaking, feeling the sun on their backs.

The seals congregated on the furthermost part of the beach, which sloped down to a wide channel of water that skipped along, shallow waves never quite breaking, to join the sea. The slope afforded the seals a good place to slide down into the water, where a dozen or so of them played hide and seek. They would disappear, then suddenly black noses would surface far from the place they had dived. Their return to dry in the sun was more difficult. Clumsily they struggled up the slope, determined, comic. When they reached the crowd at the top they flipped over, exhausted, their flippers fanning their fat bodies.

Rudolph and Prue laid their rugs at the top of the slope, but some hundred yards from the seals. They did not want to disturb them. Prue's heart was beating horribly fast. She knew that today there would have to be some sort of declaration: a temporary farewell, or a plan for some unknown future. They lay back on the rug. She rested her head on Rudolph's arm. After a while he said: 'I haven't wanted to ask what your plans are. I suppose I must, today.'

'My plans? Golly, my plans . . .' Prue felt a sense of mild panic. She tried to collect her thoughts, her words. She wanted to answer Rudolph in a way that he would not see as alarmingly ambitious for a future together, but would indicate her wild certainty. 'Before I came to stay with Stella, the idea was I should go back to Manchester, collect my things and move to this flat in Brighton that Barry seems to think will suit me nicely.'

'Right. That was your plan. And now?'

'I suppose it still is.' She turned to him. 'What are you going to do?'

Rudolph shifted himself so that he could look down at Prue. 'Jesus,' he said, 'it's hard. I'm returning to the States at the end of the month. I'm leaving the Air Force. I'm going to take over the farm from my dad. He's not in a good way. But I shall enjoy that. I've always wanted to farm. Just had to put my plans on hold when the war came.'

'Quite.'

Rudolph eased himself out of his Eisenhower jacket – a green that Prue fancied – folded it and put it under her head. 'I've liked my time over here,' he said. 'I shall miss it.'

'Perhaps you shouldn't leave. You've done so well – I mean, a captain at your age.'

Rudolph gave a small laugh. 'No great achievement, honestly. It was just that so many of us were killed – seventy thousand in the Eighth Air Force alone. More or less anyone who survived till the age of twenty-four was made a captain. It was mostly luck.'

'You're being too modest.'

'No, really.' They watched a mother seal nudge her pup up the slope, pushing it skilfully with her nose. 'But Prudence – Prue . . . I don't want all this, you and I, to come to an end, no plans. No possibilities. No future.'

'No. Neither do I.' Even as she said it, Prue felt a whisper of uncertainty. Considering her conviction that Rudolph was her man, this was confusing.

'There might be another way. You could come back to the States with me.'

'What? As your girlfriend?' Clouds, with a sudden burst of speed, raced above them.

'No, no. Of course not.' He took her hand. 'As my wife.'

Prue sat up, startled. 'Golly, cripes, goodness,' she said. 'I mean, you've never given me a sign, this week, that you thought I might be the right *wife* for you. Lover, yes. We're the best ever lovers, aren't we? But marriage . . .'

'We've been too occupied for much serious talk. I didn't want to rush in with a lot of possibilities. I just wanted to give you a good time. But it was love at first sight for me. It can happen. I firmly believe it can. You must have guessed how I felt.'

'I didn't quite know . . .'

'Well, that's how it is. How can I put it? I love you totally. You're the most marvellous girl I've ever met. I haven't bought a ring because I knew I couldn't find a decent one in the wilds of Norfolk. But I want to marry you. I want you to be my wife. Will you think about it?'

Prue flicked away a strand of hair from her eyes. Now that Rudolph had made his feelings clear, and offered her a future as his wife in America, in some puzzling way her own certainty was suddenly cracked. 'Goodness,' she said again. 'That's a very big thought. A huge thought. It'd be an enormous decision.'

'Of course. I don't want to hurry you. There's time, there's time. All you have to do is to write to me in America to say you're coming.' He fought to contain a sigh. 'Or to say you're not.'

'I could do that, yes.'

'My best buddy, Ed – he was shot down on the last day of the war – when he knew I was to be posted over here he said, "Rudi, find yourself a good English girl. Find yourself a good wife." He'd have been over the moon, Ed would, had he known I'd found you.' He paused. 'There've been a few other girls, of course. Nothing serious. I've never had my heart broken, or even dented. It's always been, why, thank you, ma'am, and goodbye.'

'Bit the same with me,' said Prue. 'Though I did love Barry One very much. I would have married him. He was killed within months of being called up . . . I haven't been so lucky since then.'

'Perhaps now?'

'What can I say? It's been one of the best weeks of my life. I shall never forget it.'

'So perhaps . . . But I should tell you a bit about where I come from, life in the Deep South. When I get back I'm going to live in the big house – not that big – and my dad's going to move to a smaller place half a mile down the road.'

'Rather like Mr Lawrence's arrangement with Joe,' Prue said, but did not explain.

'And you with your love of farming, your expertise, your skills,' he smiled, teasing, 'you'd love it there. It's a fine place, good land. We're far from rich but we do all right. I'm looking forward to it, I really am. One day I'd like a couple of sons to help, and a daughter or two. Does any of that idea take your fancy?'

'It does, yes.' For a moment she could almost see it all.

'Then perhaps you should come out, take a look, make up your mind when you've seen what I could offer.'

'That's a good idea.' She was aware that her voice was thin.

Rudolph took off his cap. Prue put it on, suddenly skittish, to scatter the solemnity of their talk.

'You look pretty good in that.' He tilted it to one side. 'I'm going to swim. Coming?' Prue shook her head. Rudolph, the extraordinary man who wanted to marry her, stood up, undressed faster than anyone Prue had ever seen. The old man digging for cockles was too far away to see them, let alone be shocked by Rudolph's nakedness. Sunlight flashed off his hard body. His eyes, as he looked down on Prue, were uncertain. He ran to the water – seals slithered away as he went – plunged into the channel. Prue watched, smiling, as he moved about among them: they were curious, unafraid. Some swam so close to him he could touch them. When they dived, he dived too, joining their game.

Prue looked up at the familiar arc of sky, the distant line of sea, the spire of a far-away church tower, the endless stretch of sparkling beach, and knew she should put her mind to contemplating Rudolph's proposal. She didn't want to because she wanted this last day, like the others with him, to be almost mindless: just hours of glorious sensations. Some instinct told her she should take her chance. She and the handsome American pilot seemed to have found a rare closeness that, surely, was love, though the actual definition of love was always elusive. She desired him every moment of the day and night, and there were flashes when, beneath the extraordinary passion, she thought she detected the kind of love that would last, that would be strong enough to overcome any difficulties. A picture of the wedding day came to mind – perhaps in a Norfolk church, as this was where they had met. Her mother would not be there, but that would be her fault. Prue would have a white dress, despite it being her second wedding, and pale feathers in her hair.

Rudolph was standing beside her, water pouring down his legs, a little towel round his waist. 'That was a swim I'll never forget. Fantastic.' As he rubbed himself with the towel drops of sea water swarmed about, gathering miniature rainbow colours. 'What've you been thinking?'

Prue gave him an enchanting smile. Certainty now swept over her, but she was determined to be double-sure. 'I was thinking we've only known each other for a week. Is that long enough? I mean, to be sure we could be for life?'

Rudolph bent and touched her cheek with an icy finger. 'As my mother used to say, God deals out His gifts according to His own plan. Sometimes He makes it so plain that time doesn't matter. Sometimes it's just completely sure, obvious, that a person is destined for you, so the chance should be taken. We should recognize the signs, have faith. I believe that. Listen: I love you.'

'I love you too,' said Prue. At that moment she did, very much. She also wanted the talking to stop. She tugged at the towel.

They made love for so long that they did not notice the tide coming in until the water had covered the banks of the channel. There was no time for their picnic. They hurried back over the sand – colder now the sun had disappeared behind cloud. The old man digging for cockles had gone. They were exhausted, dazed, chilled despite their coats. The bottoms of Rudolph's neat khaki trousers were wet and sandy. In the sudden warmth of the Sunbeam, he wrote his address on a piece of paper. He said he had to get back to the base by six, and they should say goodbye here.

The farewell kiss was long and gentle, full of tentative promise. When they finally pulled apart, Prue asked the question she had been meaning to ask all day. What kind of farm was Rudolph going to manage in Georgia?

'Why?' he asked. 'Do you have a favourite? You said you liked milking. We only have a few cows, but we've built up a good business in hogs. We've got a couple of hundred. Increase them all the time.'

'Hogs? Pigs?'

'Pigs, that's right.' He started the engine. Laughed. 'Do you have anything against pigs? You know something? They're good animals if you treat them right.' He touched her hand. 'Love you,' he said.

They drove back to the bungalow in silence.

Later that evening Prue told Stella about Rudolph's proposal. A frown flickered across Stella's forehead before she could discard it. 'That was quick,' she said.

'Exactly.'

'What did you say?'

'I said I'd think.'

'You must. You must think very hard. Do a lot of weighing up. There are so many imponderables between doubt and certainty. I imagine you'd miss living in England.'

'I would. I'd miss you and Ag. No one else, really. It would be a huge leap into the unknown. On the other hand, as soon as I met him I felt at one with Rudolph.'

Stella gave a wry smile. 'One does feel that, sometimes, dancing. Even with a stranger.'

'No, it was more than that. I was totally whirled ... The best thing was, we didn't seem to need to talk very much. We exchanged some facts about our lives, but it didn't seem necessary to give full histories, in the way some people do. Rudolph reminded me of Joe in that way. The unspoken was just as engaging as the spoken.'

Stella gave her a glass of wine. 'Does he love you? Do you love him?'

'I think so. Yes, to both those questions.'

'Because America is a very long way to go to find out if it was a mad dream.'

'I know. What should I do?'

'If you decide to join him, I think you should go with no promises, see what it's like – a whole very different culture, his friends to turn into your friends, none of your own. But you'd love being back on a proper farm.'

'I would. Although pigs . . . I'm not sure I could deal with pigs again.'

'Of course you could. You loved Sly, remember? Now the unreal week is over you'll be able to think more clearly. A week is much too short to be positive. But extraordinary things do sometimes happen. Recognition of what is right can come suddenly from heaven and remain firm, though the chance of that happening is small, I admit. You need to calm down, get some sleep. The solution will come to you. Why don't you stay on for another week?'

'No, I can't do that. It would all be different. Confusing. I must get back, move to Brighton. But thank you. You're a wise old bird, Stella. This has been an unforgettable time, staying with you and Philip.'

James came running into the kitchen in his pyjamas. Stella ruffled his hair. 'He's so like . . .' Prue stopped herself.

'He's my saviour,' said Stella.

Prue picked the child up. He was surprisingly heavy. The skin of his cheek against hers was as soft as fallen rose petals. He smelt of chocolate and milk. It was the first time Prue had ever held a three-year-old boy. Her eyes swarmed with tears. This was a might-have-been, a could-be-still. She handed James back to Stella, shaken. If she and Rudolph had a baby it would probably not have her green eyes, but Rudolph's black ones, and tightly curled hair and skin the colour of wild honey. The idea was overwhelming. Prue drank the wine very quickly, wanting to blur the imponderables.

The next morning she drove away, confused that her aching for Rudolph was as deep as anything she had ever known, though the absolute certainty of love, such as she had felt for Barry One, was not quite there: mysteriously, it had faded a little in the night. But certainty was always elusive: its vagaries were mystifying. She had no doubt it would return.

The journey to Manchester seemed, in Prue's state of exhaustion, to take for ever. Her plan was to spend a last night at The Larches, pack her things and leave for Brighton next day.

Bertha's bicycle was not in its usual place. Prue, wondering if she had already gone, let herself in through the front door. She picked up a couple of letters waiting for her in the hall and took them to the sitting room. There, it seemed to her at a glance, a few things were just perceptibly different: cushions changed round, strange candlesticks over the fireplace, two pots of hideous scarlet flowers on the window-ledge. Prue felt a stab of annoyance. Her mother, presumably already installed as house-keeper, had not been slow to make her imprint on the house.

She went to the window, looked out at the bare garden. It was bigger. An illusion, of course, she told herself: the chicken run and shed had gone. Johnny had moved them while she was away. She had forgotten that he would, and their absence added to the feelings of unease that had confronted her since returning to the house.

With a pang of foreboding Prue took her case up to the spare room she had moved into on her last visit home. Barry had been generous to her so it was her turn to be generous to him and let him have the main bedroom again.

There, the clutter she had left on the dressing-table had disappeared. In its place were her mother's myriad aids to her routine of beautifying: pots of cold cream, round boxes of Pond's powder decorated with randomly flying puffs, a bottle of lavender water – things so associated with Prue's childhood when she had stood beside Mrs Lumley as she had put on her makeup that a kind of desolation crept into her tiredness. She did not know why, for she wanted her mother to be secure in this job, happy. She opened the cupboard. Her own clothes had been pushed to one side. Mrs Lumley's homemade drooping garments replaced them, the familiar dewlap hems and flabby collars. Shoes of delicately punctured leather, their sides swollen in permanent imitation of Mrs Lumley's bunions, crowded on the floor. There was a strong smell of lavender mixed with nervous sweat. Prue turned to the bed.

On the table next to it there was an expensive-looking travelling clock in a leather case that she had not seen before. Perhaps Barry had found a substitute recipient for his presents. Prue picked up an ancient nightdress-case made of imitation fur in the shape of a cat. She could tell from its swollen belly that a pre-war nightdress was bundled inside. As a child in her mother's bed on stormy nights she had liked to use it as a pillow. Prue lay back on the bed and closed her eyes, the cat now making a childhood pillow behind her neck.

When she opened them, her mother was looking down at her. 'Oh, darling,' she was saying, 'we didn't know when to expect you. You've been gone a long time.' Prue sat up. They kissed each other on the cheek. 'Everything all right with you, is it? You look quite pale. Tired.'

'I'm fine. Had a wonderful time. Everything all right with you?'

Mrs Lumley moved away from the bed. She dithered about, snapped at a curtain that was not completely drawn back. She pushed at her things on the dressing-table, glanced at her reflection in the looking glass. 'If I'd known you were coming back to stay, of course, I would never have settled in this room till you'd gone for good.'

'I've not come back to stay, Mum. I'm here for the night, too tired to drive any more today.'

'Of course. You look exhausted.'

'Before I left, Barry said that would be OK.'

'And so it is. Of course it is.' Her voice rose higher, as it always did when she was nervous. She swivelled to face her daughter. 'But as you can see there was a change of plan.' Their eyes met. Prue had no intention of helping her mother break the news. 'It soon seemed it was a very silly idea, coming here daily, catching the bus morning and night.'

'Very soon,' snapped Prue. 'Not quite two weeks.' She was confused by her own annoyance.

'Yes, well. "Much easier if you live in," Barry said. "You won't have to be up so early to get my breakfast."' She giggled.

Prue wondered if her own giggle would sound the same, apeing youth, in thirty years' time. 'So he helped me bring my stuff round in the Daimler – or was it the Humber? I'm not sure, to be honest. Not much, though. I didn't bring much because the idea is that I spend weekends at home, leave a few things for Barry in the fridge. Well, that's the plan for the moment. One day, of course, if Barry's thinks it's a good idea, I might sell the lease. He's got a good head for business, you can tell.'

'Quite,' said Prue. A fading wash of sky now filled the north-facing window. Her mother turned on the overhead light. Its forty-watt bulb, beneath a shade decorated with a zigzag pattern, made no more than a dispiriting glow in the dimness of the room. Prue went over to look out at the front drive. She saw Barry pull up in the Humber. 'He's back,' she said.

'Good. Nice and punctual. I've got a nice piece of plaice.' She picked up a tortoiseshell hand mirror from the dressing-table, glanced at herself with smile. 'Listen, darling, I don't want you to think there's anything to it, this arrangement with Barry. It's just a job. It's safety. No more worries. You understand?'

'Of course.'

'Anything else would be quite inappropriate.' She struggled with the word. 'Anything else would never happen.'

Prue granted her a smile. 'Of course not. I can't imagine it would.'

'Very well, then, darling, that's cleared up. It's been on my mind. Now, let's go down. We can easily stretch the plaice. We can have a nice supper, the three of us. I'm sure Barry would like that. Then we can make up the bed in the other spare room.'

'I think I'll go back to Wimberly Road, Mum, thanks.'

'Very well. Please yourself. But you'd be very welcome.'

Prue saw the humour in being welcomed to what was recently her own house, and smiled.

As she came down the stairs, carrying her case, she found a cheerful husband at the bottom, arms wide open, demanding a hug. Too tired to argue, she agreed to stay for supper, but insisted on leaving afterwards. Barry gave her an envelope with the key to the Brighton flat, and a map. Over the plaice and sprouts, he and his housekeeper kept up a constant ping-pong of fatuous observations designed to lighten the tension. Prue left as soon as the pancakes had been admired. She drove recklessly fast to her childhood house, went straight to her shabby bedroom, posters of Vivien Leigh in *Gone with the Wind* still on the walls. All she could think was: Rudolph.

When she woke, early next morning, Prue allowed herself only a moment to remember the flotsam of her childhood that accosted her all round the room. Her eyes dashed past the slumped animals, dusty ornaments, the first hair ribbons of her collection hanging from the dressing-table mirror, and came finally to rest on the table by her bed, where a small snapshot of a man in air-force uniform, her father, taken by her mother, had always stood in a cheap little frame of imitation leather.

'Tom Purdy was his name, I think – though it might have been Tim,' she had explained to Prue on her tenth birthday. 'We met in a pub. He was in uniform, ever so smart, handsome. I happened to be carrying my new Box Brownie. It was my most precious possession. I took it with me everywhere. I persuaded him to stand outside the pub, let me take his picture. I think he was flattered. He was going back up north next day, where he was stationed. Anyway, I got the sun behind me, he gave a lovely smile, said "Cheese", when I gave him the signal, and that was that. You were born nine months later. I never saw him again. We were in that much of a hurry we never exchanged addresses. I often wish we had.'

Sometimes Prue had asked her mother to try to track down Tom, or Tim, Purdy, but she said there was no use, what was the point? As he'd never known about his daughter, he probably would not want to be bothered all these years later, she said. Prue's only – possible – inheritance from her father was her eyes: Mrs Lumley said she thought they were a deeper emerald than her own though she couldn't be sure, could she? Their meeting had been in a dark shed. And as she had been unsure of the spelling of Purdy (Purrdy?) she had thought it safer to pass on her own maiden name to her daughter. Prue had managed to extract from her the only facts about her father that her mother had gleaned. But there were not many, for she and Prue's father had not been concentrating on conversation, Mrs Lumley had snapped one day, when Prue was goading her. He had grown up in Yorkshire and was an electrician by trade before joining the RAF. He did not like pork crackling – a fact Mrs Lumley had proudly observed for herself in the pub – and had very shiny shoes. There was no point in asking for more, for there was no more. As Prue grew older, questions about her unknown father faded. She thought ignorance about one parent was sad but not traumatic, and for months on end she gave him no thought.

She had not been in her childhood bedroom for a long time. The sight of the small dusty photograph in its disintegrating frame made her pause for a moment. A flicker of old regret went through her, but then she was steady again. She swung her feet above the rag-rug by her bed, its scraps of material clotted and stained, to avoid it with her bare feet. Funny how she had never had anything against it as a child. She had thought it rather nice, the bright colours. She had liked her room very much, she remembered. It was her refuge, the place she could write her secret diary and try out nail polish, but she could no longer see it with a child's eyes.

Prue went to the window, looked out at the narrow strip of garden. As usual there was not a flower in sight (her mother preferred artificial), and the pattern of nearby roofs was so familiar that they slotted instantly back into her visual memory. She sighed, grabbed a skirt from the top of her open suitcase. It smelt powerfully of Rudolph. A bath was needed.

In the grim little bathroom, a threadbare mat twisted on the brown linoleum floor, both anger and sadness came upon her. She lighted the geyser. As always, it needed several attempts before the flame took hold. She listened to its tuneless wheezing, a sound she had hated for years, as she watched a thin spittle of brackish water peter out of the taps. She touched one of the aged white tiles that covered the walls and gave the room the air of a public lavatory. Then she looked at a strange version of herself in the freckled mirror above the basin, and at the well-remembered cracks in the basin. A lump of soap sat in its own slime. Prue picked it up. Blimey! Her mother's wartime habit of sticking together old bits of soap still went on . . . She examined the disgusting clutch of cream and peach scraps, hard, cracked, jammed together. What was her barmy mother up to, such useless economy? Soap was still rationed, but not hard to find if you were willing to pay a few extra pence. A flame of irrational anger seared through Prue. She vowed that she would buy a bar of Imperial Leather, out of her own rations, in Brighton and send it . . . Even as the idea came to her, melancholy replaced anger, guilt as her mean thoughts followed irritation. Her mother, after all, had had a hard time bringing up Prue on her own. She had done her best. Her economies were understandable. All the same, Prue had no wish to spend a moment longer in that bathroom. She couldn't bear to wash in the grimy tub, whose bottom was still scarcely covered with the tepid, sluggish water.

She went slowly down the steep staircase, its pre-war carpet deadening every familiar step, and into the kitchen, half wondering why she did not rush straight out of the front door. But something made her want to pause for a last moment, remember why she was glad to be going. She sat on a chair at the small square table. The unusual silence made her uneasy. She had once thought it a perfect kitchen, with its constant music of clattering saucepans and a steaming kettle. Now, deserted by her mother, the life seemed to have gone out of it. Still, Prue thought, she was leaving Manchester *for good* this time. She would resist ever returning here, to the obsessive neatness, the poppies on the china . . .

Mrs Lumley had inherited the house from her own parents and lived there all her life. Familiar to Prue were myriad stories of how, until she had become the owner, the lavatory was in the yard, which was now the small garden, and heating was provided by one small fire in the front room. Her parents had also left her their scant life savings, which she had spent on modernizing the house in 1938. It was then she had given up her job in the cotton mill, where she and 'the girls' had enjoyed working for many years. Always in search of a husband, she had decided that a position in the old Ford factory in Trafford Park, reopened to make engines for fighter planes, might be just the place to run into a good bunch of young men. But by the time she applied there were no vacancies left.

'Fate,' she had said to Prue, one day at the kitchen table. 'If I'd got a job there I wouldn't have thought of following my heart's desire, would I? Hairdressing.' She had just enough money to rent a small, dingy shop, some way from the centre of the city, which she named Elsie's Bond Street Salon. Surprisingly, it had done well, and Prue had enjoyed helping out in the school holidays.

But she could never share her mother's love of Manchester. In Mrs Lumley's view it was a glamorous place: dance halls, huge shops, banner-waving marchers keeping in time with the trumpet players, trips to the Zoological Gardens with a sandwich lunch on Sundays, the marvellous Christmas circus at Belle Vue. Prue's recollection, above all, was of darkness – the perpetual smoke hovering over the rooftops, the vast buildings of blackened stone, the cold, the dank, the endless rain. There were just a few things she did remember with some awe: the handsome cathedral, so solid in the murky dusk, its lighted clock looking no bigger than a watch-face: the grandeur of the town hall, whose windows, when lighted by occasional sun, enlivened its sooty stone walls, making it fleetingly cheerful. And the Ship Canal. Prue loved that. Often she had gone with friends to watch the great liners, pulled by tugs from the sea, cutting through water thick as melted chocolate. Her most vivid childhood memory was of an afternoon walk with her mother through a field of buttercups near the canal. A vast ship appeared to be approaching them through a sea of yellow.

'How's it sailing in a field?' she had screamed.

Her mother had clutched her, laughing. 'It's on the canal, you silly thing,' she had explained. 'Just looks as if it's coming through the field. It's what you call an illusion.'

That had been a bright moment. Frightening, then funny. Prue had made Rudolph laugh with the story. But mostly she remembered bombs, fires, the gut-splitting wail of sirens. In the 1941 air raid, when buildings had crashed down on the corner of Deansgate and St Mary's Gate, she and her mother had stood at the kitchen window watching terrifying monster flames roar into the sky. No fireman's ladder would reach beyond their base. The Manchester of her distant past she could not love, would not miss. She felt no affection either for the richer, more genteel part where she had lived with Barry. She was ready, now, to leave for good. She stood up. The chair squawked one final time. She hurried to the front door.

Her journey to Brighton was complicated. She was lost several times, but did not mind. Once she stopped in an agreeable-looking village, bought fish and chips and ate them in the back seat of the Sunbeam, parked by a pond a-flutter with ducks. She liked the warmth of the seats with their gentle smell of leather. Random thoughts jangled through her mind. Did her mother have breakfast with Barry? And, if so, would it be in her old pre-war dressing-gown, as was her custom at home? Would Barry take to giving her extravagant presents, now there was no longer a wife on whom to bestow them? Would her mother resist flirting with him? Would he resist shagging the kind of older woman he apparently fancied more than a young one? These were not disturbing questions, just questions.

But then came Rudolph. Where was he now? Zooming through the sky, his entire concentration on his piloting, no thought for her? They had left it that he would not contact her for a week. If he heard nothing after that, he had said, he would presume she had chosen to turn down his offer of life in America. What was she going to do? Go, or stay? Either decision would be alarming.

Once she arrived in Brighton, Barry's considerate, hand-drawn map helped Prue find her way to the old cinema with no trouble. As she got out of the car she could smell the sea, a sharper smell than she remembered in Norfolk. There was a breeze, too. It blew her skirt about as she stood looking up at the fine old building with its peeling paint and boarded-up windows: she could see that if Barry spent a fortune it could once again be a handsome place.

She followed his instructions to the side door, unlocked it, carried her suitcase up a single flight of steep stairs. The door to the flat opened into a small dark passage, but there was light from the sitting-room window at the end. Prue sniffed. There was a strange, hard-to-place smell. A combination of fish, soot, stale air. She went into the sitting room: one sofa covered with hideous cretonne flowers, one hard chair, small pictures hanging high on wallpaper the texture of solidified porridge. 'Blimey,' she said.

The view from the window wasn't bad: a slab of grey sea, a great slash of matching sky, a distant pier, a single boat. Prue moved to the minuscule kitchen, painted a deadly green. The surprise there was that in every drawer she opened she found knives and forks, and tins of food in the cupboard. There were a few plates, cups and saucers and bowls – enough for a host and one visitor if they washed up between courses – and in the fridge there was milk, bread, butter, six eggs, a yellowing cabbage and a lamb chop. The final surprise was half a bottle of champagne. How on earth . . .? Who could have . . .?

Prue went to the bedroom at the back where light meshed through a coarse net curtain. The bed was made up, the bedside lamp worked. Prue dumped her suitcase on the floor, opened the narrow cupboard. At least two dozen hangers were on the rail. Were they a message from the husband who knew about her collection of clothes? Prue sat on the bed, confused and a little alarmed. She did not consider unpacking her case.

A deep growling telephone rang in the sitting room. Prue ran back there, found the hefty old black instrument, identical to the one at The Larches, on the floor.

'Hello, sweetheart.'

'Oh, Barry—'

'I've been ringing a lot. I was expecting you to arrive much earlier. I was getting worried. Everything all right?'

'Fine, fine.'

'I made arrangements – food and that. Should tide you over till you can go and explore the shops tomorrow.'

'Thanks. Thanks. But Barry, what do you imagine I can do here?'

Barry paused. Prue could hear familiar indrawn breath as he inhaled on his cigar. She wondered how her mother would put up with the permanent smell of smoke.

'Well, you can have a nice peaceful time. You could find a job, if you insist, though you know that's not necessary. You'll fall in with people, I've no doubt – your looks. Soon you'll be out dancing every night. You could learn to swim. All that sea, so convenient, isn't it? You could learn to cook . . . I don't know. But you're a woman of plenty of initiative. You'll make something happen.'

'I don't know where to begin. And besides, I don't want to live in a town, you know that.'

'It's only temporary, sweetheart. I just thought it was somewhere to go while you work things out. Staying on at The Larches, the divorce going through, might have meant problems.' There was a catch in his voice – guilt? Regret? Prue wondered. 'And now with your mother here—'

'Quite.'

'But you could start looking for a cottage, roses round the door, couldn't you? Don't worry about the money. I've said I'll take care of that. I've just put two hundred pounds in your bank account to last you till we come to an arrangement.'

'Thanks. You're very generous.' Prue felt weak, almost faint. Two hundred pounds.

'So, I'll be letting you go now. We'll keep in touch. Take care of yourself, sweetheart. It's still quite strange, here at home without you.'

Prue drew the chair up to the window, sat looking at the sea, listening to the thick silence. She had not brought a book with her. There was no wireless. She hated the smells, guessed that if she opened the window even the sea breeze would not banish them.

So this was being alone: this was the solitude Ag had recommended. Hours as long as days. Silence that weighed on your head.

At five o'clock, fearing she was heading for a trough of self-pity, Prue decided to go out. She wandered up and down a few streets, bought a magazine, looked in shop windows – livelier than those in Manchester, but not exactly tempting. Curiously, knowing she had an unbelievable amount of money, she had no inclination to spend it. She liked the idea of it sitting in an untouched lump in the bank.

She came to the Ship and Gull, a shabby pub on a corner. Go to a pub, Barry had said. Make friends. Well, she'd give it a try.

Judging by the lack of customers, the place had been open only a short while. There was a soldier at one end of the bar, gazing into his beer, an old woman at the other end, headscarf tied under her chin, coat sagging almost to the ground. Although Prue doubted there was much future of lasting friendship with the sad old thing, she chose to stand next to her, far from the soldier. He had already interrupted his meditations to greet her with a lascivious look.

The old woman, who could scarcely see over the bar, asked for a ginger beer. The barman poured her one, pushed it across. She took the glass in both unsteady hands, put it to her grey lips. Prue asked for a gin and lime: she badly needed an instant silvering of the mind. A middle-aged couple came in, sat at a table and took out a pack of cards. The man shouted that he wanted the usual. Prue stayed beside the old woman who took small sips of ginger beer: streams of it ran down her chin.

'New, here, are you?' she ventured, when the drink was finished.

'I am, yes. Just arrived this afternoon.'

'I was new here thirty or forty years ago. Place's changed.'

The barman, quite roughly, asked if the old woman would pay for her drink. There was much scuffling in an over-full bag, then fumbling in her purse. 'I haven't got it tonight, George,' she said. 'You'll have to wait.'

'I'm sick of waiting, Nancy, truth be known. It's pay-up time. I've been patient for weeks, but it can't go on like this.'

'No, it can't, can it?' The old woman was now showing there was still spirit within her, a proud cheekiness. She turned towards the door. Prue quickly slipped a ten-shilling note from her purse and put it into one of the gaping pockets. The old woman swung round to her. 'You can't do that, dear,' she said, clearly not quite certain as to what Prue had done, 'but God bless you all the same.' She hurried to the door and went out.

'You get some like that,' the barman said.

Prue asked for another gin, paid for her own drinks and settled the old woman's bill. 'Does it liven up here later?' she asked.

The barman looked offended. 'Yes and no,' he said. 'Doesn't exactly throb on a Tuesday. You'd do better to try Saturday.'

Saturday was too far away even to think about. Prue thanked him, glanced at the card players and left the pub. By now the gin had tempered all the jarring sensations caused by the cheerless flat. She planned to cook the chop and heat a tin of peas, read her magazine and look out of the sitting-room window at the stars. She wanted to try to work out why they were so important to Rudolph. Perhaps she would open the champagne, drink herself into further protection against the hideous furniture, the darkness that swirled round the dim lights, the persistent smells.

Solitude, she thought. Not worth giving it a chance, really, though she would try to think hard about it one last time. Bloody solitude.

Back in the flat she poured the champagne. Whoever Barry had hired to furnish the place had provided an elegant glass from which to drink it. That was something of a puzzle, but it wasn't worth pondering on: the time had come to put her mind to higher things.

Prue had a vague idea that, through the ages, people had found inspiration in the stars. Their mystery had been an eternal inspiration to many besides Rudolph. So now, here in the horrible little flat, on a chair by the window, she was going to try. See if something would come to her. Some wise message about what she should do. She took a large gulp of champagne, swilled it round her mouth trying to get rid of the taste of tinned peas and the fatty chop. All that came to her was 'Twinkle, Twinkle': her mother jumping up and down in the kitchen, a bowl of jelly in her hand, singing the nursery rhyme. When at last she had stopped, she had said to Prue, 'I am a star, you know, darling. You'll be a star one day. Everyone should try to be a star.' Prue had had no idea what she meant. She just knew her mother looked daft, with a bit of jelly on her chin, her cheeks a funny colour and her eyes slurping about all over the place.

So much for stars. Bloody solitude.

But then, looking again at the flat black sea speared with a dagger of moonlight, and at the sprinkling of stars in the enormity of the black sky, something happened. It happened in an orderly sort of way, considering the gin and the half-bottle of champagne. First, she remembered the night – well, most of the night – she had spent under the stars with Rudolph, in a nest in the dunes. The strength of their mutual passion that night was unique in her (many) experiences, as she confessed to him, and he had smiled his smile, white as the half-moon. When at last they had exhausted themselves, and huddled together against the cold, Rudolph had begun to tell her about life in America, his family and friends in Georgia. A picture of it all had come to her: exciting, appealing. Had he suggested leaving within the hour, she would have agreed at once. As it was, in the days left to them, reasonable doubts had annoyingly pushed their way into her calculations, blurring her imaginings of a new life far from home.

But now the old excitement returned without warning. She did some very quick weighing up. What would she miss if she put Rudolph out of his misery and agreed to go with him to the States, become his wife? She would miss Stella and Ag – not that they were often able to meet, but just knowing they were there and she could always go to them was an invaluable security in her life. She would miss England, the seasons she had learnt so much about as a land girl, the trees that seemed to differ from county to county in their shapes, their variations on green. Bluebells – were there bluebells in America? Well, if not, she could probably live without them, and even without primroses. The Light Programme, her mother's bread-and-butter pudding, though perhaps she could find the recipe. Her mother? Not really. She was fond of her, but didn't quite love her. There would be no mother-love on offer once Prue was married to a black man. Mrs Lumley would disown her: she had none of Mrs Lawrence's qualities – strength, dignity, quiet sympathy and understanding, things that Prue had always believed a mother should have. As for Barry and The Larches, they were already in the past. Johnny, her friend . . . well, he'd been kind but outrageous. She would soon cease to miss him.

Instead she would thrive on a new life, married to a farmer, several children running about the place learning about animals. Rudolph would show her a new country impossible to imagine – for geography had not been pursued very hard at Prue's school. *Gone with the Wind* was her only knowledge of America. But she knew quite clearly in her dancing head that there were times you had to make a hard choice: this was one of them. As far as she could tell, now, she loved Rudolph. He loved her. It would be foolish not to take her chance, be left in grim post-war England endlessly visiting pubs in the hope of finding a lovable soldier looking for a wife.

So, her mind was made up. She would go. New country, new life. The stars had worked their magic.

Prue stumbled to her room. Without undressing she lay on the eiderdown, was asleep in a moment.

A few hours later she woke, terrified, not knowing where she was. Still half webbed in the nightmare, she switched on her light. She had dreamt of pigs, thousands of them, their snouts jostling her, trapping her, planning how best to attack her. Their mean little eyes were laughing. The blue veins in their ears were lighted, as if by an electric current. Their fat scrubby bodies barged into her. Their orchestra of screams and grunts hurt her ears.

Prue sat up, head on bent knees, trying to stop their raging in her mind. Then she remembered: Rudolph had said his family had a pig farm. Hundreds of pigs. Good animals if you treated them well. It was unlikely he would abandon them, no matter how much he loved her. And it all became clear: twice as clear as the star-induced plan of a few hours ago. She could never cope with pigs again, not after the real experience and the nightmare. She could never leave England, Stella, Ag. She wanted to visit Mr Lawrence as he grew older. She must have been mad.

For the rest of the night Prue reflected on her own foolishness. She got up at six. She knew Johnny would be awake. He liked writing his poetry at dawn, before feeding the hens.

She went to the sitting room, asked the dozy woman at the exchange for the long-distance number he had given her.

'You're an early caller,' he said. 'Where are you?'

'In Brighton. Some flat Barry found for me. But bugger solitude. I've had it.'

Johnny laughed. 'How long have you been there?'

'Not quite twenty-four hours.'

'Not quite a real test.'

'No: but enough to know it's not for me.'

'I can imagine that.' His voice was not as light as Prue remembered it. It was thicker somehow.

'Could I come and be your lodger? Any rent you like.' There was a pause. 'I mean, just till I've found somewhere of my own ...'

'Of course you can. I'd like that. You might be just what I need to stop me reverting to old bad habits.'

'What old bad habits?'

There was a pause, a slight laugh. 'Have you got a pencil? I'll give you directions.'

Within ten minutes Prue was on her way. The dread of arriving in Brighton, which had weighed so heavily on her yesterday, had disappeared. The sadness at leaving Rudolph had also receded, though there was still a shadow in her heart. But it was a bright spring morning. She drove fast, concentrating on the road. She was looking forward to seeing Johnny, and did not give a thought to his mysterious bad habits.

# Chapter 11

When Prue arrived Johnny was standing at the gate waiting for her. He was leaning against it as if for support. There was something about the set of his body that made her think he had been there for a long time. His hands fidgeted in his pockets. He was pale and unshaven, and his eyes were bloodshot. But he smiled as Prue got out of the car. 'You drive faster than you used to,' he said.

'I do. I enjoy it.'

'I'm looking forward to another spin in the Sunbeam.'

They kissed briefly on the cheek. Johnny patted her shoulder. He looked very tired. 'So glad you've come,' he said. 'Let's take a look at the chickens before we go in.'

Prue followed him round to the back of the cottage, a jumble of overgrown herbaceous borders and rampant weeds. But the chicken houses were in place. A couple of dozen hens were clucking away as they pecked at grubs in their large run. 'You've put all this up very quickly,' she said.

'Had to. I worked pretty hard, managed it in a couple of days. Now I can get down to restoring the vegetable garden. I'll enjoy that. We'll be able to have vegetable stews.'

'We will.' Prue smiled up at him. 'It's good here,' she said.

'I love the Downs. We'll go for walks.' He blinked fast.

'That'll be lovely.'

'Let's take in your stuff. I'm afraid it's a bit of a mess.'

The mess was familiar from Johnny's Manchester flat: the ailing old chairs, quantities of papers and books piled on the floor, dirty plates and saucepans piled in the small sink.

'I'll help you sort it out. It won't take long,' Prue said, more sprightly than she felt. Her eyes went to a shelf by the stove. Three bottles of vodka stood there, two full and one half empty.

'I know, I know,' said Johnny. 'But don't worry, I'm dealing with it. It'll be easier with you here.'

He showed her the sitting room, which was no less bedraggled and cheerless than the kitchen, though the view from the window, to farmland that rose up to meet the Downs, was enchanting. Her bedroom, which had the same view, was very small, barely furnished.

'There's a cupboard you could use on the landing,' Johnny said, in a voice that suggested any further practical help with her comfort would be too much for him. 'I just sling my clothes on a chair in my room.' Prue glanced through a half-open door and felt lucky that his own chaos was not something she would have to clear up. The primitive bathroom, with cracked walls, cracked floor, cracked bath and basin, all so reminiscent of the one she had recently run from, was not something she looked forward to, but she wasn't fussy. 'My cousin didn't seem to notice the inside of houses,' Johnny explained. 'The outside was what mattered to him. The thatch, as you may have seen, is in very good shape, and the window-frames were recently repainted.'

They returned to the kitchen. Prue was hungry. She opened the antique fridge. There was half a bottle of milk, and a slab of butter peppered with toast crumbs.

'I'm so sorry. Not much of a welcome. I meant to go shopping before you arrived. The morning just slipped through my fingers.' He sounded near to tears.

'Don't worry. I'll go and buy things this afternoon. Let's just have a cup of tea and a biscuit.'

'I know there's a tin of sardines somewhere.' His tone conveyed little hope. He went to a musty-smelling cupboard, took the tin from a small group of others. After a desolate hunt in another cupboard he found two clean plates, but no biscuits. 'Shall I hard-boil a couple of eggs? At least we're not short of those.'

They sat at the table in the window, sharing a single clean fork and mopping up the sardine oil with a chunk of stale bread.

'So what's the matter? What's happened?' asked Prue.

Johnny ran shaky hands through his hair, summoning the right words to answer the question. 'I don't want to bore you with the whole business, but I don't think it's going to work. Moving here, I mean . . . Big mistake.'

'But you've only been here a couple of weeks. Much too soon to make up your mind.'

'You know at once whether you can work in a place. I haven't written a line since I've been here. Nor have I made anything, which is frustrating because there's masses of wonderful elm round here, very cheap. But so far no commissions.'

'Patience, Johnny,' Prue said. 'You'll have to put the word around. People always want good carpenters.'

'I know, I know. But I haven't managed to work up the impetus to advertise myself. Not a week after I moved into this gloomy place I went into a decline.' He paused. 'And so after five years without touching a drop . . .' He looked towards the vodka bottles. 'I'm back on it, Prue, and I've got to stop. You've got to help me.'

'I didn't know. You never told me.' Prue touched his hand. He flinched. 'Of course I'll try to help you.'

'I didn't tell you because I thought I'd beaten it. And I had, for all that time. But there's another thing to add to the good news. I'm totally, utterly broke. Four and sixpence left from selling a

253

few eggs, and that's it. I'd been making a huge gate for someone before leaving Manchester. I was rather proud of it. I delivered it, the man seemed delighted, gave me a large cheque. I could have lived off it for months. But it bounced, and he's disappeared off the face of the earth. House deserted, no one has a clue where he is. So . . .' He shrugged.

'That's awful,' said Prue. 'The bastard. But you don't have to worry about money while I'm here. Barry's put the equivalent of gold bars in my account. I've been wondering what to spend it on. I'll start by going shopping now. Food, cleaning things – what else do we need? Why don't I get an electric iron? And I've got my ration book. Stella said she didn't need it in Norfolk. So give me yours and I'll be able to stock up. And as for rent, why don't I pay you three pounds a week?'

'Three pounds a week? You can't possibly.'

'I can, and I'd like to. I like the thought of providing for an artist like you.'

'You're an angel.' Johnny touched her hand, then quickly snatched his away. He seemed shaken by her generosity.

'Tonight we'll have supper in a pub,' Prue went on, 'wherever you choose. On condition you shave first, and put on a clean shirt.' They both laughed. They were uncertain, still, in these new circumstances, how to approach each other.

Prue spent the afternoon in Marlborough. She came back triumphantly with several bags of the best food she could find. 'And,' she said, as they sat at the kitchen table crowded with her purchases, 'guess what. A Mars Bar! I found the last one in some sweet shop. If we cut it into thin slices, we can make it last a week.'

'I don't believe it – Mars! You know how I love it.' Johnny's cheeks were suddenly pink. 'Thank God you've come.'

'Well . . .' Prue sat back, looking round the kitchen – almost as depressing, she thought, as the Ganders'. 'You know what I've been thinking? I'm going to clean this place up for you, starting tomorrow. I've bought scrubbing brushes, Sunlight soap, Dettol, everything.' She giggled. 'This time next week, you won't recognize the place.'

'You're an angel,' Johnny said again, too grateful and relieved to think of a better compliment. 'If you really don't mind.'

'You know me. I love hard work. A project. I'll enjoy it.'

'I'll keep out of your way. I'll be in the shed all day, working on a new table which I'm hoping to sell to some man of impeccable taste, though I haven't come across him yet. I'll have to advertise, as you say.' Once again he touched her hand very briefly, as if he didn't dare let his skin meet hers for more than a second. 'I'll be in charge of the chickens. You be in charge indoors.'

'Fine.' There was a waft of doubt at the back of Prue's mind. For how long would she be happy spring-cleaning someone else's cottage – she who yearned to be outside working the land, milking cows, dagging sheep, ploughing? She decided not to think about that for the moment, and began to pile tins of soup into a dirty cupboard which, later, she would scrub.

That evening, Johnny drove the Sunbeam to a pub beside the nearby canal. There was a lighted fire, and a few locals at the bar. Having chosen a table, Prue went quickly to order two ginger beers – she remembered Johnny had once said it was his favourite drink. He smiled when she put the tall glass in front of him.

'So.' Shaven, and in a clean shirt as requested, Johnny looked more like his old self. 'I'm out of touch with all your activities. What went on in Norfolk?'

As she began to tell him, Rudolph came stingingly back to Prue. She realized she had only three days before the letter she had promised was due. She also realized that for one whole day, occupied with Johnny's problems and his filthy cottage, she had not given Rudolph a thought. Johnny, a rather sad friend, as she now thought of him, had shown apparent approval of her

Norfolk adventure. He seemed to be uncritical of her lively week. Perhaps it was his understanding that made Rudolph fade a little.

'My guess is,' said Johnny, at the end of the story, which had taken them from tinned mulligatawny soup through tough liver and on to blancmange the colour of sore bunions, 'is that you'd soon be homesick, so far away. You're so deeply rooted in English earth. I think you'd be happier . . . here.'

Prue longed for a gin and lime but did not dare suggest it. 'If I stay, I must get a proper job,' she said. 'I can't just stay in your cottage scrubbing and cooking, grateful though I am for a roof over my head.'

'Of course not. We'll start looking next week,' Johnny agreed, in a voice hollow with reluctance.

'We will. That is, if . . . I decide not to go to America. If . . .'

'But you said you'd definitely decided not to go?'

'I have. But perhaps not completely. It's so difficult to be absolutely sure. One moment I'm certain about one direction, the next I'm certain of another.'

'I'll have to try to help you make up your mind.' Johnny looked down at his empty glass. His fingers tightened on it. Prue could see he was exercising control. She suggested it was time they left, and gave him her purse to take to the bar to pay. 'You think of everything,' he said, when he returned with the change.

When they got back Prue went straight to her room. She said she had to write to Barry and Rudolph.

This caused Johnny anxiety about the lack of a table in her room. He ignored her declarations that she was happy to write on her knee, and went out to his shed with a torch. He returned a long time later with a wooden packing case, which he heaved slowly upstairs, apologizing for not having anything better. Finally, the packing case placed by the bed, he left her with a wistful look that he quickly replaced with a smile. She heard the door of his bedroom bang very hard.

Prue took out her pack of Basildon Bond paper, chosen for its useful undersheet of ruled lines, and her fountain pen.

Dear Barry, [easiest to start with him]

I want to thank you very much for all the trouble you took to find me somewhere to live. But I have to say that the flat and Brighton were not really for me. It was never going to work out. I wonder if you ever saw it yourself? It was dark and pretty gloomy. I did go to the pub, not exactly crowded with potential friends, and wandered round the streets, and just felt there was no future there. Besides, I really didn't want to be in a town or by the sea. So after one night I left. Now I'm staying with Johnny – I'm his lodger – in a cottage he has been lent in Wiltshire. It's a terrible dump, which I'm going to clear up, but a most lovely part of the country, the Downs nearby. I do promise I am only a lodger, not that I think you would mind if I was anything else. Johnny is sad and lonely and thinks he has made a mistake leaving Manchester. I'm sure I won't be here long as I will put my mind to settling somewhere.

Thank you for all that money. You are very generous. It makes me feel safe. I hope Mum is happily settled. You've been very good to her. Give her my love. I'll keep in touch.

Love, Prue

As Prue stuck up the envelope, she remembered both Stella and Ag saying how much they enjoyed writing letters, what a pleasure it was to try to convey to someone exactly what you were doing or feeling at the time of writing. Ag had said she sent her father long descriptions of her progress in hedging, of Ratty's eccentricities and Mrs Lawrence's pride in her fruit trees. Stella had declared she wrote pages to Philip about everything on the farm, but always ended with a paragraph describing her undying love for him. Prue had said that if ever anyone besides her mother wrote to her, perhaps she would be inspired to write a good letter back. But she received almost no letters while she was at Hallows Farm, and didn't mind about this: what she had, which the others did not, were boyfriends nearby who gave her much more fun than letters.

As she picked up her pen to write to Rudolph, she still did not know what she was going to say: 'Yes, I'll come to America', or 'No, I'm staying in England.' She thought she would see what came out of her pen.

Dear Rudolph,

I'm not much good at writing letters, as you will see. I hardly ever need to write them and nobody but my mother writes to me. But I promised to let you know the Answer, so here goes.

Rudolph, I've thought and thought and thought and I still don't really know what to think. I've weighed everything up a thousand times. On the one hand there isn't a scrap of doubt that you gave me one of the best weeks of my life. It was like a dream, completely unreal. Every day I felt we were floating. I wanted it to go on and on and on. But you see it probably was a dream: two people meeting, dancing as one till they could dance no more, bound together by the music and the mutual wanting. But in that glorious week I'm not sure we really got to know each other, did we? I mean, we were so full of sky and sea and seals, and that scratchy grass stuff on the dunes and the rain coming through the leaves that first unforgettable time that we didn't have any need to talk. I liked that very much. I've had boyfriends who want to analyse progress every five minutes and I think that's very boring. I just like being, as I was with you. But is perfect being the same as long-lasting love? I don't know. I don't know how anyone can ever tell if something is for life, so a decision either way is always a risk, isn't it?

When I first saw you, and then soon after we started dancing, I said to myself I'd found my man. But then, like all single girls in search of love and a husband, which is how I see myself now it's come to an end with Barry, I was full of hope. And it seems to me that when you're really full of hope you can imagine things. So how do I know whether what I felt for you was real love instantly recognized or hope in disguise? I do believe we both felt the same, but perhaps you were full of hope too, and you just plonked it on me and imagined it was real. I don't know. Maybe all my thoughts are rubbish – I wish Ag was here to sort it out for me, or Mrs Lawrence. I wish you'd met her. She was the most wonderful woman in the world, so wise. She would have known what we should do. I would have liked her to be my mother.

Anyhow, I think what has always been my dream is very ordinary: married to a farmer, living in the West Country, several children. Well you of course are going to be a farmer, we could have lots of children, but the only problem is that your bit of country is thousands of miles away. And that, to be honest, is my great worry. I'm rooted here. I passionately love England – it came to me when I was a land girl and we all had the feeling we were actually doing something for our country, helping in a small way. America is just a shape on a map to me. I know you would do everything in your power to make me feel at home, but I would never feel at home. I really believe that. I would be in a state of constant missing.

You will say this is daft as I haven't actually got a home here – The Larches was just a house, and my mother's house I never thought of as home, and now I just wander about from Ag to Stella to lodging with friends. Hallows Farm was the nearest ever to home for me, and I know it's probably stupid but I want to make something like that in England. I think I wouldn't be any good at a great leap both of miles and culture. I'm afraid that the a desire to explore the world, travel, live in foreign countries isn't for me: my happiness is to live in a few small acres of home land, the local community.

There is one other thing – your pigs. I feel very foolish telling you this, ashamed at my feebleness. But I think I must explain. Your pigs are perhaps the strongest reason of all I have against emigrating to America. I didn't tell you in detail, but when I gave birth to the baby in a barn I was attacked by dozens of pigs and it was the most horrible, horrible experience of my life. I honestly don't think I could ever go near a pig again, let alone a herd. I couldn't cope, so I couldn't help. Pigs are your livelihood. Of course you couldn't give them up. I couldn't ask you to or want you to. So . . .

Since leaving you in Norfolk I tried the Brighton flat for one night and decided to leave next morning. There was no hope of that being the answer. Now I am staying with my old poet friend Johnny, who lived next door in Manchester and has a very dirty old cottage in Wiltshire, which I am going to spend the next week putting to rights. Just in case that thought is painful, please believe me when I say Johnny is not a lover. He will never lay a finger on me, but he is kind, lonely and struggling against drink. So I'll stay with him till I work out what to do. I hope that will be soon.

Dear Rudolph, I'm so sorry. I hope you will forgive me. I do love you and there are shooting stars all through my body when I think of you. I ache with missing you and I know I will always be haunted by the thought that I have made the wrong decision. But, uncertain about the strength of our love – would it last, would it? – and cowardly about leaving a country I love so much, I have to say I won't be coming to join you in Georgia. Please put me to one side and find a nice girl from Savannah who will deserve you more than me, and please keep the memory of our Norfolk week, as I will, till you are very old and can look back on it with a smile.

I told you I'm no good at letters but hope you can understand what I've tried to say, and I send you very very very much love,

Prue

Prue let her writing pad, pen and ink slide to the floor. She lay on the bed and began to sob. She remembered Stella saying to her – they were haymaking at the time – that if you had a single doubt about the man you had decided to marry, you shouldn't go ahead. Stella had not a doubt in the world, she said, about Philip. But then she had fallen in love with Joe. And because both she and Joe were so honourable they had trapped themselves for married life with spouses they did not love in the same way. It was all so confusing.

Exhausted by sobbing, not long before dawn, Prue decided not to post the letter. This, she knew, would mean all the struggle and heartache of writing another, and the uncertainty would still be there.

But she got up when it was light, went out into the rain and walked to the scarlet Victorian postbox, attached to a pole at the foot of the Downs, that reminded her of a red-breasted parrot on a perch. It was the kind of surprise that is sometimes found deep in the English country that she loved. Smiling at the final change of her quicksilver mind, she posted the letter. Done it. In two hours' time it would be collected by a postman on a red bicycle who had no idea of the depth-charge he had in his sack. Tomorrow Rudolph would have his answer.

On the way back to the cottage, an amber sky pushing past the grey, she began to plan her day of housework. By the time she had had breakfast with Johnny she felt calm, strong. She looked forward to scrubbing the kitchen floor. Doubts as to whether she had done the right thing chimed deep within her, but she knew she would have to live with them for the rest of her life.

It took Prue a week to transform the cottage. Each day she carried out a blitz on one room: scrubbed, dusted, shook the cushions, threw out a mass of junk, cleaned the filthy windows. She left the washing till last, for she most dreaded that. But she got down to it, in batches, with her usual determination. There was an old mangle in an outhouse: there, she spent hours persuading sodden things into the jaws of the wringer, and listening to the water squeezed from them dripping into a tin bucket. On a couple of fine days she set up a line in the garden and enjoyed watching the clothes and sheets billow about as the wind turned them into dancing balloons.

Then there was the ironing. Prue had watched Mrs Lawrence and Stella, both accomplished in the art, while the iron sizzled over sprawling shirts, which, within minutes, were transformed with neat folds. Prue had rarely tried ironing. But one gloomy afternoon – the week she had allowed for the transformation was nearly up – she plugged in the new decent-looking iron and began her experiment on the newly scrubbed kitchen table. There was a programme on the Home Service about foot-rot in sheep, which, she thought, Mr Lawrence was probably listening to in Yorkshire, perhaps Joe, too. It was an oddly comforting thought. There was a pleasing smell of damp cotton, and an undersmell of the bacon she had fried for lunch. Prue picked up the heavy iron, poised it over one of Johnny's shirts, and began.

It wasn't easy, but it was less difficult than she had imagined. A couple of hours later several triumphant piles of ironed clothes and sheets lay at the other end of the table. Prue was surprised by her own pleasure. Quite an accomplishment, in her estimation. She felt the same elation as the day she had finally mastered milking. All she needed now was a mite of appreciation.

She picked up two of the folded shirts and held them on the flat of her hand. Her idea was to take them to show Johnny now, rather than wait for him to come in for tea. Surely his surprise, and delight, would equal her own.

She walked across the garden, holding them carefully. The door of the shed was shut. She pushed it open and went in, holding out the shirts on her hands as if she was offering an omelette. Waited for the surprise, the praise.

Johnny was sitting on a low bench, head down, studying the wood shavings at his feet. He held a hammer in his right finger and thumb, swinging it backwards and forwards. Each time the hammer thrust forward, it just missed a bottle of vodka, almost empty, on the floor.

'Johnny?' Prue stayed by the door. 'I thought you . . .?'

He looked up, mouth downturned, eyes red. 'So did I,' he said.

Prue took a deep breath. 'I've been ironing,' she said, aware of the banality of her announcement. 'I just brought these to show you . . . that somehow I managed—'

Johnny stood up so fast that Prue, caught off guard, stepped back, hitting her head against a shelf that jutted from the back of the door. He was beside her in a single stride. 'Bugger the ironing,' he said, and swiped the shirts from her hand onto the floor. They looked at each other.

'You didn't have to do that,' said Prue.

'You're taking over,' shouted Johnny. 'Whole cottage antiseptic as a hospital. I was quite happy with things as they were.' His words were slurred.

Prue was not sure she had heard correctly. 'I'm sorry. I thought you wanted me to – I mean, I thought you were pleased at the idea of my getting it all straight for you.'

'That's what you thought. That's where you were wrong. You're often wrong, Prue Morton. You're just no bloody good at reading people. I'd be grateful if you went away now. Take the bloody shirts with you.'

He stumbled back to sit on the bench. Prue picked up the shirts, now crumpled and dirty again. She hurried out of the shed, shutting the door behind her.

Back in the cottage, the discussion on foot-rot was still going on, which, for a moment, tricked her into thinking that the scene of the last few minutes had not taken place. But the piles of laundry had lost their charm. Plainly, she was bad at reading people. Her foolish pride about her achievements of the last week, when she had been convinced that Johnny really hadn't been drinking, was blasted. He'd been at it secretly in the shed, and had disguised it very well. What, now, should she do? Perhaps the answer was to leave all this very quickly, just as she had left Brighton. It would be a relief to abandon the probably insuperable problem of Johnny, and send a telegram to Rudolph, saying, 'I'm coming after all.'

With this plan firmly in mind, Prue went out to the car. To her annoyance, she saw that one of the front tyres was flat. Johnny could have changed it easily, but to ask him was the last thing she wanted to do. She returned to the kitchen, took the clean linen upstairs. Then she concentrated on making a lamb stew – a local farmer had given them a few chops in return for eggs. She tried to remember what Mrs Lawrence had thrown into her stews. Then she switched the radio to the Third Programme. A cello, she thought it might be, was playing the saddest music she had ever heard. If Johnny returned while it was still on she would ask him what it was.

But he did not come in till long after the music had finished. It was dark. Prue had drawn the curtains and switched on the lights. The place looked unrecognizable, but she reminded herself not to feel any pride in this because she had misunderstood Johnny, and it was not what he wanted. When at last he came in he went immediately to the table and sat down, apparently sober.

'Smells good,' he said. Prue gave him a plate of the stew and a baked potato. 'I'm ravenous. Thanks.'

Prue took the seat opposite him, faced her own small helping. The internal churning had blasted her appetite.

'I'm terribly, terribly sorry, Prue,' Johnny said. 'Please forgive me. I do promise you that until today I haven't touched a drop of anything. Your being here has made a magical difference. Made it easier. Honestly. But today I woke up in one of those amorphous glooms that sometimes accost me, and then . . . something hit me that was the last straw.' He paused to cut his potato in half, mash into it a small slab of margarine. Prue had miscalculated the length to which their combined rations of butter would go, and once again they had run out. 'When I went out to see to the hens this morning, I found a fox had got in – it's never happened before. There were feathers everywhere. And poor old Dolly, one of the first birds I ever bought, was lying there without her head. I put her in the shed – should have buried her straight away. When I went back to get her after lunch and saw the disgusting sight of her, blood dripping from the gaping neck, I just became enraged. Once I'd buried her I came back to the shed and couldn't face getting down to work. Feeble, I know, but I was oddly upset. I thought, Just one swig, calm myself down. Unfortunately there was a bottle in the shed from when I'd had my bad week before you came. So I opened it, cursing myself.'

'First thing tomorrow morning,' said Prue, 'you must do something about mending the run.'

'I've fixed the weak place for tonight and I'll mend it in the morning. I will, I will. And I've thrown away the rest of . . .' Johnny sat back, held out his plate for more. 'God, I feel better. That was so good. One day you'll be a cook.' He gave her a smile, then his eyes roved round the room. 'I suppose I haven't really said anything, have I? Shown appreciation. What you've done to this place? It's an absolute wonder. It's marvellous.'

'Almost as hard work as farmwork.'

'Thank you for all your efforts. I never quite understand you, Prue. There you are, a dotty flibbertigibbet, apparently no thoughts in your pretty head beyond dresses and bows and seducing young men, yet you're the hardest worker I've ever met. All that rubbish I think I said to you about not being able to read people is completely untrue. I'm so sorry. I didn't really know what I was saying. You're amazing. You've been kinder to me than anyone in my life. If I was a different sort of man I'd like to marry you, look after you, have children with you. But I'm not that sort of man. I'm a loner. I get irritated by another presence, however sympathetic and untroublesome that presence is.'

'Does that mean you're giving me my marching orders, now the cleaning's done?' asked Prue.

'Good heavens, no. I love your being here. It's changed everything. We seem not to get in each other's way. It's a perfect arrangement.'

'It won't go on for that long,' Prue said. 'I've got to get a job that I love. I've got to find somewhere permanent to live, settle down.'

'Not too far from here, perhaps.'

'I hope not.'

'Don't give up on me.' Johnny took one of Prue's hands. She expected him immediately to withdraw, as he had done several times, but he kept hold of it. 'I'm determined to get over this drink business. I've done it once – for five years – so I can do it again. I can do it for ever. What I have to guard against is flying to the bottle when something unexpected, something disturbing, takes me unawares. Like the chickens. Thank God you were here, or who knows what might have happened?' He released her hand.

'I've tried to make a treacle sponge pudding,' said Prue. It was so heavy, so dry, so lacking in syrup that they could only laugh, throw it away and make a pot of tea.

Later Johnny gave Prue her first lesson in backgammon. She went to bed feeling quite proud that she had understood a few of the rules, and relieved that the air between them was clear again. All the same, the scene in the shed that afternoon had alerted her to a wild, alarming streak in Johnny. There was no guarantee that something unexpected would not trigger his drinking, or his temper, again. That was unsettling. She did not fancy the idea of living with him for too long, for all that she liked the place and her fondness for him remained.

The novelty of spring cleaning had worn off by the end of the week and the urgent need for Prue to find a new and challenging job spurred her to look in the local paper for work. Nothing of interest was advertised. She asked in the village if anyone knew of a Young Farmers' Club: the idea of a strapping young farmer, and going to village-hall dances with his equally strapping farmer friends, suddenly appealed to her. There was, indeed, just such a club, and they were to have an Easter Knees-up, as it was described on the posters, in a nearby village. Prue toyed seriously with the idea of going to it, without Johnny, but her enthusiasm waned as quickly as it had come.

A letter came from Barry. Prue waited till Johnny – in a much happier mood for the last few days – had gone to his shed before she read it at the kitchen table.

Dearest Prue,

Thanks for your letter and news. Of course it doesn't matter about the Brighton failure. My mistake, that. But I'm pleased you're settled with Johnny, a nice enough young man, though I always thought there was something a little troubling about him. I couldn't quite put my finger on it. So take care. I very much hope you will come across the perfect place to live soon, and settle. You only have to alert me and the money will be there. At the moment I'm spending a fortune on run-down cinemas.

The divorce, Prue, is going through. I have to be found in a hotel bedroom with some floozy. But who? That is my problem. I can see it will cost me. A friend of mine in the same situation got so desperate trying to hire someone that in the end he persuaded his wife to be the special co-respondent – bought her a wig and a pair of glasses! I believe they had such a good time they almost cancelled the divorce.

I'm so sorry about our marriage, I really am, but I'm relieved it all remains so civil between us. You know you can always count on me for anything. I rather miss you scuttling about in your funny bows. I think your mother is settled in and happy. She sends her love. She looks after me well, does wonders with the pathetic rations we still have to put up with. She never complains about the constant queuing and likes to do her shopping in the hat she wore when you and I were married! Despite running the house so well, she seems to have time on her hands so I've suggested she joins the British Housewives' League – fed-up women who write to ministers to complain about food shortages and so on. She'll enjoy that. How is the Sunbeam? Daimler and Humber still in good shape. I can never make up my mind which one I like best.

With love, Barry

Prue read the letter again. She smiled at the story of the co-respondent. During their marriage he had never told her funny stories. He never reported his private observations. Why hadn't he mentioned his misgivings about Johnny? And why had she herself not noticed warning signals beneath her friend's agreeable but detached exterior? The only time she had been jolted was the occasion in the barn. But that wildness had been driven by pure lust, and she had long ago forgiven him. Barry's letter, Prue thought, was altogether surprising. Sometimes he had seemed so coarse, dull, insensitive. She would never have guessed he could write such a letter, and began to question herself. Perhaps much of the blame for their marriage breakdown was hers. Come to think of it, she hadn't tried very hard either to discover things about him or to please him. She had always appreciated his generosity, but scoffed at his belief that endless presents were the way to a wife's heart. She had learnt very quickly, married to her rich man, that material goods did not make up for so much else that was missing. Perhaps if she had been more sympathetic she would have unearthed a man of more value than she had imagined existed. There was nothing she could do now, of course: she had no desire to return to the claustrophobia of The Larches, and she and Barry probably had too little in common to flame real happiness. His liking of older women meant Prue could never have satisfied him sexually, and his perfunctory approach to making love would never have fulfilled her. All the same, this bright morning, daffodils jigging at the edges of the garden, Prue felt a kind of guilt, a patina of shame. She decided that the least she could do was to write him another letter and try to convey a kind of apology.

Prue drove slowly to Marlborough – now she could no longer get Barry's black-market petrol she had to try to be economical – to buy stamps. Then she went to the newsagent for *Picture Post*. On the way out of the shop she stopped to look at the handwritten cards in the window advertising for baby-sitters, gardeners and shop assistants. One card stood out from the rest, thick, shiny, expensive, with a printed line at the top: 'From the Hon. Mrs Ivy Lamton'. Beneath this, in sepia ink, her require-ment was written in the most beautiful script Prue had ever seen, rather like the writing in an old manuscript, reproduced in a magazine article that she hadn't bothered to read. 'Would anyone be willing,' it said, 'to spare a few hours a week with an old lady? Companionship, conversation, potting out a few plants, nothing very taxing, agreeable surroundings. Please be kind enough to write.'

The address given was a few miles from Johnny's cottage. Prue's first thought was that, should she get the job, she could bicycle there to save petrol. She read the card again. She would have done anything to take it away, send it to Ag – it was her sort of thing. As the job was still advertised, she thought, it was probably still available – if you could call it a job. There was no point in waiting, postponing. Why not go at once, apologize for arriving with no warning?

She found the house at the end of a small village of scattered grey stone cottages. The Old Rectory was up what Prue considered to be a long drive – almost as long as the Ganders' rough road, but with an immaculately tarmacked surface, and hedged in with trimmed yews. The house was a real-life dolls' house: red brick, symmetrical windows with glossy white frames, a shiny black front door with a brass knocker. Prue parked, but didn't move for a few moments as she determined whether or not to call unannounced on the Hon. Mrs Ivy Lamton. What was an Hon.? Was Ivy really a name? Why didn't a vicar live in the Old Rectory? All so peculiar. But now she was here she might as well . . .

Prue tried to tug her skirt a bit further below her knees. She dabbed at the bow in her hair, wishing it wasn't the yellow one with red spots. For some time she stood looking for a bell to press before she realized a wrought-iron handle, attached to an iron pole twisted like barley sugar, was the sort of bell that came with old rectories. She pulled it. Silence, for a moment. Then a deep, growling, far-away ring like a noise that might come from the bottom of the sea. But no footsteps.

Prue was about to turn and go back to the car when the door opened. An old lady stood there, one hand on a cane. She was very upright, as if she had learnt to balance books on her head and never lost the habit. Her soft white hair was piled up, a bun on top like a cottage loaf. She had the smallest eyes Prue had ever seen, set far back in hollows the colour of black grapes. Prue bit her lip, worried that the Hon. Ivy could read her astonished thoughts.

'Can I help you?' The voice was thin, high, sweet.

'I've come – I mean, I saw your card and I thought I'd better come right away before the job had gone.'

'Oh, that.' The old lady laughed. 'Do come in. That card's been there for months. No one remotely interested. I don't know why I thought anyone would be . . .'

Prue stepped into the hall. No wonder there had been no footsteps: the carpet was so thick she felt the heels of her red shoes sinking into it.

'I was about to give up. How very good of you to come, how delightful. Let's go into the sitting room.'

Sunlight on the brass face of a grandfather clock in the hall made a sudden flash, like a wink, acknowledging the oddness of the encounter with the Hon. Ivy who, tapping her cane on the carpet, which changed from grey to dark red as they went through a heavily panelled door, led Prue into the sitting room. There, Prue came to a halt, suddenly overcome.

'Blimey,' she said. 'If you don't mind me saying so, I've never seen anything like this. Such a room.'

Ivy looked at her. One pale eyebrow twitched. She smiled. 'Well,' she said, 'its heyday's long past. I don't mind the fading or the threadbare tapestry, but it's all a little . . . lifeless now. Everyone gone.' For a second she was melancholy, then instantly righted herself to brightness. 'Why don't we have a pot of coffee, and you can tell me all about yourself?'

'Lovely. Thank you.'

'And do sit down.'

'Lovely. Thank you.'

Prue was cross with herself for the silly repetition. She could not imagine why she felt so nervous, ill at ease, but supposed it was because she hadn't come prepared to find herself in a world so far from her own. She looked around, wondered how many books there must be in the shelves that lined an entire wall, and chose the corner of a sofa by the fire. She put out her hand to move a cushion covered with what must be real satin. Ivy crossed the room to a desk of dark wood with brass trimmings. She picked up a small bell and rang it. The tinkle, in the deep silence, was almost impertinent.

'Alice will bring us a tray in here,' she said. 'Dear Alice has been here for ever. She's not the fastest but she's a treasure, one of those saints who spend their lives in English villages helping people. She probably didn't hear the bell. I'll just go and tell her.'

Ivy loped towards the door faster than she had previously moved. Prue stroked the satin cushion and looked round the room. Old furniture glowed from decades of polish. The sage green walls that were free of bookshelves were crowded with portraits. The stern faces shone out from dark and gloomy paint – they all looked either cross or sad. A bit spooky, Prue thought. She wouldn't much like to be alone with them in this room on a winter's evening. At the high windows curtains hung from elaborate pelmets – the word suddenly came to Prue: her mother had once expressed an acute desire to live in the kind of house that had pelmets. They were gathered into breathtaking pleats. The curtains – brocade, was it? – were the colour of the wet sand on the seals' beach. Oh, how she wanted to tell Rudolph all this. But their edges, where the sun had touched them, had paled to the colour of candle wax. On a table beside Prue stood a precise arrangement of photographs in silver frames. One was of a very grand-looking man in uniform, medals all over his chest. On another table there was a bowl of white hyacinths. Their scent reached across the room.

Ivy returned.

'So sorry, my dear,' she said, and lowered herself into an extravagant armchair opposite Prue, hitching up the back of her long black skirt before her behind touched the cushion. 'Now, you must tell me why you've come. Were you really attracted by my plea? If so, I can't imagine why. Who knows? Maybe I'm in luck. Who are you? What's your name?'

'Prudence. Prudence Lumley.'

'Such a lovely name. I fear it's destined to go out of fashion. My sister-in-law was a Prudence – very aptly in her case. Over-Prudence, I called her . . .' She smiled.

As Prue had no idea how to respond to this observation, she kept quiet. She hoped the Hon. Ivy's questions would not be too hard to answer.

A bent old woman came through the door carrying a tray of clattering china. The chances of her crossing the room without it crashing to the floor, Prue reckoned, were small. She leapt up, hurried to take it from her.

'Thank you so much. Put it here.' Ivy patted a brocade ottoman. Prue put the tray on a copy of *The Times*, wondering if that was the right thing to do. Perhaps she should have moved the newspaper. Her heart was battering. Never had a room made her so uncertain. But the Hon. Ivy looked on with approval, so she guessed she had done the right thing. Blimey, relief. The cups and plates, the coffee pot and milk jug were almost transparent in their thinness – they made Barry's 'best' china look thick, clumsy. They weren't decorated with prissy roses, like Barry's: there was just a thin gold line round the rims. Ivy turned to Alice, who swayed like a statue poorly soldered to its base, her mouth open, indignation stiffening her clenched hands. She was not accustomed to having her tray snatched away by some young whipper-snapper with a film-star bow in her hair. 'Thank you, Alice,' said Ivy. 'This is just what we need. I said, thank you.'

Alice, further affronted, shuffled out.

Ivy leant back in her chair, ignoring the tray. It occurred to Prue that a companion's job would be to pour the coffee. This she suggested.

Ivy, whose tiny eyes had glazed, brightened. 'Would you be a darling? That would be so kind.'

Not that kind, really, Prue thought. All she said was 'Cripes'. As Ivy did not question this, she imagined she should explain. 'Your house, this room . . . everything,' she said. 'I'm afraid I'm overwhelmed. It's perfect—'

'Now, now,' Ivy interrupted. 'It's just an ordinary old rectory filled with some nice things my husband Edward and I collected over the years. He was in the diplomatic service. We moved about all over the world. I insisted we take all this clutter everywhere, so a bit of each foreign embassy would feel like home. Most of the places were so hot it all looked a bit heavy. I can't tell you how grateful I was to get back here. I've always loved England better than anywhere. Give me just a speck of milk, would you mind? And help yourself. But I want to know about you. Tell me all about yourself. Tell me why such a pretty young thing as you – oh, I do love your shoes, I've always loved red shoes – would like to be a companion to a very old lady like me.'

Prue settled deeper into the cushions. It was like being on a firm cloud. Had she not been juggling in her mind how to start, she might have fallen asleep, lulled by the scent of the hyacinths. She was about to begin, having drunk her fragile cup of coffee very fast, and returned it to the saucer where it skidded about, when the clock in the hall struck eleven: each note echoed, and the echo thinned till the next strike took its place. Prue waited for absolute silence to return.

'OK,' she said at last. 'I'll try to explain.'

She began her story.

# Chapter 12

Occasionally, during the hour that Prue recounted (most, but not quite all of) the events in her life, the Hon. Ivy flicked at specks of invisible dust on her skirt. Occasionally she moved her deep-set eyes towards the hyacinths and gave the beginnings of a smile, which never matured. For the most part she sat absolutely still, seeming to listen with her whole being. When Prue judged she had nothing left to tell this stranger, on whose grand sofa she sat, she shrugged, and fell silent.

Ivy sighed. She tipped back her head, closed her eyes. 'Well, well, dear Prudence,' she said, 'what a life in so few years. So much of it sounds familiar. I felt I knew so many of those people. You're a wonderful raconteur.'

Prue didn't know what a raconteur was, and did not like to ask. But she took it as a compliment, given it was preceded by 'wonderful'. 'Thanks,' she said. She wondered which way the interview – which didn't feel like an interview – would go now.

Ivy opened her eyes. 'Oh, that land-girl life. What would we have done without you? My sister, you know, joined the Land Army just as it was starting up at the end of the First World War. It lasted such a short time because, of course, the war ended. So fortunate it was reinstated for this war, though by then Maud was too old to join up.'

Maud? Maud and Ivy? The Hon. Mrs Lamton and her sister plainly came from another world. Prue felt a strange keenness to know more about it just as, coming from Manchester, she had been keen to discover about the Lawrences' rural life.

'Now,' Ivy was saying, 'there must be some questions you'd like to put to me.' The pale eyebrows rose and fell.

Prue hesitated. The question she had in mind might be considered cheeky, but she was convinced Ivy wouldn't be offended. 'What exactly is a Hon.?' she asked. 'I've never met one before.'

Ivy laughed. 'Well, how can I best explain it? It's all to do with the weird English system of titles and so on. My father was a viscount. The children of viscounts, who are themselves the children of earls – oh, it's all too complicated to go into. Pretty silly, not to say confusing, really. It'll all come to an end one day. But I'll tell you another silly thing.' She clasped her hands, working out how best to put it. 'A Hon isn't actually pronounced . . . the H is silent. Daft, I know.'

'You mean you're an On, really?'

'That's it.'

'Cripes. Can't wait to tell my mum all this. She'll never believe it – me meeting the daughter of a whatever . . .' Prue giggled.

'But what I actually meant, when I said had you any questions, was have you any questions about the job I'm offering?'

'You're offering?'

'I don't see why not. I'm not quite clear in my mind the exact nature of the job, but I'm sure we could work it out once you're here.'

'I'm sure we could.'

'It would just be sharing a few hours of my day, really. Two or three times a week, perhaps. We could see how it goes.'

With surprising agility Ivy, suddenly scorning her cane, now rose from her chair as easily as someone half her age. She looked, it occurred to Prue, exactly as she imagined the ghost of an old lady would look. For a second she wondered if she was a ghost, and this whole peculiar visit was no more than a dream. But Ivy was speaking very firmly: nothing insubstantial about her.

'One little idea came to me while you were telling me about Johnny and his bad luck,' she said. 'A couple of stable doors in the yard are completely rotten and the wonderful old carpenter who lived in the village died last week. I wonder if your friend Johnny could make two new ones?'

'I'm sure he could. He'd be thrilled.'

'That would be such a relief. I didn't know where to turn.'

Prue felt that she, too, ought to stand now. But Ivy had picked up one of the silver-framed photographs and handed it to her. 'If you ever fancy another husband, you could do worse than Gerald, my nephew.'

'What?' Prue had no notion of how to respond to this extraordinary idea.

Ivy was laughing, enjoying her joke. 'Awfully clever. Scholar at Eton, classics at New College, Grenadier Guards, and now the City.'

None of this meant anything to Prue: a different language was used at the Old Rectory, which she found hard to understand.

'What City?' she asked.

'The City of London, dear girl. Banking. Bores him stiff. Still, once I've gone, he'll take over all this. He loves it here.'

As Prue got to her feet she studied the photograph of an impossibly handsome man in soldier's uniform. Gerald. Wow. 'How old is he?' she dared herself to ask.

Ivy waved a hand vaguely. 'I don't know – thirty-five, forty, maybe.'

'Bit old,' said Prue.

'What? For marriage? Older husbands are a darn good idea. Of course, they usually die first, but by then the wife has got used to the idea. Edward was fifteen years older than me, looked after me wonderfully well, gave me good advice about what I should do once I was a widow. And I don't want you thinking, Prudence, that because I fancy a little companionship I'm a lonely old thing. For I absolutely am not. I love living alone. I've never been lonely for a moment. There's so much to do.' The beginning of this declaration had been made in a firm voice, which was now petering out.

'I can imagine,' said Prue, though in truth she couldn't. 'In this house no one could be lonely for a moment.'

'Quite. There are all the books. The piano. The gramophone. The garden. Are you a reader, Prudence?'

Prue felt herself blush. 'Not really,' she said. 'There were no books at home, though there were lots at Hallows Farm – but not much time for reading, there.'

'Of course not. All that farm work. Still, I dare say you managed a few pages of Hardy, from time to time, as you were in Dorset?'

'I didn't, no. I sometimes looked at Mr Lawrence's copy of the *National Geographic* magazine. And Mrs Lawrence's *Picture Post.*'

'Oh my dear girl, you've got a long and exciting road to travel.' Ivy moved to the bookshelves, took a leatherbound volume from a row of identical ones. 'Dickens?' Prue shook her head. 'Well, then, I think you should begin with the master. *Great Expectations*. Here, take it. Bring it back when it's finished, and we'll replace it with something else.'

Prue looked at the tooled leather, the gold writing. 'I'd be terrified of something happening to it,' she said. 'I've never seen such a beautiful book.'

'Books are for reading. If it falls on Johnny's kitchen floor, well, that's not important.' She took the photograph from Prue, returned it to its place on the table. 'I'll try to get Gerald over one day when you're here. You might find him quite amusing.'

'Thank you so much.' Prue's sudden flare of great expectations concerning Gerald seemed to be far stronger than those for the book.

'And please mention my stable doors to your friend.'

'Of course.'

Ivy held out a papery hand, which Prue took care to shake gently.

'Come on Monday morning, why not? We won't talk about money, wages, that sort of tedious thing now. We'll see what happens.'

When Prue went through the hall to the front door, the grandfather clock struck twelve. As she wrote to both Stella and Ag later, it was the weirdest, maddest morning of her life. Although the nature of the work remained not quite clear, she found herself looking forward to it with peculiar excitement.

Johnny was pleased by the idea of the Hon. Ivy's job: he liked making doors. He did not show much interest in Prue's descriptions of the house, or of its elderly owner, and spent most of the weekend in his shed. From time to time Prue went in with cups of tea or coffee, but really to check that he wasn't drinking. He had convinced himself he had given up, at least for the time being, and was happy with the quantities of ginger beer she provided.

The weekend, for Prue, went very slowly. She was bored by now with housework and reduced it to half an hour every morning after breakfast. She was impatient to start working for Ivy, and tried to imagine what the job would entail. A restlessness came over her: there was no reply to her letter from Rudolph. On the occasions she thought of him, she still felt uneasy about her decision, but the pictures of him grew more distant.

Johnny, she quickly realized, with his fluctuating moods and his evident unhappiness, was not going to be easy to lodge with. She had constantly to guess what best to do for him. He seemed to be a different man from the neighbour she had known in

Manchester – but then, of course, she had seen him only from time to time. She knew that it would be much better to live alone than with an imperfect man, though she wasn't sure she was ready just yet for solitude.

She paced about, made a bread-and-butter pudding to use some of the many eggs and in the hope of disguising the hard bread (Johnny was appreciative of her cooking). She went for a walk, but in a state of such agitation that, for once, the swooping Downs and hovering skylarks were no comfort. When she returned to the cottage, cross with herself for such unreasonable discontent, she went to the sitting room and picked up *Great Expectations*.

At first Prue just held the book, turning it in her hands, in some awe. She ran a finger along the gold-tooled patterns inset in the claret-coloured leather with its soft smell of . . . what? she wondered. Rain, perhaps? A lighter smell than the rough leather of Noble's harness, but a reminder. She turned over a few of the thick, cream pages with their rough edges, as if they had been gently torn. She had not held a book, let alone read one, for a very long time. This beautiful volume made her oddly nervous, but she was determined to have a go. She could not possibly go back to Ivy and say, no, she hadn't tried it. She glanced at the print – very small. Very dense paragraphs. She was going to have to try very hard.

Within a moment she was in the churchyard with Pip – amazed that a writer could make her see a picture so clearly. The marshes were just a long black horizontal line . . . and the river was just another horizontal line, not nearly so broad or so black . . . and the sky was just a row of angry red lines and dense black ones intermixed . . . She could see it all, feel the cold, the damp. She was there.

Prue read for the rest of the day, stopping only to eat. Her enthusiasm for Dickens seemed to please Johnny. He said she should try *David Copperfield* next. And there was much more to come. Dickens would keep her going for a long time. Prue read most of Saturday night, and much of Sunday. On Monday morning, tired but exhilarated, she took the book back to Ivy, pleased at the thought of surprising her, and longing for the next one.

Johnny followed her to the Old Rectory in his van so that he could get back to the cottage and start work once he had measured up for the stable doors. He parked in front of the house, beside the Sunbeam, and came over to Prue. 'Nice house,' he said, fighting against extravagant praise. He took Prue's elbow with a tense hand.

She had the fleeting thought that, were he a husband, he would be good about keeping to his wife's side. Then she realized he only kept close to her on this occasion because he was nervous about meeting Ivy.

Ivy opened the front door even before they were climbing the steps. She stretched out both hands in greeting and Johnny, on reaching her, took both her hands in his with all the ease of one who is used to unusual handshakes. Prue smiled. She and Ivy did not shake hands. 'How lovely of you to come,' she said to Johnny. 'I can't tell you how much I need a master carpenter. The stables are falling to pieces. Wasn't it lucky, Prue being your friend?'

She led them into the sitting room. Johnny glanced surreptitiously about him, trying to disguise his interest.

'Now, why don't Johnny and I go and look at what's to be done? Then we can all have a cup of coffee. Oh, Prue, my dear girl, you've brought back the book. How quickly you've read it! And what did you think?'

'I was astonished, overwhelmed,' said Prue, unable immediately to come up with more literary praise.

'That's marvellous! Why don't you go and choose yourself another Dickens?'

'I recommended *David Copperfield*,' said Johnny. He seemed pleased to show he shared his new employer's literary knowledge.

'Good idea, dear boy,' said Ivy. 'And when I come back I'll get you, Prudence, to run me to the post office.' Her eyes twinkled. 'You know what? I rather fancy a little run in your lovely red car.'

'It's terrific,' said Johnny.

When they had gone, Prue replaced the book in the shelf and took out *David Copperfield*. She sat on her old place in one corner of the sofa, and looked about her. She wanted to check it was all just as magical and extraordinary as it had appeared on her first visit. Though as she was in a calmer state, she was able even better to enjoy the room. She realized that, amazingly, she felt almost at home here. She could imagine living in this house. Arranging the flowers on the desk. Drawing the curtains on winter evenings. Coming down in the mornings to find sun on the fragile carpet, which must have come from one of the eastern countries Ivy had lived in. Boldly, as these sensations swept over her, Prue picked up the silver-framed photograph of Gerald. She stared at it for a long time, consigning every inch to memory. Gerald. Very distinguished name. 'Prue and Gerald', she said to herself, for she always liked trying out her own name with other possibilities. They went well together. One day, perhaps, there could be thick white invitations propped up on the mantelpiece, 'Prue and Gerald' in fine handwriting at the top . . . Somehow, she must subtly remind Ivy that she'd be very interested to meet her nephew.

Prue had no idea how much time went by caught up in her day dreams. She was conscious of an almost tangible happiness – the sort of happiness she used to sense sometimes when she was ploughing Lower Pasture, and the chimes from the hall clock scarcely interrupted her thoughts.

When eventually Ivy came back, she seemed thrilled by the promises Johnny had made. 'What a talented young man,' she said. 'I dare say I can find all sorts of jobs for him on the estate.

There's always so much repair work that needs doing. He wouldn't even stay for a cup of coffee – said he wanted to get going straight away. He's gone off to order the wood. So: how about you and I making a small trip to the post office? Only a mile or so. I usually walk it, but . . . Edward and I loved fast cars. Once, we had a Lagonda.'

Prue took the precaution of not driving at speed along the narrow lanes, but Ivy did not object. She moved about in her seat like an excited child. At the post office Prue saw her reluctance to get out, so offered to post the letter for her.

'You're a good girl,' Ivy said. 'We must go for a proper drive one day. I only have a tiny Ford. Not much more than a perambulator – no fun at all.' Suddenly she fell silent. Then she said, 'You know, I've been taxing my mind about this job I've asked you to do, and I'm still not quite sure what it should be. Still, we'll see what comes up. This afternoon we could perhaps attack the linen cupboard, and when that gets boring, well, you could begin *David Copperfield* while I have my rest . . .' She trailed off, uncertain of the appeal of her idea.

'That would be lovely,' said Prue. 'I don't mind what I do.'

'And then one day, I suppose, we could go through all the clothes I had as a young girl, box them up and send them somewhere.'

'That'd be good, too.'

As she turned into the drive, for Ivy's sake she accelerated very slightly and was rewarded with a shout of delight. Then the old lady clamped a hand over her mouth, for a moment, cutting off the scream. 'Oh, my goodness, Prue. Look who's here! Isn't that an astonishing coincidence? I was going to telephone Gerald today. He needs to meet a few bright young things. I have a notion his life is quite dull.'

A large car was parked by the house – not as large as the Humber or the Daimler, but sportier. There was no sign of the driver. Prue wished she'd been less economical with her mascara. She and Ivy got out of the car. Ivy called Gerald a couple of times, her voice scarcely audible over a sudden clatter of rooks in the high trees.

He appeared round the corner of the house and sauntered over to his aunt, apparently not noticing Prue. He wore the kind of clothes that Prue had only seen on the gentry in church on Sunday at Hallows Farm: sharply pressed trousers, beautiful tweed jacket, fine shirt with regimental tie, yellow silk handkerchief flopping from his top pocket. He drew on a cigarette whose smoke, even in the sharp air, indicated it was some kind of exotic brand. He waved it about in an amber holder, then held it above his head as he kissed his aunt.

'Gerald, what a lovely surprise,' she said. 'I was about to ring you.'

'Thought you wouldn't mind if I dropped in. I'm not skiving.' He smiled at his aunt. 'I'm on my way to Salisbury Plain. Business, I promise.'

'Now come and meet Prudence. She's going to help me a few days a week. Prue, this is my nephew, Gerald Wickham.'

As Gerald did not move, Prue stepped towards him. They shook hands. His eyes, Prue noticed at once, slanted upwards from each side of his nose like two small wings. In repose, his mouth was severe, almost sneering, but when he smiled again, as he did shaking hands with Prue, it cracked his face making friendly, endearing wrinkles. She felt relieved.

The three of them went to the sitting room. Gerald sat on Prue's sofa. Ivy fetched a glass ashtray and put it on the table beside him. Prue chose the chair opposite. She wished Gerald did not have his back to the light, and she herself was not so exposed to it. Ivy suggested Gerald stayed for lunch. He declined with apologies, said he could only stay for a short time.

'Duty calls, I suppose,' said Ivy. 'I'll just go and . . .' She whipped out of the room, once again scarcely leaning on her cane.

Gerald crossed his legs, studying Prue with the intensity of a man looking at some rare object for which he might be persuaded to put in a bid. Prue noticed that his kneecap was a sharp little plate showing through the thick material of his trousers. Good sign, that. Meant he had good legs. Barry Two's knees she had always found unappealing.

'So what on earth are you doing here?' he asked. His voice was a languorous drawl, something like Rudolph's but minus the charm of the Southern accent.

'I'm not really sure.' Prue giggled. 'I'm not sure your aunt knows, either. She said we'd see how it goes. See what comes up.'

'I see.' Gerald inhaled deeply. 'What do you like doing? What kind of work?'

'Looking after animals. I used to be a land girl. I love cows. I love ploughing, driving a tractor.' She fluttered her eyelashes. 'As a matter of a fact, I got pretty good at straight furrows.'

'I bet you did.' Gerald smiled very slightly. 'Well, I'm afraid there are no cows here, no animals at all, though there will be again when I take over. Like everyone else, Ed and Ivy had to turn to arable during the war and still haven't changed back. Still, I dare say we could find somewhere for you to do a bit of ploughing one day.'

Prue dismissed the thought that he was faintly sarcastic. She didn't really care what he said or didn't say. She was happy just to look at him. She loved his very shiny shoes, and the way he looked serious when he inhaled his cigarette. She would be quite happy as Mrs Gerald Wickham.

Gerald stirred her cogitations by asking her where she was living.

'I'm lodging nearby with an old friend, Johnny. Just for a while, until I find somewhere. He's a carpenter.'

'A carpenter.' It wasn't a question. Gerald thought about Johnny's profession for a long time in silence.

'And a poet,' said Prue, eventually, wondering whether this might inspire more approval.

'A carpenter and a poet? What a combination. As a matter of fact, probably rather a good one.' His eyes strayed about, avoiding Prue, as if he was thinking seriously about this, too.

'Actually,' said Prue, wishing she had never mentioned Johnny, 'he's going to do some work for your aunt. New stable doors.'

'Good, good.' At last Gerald looked at her. 'Aunt Ivy enjoys employing people. Though I really can't imagine what she'll find for you to do.'

'I think she'd just like a bit of company.'

'Well, you could learn a lot from her. She's very clever, full of arcane knowledge.'

'She's already started me reading.'

'Reading? Started you reading?'

'Real books, I mean.' Prue giggled. 'Usually I just read magazines. Film-star gossip. I love *Picture Post*.'

'Quite.' Gerald stubbed out his cigarette, immediately reached for a gold case in his inside pocket and lit another.

Prue had a flash of all those evenings at The Larches when, before her pregnancy, Barry would go through the palaver of choosing a cigar from his less delicate gold case and lighting one after another. 'In fact,' she said, squirming slightly in the deep chair, her spirits rising as she felt she was making a little progress, 'she lent me *Great Expectations*. I read the whole thing over the weekend, and I'm not a quick reader.'

'Good,' said Gerald, with less interest than she had expected. 'You must carry on. You'll have a good time. But it might be a little dull for you here. Don't you ever feel like going to London?'

'Not really. I've been just the once.' Her spirits were rising fast for she had a boast that she bet even Gerald rather-snooty Wickham couldn't match. 'Few years ago the King and Queen gave a tea party at Buckingham Palace for land girls. I was one of the lucky ones chosen to go.'

'Lucky you.' Gerald's eyes were drooping.

Was her news that boring? 'I actually had the chance to curtsy to all of them. And at one moment I was so near to Princess Margaret I . . .' Gerald's eyes were now shut. Was he asleep? Rude bastard. Most men didn't find her that dull.

He opened his eyes, kept looking at her as if to sum her up and store her away for some future decision. 'The place I like,' he began, in his languorous way, 'is the Savoy.'

'The what?'

'It's a grand hotel down by the river. Before the war it was absolute heaven. Lots of good nights there, masses of friends, a big band, dancing . . . I've often thought that if ever I get married that's where I shall spend the first night of my honeymoon. Suite overlooking the river.'

'What a good idea,' said Prue, who could suddenly imagine both the suite and the first night in the unknown hotel, which probably had gold taps. Funny thing was, he might be looking at the very woman with whom he would be sharing that night with . . . It was all she could do not to mention this.

'Would you like me to introduce you to the Savoy one day? Few weeks here, and you'll be dying for a bit of fun.'

Prue stared at him, unable to answer. A night in London with this amazing, sleepy, curious man . . .

'Would I like it?' she whispered. 'I'd be over the moon.'

'Then we'll make a plan,' he said, got up and went to the window, where he lit another cigarette.

Johnny's enthusiasm for the Old Rectory did not match Prue's. 'Usual sort of thing for an English village,' he said. 'Very average. But, yes, some good pieces of furniture. The whole place could do with a lick of paint.'

'I like it as it is,' said Prue 'How about the stables?'

'They're wonderful. The old tack room is still full of saddles and bridles that look as if someone keeps polishing them. I shall enjoy doing the new doors. Thanks for that. Mrs Lamton suggested a huge fee. I didn't argue.' Johnny sat at the kitchen table, poured tea. He seemed happy.

'I met her nephew, Gerald. Rather odd, rather nice. Almost middle-aged, I think.' She paused. 'Anyhow, he's asked me to dinner at a place called the Savoy.'

'The Savoy?' Johnny slammed his hand on the table. A wave of tea slopped over the edge of his mug. 'But that's in London.'

'I know it's in London. Have you been there?'

Johnny dabbed at the spilt tea with his handkerchief. 'Of course I've been to the Savoy.'

Prue knew he was lying. 'I don't know where you've been, what you've done. I just know you've led a much more sophisticated life than me.'

That seemed to please him. But then he frowned. 'I can't quite picture this planned evening,' he said. 'How do you get to London? Does this Gerald drive you? Going to London'd eat into the petrol coupons, all right. Train? Come back in the middle of the night – what?'

'I don't know. He didn't say. I don't even know when it's to be. Why are you so cross?'

'I'm not cross.'

'I mean, I'm only your lodger. We lead independent lives. So far, I haven't been out at all, have I?'

'I thought you were happy here.'

'I am. But given a chance to go dancing somewhere posh, I can't turn it down, can I?'

'Suppose not.' Johnny sighed. 'But you be careful. Middle-aged men are good at flashing their money, inveigling young girls.'

'What's inveigling?'

'Ensnaring, capturing.' Suddenly he shouted. 'Getting them into their beds.'

'Oh, Johnny. Don't be so stupid.' She put a hand on his. He snatched it away. 'You can't deny me a few hours' fun, can you? What do you think I am? A serial seducer?'

'Yes,' said Johnny. 'Exactly. There's scarcely a man in the world you don't flirt with, imagine you could marry and be with happily ever after. It's pathetic, your constant search for love, your self-delusion.' He scraped back his chair, got up from the table. 'Well, you go and enjoy yourself at the Savoy, a place so far above your station you won't know what to do, but I don't want to know about it, see? I'll stay here with a nice bottle of vodka.'

'Johnny!' He sped out of the room, banging the door behind him.

His mysterious anger had little effect on Prue: she was too engaged imagining the evening with Gerald. The more she thought about him the more she saw that he was a real possibility. And when Johnny returned for supper he seemed to have forgotten about his previous rage and its cause. They had a perfectly normal evening: ginger beer, chicken talk and a few games of backgammon.

Over the next two weeks Prue found herself going to the Old Rectory most weekdays, always uncertain of what each might hold. Sometimes she went to the greenhouse with Ivy and helped with planting out seedlings. Once she trimmed a hedge, a job with which she felt more familiar, though Ag, as she told Ivy, would have done it much better. She 'sorted out' an address book, neatly writing names and addresses into a new leatherbound book, leaving out those with a line through them. 'So many dead,' as Ivy said.

They did, one rainy afternoon, go through the linen cupboard, as Ivy had suggested the day Prue arrived. A mutual reluctance about this job made them slow. They unfolded and refolded enormous initialled linen sheets, then wondered on which shelf to put them, while Ivy told stories of life under the Raj. Every day they had shortbread biscuits and a cup of coffee in the sitting room at lunchtime.

'Alice uses up my entire ration of sugar and butter with all this shortbread,' Ivy said, 'but she knows I love it and I don't like to discourage her. I've had to get used to sugarless porridge.' When Prue suggested it would be easier to eat in the kitchen, Ivy looked mildly shocked. 'I daresay, Prue, in this modern world, dining-room people will spend more of their lives in the kitchen. But I'm not one of them, thank goodness.'

'So what do you do at night, alone here for supper?' Prue asked.

'Alice leaves me something in the oven and a place laid in the dining room. I light the candles, listen to a concert on the wireless. I reflect, I remember. What could be nicer?'

Never once, over their shortbread, did Ivy try to describe the nature of the job she had in mind for Prue. It soon became clear that, despite her enjoyment of solitude, someone just there, in the house, was all she really required. Always, shortbread finished, she struggled to think of something for Prue to do while she had her rest. Every day she came up with the same solution. 'Why don't you make yourself comfortable in here, Prue, carry on reading?' Prue always agreed, for her afternoons with Dickens had become an extraordinary pleasure. Her aim was to read his entire works. Most days, mid-afternoon, she would hear Ivy come downstairs but not into the sitting room, as if by design she was leaving Prue to read, having no jobs for her. This arrangement became so satisfactory to both of them that it was never mentioned.

One day Prue asked if she might write a letter to Ag while Ivy slept. She was immediately offered ink, pen and as much writing paper as she wanted. Prue sat down at the huge leather-embossed desk, glancing from the brass inkstand, 'given to us by the high commissioner in India', to the silver dagger for opening envelopes and the pristine blotting-paper in the embossed blotter. Cripes, she thought. The cream writing paper, sharp-edged and thick, had the Old Rectory's address engraved at the top. Prue ran a finger over the raised letters, marvelling. She dipped the pen into the depths of a bottle of Quink, and began her letter in royal blue. So engrossed did she become, trying to describe her new life to Ag, that she did not hear Ivy come into the room.

'I've just had Gerald on the telephone,' she said. 'He suggested you might like to go through with the Savoy plan next Wednesday.'

There was a trace of something – anxiety? doubt? – in her voice. Prue could not be sure what it was.

'Gosh, I thought he'd never ring,' said Prue. 'Wednesday would be fine.'

'Gerald's never very speedy in executing his plans,' said Ivy, 'but he gets there in the end.' She pursed her lips, trapping a few remembered incidents.

'What shall I wear?' Prue's thoughts had leapt immediately to the inadequate crowd of dresses squished into the musty cupboard in Johnny's cupboard.

'Oh, my dear girl, it has to be long, of course.'

'Long? But I haven't got a long dress. I've never had one.'

'Then you'd better come with me.' Prue followed her upstairs to a room she had never been into before: floor-to-ceiling cupboards on each wall. 'My cupboard room,' explained Ivy. 'The collection of things I've never thrown away. I suppose it'll all be sent to a sale when I'm dead.'

They spent the rest of the afternoon going through rails of clothes in all the colours of a peacock's tail and rainbows: silk, velvet, crêpe-de-Chine, chiffon, sparkling buttons, fur collars, lace jabots. For each dress there was a story of some dance in Peking, an ambassadorial ceremony in Washington or Rome . . . Ivy held up hanger after hanger, letting a wisp of her past sway again a little as she held out the skirt, puffed up the sleeves. The clothes came with a faint smell of mothballs, and an even fainter waft of scent – 'Mitsuko, always Mitsuko, Ed loved it,' Ivy said. She was jumping from foot to foot, her voice high on memory.

The light began to dim. Purpureal sky appeared in the single window. They could hear the snarling of thunder. It began to rain. Well-spaced spots clattered against the glass. Quickly the light became so poor it was difficult to depict detail of fabric and embroidery, pleats and ruffles. Ivy thrust a long dress of Quink blue into Prue's hands. Its stuff pulsed through her fingers, the softest velvet she had ever touched.

'Try it, why not?' Ivy went to the single piece of furniture in the room, a cheval glass, and tipped it so that it could accommodate what light there was from the window. 'I do believe I was exactly your size when I wore this – early twenties, it must have been, a New Year's Eve party in Derbyshire.'

'You're still so . . .' Prue tried to appraise, but avoid cheekiness.

'Well.' Ivy lowered her voice modestly. 'I have tried not to let myself go, as so many do.'

In the increasing dark Prue slipped off her clothes and poured the tunnel of soft darkness of the dress over her head. A moment later she was dipping and swaying in front of the mirror, unable to believe her own reflection as the long skirt, with a mere flip of encouragement, danced round her legs.

'Perfect,' said Ivy. 'We need look no further. It's too dark now – I can't think why there's no light in this room – but tomorrow I'll find you a wrap, and some jewels. Perhaps Gerald will buy a gardenia for your hair, if you wouldn't mind abandoning the bow just for one evening . . .' She could not contain a small smile.

'I wouldn't,' said Prue.

She drove back to the cottage through a thunderstorm and violent rain, wondering how to describe her afternoon. She began by telling Johnny that her date with Gerald was on Wednesday, and as she needed a long dress Ivy had lent her something.

'Really,' was all Johnny said. As he showed no interest in hearing details, Prue abandoned her plan of trying to tell him about London. She decided instead to keep it to herself: it would be something extraordinary to look forward to and then, with luck, to look back on.

There was no communication between Prue and Gerald before Wednesday afternoon when he arrived at the Old Rectory to collect her. All plans had been made through Ivy. Prue packed a case, as Gerald had requested, for they were to change at the Savoy. Ivy had shown her how to protect the dress in a cloud of tissue paper. She had also lent her jewellery – 'only paste for safety's sake' – which she slid into a drawstring velvet pouch.

'You'll be staying at the Savoy,' said Ivy, as Gerald's car came to a punctual stop in the driveway. Her pursed lips indicated some private imagining.

Gerald kissed his aunt, moved to shake hands with Prue – she quickly withdrew her proffered cheek, hoping he had not noticed her intention. Again, Gerald was sartorially perfect, in a grey suit and a blue spotted tie of silk so thick Prue wondered how he could tie the knot with such skill. She was keen to know if Ivy's prediction about the night's plan was right. They had not sped a mile down narrow lanes when she asked, diffidently, what the arrangement was to be.

'We'll stay at the Savoy, of course,' said Gerald. 'Why would we want to go anywhere else?' Prue, snubbed, fell silent for the rest of the journey. She brightened as they passed Buckingham Palace, but judged that her memories of tea with the King and Queen might not be of interest to the surly – was he surly, or just concentrating on the driving? – Gerald. She carried on silently imagining the magnificence of the room overlooking the Thames that she and Gerald would share.

As they drew up at the hotel entrance, huge men in top hats and coats with two rows of buttons, like pre-war children's coats, surged forward to take the small cases and the car key, and to push open the vast glass doors. Prue felt her red shoes dipping into inches of carpet as she followed Gerald to the reception desk. There, uniformed men gave the impression of knowing him well, though she could not hear the exchanges between them. A pageboy wearing a pillbox hat, exactly as she had seen in a Christmas production of *Aladdin*, appeared beside them. He had a bright, eager face and a chunk of fair hair flopped over one eye. If things had been different, Prue would not have minded going to a pub with him for a drink. She smiled at him. The pageboy glanced at Gerald's back view, flashed a wicked grin in return.

They followed him to a lift. For a moment there was an illusion that a dozen people were crammed into the small space, as their reflections crowded together, eyes not meeting. They came out into a long passage of extravagant carpet, followed the pageboy to one of the doors. He unlocked it with a show-off flourish, gave a bow (a secret signal, perhaps) as they entered the room. In a trice Prue took it all in: satin-covered bed, glossy cupboards, a great deal of glass, pleated lampshades, a marble bathroom visible through a half-open door.

'All right?'

'Amazing.' He turned to the pageboy. 'I'm one floor up, I believe,' he said.

'You are, sir.' He fiddled with another key.

One floor up? Prue considered this odd state of affairs. So who was to visit whose room? Why on earth had Gerald not booked a double? Was he afraid for his reputation? In a moment of fury, Prue gave the pageboy another smile, as Gerald pulled back a net curtain to look at the view. The pageboy blushed and did not smile back.

'Afraid this isn't actually overlooking the Thames,' said Gerald, who did not sound remorseful. He turned back to Prue, looked her up and down in his cool, auctioneer manner. 'Plan is, you have a bath and change, why not? I'll collect you at seven and we'll go down to the bar for a drink before dinner.'

'Fine.' Prue gave a small toss of her head. She was determined he should know she was put out by the room arrangements, but supposed it must be for good reason, so would go along with it.

'See you later, then.' He and the pageboy left the room.

Prue stood looking at her suitcase, the enthusiasm to unpack the glorious dress suddenly vanished. She went to the window, pulled back the curtain to see a roofscape of dark and gloomy stone. The oppressive silence of the room made a heaviness about her: hundreds of people must have spent nights there, but none had left an impression. She supposed that was the thing about hotel rooms. For all their grandeur, they were impersonal, bland. This was another disappointment. She had expected to feel the excitement of an unknown room – but then she had expected to see Gerald laying out silver (or ivory?) brushes on the chest of drawers, and hanging his suit in one of the cavernous cupboards . . .

When she looked back on her night in London with Gerald Wickham, Prue remembered the hour after he had left her alone to change as lonely in an icy way she had never before experienced. Describing it to Stella and Ag, she had not mentioned that part, for she felt it was feeble and unreasonable to sense disappointment on an occasion that would commonly be considered a luxurious privilege. But in her imaginings she had seen Gerald zipping up the back of the velvet dress, then fastening the necklace of paste sapphires that Ivy had lent her. As it was she had had to struggle alone with these things. Also, there was no sign of a gardenia and she hadn't, on Ivy's advice, brought a bow. Without her normal prop she felt uneasy. She looked at herself in a long mirror and thought the dress had lost some of its appeal in the dull electric light. The quality of magic that had been so powerful on that thundery afternoon seemed to have vanished.

She was ready long before the hour was up, wishing she had brought *Bleak House* with her. Having decided against a bath, she explored the bathroom, touched the slabs of marble which were tepid, not cold, and looked into the huge cupboards, wondering if there were some guests whose clothes would fill them, use all the hangers. She longed to be transported to a bedroom in a familiar place. Which one? Certainly not her room in her mother's house, or at The Larches, or Johnny's soulless cottage. The attic at Hallows Farm: that was the bedroom she had most loved. She shut her eyes, remembering every detail, wanting to be there, scoffing at her childish feelings.

Promptly at seven there was a knock on the door. Gerald stood there. He wore a dinner jacket and smelt strongly of a cologne that Prue did not recognize.

'Everything all right?' He stayed where he was in the passage, looking at her, as he always did, assessing, silently judging.

'Everything's fine.'

'Let's go down to the bar, then.' They moved towards the lift. Their progress over the silent carpet gave the short journey a dream-like quality. 'The Grill, of course, is the place to eat, but I thought that as you'd like to dance we might as well be in the restaurant.'

'Fine,' Prue said again. She had no idea what he was talking about.

In the bar, settled into a dark and comfortable corner, Gerald suggested they should drink White Ladies. 'Not quite the fashionable cocktails they once were, but beguiling. Like to try one?'

Prue, realizing she had already said 'fine' twice, and unable to think of another word of agreement, nodded. Her head spun with the jumble of new experiences, new references. The Grill: she'd thought that was part of an oven. White Ladies – at least she knew and liked them . . . But 'beguiling'. She would have to look that up in the dictionary when they got back. But, determined to seem at home in this unknown world, she tipped back her head, fluttered her eyelashes – a gesture that usually eased the way to whatever the next level might be. On Gerald Wickham it made no impression at all. He was attending to his cigarette with a gold lighter, his initials engraved in one corner.

The waiter appeared with two glasses, shallow, wide Vs of the most delicate glass – aristocratic, haughty, perhaps made to intimidate, Prue thought with a smile. She raised her glass. Gerald raised his. Prue waited for him to mutter some witty toast, or perhaps to say 'Cheers'. He remained silent. She did likewise, not wanting to say the wrong thing. So many lessons this evening: no wonder her usual cool was disturbed. They drank.

'What do you think? Like it?'

Prue, determined not to be outdone, was suddenly inspired. 'Very *beguiling*,' she said. 'You're quite right.' Her flash of well-chosen praise went some way to melting the upright Gerald.

'I must say, you're looking extraordinarily pretty,' he said, after a while. Like Rudolph, he was unhurried in his responses.

'Thanks.' That was better. Possibly a beginning.

'Wondrous dress.'

'Your aunt lent it to me. And the necklace.'

'She'll have enjoyed that, reliving her youth a little. She was always beautifully dressed, turned heads wherever she went. Are you liking working for her?'

'I am. Though you could hardly call it working.'

'I think she fancies the idea of someone just being in the house from time to time, helping her out in the greenhouse or whatever.'

'I spend a lot of time reading Dickens.'

'Well, as long as you don't mind doing so little, it sounds like a good idea for both of you.' There was a sneer so faint in his voice that it was barely distinguishable, but it was there.

'It is.'

'What does your boyfriend think?'

'I don't have a boyfriend.'

'I thought you lived with a man called Johnny who's going to make new stable doors.'

'I do. But I'm just his lodger.'

'Ah.' He gave a sigh of smug understanding. 'Shall we have another?' He beckoned the waiter with a wave of his cigarette. Prue noticed his fingernails: perfectly matching, their crescent shapes. She was cross to think he imagined Johnny was her boyfriend. Better relieve him of that impression fast.

'I'm trying to find somewhere to buy, be on my own,' she said, eyelashes a-flutter again. Two more White Ladies were put on the table.

'Be alone, a young girl like you, in the country? Whatever for? Sounds a crazy idea.'

'Whatever for?' So that you, Gerald Wickham, she said to herself, can call on me, bring me White Ladies, make love to me all night until your stuffiness is beaten out of you and we can laugh and walk and drink and sleep . . . 'You'll never guess.' She aimed to sound mysterious but the words tipped up, slid a little. 'You may think it's a crazy idea, but I want my own farm. Friesians, sheep. Acres of wheat and corn.'

By now Gerald had a constant half-smile. Whether it was teasing or scornful, Prue could not judge. But she thought he was beginning to unbend.

'You know what?' he said. 'This is the first time I've ever talked about farming in the Savoy bar. Rather refreshing.'

'But we haven't actually talked about it,' said Prue. 'I could tell you all my plans about the size of the herd and so on, if you like.'

'Another time,' said Gerald, retreating again. 'Let's go and eat.'

They left the bar and moved over acres of purplish carpet whose waves rose up to greet them. They arrived at a long stretch of shallow steps. Gerald glanced at Prue. He put a hand on her elbow. 'Can be lethal, White Ladies,' he said.

Prue tossed her head. Tipsy, did he think? She'd show him she could deal with a couple of fancy cocktails. She tested the edge of each stair with a foot before lowering it to the next one, and made an effort to dislodge Gerald's hand. He gripped her more firmly.

'This,' said Prue, measuring her words as she looked ahead at the pink glow of the huge restaurant, 'is like walking into an indoor sunset.' She had had no time to think of something witty to deflect his opinion that the White Ladies had unsteadied her, but her spontaneous thought seemed to appeal to him.

'That's a funny idea,' he said. 'I see what you mean. I like that.' He gave her a warm smile, the first of the evening.

They were led to a table near the dance-floor. Its brilliant white cloth, starched creases sharp as knives, made her think of Barry's favourite hotel in Manchester. But here everything was somehow better. The single rose in a silver flute was just beginning to unfurl. There were four long-stemmed glasses at each place, in whose sides smoky pink reflections wound like ribbons. The waiters, constantly on the move between the tables, were younger and better-looking. The other diners were similar, if only in age, to those in Manchester. Prue looked over to the band for a further comparison.

The musicians, in blue jackets, were on a platform thumping quietly through 'Tea For Two'. Prue's bottom squirmed in time to the music on the seat of her chair. 'Blimey,' she said, before she could stop herself.

They were handed menus the size of posters. The waiter gave Prue a look of such undisguised lust, she liked to think, that she felt herself blush.

'Quite an effect, you have, don't you?' Gerald sounded faintly weary, but he was still smiling. 'What'll you have to eat? They don't do badly, considering the shortages.'

Prue glanced at the menu and saw she couldn't understand a word: it was all in French. 'You decide. You know best.' She heard Gerald giving instructions: whatever it was sounded exotic in the foreign language, so Prue was surprised when their first course, a few mushrooms on fried bread, was put before them.

Although Prue tried to convince herself that the effect of the White Ladies had worn off, she could not deny that after two quick glasses of red wine the entire sunset scene started to quiver, to roll at the edges. Ask questions, she told herself. Listen.

But questioning Gerald about his life brought little reward. He talked of his army life, his love of golf, and of some scandal at his local golf club – a tediously long story. Prue detected occasional moments of warmth in his answers, but still he seemed at arm's length, distant, though always polite. Maybe, she thought, dancing would unbend him. There was something about him she failed to understand, but she was determined to keep trying. The band struck up with 'Dancing On The Ceiling'. She glanced at the floor, thick with lumbering elderly couples, the men with heads thrown back looking down on the grey permanent waves of the women, most of whom had chosen to expose their unsteady arms.

'Let's go,' said Gerald.

They got up, moved to the dance-floor. Prue, wavering a little, took the precaution of clutching Gerald's arm. For a second, just as they stepped onto the floor, Gerald looked down at her. She was convinced his look was one of pride.

He put out his arms, held her in the accustomed manner of those about to quickstep. Prue manoeuvred her whole body close to his, looked up with another flutter of her lashes. No smile. No returning look. The evening in Norfolk flashed through her mind: the moment Rudolph had strode across the dance hall, whisked her into his arms and they had instantly welded into one body, one spirit, one flare of mutual desire.

Here, in this grand hotel, in the beat of the irresistible music, in the arms of this handsome officer, nothing happened. Nothing, nothing. It was like dancing with a block of wood carved in imitation of a man, but with no male response. Prue wriggled herself even closer. What was the matter with Gerald Wickham? Was it her fault? Never had she felt such a failure.

He danced well, kept in time, she had to admit that. Sometimes he pushed her away so that she could give an independent turn, wiggle her hips, return to him with a wicked smile, but still she got nothing more than a brief nod. They returned to their table for minute cutlets, the bones dressed in paper ruffles, like those in Manchester, and small grilled tomatoes. By now a fatal combination of drink and disappointment had taken hold. Prue felt a recklessness come upon her. She had no intention of asking more about Gerald's boring golf club or listening to his dreary answers.

'Are you planning to get married?' she began.

'Not a question I've ever asked myself.' Gerald seemed faintly surprised. 'And you?'

'I tried it once. Didn't work out. I suppose I might be prepared to try again, but it would have to be someone pretty bloody special.'

'Quite.' A waiter filled their glasses. Prue put her elbows on the table and supported her head in her hands. Her mother had once given her what she called an invaluable tip: if you hold your head in a certain way in your hands, your eyes increase their sparkle. If this was the case, it was lost on Gerald. He merely lighted a cigarette, postponing the moment of trying the cutlet.

'But my theory about marriage,' Prue said, trying to control the slight slur of her voice, 'is probably a little unusual.' Gerald raised one eyebrow politely. 'I reckon that as it's so difficult to know how things are going to work out, even when you've found someone you think you love, you might as well just weigh things up in a cold and calculated way and take a chance. If there's enough in common, you just might find that in the end you really do love each other and it all works out . . .' She was conscious that her words were skittering, some falling like dominoes. 'So you could say that, for instance, you and I might make a happily married couple. We seem to get on, even though we don't know each other very well. We want the same things . . .'

'Do we?' Gerald flicked ash onto his side plate, ignoring the ashtray.

'Well, I imagine we do. Quiet happy life. Children. All that sort of thing. I think I could get you to like cows.'

Gerald nodded. 'Possibly,' he said. Then, looking straight at her, frowning: 'Is this by any chance a proposal?'

Prue, startled, laughed. 'I hadn't really thought about that,' she lied. 'It was just a theory – a theory that was meant to show you that, should you and I want to be man and wife, it could work.' Gerald stopped frowning but said nothing.

'To be honest, I think I'm a little drunk.'

'I think you are. Shall we have another dance? Then, perhaps, ice cream?'

This time, when she stood up, Prue sensed the room was in the grip of a volcano. The floor heaved, the walls caved in, but Gerald supported her. She was grateful for his kindness. She wanted him to know that although she was a little muddled from the drink her silly proposal had not been meant to sound serious. 'Usually,' she whispered, 'people propose to me. Dozens of men propose to me. Just for once I wanted to be the pro-poser . . .'

They waltzed on among the collapsing walls, the staggering dancers, the exploding lights. Then they were back at the table, Prue safe at last in her chair. 'Just one last question,' she said, making a supreme effort to control her voice, 'why did you book separate rooms?'

Gerald turned to her. 'My dear girl, why do you think?' His look was one of utmost scorn.

'I don't know what to think. That's why I asked. It seems to me if you drive a girl to London, take her to stay in this place, pay all that money, you must want to sleep with her.'

'How very wrong you are. Think about it. We scarcely know each other. Aunt Ivy told me you don't have much fun, stuck in the country. I liked the idea of giving you a little innocent amusement. In my book, that doesn't have to include sex.' He regarded her, now, pityingly. 'You go too fast, Prue. You go too fast. You must learn to slow down or you'll drive away what might be possibilities of some real thing. Do you know what I mean?'

'I suppose I do, though I've never thought of that before. I've always reckoned, fuck first, see what follows.' She saw Gerald flinch and decided, recklessly, on one last chance. 'If you want to change your mind – well, think of me as one of those fast loose girls who enjoy . . . What I'm trying to say is – I'm willing, even at this last moment.'

'I know what you're trying to say, and I'm not willing. I'll get the bill. Bugger the ice cream.'

Battered by her own foolishness Prue followed Gerald upstairs. She was still unsteady on her feet but now he did not support her. He walked ahead, ignoring her condition. But he did unlock the door, come into the room with her. Prue turned her back to him.

'Would you mind?' she said. This was not a final attempt in her dazed mind: this was practicality.

Gerald slowly unzipped the dress. Prue was about to move when she felt a finger travelling down her spine. 'I'm sorry,' he said. 'I'm sorry to be the first to turn you down. But it wouldn't work, you and me, not in a thousand years.'

Prue gave a small, snorting laugh. 'That's OK. Honestly. Thanks for a nice evening.'

'I've ordered your breakfast for eight. We'll leave at nine.'

'Fine.'

'Here, I'll undo the necklace.' All his brusqueness had left him, now the evening was nearly over. 'I hope you might still like to come out sometimes. We could go to a theatre, a film. Talk about cows, if you like. And Dickens. Not about ourselves.' He lifted her hair, undid her necklace, handed her the pile of glittery stones which were warm in her hand.

With no plan in mind, but with an invisible movement she tugged at the undone dress. It fell to her waist. She turned to Gerald, breasts bare. He did not look at them, but kissed her lightly on the cheek. 'Sleep well,' he said, and left.

Prue, in bed, laughed at herself: a laugh that turned into a howl, then tears, then more laughter. No sleep at all.

Gerald drove her back to Wiltshire very fast: he had another meeting near Salisbury. He dropped her at the Old Rectory. Prue, not wanting to face Ivy's enquiring look immediately, took her own car back to the cottage. Once again, Johnny was waiting for her at the gate. 'I've got news for you,' he announced, as soon as she was out of the car. 'I found a gun.' He held it up, smiling.

Prue, carrying her case, followed him into the kitchen. On the draining board lay two headless pigeons, their mauve feathers faintly luminescent in the morning light, their claws scrunched up like the hands of aged dowagers. Blood dripped from their necks into the sink, where Johnny had thrown their heads. They had fallen so that they looked at each other in death, beaks almost touching, eyes half shut.

Prue, sickened, turned to the kitchen table. Beside the remains of Johnny's breakfast lay two rabbits, their stomachs split wide, the red-brown empty caverns showing.

'Just got to skin them,' he said. 'Rabbit casserole tonight, pigeon tomorrow. No more worry about the shortage of food. Isn't that good news?'

'I suppose it is, yes,' said Prue.

Johnny propped the gun in a corner, turned and looked at her. 'Not a word,' he said. 'Don't forget, not a word about your night. I don't want to hear. I don't ever want to hear.'

'OK, OK. Fine.' Prue picked up her case and went upstairs to her room.

# Chapter 13

'I heard from Johnny it all went very well,' Ivy said to Prue, the next day.

'I think it did. Though I'm not quite sure what to make of Gerald. I wasn't certain how to interest him.' She caught Ivy's fleeting look, but ignored it. After a good night's sleep she was feeling strong, normal. The night at the Savoy was reduced to a distant bad dream. Her worry now was not Gerald but Johnny.

'I have to say I've always thought of my dear nephew as something of a dark horse. I'm not sure what to make of him either. Never have been. Now, let's have a cup of coffee. Then perhaps you could run me down to the post office.'

They sat in the sitting room, the tray of coffee things arranged in their usual orderly fashion on the table between them. Ivy asked if the dress had been a success.

'I loved wearing it,' said Prue. 'And again, thank you so much. I'll never have a dress like that.'

'Did Gerald notice it?'

'I expect he did.'

'Huh. Did he dance well?'

'Oh, yes. I loved the band.'

There was silence for a while, chipped by the clink of silver spoons against porcelain.

'Now, there's something I've been meaning to say to you, Prue.' Ivy cleared her throat, touched her hair. 'My will, inheritance matters, if you'll forgive my speaking about such things. All very easy, with no children. Everything was decided and signed some time ago, as you can imagine. Everything except the contents of my cupboard room. Somehow I wanted them to be left unassigned. I wanted to be free to leave them to someone who might come along and appreciate them. I could well be dead by the time Gerald's married, if he marries, and who knows if his wife would fancy all that old stuff? But you, Prue, it seemed to me you loved and appreciated it. So strange we're the same size, and you looked so beautiful in that dress. You'd look beautiful in all of them. So this is my wish. When I die, you must assure Gerald that my clothes go to you, and I'd like to think you'll have fun in them.'

'But you can't! I mean, you can't just give them all away. I couldn't possibly accept – we've only known each other for a very short time—'

'Ah, but I felt we were kindred spirits from the start. You were one of those bonuses, sudden from heaven. Now I can't imagine you not here, lighting my days, reading my books.'

Prue's eyes were cluttered with tears. Ivy's were dry. Prue tried again to protest at her generosity but Ivy tossed aside her objections with an imperious wave of her hand. Had it been almost anyone else, Prue thought, she would have hugged them with gratitude and delight. But her employer was not the sort of person who would welcome being hugged, any more than she would agree to being addressed by her Christian name. These things Prue found strange, but supposed it was a matter of age, and she had grown to appreciate the formality. It gave a polite distance to proceedings but in no way deterred warmth, merriment, humour or the exchange of ideas.

'So that's it,' said Ivy, putting down her empty cup. 'Done.

Finished. It's been on my mind for a few days so I'm glad it's settled. You must promise me you'll make sure—'

'I promise I will.'

'Now, off to the post office, shall we? In the car.'

Prue helped Ivy into the low passenger seat of the Sunbeam. Then she revved up the engine, which always brought a squeal of delight, but drove quite slowly through the lanes ablaze with hedgerows of May green. Ivy kept a silent smile. Prue was conscious of a strange longing to say something about the affection she felt for her. If she had dared, she would have told Ivy that she loved her in a funny way – a granddaughterly sort of way. But she said nothing, made herself concentrate on the cheerless prospect of looking for somewhere of her own to live, finding a job and a husband. But for the time being, as Ivy's 'companion', she could not have been happier.

That summer, the pattern of life with Ivy did not change. Prue went to the Old Rectory every day of the week. There were few new tasks, apart from deadheading the roses. After lunch she would go to the sitting room, or to a chair on the terrace, and continue her way through Dickens. When Ivy came downstairs from her rest, she would urge her not to stop: 'Take your chance, take your chance – the rest of your life might be too busy,' she often said. When they were together she would speak of moments in her own life that revealed to Prue unknown and unimagined worlds: she spoke so eloquently, with such humour and twists of language that Prue was enchanted. She spent less and less time at the cottage, and saw little of Johnny.

He was happily engaged in making the stable doors: Ivy declared herself very pleased when they were finished and immediately commissioned a new five-bar gate for one of the fields. When he wasn't working at his carpentry he was shooting rabbits, pigeons, pheasants. Suddenly fascinated by cooking, he produced suppers made from whatever he had caught, and vegetables from the garden that he had begun to resuscitate. There was no longer time for writing poetry, he said, but this did not seem to trouble him. Prue judged him happy, more as he had been when she had first known him. There was no sign of any vodka, or of his drinking.

No word came from Gerald, no suggestion of another night out. But a postcard arrived from Rudolph, now back in America, sent on by Stella. 'Thank you for your letter,' he wrote. 'This is just to give you my home address, should you ever change your mind. My love, Rudolph.' The picture was of the azalea avenue leading into Savannah. It was one of those cards that would remain for ever on a shelf, its picture fading as it gathered a bloom of dust – the kind of card that would be taken to a new shelf when there was one. Rudolph seemed a very long time ago, but she did not throw the card away.

In July there was a heatwave. Ivy said that, despite her many years in hot climates, she could never like great heat. It sapped her energy, she said. Her mornings were spent on a *chaise-longue* on the terrace, in the shade, reading *The Times*. She wore a straw hat with a ribbon round its crown. When she emerged from under the buddleia tree, which flickered with butterflies, sunlight pierced the loose weave of the brim, scattering gold freckles on her pale skin. After lunch – in celebration of summer, the shortbread was briefly replaced by home-grown peaches – she took a much longer siesta in her room, blinds drawn. Prue noticed that she leant more heavily on her cane, but there seemed to be nothing wrong with her beyond inertia caused by the relentless heat. Prue would make lemonade every day. It seemed to revive Ivy for her daily watch of the light fading from the terrace. She would return to the *chaise-longue* with a jug and a glass, her blue-tinted spectacles and an anthology of poems.

'You hurry back to Johnny,' she would say. 'Have another nice rabbit casserole.' This had become a joke between them. 'Don't worry for one moment about me. Autumn will soon be here and I'll be lively as a cricket again.'

One evening Prue, engrossed by a story Ivy was telling about her husband's big-game hunting, left later than usual. When she arrived at the cottage Johnny was standing at the gate in the same sort of agitation as he had been on the day Prue had first arrived. 'I've been waiting for you for ages,' he snapped. 'What happened? Where've you been? I was worried.'

Seeing that he was oddly upset, Prue put a hand on his arm.

'Don't you touch me,' he said, and hurried into the kitchen. There, the heat of the day had begun to wane. The room was unusually tidy. There was a jam jar of lavender on the table, and a small box crudely wrapped in tissue paper. 'Got something for you. Sit down. Sorry. I'm jumpy today. This bloody heat. Here.' He pushed the box towards Prue, who took the seat opposite him.

'What's all this?'

'Just a little something. Thank-you present for the stable-door job – entirely your doing and old Mrs L paid me very generously. So now I can contribute a bit to everything.'

'No need,' said Prue, 'unless you really want to.' She took off the paper, opened a small box. It held an embossed silver locket on a silver chain. She took it out, swung it back and forth, laughed with delight, 'Oh, Johnny. It's lovely. I've always wanted a locket. Thank you.'

'I found it in Marlborough. Open it.' Prue did so. The two spaces for photographs were empty. 'I was hoping,' Johnny went on, 'there'd be a picture of you one side, me the other . . .' He spoke jokingly, so Prue smiled.

'We'll get a Box Brownie,' she said. 'Take pictures of each other. I'm thrilled with it, I really am.' She fastened it round her neck. 'All right? How can I thank you?'

310

'You don't have to. Just glad you like it.' Johnny got up, went to the tap and filled two glasses of water. 'I'd do anything in the world for an iced lager now. But I don't dare.'

'No. You've been so strong.'

Johnny sat down again. 'I've tried,' he said. He looked at Prue, stretched out a hand and touched the locket with a finger. 'It looks good. Something I must say, though.' He withdrew the finger, paused. 'I'm going to have to ask you to start seriously looking for your own place. I can't take much more of this landlord business. I'm sorry.'

'What do you mean?'

'I mean we can't go on living like this, under the same roof. It's agonizing. For me, that is. I thought it would be all right. Just the one brief occasion, a long time ago. I thought I could bury it, but I can't.'

'I don't know what—'

'I mean you – there, here, every morning, every evening, every weekend – bobbing about, breasts half exposed under some summery little dress, not giving a thought to what you do to me – would do to any man. It's unbearable. God knows how many times I've been close to forcing myself upon you. Don't worry, of course I'd never do that. Never, ever, I promise you.'

'Oh cripes. I never realized . . .' Prue winced internally, alarmed. She cursed herself for having been so blind. The idea of her presence being difficult for Johnny had never occurred to her. She had taken care not to flirt with him for a single instance, and he had given no sign of the frustration he now admitted. 'I never realized you still fancied me. You never gave a sign.'

'You don't look very closely, Prue, sometimes. There's so much buzzing round in your half-empty head. One of your charms is that you've no idea what you do to men – or perhaps you have? I don't know. Perhaps this whole arrangement was daft in the first place. I'm so sorry I ever suggested it. How can a man and a

311

woman of ordinary desires hope to live together without . . .? And the other thing is, it isn't just that I want you in my bed. I seem to have fallen in love with you. That never occurred to me. You're not the sort of girl I've ever gone for.' He finished his glass of water.

There was silence, but for the slow drip of a tap. Prue blinked rapidly. 'What can I say? This is the most awful surprise. What can I do?'

'Go,' said Johnny. 'Go as soon as possible, if you don't want to drive me mad.'

'Blimey. All right.' Prue nodded, thinking fast. 'It shouldn't be too hard to find somewhere . . .'

'And then, you can imagine what it's been like for me. Hearing about all your other men. How did you think I felt when you described with such relish the "glorious" fucking with Rudolph? And now this Gerald man. God, how was that, in the Savoy?'

'Nothing happened. I promise. We had separate rooms. It was all a disaster. Utter failure. It'll be a funny story one day.'

Johnny looked at her, disbelieving. 'More fool him, then. My night, imagining you both, was hell.' He spat the word.

'I'm so, so sorry. I'll go as soon as I can.' Prue touched her locket. Johnny watched her finger trace the pattern on its silver case. His desire for her to be gone seemed to be dwindling.

'It's not that urgent, I suppose,' he said. 'Dare say I can put up with the torture for a bit longer. I can't decide which would be worse – missing you, or having yet not having you here – Anyhow, start looking around and don't worry about me.'

'I'll do my best.'

'I've made roast rabbit with dill and cider.' Johnny went to the stove.

'Lovely.'

'You don't by any chance love me just a bit? Even in a vague, brotherly sort of way?' He stayed with his back to her, stirring. The question's lightness of touch did not deceive.

'Of course I love you a bit. You've been good to me. We've shared a lot. But I don't love you enough, or anyone else, to commit my life in some way.'

'OK. Thought as much. Dare say I'll get used to the idea, make myself understand.'

'Oh, Johnny. Such muddles we all get into.'

'We do.'

Somehow they managed a peaceful evening: rabbit talk, a game of backgammon. A new moon hung from a thread of cloud in the window. They heard a fox bark nearby.

'Better just check the chickens,' said Johnny.

Prue went up to her room when he had gone. Just as a precaution, for the first time, she locked the door.

Cooler weather came with September. Ivy's old energy returned and she spent less time resting. Eager for more rides in the Sunbeam, which had stopped during the very hot days, she suggested she should accompany Prue on visits to see possible cottages for her to live. There was little on the market and they saw nothing that was remotely suitable. Often Ivy would dismiss the estate agent who was waiting for them. 'Don't think we'll bother to go round, thank you very much,' she would say, after a cursory glance at the outside. 'We can see straight away that it's not what we're looking for.' She seemed to know more clearly than Prue what would be the perfect thing, and with one look knew instinctively whether or not it was worth considering.

As the weeks stretched into autumn Prue became anxious about lingering in the cottage with Johnny. But since his outburst urging her to go he seemed to have calmed down. On several occasions he had apologized for berating her, and said his real wish was for her to stay as long as she needed. Her presence was difficult, he said, but her absence would be no less so.

Prue reported to him every sighting of a rural cottage, to show she was trying, and they carried on living together in cautious harmony. Johnny made several more gates for Ivy. Prue, who had moved from Dickens to Jane Austen, spent most of her time at the Old Rectory.

Gerald turned up unexpectedly one afternoon. He stayed for a polite hour, talking mostly to his aunt, then was gone again. There was no mention of another evening out. Must have forgotten, Prue thought, and felt pleased not to mind very much.

One day in early October Ivy came into the sitting room, where Prue was reading *Emma*. She looked excited. 'I've just had a call from my old friend Arnold Barrow,' she said. 'Such a surprise. I thought he was living in Switzerland. Well, it seems he's not. He's back in his house near Amesbury and he wants us to go over, look at his garden. Would you mind?'

'Of course not.' In truth Prue, happily engaged in her book, was not overjoyed by the plan but she managed to look enthusiastic.

Ivy sat down on the sofa, a little breathless. She put one hand on her chest. 'You may think I have a curious lack of friends,' she said. 'I sometimes think the same myself. But then after so many years abroad a lot of them are scattered. And of course a good many of them are dead. But Arnold! I'm so pleased he's still around. What a lovely surprise. He was a colleague of Ed's. We shared a house with him for a while in Delhi. Ed was so fond of him.' She paused, smiled to herself. 'To be honest, I rather thought he was particularly fond of me, though of course he was much too much of a gentleman to indicate any such thing . . . But let's be on our way, shall we? It's not far.'

Not long after they had set off in the Sunbeam, the gold October air dulled a little and there was a brief shower.

'Never mind,' said Ivy. 'Arnold will have umbrellas. I seem to remember he had a proud collection from all over the world.'

They drew up at a handsome house, though smaller than the Old Rectory. 'Queen Anne,' Ivy said, who took every opportunity to educate her companion. Prue had never seen her get out of the car so fast: the cane thrashed about, hindering rather than helping, and her long black skirt became tangled in her eager legs. Briefly she agreed to Prue's help in untangling the muddle, then almost ran to the front door.

When Arnold opened it Prue felt close to laughter, for he was so exactly like the illustrations of old men in Dickens's books. Silver whiskers encircled his red face and merged at some imperceptible point with a splurge of white hair. His screwed-up eyes looked as if they had set that way from constant laughter. Prue tried hard to imagine that he had ever been attractive, the object of a sly glance from Ivy. Old age plays such tricks, cheats so cruelly on remembered youth.

'Ivy! My dear, dear Ivy!'

'Darling Arnold! Such a long time.'

They embraced. Arnold's lumpen fingers played on Ivy's shoulder: hers played the other half of the duet on one shoulder of his fine tweed jacket. At last they drew apart, observed each other with fond honesty.

'Just as beautiful! Just a shade paler, your hair.'

'Are those new teeth, Arnold? They're wonderful.'

They laughed.

Prue was introduced, her presence not explained. The plan was to go round the garden before it rained again.

Prue followed them at a distance. They tottered along, side by side, Arnold so stooped it was an effort for him to raise his eyes to the tall hollyhocks. Ivy was particularly upright, scorning her cane for moments at a time as she pointed to things in the buxom herbaceous border. From time to time Prue heard squeals of delight and laughter. Then they would pause in their horti-cultural journey, move their heads closer, recall something, somewhere, that Prue would never know. She wondered if in sixty years' time she herself might be tottering round a garden with some old man, and if so, who would he be?

The subtleties of planting had never interested her: Mrs Lawrence, she remembered, used to tease her for her lack of knowledge about plants. 'Daffodils are the only things you recognize,' she would say. Well, daffodils had been the only flowers she'd seen in Manchester, Prue had snapped back. At the Old Rectory, she had tried, for Ivy's sake. She'd learnt to recognize a few papery shrubs, and had come to love the scent of roses, but to study plant after plant, as Ivy and Arnold were doing with such pleasure, she found infinitely boring. She hung back. Eventually she made her way to a small terrace by the house, and sat on one of the ironwork chairs. She could still follow the old things' progress. They did not notice that she was no longer close behind them.

She had no idea how long she sat, no thoughts troubling her. The lawn was a glorious smoothness of emerald green, faintly glittering from the last shower of rain. A cat ran along a wall and jumped onto the branch of an overhanging tree. A bird tried out a complicated song – blackbird? She knew a certain amount about stormcocks, but she had had only one chance to exercise her knowledge. There were no stormcocks in the Old Rectory's garden, though Ivy had seemed interested in all Prue had had to say about them.

She saw the old couple pause. Ivy stretched out a hand. Arnold took it. The knot of their arthritic fingers moved up and down, in some secret agreement, then parted. A large dark cloud, with no warning, rose over the herbaceous border and covered most of the blue sky. A few single drops of rain, heavy as coins, fell onto the flagstones of the terrace.

Ivy and Arnold were now approaching the house as fast as they could. There were darker spots on Ivy's skirt. Arnold's hand was under her elbow, perhaps more for his own support than hers.

Time, Prue felt, slowed in a strange way, dream-like. But at last the two friends were through the french windows of the sitting room. They made no mention of the rain. Ivy filtered round the room admiring a collection of faded watercolours. Arnold rang a bell.

Again, Prue kept herself a little apart. She sat on a velvet stool by the fireplace when she wasn't handing a plate of cucumber sandwiches or pouring China tea. Never had she felt so invisible, and she was glad to be so. She was fascinated listening to the two old friends recount tales of the Raj. They spoke of many people with peculiar names – Calypso, Euphemia, Lalage, Candida, Eugénie – the last pronounced by Ivy with a perfect French accent. Prue tried to imagine them all at parties under a full Indian moon, dancing with Clarence, Edgar, Erskine: the names came tumbling out as Ivy and Arnold seemed high on remembrance of their long-dead world. The mutual pictures of times past gave them such pleasure that they kept unconsciously touching each other. A finger alighted on the other's knee or an arm, briefly as a butterfly.

Ivy did not suggest leaving till after six. 'Oh, Arnold, such, such fun.'

'So good we're so near at last. You must come often.'

'And you to me. Soon, soon.'

'I most certainly will.'

'Dear Arnold. Thank you so much.'

'Dear Ivy.'

They stood in the stone porch, the three of them, looking at the rush of hard rain that bent the trees. The sky was nightfall dark, no streak of light. Arnold did not suggest fetching an umbrella from his collection. Perhaps Ivy had misremembered that part of the past. He suggested, in a brave voice, that they all make a dash.

The short journey to the car, through thrashing rain, was perilous. Prue took one of Ivy's arms, Arnold the other, which impeded rather than helped the treacherous journey. Somehow the door was opened and Ivy was bundled in. Prue stooped to pick up her long damp skirt, Arnold bent awkwardly into the car to give his old friend a farewell kiss. Prue stood patient, soaked, while his face awash with raindrops slid across Ivy's sparkling cheek, and they both muttered promises Prue could not hear.

Farewells over, Arnold had difficulty in regaining an upright posture outside the car. Prue heaved at one arm. Ivy pushed at him with both her small hands while he uttered several ancient curses that made both women laugh. At last he was securely on his feet, rain pouring through white whiskers and hair, and dazzling his scarlet cheeks. Prue ran to the driving seat.

'That's right! Make a dash! Good girl.' Arnold waved. They drove away.

'Oh, what fun that was, wasn't it? I haven't enjoyed myself so much for ages. Isn't Arnold a dear?' Ivy wiped the rain from her face with a tiny handkerchief.

Prue was peering through the fan shape of clear windscreen made by the wipers. It only lasted a second before rain obliterated everything again. It was impossible to see anything clearly. She switched on the headlights.

'I think we should hurry home, dear Prue,' Ivy said.

'I can't hurry in this. I can't see anything.'

'Oh, I don't know. Ed used to drive fast in all conditions. He said he liked a challenge. He was very skilled, but I must admit we did have a few mishaps. It was exciting, though. But I'll let you concentrate.'

Prue drove slowly along the lanes, listening to the noisy swish of water parting beneath the tyres and the battering of rain on the windscreen. She considered stopping altogether till the worst had passed, but thought Ivy would regard that as feeble. On a straight stretch she put her foot on the accelerator harder than she meant to – her wet shoe slipped – and the car bounced forward. Ivy squealed with delight.

Two headlights appeared round an invisible corner in the middle of the road, coming straight towards them. Prue's hands on the steering-wheel turned to liquid.

'Fast, Prue! Left, and we'll miss him. There!' Ivy shouted, her voice so high it tumbled over itself, prepared for one last screech of encouragement. 'Good girl!'

Prue missed the oncoming vehicle but skidded violently into the trunk of a huge oak tree by the side of the road. There was a very loud bang, a crunch, an almost inaudible whimper from Ivy. Then, just the thud of the rain.

Prue glanced to her left. Ivy had been thrown forward onto the windscreen, which had shattered. Prue herself, also thrust forward, had been saved by the steering-wheel. She tried to sit upright, but acute pain severed her ribs. She tried again, succeeded, and pulled Ivy gently back into her seat. Strings of blood moved in various directions over her face. She was deadly pale. Her eyes were shut. Prue whispered her name. There was no answer. She looked through the clouded liquid windscreen, could see that the scarlet bonnet of the Sunbeam had reared up and was scrunched into a weird shape. The ghostly outline of a van, or a large farm vehicle, was just visible.

Prue held Ivy's hand, kept whispering her name. The passenger door, which she tried to open – the effort pierced her ribs agonizingly – was stuck. She did manage to wind down the window a few inches. A blast of horizontal rain shot through the space. It would not shut again. She sat there, in the cage of attacking rain, wondering, stunned, and moved her hand to Ivy's wrist. She thought there was a very faint pulse. She did not like to feel Ivy's heart, did not know if she could even tell if it was beating. In a misted way she wondered what to do. How long till someone came?

She had no idea how long it was – minutes? half an hour? – before a scared face loomed at her through the passenger window.

A farm worker, she thought he must be, his clothes sodden and dark.

'Awfully sorry, my duck,' he said, his voice shaken. 'I was trying to avoid . . . You all right?' He peered into the car. 'The old girl looks . . . There's a pub up the road. I'll go and ring for an ambulance.'

'Thanks,' said Prue. She bent forwards, trying to ease her own pain, but did not let go of Ivy's cold wrist. The rain began to jitter before her eyes in a way rain did not normally behave. The raised smashed bonnet of the car moved sickeningly from side to side. Prue wondered if she was going to faint. Several times she begged Ivy to say something. But still there was no answer.

An immeasurable time later, from a long way off, she heard the wail of an ambulance, the now familiar slash of tyres cutting through water. She felt a rush of cold as the stuck door was pulled open. Then there were gentle hands and gentle voices. She heard distant words: 'old girl unconscious' . . . 'could be broken ribs, the young 'un' . . . 'Better hurry.'

They must have hurried, these gallant men, for suddenly – time was unaccountable – Prue saw curtains jumping with bleached flowers all round her. A dull ache had replaced the acute pain. There was a stifling smell of cleanliness. A young nurse, blown about by her starched white headdress, pushed through the curtains like a modest singer. A word came up in Prue's mind as if it was being typed on a sheet of white paper, each letter separate: 'h o s p i t a l'.

'How's Mrs Lamton?' she asked, surprised to find she had a clear voice. 'Where is she?'

Ivy was in a room some distance away, but Prue was not allowed to see her until her condition had been further assessed by the doctors.

'So she's not dead, then?'

The nurse looked shocked, ignored the question and enquired how Prue felt.

'I'm fine,' she said, swinging her legs over the side of the bed. There was some kind of strapping round her ribs. She could feel it beneath the hospital nightdress. The nurse moved to help her try to stand. She felt nauseous, still, and dizzy, but remained on her feet.

'I should get back into bed just now,' said the nurse. 'Someone will be coming round for details.'

'Details?'

'Names of relations to be telephoned. The old lady's name and address. And someone who could bring you clean clothes. They'll want you in overnight, but I'm sure you'll be able to go home in the morning. Cracked ribs heal quite well once they're bound up.'

'Right,' said Prue. 'But please tell the doctors I want to see Mrs Lamton as soon as possible.'

'Are you a relation?'

'She's my grandmother.' The lie might be her only pass to see Ivy.

'I'll see what I can do,' said the nurse, and sailed back through the horrible curtains.

Prue was taken to see Ivy later that evening. A young doctor in a white coat led her along passages that smelt of disinfectant mingled with another, more lurid, smell. He had a wide, appealing face. Different time, different place, Prue might have thrown him an interested look. As it was, walking was painful. She found it difficult to keep up with him.

'Your gran, is she?'

'That's right.' The doctor opened the door into a small white room.

Ivy lay propped on a mound of pillows in the high bed. Her eyes were shut, her face had been cleaned of the blood. Now the white skin was covered with a tracing of thin scratches, as if she had been caught by a bramble bush, nothing more. A single piece of plaster secured a wad of lint at the corner of one eye. Prue put a hand on the bed, avoiding the ridge of Ivy's legs. 'Will she be all right?' she asked. 'How long till she comes round?'

The doctor shrugged. He put a large hand round Ivy's wrist. 'Who knows? We don't think there's any internal bleeding. Could be just shock. Chances are she'll be OK. But she's not in her first youth, is she?'

'Can I stay with her?'

The doctor gave a sympathetic smile. 'As far as I'm concerned, but I'm not in charge – I'm very junior,' he added modestly. 'Why don't you just stay till someone turns you out?'

When he had gone, Prue moved closer to Ivy's head, very small on the large pillows. The white hair, the bun, was awry. One side of her mouth was turned down, the other seemed stuck at the beginning of a smile. Her hands were clenched into two small fists: Prue had never seen them like that. Gently she tried to prise open the fingers of one hand, so that they could lie straight out, as they always did on her skirt while she talked. But they would not move. It was as if rigor mortis had already set in. This thought made Prue back away. She did not want to see Ivy dead: she wanted to remember her alive. At the moment she did look dead, but the fact that her heart was still beating made her less alarming.

Prue sat on the chair beside the bed. She could not think what to do. She could not think what might happen. She shifted her position to try to relieve the aching of her ribs, but it did no good. Above her was Ivy's profile: beautiful cheekbone, closed eyelid the shape of a horizontal petal nesting in its purple hollow. The side of her mouth that was turned down made a long thread to her jaw. Prue longed for her to wake, smile, so that the line would disappear. She turned away. She could only think that it was her fault.

It was getting dark, but she did not want to put on a light, make new shadows on Ivy's face. For something to do, she got up and drew the curtains. They were made of hard green rep, covered with bad drawings of parrots, hardly the sort of thing to cheer a patient. But maybe this room was reserved for patients who were too ill to be affronted by hideous birds.

There was a knock at the door. A nurse Prue had not seen before came in. 'You've a visitor,' she said. Johnny followed her into the room. He carried a small case. The nurse left.

'Oh my God,' he said, quickly glancing from the bed to Prue. 'I'm not staying.' He put down the suitcase, laid a hand on Prue's head. 'Just brought you something to wear, your toothbrush. They rang me, said you'd given our number. How badly are you hurt?'

'Hardly at all. Just my ribs.'

Johnny nodded. 'And Mrs Lamton?'

Prue shrugged. 'No one seems able to tell me. Apparently there's no huge physical damage. Perhaps it's just shock.'

'Hope so. Some of these old things are tough as anything. What happened?'

'Terrible rain, I could hardly see a thing. Then two headlights in the middle of the road. I knew I had to avoid them.' Her voice sounded faraway, flat, metallic. 'I did avoid them. But I skidded. I couldn't see a thing in the mist. There was this tree . . .'

'What about the car?'

'I don't know. Pretty bad. I don't know what to do about it . . .' Her eyes went back to Ivy.

'Don't worry. I'll get all that seen to. Are you coming home?'

'Of course I'm not coming home. I'm staying with her till – she comes round.'

'Right. Well, let me know when you want to be collected.' He tipped up her chin, kissed her gently each side of her nose. 'So sorry,' he said. 'What a ghastly . . .'

The door opened again. No nurse preceded Gerald. He strode into the room, tweed jacket, yellow tie, a look of curiosity rather than concern. He stopped dead when he saw Johnny. Prue had no time to think. 'Johnny, this is Gerald,' she said. 'Gerald, this is Johnny.' The two men nodded at each other. 'Johnny's making gates for Ivy,' she heard herself say.

'I'm just on my way out.' Johnny, after a look at Prue, hurried from the room avoiding a further glance at the figure in the bed.

Immediately, astonishingly, Gerald came up to Prue and put his arms round her. She gave a great, quivering sigh. 'You poor darling,' he said, and moved to stand by the bed. He stood looking down at his aunt for a long time without speaking.

The embrace he had given Prue remained ghost-like round her. It was not a comfort, but it was there.

'What do they think?' Gerald asked, after a while. He touched his aunt's clenched hand.

Prue went to look out of the window. 'They don't seem to know. Nothing broken. Just unconscious.'

'She's a tough old thing. I reckon she'll pull through.'

'Hope so.'

'And how about you?' Gerald came over to Prue and again put an arm round her shoulders. He smelt of his expensive smoke.

'I'm OK.'

'I'm not going to ask you about it now, but you can tell me what happened some time.' Prue nodded. The tweed of his jacket was scratchy against her neck. 'I'm going to take a week's leave, stay at the Old Rectory, come in every day. What about you?'

'They said I can go home tomorrow, but I'm going to stay with her.'

'Are you sure?'

'Positive.' Prue shifted a little to ease her own pain, which came and went in unnerving gusts. Gerald moved his arm. 'At least she had a lovely afternoon with her old friend Arnold.' Prue heard her voice break, so did not try further to explain.

'Arnold?' Gerald smiled. 'That old bugger. They were very fond of each other. Now, I'm going to leave you, organize a few things. I'll have a word with the matron, see what I can do about making things comfortable for you.'

'I'm afraid I said I was Ivy's granddaughter. I thought it was the only way they'd let me see her.'

'Quite right. I'll stick to the story.' He went back to the bed, lowered his head and silently kissed his aunt on the cheek without the dressing. 'Ring me any time at the Old Rectory if you want me. I'll be back in the morning.' He gave Prue an identical kiss, and left.

When he had gone, Prue returned to the chair. She thought how odd it was that Ivy, lying unconscious in hospital, had inspired a certain warmth and affection in her nephew who, when offered Prue on a plate at the Savoy, had shown neither warmth nor interest.

Some time later an orderly came into the room, switched on the light, and gave her a cup of tea and a Digestive biscuit. She realized she was hungry, but the biscuit stuck in her throat.

Later still, someone brought in a camp bed with a rubber mattress, a blanket and pillow. Gerald had obviously pulled rank somewhere.

All through the night nurses, and sometimes a doctor, came regularly into the room, looked at Ivy, touched her closed eyelids and left without a word. When she was alone again Prue would get up and look at her, too. She had drawn back the curtains. An almost full moon filled the small room with a pallor that matched Ivy's skin. Prue didn't touch her again: she thought she might be cold, turned to marble. She did not want to witness the moment her heart stopped beating – if it stopped beating. As the night lumbered on, a strange optimism came to Prue. Ivy wouldn't die because she was so capable: capable of everything which included surviving to a very old age. Mrs Lawrence had been beaten by cancer. Ivy had suffered merely a bad jolt. She would come round, recover, live a good while longer in the Old Rectory, teaching things to Prue.

She slept scarcely at all. Sharp clouds of thought moved across the taut sky of her mind. If she married Gerald, perhaps she could tease out the hidden, loving side of his nature. They would live in the Old Rectory among Mrs Lamton's things. It wouldn't be quite the same as when she was alive, of course. A few alterations would have to be made. The kitchen repainted, the treacherous stairs carpeted. But she would love it, as Ivy had loved it.

If she stayed with Johnny she could perhaps help him to resist drinking. They could put all their energies into transforming the cottage into a comfortable and happy place. They could buy more land, sheep, cows . . .

If she replied to Rudolph's invitation, she could perhaps persuade herself that to live in America would be ideal, so long as he agreed to get rid of the pigs.

So many perhapses. And perhaps all the possibilities were ridiculous, because she didn't love any of the men in question in quite the right way – not in the way Ivy had loved Ed, or Mrs Lawrence had loved Mr Lawrence, or Ag loved Desmond or Stella loved Joe . . . No: the fact was Prue didn't love, absolutely, any of the men she had thrown into these dawn calculations.

The young doctor looked round the door. 'Everything all right?' he asked, looking down at the muddle of Prue's camp bed. She nodded, thanked him. Out of an old habit that returned whenever she saw a man she fancied, she fluttered her eyelashes. The doctor didn't seem to notice. Hardly surprising, really: the mascara had long gone. 'We'll be looking in on Mrs Lamton all the time,' he said, and left the room.

The thought came to Prue that she wouldn't mind being married to a doctor, and he had such a friendly face. She wondered if it would be possible, once Ivy was better and back at home, to get in touch with him. She could explain to Ivy how good he had been when she was unconscious, and perhaps suggest asking him to the Old Rectory for tea. Then it would be easy. A walk in the garden, a certain kind of giggle when she explained she didn't know one flower from another ... Prue's imaginings gathered speed. She looked again at Ivy, trying to gauge how likely the tea invitation would be, and felt a shadow of guilt about the trivial nature of her hopes when Ivy was not really there.

She tried to shift herself into a comfortable position. There was no hope of sleep. She watched the dawn press through the parrot curtains and turn the walls of the room the colour of an unripe apple. She cursed herself for all the preposterous thoughts that came to her while the old lady lay there knowing nothing.

Gerald returned early the next morning. 'No change?'

'Doesn't seem to be.'

'But they got you a bed?'

'Thanks so much.'

'Ed and Ivy gave pretty generously to the hospital.'

Prue said she would go and wash, and dress. Her head felt unbalanced from lack of sleep. Top heavy. Full of strange weights. Her ribs continued with their dull ache, which every now and then accelerated into acute pain, surprising her. When she returned to the room she found Gerald in the chair reading *The Times*.

'Brought you something,' he said, and reached into a briefcase. 'Here.' He handed her the copy of *Emma* she had been reading before the accident and a bag of plums. 'I'll go shopping later today, try to find you something decent to eat.'

'You mustn't go to any trouble, really – I'm not hungry.'

'If you're going to keep watch, you must be looked after. Ivy would be furious with me if I hadn't taken care of you.' Gerald opened his paper.

327

All day long nurses and doctors paid brief visits to the room. Looked at Ivy. Felt her pulse. Expressionless. They said nothing, gave no news. Gerald came and went. He asked for another chair. Prue read her book, occasionally forcing herself from Mr Knightley's wisdom to look at the unmoving Ivy. Gerald took to reading a few snippets from his paper aloud: humorous bits that made them both smile for a scant second. Prue liked his quiet presence, hated the moments he left. Johnny did not appear again.

For three days Prue and Gerald lived their odd, camp-like existence in the small room, one each side of the effigy-like figure on the bed. A kind of rhythm came to the days: exits and entrances, looks exchanged between the nursing staff, cups of hospital tea, moments of escaping it all while reading, attempts to eat the things Gerald brought in paper bags. From time to time they were both asked to leave the room. They would stand adrift in the corridor, brushed by the sweep of passing nurses, trying not to imagine. Sometimes Gerald would take Prue's hand, but only for a moment, and with a politeness suitable to the situation rather than growing affection. When they returned to the room the pillows had been replumped, the sheet beneath Ivy's clenched hands pulled taut again. But her demeanour had not changed.

Prue observed that Gerald was becoming distracted, anxious about something far from the hospital. He explained he was needed for a meeting that he kept having to postpone. But he would stay a couple more days. 'And then,' he said, 'you should go home. You can't stay here for ever. She might hang on for months. People do.'

'But I want to be here when she comes round,' Prue said, dreading his departure.

'I think you should realize,' Gerald replied quietly, 'there's a chance she may never come round. I had a word with her doctor. I'll be back this afternoon.'

The third day passed more slowly than the others. Dazed from lack of sleep, Prue felt a curious longing to talk to Johnny. But she had no energy to walk to the sister's office and ask if she could use the telephone. She merely wanted to hear from the outside world, but gave up the idea, returned to her book, and more cups of tea. Occasionally she went to the window to look out on a jagged landscape of roofs. She had discovered how to move about the room without looking at Ivy. Gerald sent a message to say he had been held up, couldn't get back, but would be there early next morning.

That night, exhausted, Prue fell asleep as soon as she lay on the camp bed. She woke at first light. The parrots, through her sleep-clouded eyes, were a jumble on the curtains, their orderly lines in a muddle she could not sort out. She sat up, sensing a depth to the usual silence. She glanced up at Ivy. At first she saw only that her hands were no longer lying outside the bedclothes but were under a sheet, which stretched right over her head. Prue sat holding her knees to her chest, making her ribs throb: she needed the physical pain.

A nurse, an older one she had not seen before, came into the room.

'I'm so sorry, Mrs . . . Your grandmother passed away at four twenty-eight this morning.' She took a fob watch on a chain from the pocket of her starched apron. 'Just a quarter of an hour ago. I didn't like to wake you.'

'No,' said Prue.

'There was nothing to be done. She wouldn't have known you were there. She passed away peacefully.'

'Good.'

'Would you care to see her? Be alone with her a while?'

'No, thanks.' The nurse looked surprised. 'I want to remember her alive. Not dead.'

'Very well. I'll get you a cup of tea.'

Prue stood up. 'If it's all right,' she said, 'I'd rather stay in the passage till Mrs Lamton's nephew arrives. I don't much want to be alone with . . .' Her voice was so taut she knew it would break if she tried to explain.

Again the nurse looked surprised, but she said, 'There's a little reception area just down to the left, sofas and chairs. I'll bring your tea there.'

'Thanks,' said Prue. She picked up the bundle of her clothes and quickly followed the nurse out of the room. Her last sight of Ivy was of a small shape, a narrow ridge, under a sheet. It was only then she noticed the precise angle of the elegant nose. It made a small, sharp point under its deathly covering, which Prue had never noticed when Ivy was alive.

On the sofa in the reception area she could not read. She sat staring out of the window at early-morning life in the street: people queuing for buses, hurrying along pavements bent against a shower of strong rain. It occurred to her that many people must feel as she did when someone they love dies: shock, surprise that life goes on, impervious. Rage against the continuing of the day welled up in her. She could not drink the tea. She stared at patients wheeled down the corridor, wondering when they were going to die. Some of the passing nurses threw her a sympathetic look.

Gerald appeared soon after ten. 'They told me at the desk,' he said. 'I saw her. Said goodbye.'

Prue fell forward into his arms. He held her silently for a long time. Then he said, 'Shall I tell you something? She told me only a few days ago, before the accident, what a joy you'd been to her. Brightened her life, she said. So, though neither of you knew it, you made her last year very happy. Remember that.' He pushed Prue a little away from him. 'Here, don't cry.'

'I'm not.'

'Why don't I run you back to the Old Rectory? You could stay a day or two, get some sleep. I'll have to take care of the funeral and everything.'

Prue thought about this suggestion. 'Think I'd better go home. Johnny'll . . .'

'Whatever you like.' Gerald stiffened slightly. 'I'll drive you there, then come back to make arrangements, do whatever's needed.'

'Thanks.' Prue nodded.

Gerald held her again, put his cheek against hers. 'God I'll miss Aunt Ivy,' he said. 'Wish I'd done more for her. I loved her.'

'So did I,' said Prue.

They drove to the cottage in silence. There, Gerald dropped her at the gate. He did not get out of the car, and drove away with no word. Prue looked up the path to where Johnny was leaning against the door, waiting for her.

# Chapter 14

Prue wanted to hurry towards him but her feet would not obey her. When she was halfway up the path Johnny turned from his place in the doorway and ran to his shed. He went inside, banged the door. Prue was too exhausted to care, or to put on the kettle once she was in the kitchen. She tried to remember how the room had looked before Ivy died. She had always found it strange, the way events change the look of familiar, solid things.

A letter from Barry was waiting for her. She took a knife, opened it. Something to do, this empty day, when nothing mattered.

Sweetheart,

Do hope you're in good heart, all settled and well. Here, everything is tip-top. The divorce is going through with no hitches. There are papers to be signed, though, so you'd better come and see the lawyer as soon as you are able. I spent the night of 'sin' in a different hotel from usual as I could not face that friendly porter. Guess who with? No, not your mother – she refused. Bertha. I offered her so much money she couldn't refuse and it was hardly a difficult job. We played card games most of the night. I tried to introduce her to the good new game of Scrabble, but she didn't seem able to understand it. I wonder if you have found anywhere to live yet? By that I mean of your own. There's money all ready to pay over soon as you need it. One piece of good news is that we've purchased a new-fangled washing-machine, a wonderful invention that has made all the difference to your dear mother's life. You must definitely have one when you are settled. Good luck with everything, sweetheart.

Love,

Barry

Prue put the letter to one side, looked up to see Johnny slouching past the kitchen window. He came in, sat beside her. 'So sorry,' he said. 'I suddenly couldn't face you, couldn't think what to say to you. I'm all over the place.' Prue nodded. She didn't much care where he was. 'I know how much Ivy meant to you. At least, I think I do. I'm not much good at gauging that sort of thing.' He got up, went over to the kettle, made coffee, returned to the table. He looked very far away. 'They told me at the hospital she died at four this morning. Except they said "passed away". I suppose that's meant to sound gentler, take the edge off the actuality.' Prue nodded again. Johnny's words were a skein of wool, dipping and twisting, not making much sense. 'Is there anything I can do to help? What are your plans?'

Plans? Prue asked herself the question, drank some of the coffee. 'I haven't slept much for three nights,' she said, 'so I suppose I should go to bed now for a while if I want to make any sense. But I need a car till the Sunbeam's repaired. Could you find somewhere that hires cars by the week? Just some small thing so I don't have to keep asking you for lifts.'

'Of course,' Johnny said.

They sat in silence for a while, their hands flat on a square of sun that had appeared on the table.

'You'll soon find another job, I'm sure. Maybe looking after people is what you're cut out to do. And forget, please forget, what I said about leaving. You can stay here as long as you like. I know I said I find it difficult, but it would be much worse without you. All right?'

Prue looked at him, gave a disinterested nod. 'I'm going up to bed,' she said.

As she crossed the room to the door Johnny spoke in a voice that had lost its gentleness. 'I could have come and fetched you from the hospital,' he said. 'I waited for hours for a call from you.'

'Gerald was there. It was easy for him to drop me here.'

'I suppose so. Gerald has obviously been a great comfort.' Johnny began to rearrange eggs in a basket on the table.

Prue made a dazed journey to her room where she opened the window. She could hear the ebb and flow of the chickens' clucking, and thought it might help her to sleep.

The funeral took place at the end of the week. It was a fine October day, blue sky blotted with small white clouds that seemed keen to disappear once the event was over. Prue noticed that as soon as the six pall-bearers had heaved the coffin from the hearse, the gathering of clouds, like spectators who had seen enough, vanished, leaving a clear sky.

Prue had parked the small Ford 8 that Johnny had hired for her by the front door of the Old Rectory and walked down to the church through the garden. She had never been into it before. Ivy went to the service every Sunday, when Prue was not there. She had stated many times her intention to take Prue to see the fine altar window, but somehow they had never gone. She would study the window, thought Prue, all through the service. Keep her mind firmly on the coloured glass.

There were few people in the church – some half-dozen farm workers, Alice, top heavy in a hat flaming with black feathers (some long-past present from Ivy), one or two villagers, and the old woman from the post office to which Ivy and Prue had driven so often to post a single letter.

Gerald had told Prue to go to the left-hand front pew. He would join her there. She moved up the aisle with a small toss of her head, aware that her long black New Look skirt – from now on to be called her funeral skirt – swished round her legs in a frivolous manner that Ivy would have approved but staider folk might have found inappropriate. She wore a black bow in her hair, and a pair of black suede gloves – one of many presents from Ivy in lieu of wages.

The front pew was perilously close to the coffin on its stand.

Prue wondered if Ivy, within it, looked as she had before she had died in the hospital, or if she had changed. A large bunch of white chrysanthemums lay on it, with a card from Gerald. Pity it wasn't rose-time. Ivy would have liked a covering of 'Himalayan Musk', a name she had taught Prue just a few weeks ago. Beside the soulless chrysanthemums lay Prue's small bunch of the only three gardenias she had been able to find: knowing she wanted them, Johnny had driven all the way to a florist friend in Winchester who had some in her greenhouse. The journey had used the last of his petrol ration. He'd been good, helping her like that, in the face of her determination. Ivy had said so many times they were her favourite flower. Their scent smelt of extravagant parties in the twenties, she said, and Ed had worn one in his buttonhole on their wedding day. It had been good, too, of Gerald to let Prue put her flowers, and her card – 'love, love from Prue' – on the coffin beside his. Everyone had been good.

Gerald was suddenly beside her. Very dark suit, black tie of ribbed silk. Prue went on looking at the altar window, the sun making brilliant the angels' wings. She turned to see the vicar come in through the door and close it behind him. In the moment of light at the back of the church, she also saw Johnny standing by the font. He'd said he wasn't coming. Didn't think he'd be wanted, he said. He, too, had found a black tie: a thin, stringy thing, a single pencil line on his white shirt.

Prue turned back to concentrate again on the window. The primary colours confused her eyes. She shifted her gaze to the two lighted candles on the altar. Beside her, Gerald moved slightly. She knew he kept glancing at her. She remained looking at the candles.

The small organ, at the side of the altar, wheezed for a moment. Then it produced so thin a sound from its fat sides that Prue felt herself smiling. 'Lead, kindly light', it began. It's my fault, all this: Prue's inward words went with the tune. I killed the Hon. Ivy Lamton. The small congregation stood: 'Amid the encircling gloom', they sang.

Ivy was buried beside her husband in the churchyard. A yew tree stood by the two graves, its black-green mocking the livid colour of the false grass that had been laid over the mounds of earth dug from the ground. The few people who had been in the church gathered round the grave, but Johnny was not there. Gerald stood close to Prue until he had to step forward, pick up a clod of earth and throw it down onto the coffin. He did not signal to Prue to do the same. Rooks, cawing in the trees overhead, meant the vicar had to raise his voice for the final prayer.

Back at the rectory there was not much of a wake. Alice had insisted on being in charge. Her idea of all that was necessary was pots of tea and plates of the last of the shortbread biscuits. No one stayed long. They shook Gerald's hand before they left, muttering their condolences.

When they had gone, Gerald and Prue sat in the sitting room. Though nothing had been moved – today's *Times* was on the stool and everything was the same – it was desperately empty now that Ivy was not going to potter in with her cane.

'What now?' asked Gerald. 'What are you going to do?'

His look was so concerned that Prue felt a prickle of amorphous hope. 'Don't know. I've got to leave the cottage. Johnny's being unpredictable. Find somewhere of my own.'

'You can always stay here while you're looking,' said Gerald. 'I know Ivy would have suggested it. I won't be moving in for some time. Lots to sort out.' He undid the black tie, pulled it off. Undid the top button of his shirt.

'Thank you,' said Prue, 'but I don't think I could do that. I'd find it too strange.'

Gerald nodded. There were small angular shadows under his eyes that were not usually there. He smiled, which banished the tired look for a moment. 'It's probably not an appropriate moment to say this, but you look beautiful in all that black,' he said, not looking at her. Prue felt herself blush. 'I dare say,' he went on, 'that sitting together in the front pew we've given the village something to gossip about.' The blush did not fade. 'You must promise to let me know wherever it is you go, when you do. Promise to keep in touch. When you're finally settled I'll hire a removal van to deliver Ivy's clothes. She left me a note saying you were to have the entire contents of her wardrobe. Such a good idea.' He crossed his legs, looked round the bookcases. 'And I'm going to add to that her complete works of Dickens. I think you should have them.'

Prue felt her eyes blink unsteadily. 'I don't know what to say.' She stood up, reluctant to go but feeling she should. 'It's a very generous thought, but it would break up the library.'

'Well, that's what's going to happen.' Gerald stood too. 'Awful thing is, I've got to get back to London. I see you've rented a car.' He smiled, glancing out of the window. 'Should just about get you back to the cottage. You can always borrow Ivy's . . .' For some reason this thought ungrounded his voice.

'I couldn't do that.'

'Anyway.' He came towards her.

Prue knew there was only a moment left. 'Do you think it was my fault?' she asked. 'Did I kill Ivy?'

Gerald put his hands on her shoulders quite roughly. 'Don't be ridiculous. It was a ghastly accident. You managed to avoid a worse one. You're never to think that again – please. For me. What you must remember is that it was the perfect day for Ivy to die. She'd had a lovely afternoon with Arnold. She was with you, to whom she'd become devoted, and she was in the Sunbeam. Remember that.'

He drew Prue to him. Their cheeks did not touch but they stayed pressed together for a long, silent moment. Then Prue said she'd like to go round the garden when Gerald left. He said please do, go where you want, stay as long as you like. There was no need to lock the front door. Ivy had not believed in locking front doors. He said all this in a great hurry, the words tumbling together. Then he roared down the drive in his powerful car. They did not wave.

When he had gone Prue spent the rest of the afternoon wandering round the garden, sitting on the terrace, looking at the trees, which were turning to autumn colours – 'hectic red', Ivy had said only last week, a quote from a poet called Shelley whom she had put on Prue's list to read. As she went from place to place in the garden, she tried not to remember, because she knew remembering too much would break her, and she had to stay strong.

When it began to grow dark, she sat in the sitting room for a while. The unfinished *Emma* lay on the table. She put it back in its space on the bookshelf, then drove to the cottage in the small rackety car.

Johnny was at the kitchen table playing patience. A bottle of vodka stood beside him, and two glasses. 'I was there after all,' he said.

'I know. I saw you.'

'You look washed out,' he said, 'but beautiful in all your black.'
Prue winced. 'What you need is a drink. I promise I haven't
touched a drop.'

'Good. That's good.'

'Here.' She drank the vodka he gave her in one go, something
she had never done before. It burnt her throat.

Johnny refilled the glass. 'Where's Gerald?'

'Gone back to London.'

'I suppose he'll be moving to the Old Rectory soon.'

'I don't know.'

'He'll need a woman – a wife – to look after it.'

'Dare say he'll have no trouble finding one.'

'I hope he'll keep ordering more gates.'

'I'm sure he will.' It was as if she was throwing pebbles, the way
the words came out. They landed randomly.

'I've almost finished the last one.'

'Good.'

'It'd be wonderful to live in that house, wouldn't it?'

'I suppose it would.' Prue raised her eyes to Johnny. She couldn't
see him clearly for the tears that suddenly came. She knew he
was urging her to have more vodka, and that she obediently
swallowed several glasses between the sobs that shook her. Very
quickly she was completely disoriented. Solid things liquidated,
spun, came at her and receded in a hideous dance. Through
bemused eyes she saw Johnny stand, a strange, kindly, determined
look on his face.

He picked her up, carried her upstairs. He laid her on her bed,
undid her black shirt, pulled off the funeral skirt, lay down beside
her. Through the chaos of vodka and tears she was vaguely aware
of the comfort of another human being. Then he began to act far
beyond mere comforter, and it was not in her power to stop him.

\*   \*   \*

Very late next morning Prue came down into the kitchen. She carried her small, packed case. Johnny was sitting at his usual place at the table, his head in his hands.

'So you had your way after all,' she said.

Johnny looked up, bleary-eyed. 'You needed comforting. You seemed to appreciate it.'

'Appreciate it? I didn't know what I was doing. You took outrageous advantage of me, you know you did. You call that comforting?'

'Sorry,' he said dully. He looked at her suitcase. 'You know if you leave now what will happen.' He touched the bottle of vodka still on the table, empty.

'That's blackmail. And I'll tell you something, Johnny, I don't care. I don't care what you do to yourself. I don't care about you any more. We've had some good times, you've often been kind. But you knew I could never give you what you wanted, and your near-rape last night spoilt every last hope of our living peacefully together.'

'I didn't force myself on you, I swear to you I didn't. Though you were probably too drunk to remember your own willingness. Too drunk and too sad about some dotty old lady who seemed to have so much influence over you, who you seemed to love—'

'Don't go on. I'm going.'

'Where to?'

'I don't know. I'll stay at some pub or hotel. Miles from here.'

'You'd better keep in touch. I may have to send on letters.' He covered his eyes with his hands.

'Maybe.'

'What about the Sunbeam? What about the chickens?'

His playing for time was pathetic, Prue thought. Her head throbbed. 'I gave mine to you, remember?'

'I'll take care of them.' Johnny broke a moment's silence by banging his fist hard on the table. 'Go, then, woman,' he shouted.

'If you're really going, just go . . .' Prue moved quickly towards the door. 'Just imagine my evenings, sometimes' – he picked up the bottle of vodka, waved it – 'and remember I was another of the idiots who loved you.'

Prue hurried out of the door and down the path. She had trouble starting the small car, but jerked forward after an alarmingly long wait for the engine to engage. Glancing back at the cottage she saw that Johnny was not at the kitchen window watching her departure. She drove away as fast as she could. Her only thought was to buy a road map.

That evening she drew up in front of the pub at Hinton Half Moon. Earlier, studying the map while she ate sandwiches at some roadside, the idea had come to her that, rather than be anywhere near the Old Rectory and the cottage, she would like to return to the part of the country she loved more than anywhere else. She remembered that the pub had a couple of rooms and decided to take her chance.

The man behind the bar was a stranger. He had only taken over the place a year ago, he said, and was delighted to let her have the big room at the front for as long as she liked. Prue ordered a ginger beer and explained she used to work as a land girl a mile or so up the road at Hallows Farm.

'That was the Lawrences' place, wasn't it?' he said. 'People still talk about them. A couple from London have it now. I gather they don't do much farming, just like owning the land. Now I come to think of it, a young man dropped in here not that long ago. Said he was the Lawrences' son. Said he'd come to see if the new people would sell the old tractor if they hadn't got rid of it.'

'Joe,' said Prue.

'And there's talk that the people at the farm are thinking of pulling down the barn, building something else.'

'Really?' said Prue. The barn, the barn. She asked if she could have a bowl of carrot soup, the only thing suggested on the menu propped up on the bar.

'That's more on the lunch menu,' the man explained, 'though I dare say my wife would heat some up for you.' He came back with the good news that it was being prepared.

Prue explained she had come to look around, see if she could find herself somewhere small to live.

The man shook his head. 'There's nothing I know of, but I don't get out much. I'm mostly behind this bar. But you're welcome to stay as long as you like.'

Later, the publican's wife showed her to the room: sparsely furnished but comfortable. She slept deeply, and set off early after breakfast next morning.

Her plan was to drive for a few miles, remembering the land, looking out for a tumbledown cottage, before she consulted an estate agent. She pottered about all day, glad of the fine, brisk autumn air, only stopping to scan each row of buildings in various villages. Sometimes she parked the car and walked across a well-remembered field, no longer full of sheep. She avoided the Barry One wood, and had no desire to go anywhere near the barn. That one time, with Johnny, had been enough.

Late afternoon, and no luck. Prue told herself there was time, endless time: no need to become anxious. In order not to pass Hallows Farm, she took the lane that went past Ratty's cottage back to the village. At his gate there was a small, dull board: 'For Sale' it said. Prue braked so hard she hurt her ribs again, but did not care. To make sure this was no mirage, she hurried out of the car to examine the notice more closely. There was the name of the estate agent, the telephone number.

Prue stood by the small wooden gate looking up at the cottage. The ugly new paint, which had been there when she and Johnny had passed by, was blistered. She could see it had never been put on properly in the first place. The windows were filthy. The front door was cracked. The garden was a wilderness of weeds. They ran right across the small front path that Ratty had always taken such pride in keeping trim.

With a burst of energy that sliced through her exhaustion, Prue made things happen very quickly. She drove first thing next morning to the estate agent in the local town. The cottage had been on the market for ages, he said. Most people did not want to be so 'cut off', as he called it. He gave her the key, warned her the place needed quite a bit of attention. She would find it was even worse inside than out. He also said, if she was interested, she could have more land: the people at Hallows Farm had come to him in search of a buyer. They didn't want the bother of all the acreage.

Later that morning Prue, frustrated only by the rotten acceleration of the hired car, unlocked the front door of Ratty's cottage. She had not been inside more than a couple of times – mad Edith had not been one to encourage visitors. But she remembered it had been overcrowded with too much gloomy furniture, and there was always a sour smell of old tea, rotting vegetables and cats.

The smell was still there, in the empty rooms with their walls of hemp-coloured, battered paint. Dark squares of cobwebs, where pictures had once hung, made ghost frames. There were still cinders and ash in the hearth, mould where rain had come through the windows. In its present state, Ratty's cottage was not appealing. But what seemed important to Prue was that the front room, and the bedroom above it, looked over Lower Pasture. She had not realized those rooms faced that field, which needed ploughing, harrowing, bringing back to life. An overgrown lilac tree, where the blackbird Ratty loved used to live, hid much of the view, but it only needed a bit of pruning.

Prue stood at the window looking out for a long time. In the empty fields she could see Friesians, sheep, lambs. The hedges would be neatly laid again, just as Mr Lawrence would like. The old shed could be expanded to shelter a new tractor. Inside the cottage there would be white paint, and furniture from local auctions. There would be a more modern telephone than the one at The Larches, a book of useful numbers, and Rudolph's card propped up somewhere. Upstairs there would be a whole room of cupboards for Ivy's clothes, with bookshelves for Dickens and all the other writers she had urged Prue to read. Outside, the tangled garden would have the sort of flowers that Ivy had recommended, and the plum trees that Mrs Lawrence and Ag so enjoyed. Prue realized how hard she would have to work to transform the place. It might take her years. But here was the project she had been looking for. The idea of the effort that would be needed was thrilling. Here, to be alone, so much to do, solitude would be just what she would need and love.

Prue moved away from the window, made her way back to the kitchen. Leaving the view did not dislodge the pictures of the fields and garden from her mind – how they were now, how they would be. And downstairs, superimposed over the darkness, was the bright light of her imaginings. She could see it all.